HIS CO
VIRG

BY
BARBARA DUNLOP

AND

SEDUCTION ON
THE CEO'S TERMS
BY
CHARLENE SANDS

MILLS & BOON

"You're here for a shotgun wedding…?" she asked, her brow raised.

"Something like that," he admitted.

Stephanie shook her head. "Thanks for stopping by, Alec. You're an honorable man. But your baby is safe in my hands. I'll drop you a line once it's born."

"Not quite the way things are going to happen," he said as he stared down at her with intense purpose.

"Get this straight in your mind, Stephanie. You *are* marrying me."

She squinted into his dark, intense eyes. "That was a joke, right?"

"Am I laughing?"

HIS CONVENIENT VIRGIN BRIDE

BY
BARBARA DUNLOP

DID YOU PURCHASE THIS BOOK WITHOUT A COVER?

If you did, you should be aware it is **stolen property** as it was reported
unsold and destroyed by a retailer. Neither the author nor the publisher
has received any payment for this book.

All the characters in this book have no existence outside the imagination of
the author, and have no relation whatsoever to anyone bearing the same name
or names. They are not even distantly inspired by any individual known or
unknown to the author, and all the incidents are pure invention.

All Rights Reserved including the right of reproduction in whole or in
part in any form. This edition is published by arrangement with Harlequin
Enterprises II B.V./S.à.r.l. The text of this publication or any part thereof may
not be reproduced or transmitted in any form or by any means, electronic or
mechanical, including photocopying, recording, storage in an information
retrieval system, or otherwise, without the written permission of the publisher.

This book is sold subject to the condition that it shall not, by way of trade or
otherwise, be lent, resold, hired out or otherwise circulated without the prior
consent of the publisher in any form of binding or cover other than that in
which it is published and without a similar condition including this condition
being imposed on the subsequent purchaser.

® and ™ are trademarks owned and used by the trademark owner and/or its
licensee. Trademarks marked with ® are registered with the United Kingdom
Patent Office and/or the Office for Harmonisation in the Internal Market and
in other countries.

Published in Great Britain 2011
by Mills & Boon, an imprint of Harlequin (UK) Limited,
Eton House, 18-24 Paradise Road, Richmond, Surrey TW9 1SR

© Barbara Dunlop 2010

ISBN: 978 0 263 88237 7

51-0711

Harlequin (UK) policy is to use papers that are natural, renewable and
recyclable products and made from wood grown in sustainable forests. The
logging and manufacturing processes conform to the legal environmental
regulations of the country of origin.

Printed and bound in Spain
by Blackprint CPI, Barcelona

For my husband

Barbara Dunlop writes romantic stories while curled up in a log cabin in Canada's far north, where bears outnumber people and it snows six months of the year. Fortunately, she has a brawny husband and two teenage children to haul firewood and clear the driveway while she sips cocoa and muses about her upcoming chapters. Barbara loves to hear from readers. You can contact her through her website at www.barbaradunlop.com.

Dear Reader,

Welcome to the MONTANA MILLIONAIRES: THE RYDERS series from Desire™. I have a great time writing siblings, and I hope you enjoy Stephanie's story in *His Convenient Virgin Bride,* along with the stories of her brothers, Royce and Jared, in the companion books.

I also love a ranch setting and a smart, protective hero. Add to that a little mystery and a long-ago family secret, and you have the ingredients for a really fun write. I enjoyed exploring the Ryder family history in this book, and it was great to touch base again with the characters from *Seduction and the CEO* and *In Bed with the Wrangler.* I hope you enjoy the finale to the Ryders' series.

Happy reading!

Barbara

One

Stephanie Ryder felt a telltale breeze puff against the skin of her chest. She glanced down to discover a button had popped on her stretch cotton blouse. The lace of her white bra and the curve of her breasts were clearly visible in the gap.

She crossed her arms to block the view, arching a mocking brow at the man silhouetted in the tack shed door. "You, Alec Creighton, are no gentleman."

Wearing a dress shirt, charcoal slacks and black loafers that were at odds with the rustic setting of a working horse stable, his gaze moved indolently from the wall of her forearm back to her eyes. "It took you twenty-four hours to figure that out?"

"Hardly," she scoffed. "But you keep reinforcing the impression."

He took a step forward. "Are you still mad?"

She swiftly redid the button and smoothed her blouse. "I was never mad."

Disappointed, yes. Wesley Harrison had been inches away from kissing her last night when Alec had interrupted them.

Wesley was a great guy. He was good-looking, smart and funny, and only a year younger than Stephanie. He'd been training at Ryder Equestrian Center since June, and he'd been flirting with her since they met.

"He's too young for you," said Alec.

"We're the same age." Practically.

The jut of Alec's brow questioned her honesty, but he didn't call her on it.

With his trim hair, square chin, slate-gray eyes and instructions to go through her equestrian business records with a fine-tooth comb, she should have found his presence intimidating. But Stephanie had spent most of her life handling two older brothers and countless unruly jumping horses. She wasn't about to get rattled by a hired corporate gun.

"Shouldn't you be working?" she asked.

"I need your help."

It was her turn to quirk a brow. Financial management was definitely not her forte. "With what?"

"Tour of the place."

She reached for the cordless phone on the workbench next to Rosie-Jo's tack. "No problem." She pressed speed dial three.

"What are you doing?"

The numbers bleeped swiftly in her ear. "Calling the stable manager."

Alec closed the distance between them. "Why?"

"To arrange for a tour."

He lifted the phone from her hand and pressed the off button. "You can give me a tour."

"I don't have time."

"You are still mad at me."

"No, I'm not."

She wasn't thrilled to have him here. Who would be? He'd be her houseguest for the next few days, and he was under orders from her brothers to streamline the family's corporation, Ryder International. She was a little worried, okay a *lot* worried, that he'd find fault with her management of the Ryder Equestrian Center.

Stephanie didn't skimp on quality, which meant she didn't skimp on cost, either. She was training world-class jumpers. And competing at that level demanded the best in everything; horses, feed, tack, trainers, vets and facilities. She was accustomed to defending her choices to her brothers. She wasn't crazy about defending them to a stranger.

"Are you proud of the place?" he asked.

"Absolutely," she answered without hesitation.

"Then show it to me," he challenged.

She hesitated, searching her mind for a dignified out.

He waited, the barest hint of a smirk twitching his mouth.

Finally she squared her shoulders, straightened to her full five foot five and met his gaze head-on. "You, Alec Creighton," she repeated, "are no gentleman."

The smile broadened, and he eased away, stepping to one side and gesturing to the tack shed door. "After you."

Stephanie waltzed past with her head held high.

It wasn't often a man talked her into a corner. She didn't much like it, but she might as well get this over with. She'd give him his tour, answer his questions, send him back to the ranch house office and get back to her regular routine.

She had an intermediate jumping class to teach this morning, her own training this afternoon and she needed to have the vet examine her Hanoverian mare, Rosie-Jo. Rosie had shied at a jump in practice yesterday, and Stephanie needed to make sure the horse didn't have any hidden injuries.

They headed down the dirt road alongside a hay barn, moving in the direction of the main stable and riding arena. She was tempted to lead him, expensive loafers and all, through the mud and manure around the treadmill pool.

It would serve him right.

"So, what exactly is it that you do?" she asked, resisting temptation.

"I troubleshoot."

She tipped her head to squint at his profile in the bright sunshine. Last night, she'd privately acknowledged that he was an incredibly good-looking man. He also carried himself well, squared shoulders, long stride, confident gait. "And what does that mean?"

"It means, that when people have trouble, they call me." He nodded to the low, white building, off by itself at the edge of Melody Meadow. "What's that?"

"Vet clinic. What kind of trouble?"

"Your kind of trouble. You have your own vet?"

"We do. You mean cash flow and too rapid corporate expansion?" That was the Ryder's corporate issue in a nutshell.

"Sometimes."

"And the other times?"

He didn't answer.

"Are you proud of it?" she goaded.

He gave a rueful smile as he shook his head.

She tilted her head to one side, going for ingenuous and hopeful. It usually worked on her brothers.

"Fine. Mostly I identify market sector expansion opportunities then analyze the financial and political framework of specific overseas economic regions."

She blinked.

"On behalf of privately held companies."

"The vet's name is Dr. Anderson," she offered.

Alec coughed out a chuckle.

"It sounds challenging," she admitted, turning her focus back to the road.

He shrugged. "You need to develop contacts. But once you learn the legislative framework of a given county, it applies to all sorts of situations."

"I suppose it would."

The breeze freshened, while horses whinnied as they passed a row of paddocks.

"Tell me about your job," Alec prompted.

"I teach horses to jump over things," she stated, not even attempting to dress it up.

There was a smile in his voice, but his tone was mild. "That sounds challenging."

"Not at all. You get them galloping really fast, point them at a jump and most of the time they figure it out."

"And if they don't?"

"Then they stop, and you keep going."

"Headfirst?" he asked.

"Headfirst."

"Ouch."

She subconsciously rubbed the tender spot on the outside of her right thigh where she'd landed hard coming off Rosie-Jo yesterday. "Ouch is right."

The road tapered to a trail as they came up to the six-foot, white rail fence that surrounded the main riding arena. Alec paused to watch a group of young jumping students and their trainer on the far side.

Stephanie stopped beside him.

"I didn't mean to sound pretentious," he offered.

"I know." She had no doubt that he was accurately describing his job. Her brothers wouldn't have hired him if he wasn't a skilled and experienced professional.

Alec hooked his hand over the top fence rail and pivoted to face her. "So, are you going to tell me what you really do?"

Stephanie debated another sarcastic answer, but there was a frankness in his slate eyes that stopped her.

"I train horses," she told him. "I buy horses, sell horses, board them, breed them and train them." She shifted her gaze to the activities of the junior class. "And I jump them."

"I hear you're headed for the Olympics." His gaze was intent on her expression.

"The Olympics are a long way off. I'm focused on the Brighton competition for the moment."

As she spoke, Wesley appeared from behind the bleachers, leading Rockfire into the arena for a round of jumps. Even from this distance, she could appreciate his fresh-faced profile, lanky body and sunshine-blond hair.

His lips had been *that* close to hers.

She wondered if he'd try again.

"What about management?"

Stephanie blinked her focus back to Alec. "Hmm?"

"Management. I assume you also manage the stable operations?"

She nodded, her gaze creeping sideways for another

glimpse of Wesley as he mounted his horse. This was his first year on the adult jumping circuit, and he was poised to make a splash. He grinned as he spoke to Tina, the junior class instructor, raking a spread hand through his full, tousled hair before putting on his helmet.

"Your boyfriend?" There was an edge to Alec's voice.

Stephanie turned guiltily, embarrassed that her attention had wandered.

Alec frowned at her, and the contrast between the two men was startling. One light, one dark. One carefree, one intense.

She shook her head. "No."

"Just a crush then?"

"It's nothing."

Alec dropped his hand from the rail as Wesley and Rockfire sailed over the first jump. "It's something."

She glared at him. "It's none of your business, is what it is."

He stared back for a silent minute.

His eyes were dark. His lips were parted. And a fissure of awareness suddenly sizzled through her.

No.

Not Alec.

It was Wesley she wanted.

"You're right," Alec conceded into the long silence. "It is none of my business."

None of his business, Alec reminded himself.

Back inside her house that evening, he found himself staring at Stephanie's likeness in a framed cover of *Equine Earth* magazine that was hanging on the living room wall. The fact that her silver-blue eyes seemed to hide enchanting secrets, that her unruly, auburn hair begged for a man's touch and that the light spray of freckles across her nose lent a sense of vulnerability to an otherwise flawless face, was none of his damn business.

The equestrian trophy in her hand, however, was his business, as was the fact that the Ryder name was sprayed across the cover of a nationally circulated magazine.

"That was at Carlton Shores," came her voice, its resonance sending a buzz of awareness up his spine.

"Two thousand and eight," she finished, coming up beside him.

He immediately caught the scent of fresh brewed coffee, and looked over to see two burgundy, stoneware mugs in her hands.

"You won," he stated unnecessarily.

She handed him one of the mugs. "You seem like a 'black' kind of a guy."

He couldn't help but smile at her accurate assessment. "Straight to the heart of the matter," he agreed.

"I take cream and sugar." She paused. "Dress it up as much as you can, I guess."

"Why does that not surprise me?"

She was in a business that was all pomp, glitz and show. Oh, she worked hard at it. There was no way she would have made it this far if she hadn't. But her division of Ryder International certainly wasn't the bedrock of the company's income stream.

He took a sip of the coffee. It was just the way he liked it, robust, without being sharp on the tongue.

She followed suit, and his gaze took a tour from her damp, freshly washed hair, pulled back in a sensible braid, to her clingy, white tank top and the pair of comfortable navy sweatpants that tapered down to incongruous lime-green socks.

"Nice," he observed.

She grinned, sticking a foot forward to show it off. "Royce brought them back for me from London. Apparently they're all the rage."

"You're making a fashion statement?"

"Everything else was in the laundry," she admitted. "I'm kind of lazy that way."

"Right. Lazy. That was the first thing I thought when I met you." It was nearly nine o'clock in the evening, and she'd only just stopped work to come in and shower for dinner.

"I'm going to assume that was sarcasm."

"The outfit works," he told her sincerely. Quite frankly, with her compact curves and toned muscles, she'd make a sackcloth work just fine.

She rolled her eyes. "Can I trust *anything* you say?"

Alec found himself captivated by the twinkle in her blue irises and the dark lips that contrasted with her creamy skin. She was charming and incredibly kissable, and he had to ruthlessly pull himself back to business.

"Are you aware that Ryder Equine Center has next to no income?" he asked, his blunt tone an admonishment of himself, not her.

When the sparkle vanished from her eyes, he told himself it was for the best.

"We make money," she asserted.

"A drop in the bucket compared to what you spend." Sure, they sold a few horses, boarded a few horses and took in tuition from students. And Stephanie had won some cash prizes in jumping competitions over the years. But the income didn't begin to compare with the massive expenditures necessary to run this kind of operation.

She gestured to the magazine cover. "And there's that."

"Nobody's disputing that you win."

"I mean the marketing value. That's the front cover of *Equine Earth*. It was a four page article. Check out the value of *that* on the open market."

"And how many potential lessees of Chicago office tower space do you suppose read *Equine Earth* magazine?"

"Plenty. Horse jumping is a sport of the rich and famous."

"Have you done an analysis of the demographics of the *Equine Earth* readership?"

Her lips compressed, and she set her coffee mug down on a table.

Alec regretted that she'd stopped smiling, but he forced himself to carry on. "I have no objection to assigning a value to marketing efforts—"

"Well thank you *so* much, oh guru of the framework for overseas economic regions."

"Hey, I'm trying to have a professional—"

The front door cracked sharply as it opened, and Alec instantly clamped his mouth shut. He turned to see Royce appear in the doorway, realizing how loud his and Stephanie's voices had risen.

But Royce's smile was easy, his nod friendly. Obviously they hadn't been overheard.

"Hey, Royce." Stephanie went to her brother, voice tone down, smile back in place.

Royce gave her a quick hug, then he turned his attention to Alec. "Am I interrupting something?"

"We were talking about my career," Stephanie chirped. "The publicity Ryder Equestrian Center brings to the entire corporation." She looked to Alec for confirmation.

He nodded, grateful she seemed willing to keep their spat private.

"Did you show him the video?" Royce asked.

Stephanie looked instantly wary. "He doesn't need to see the video."

Royce set her aside and strode into the room. "Sure he does. What better way to understand your career. Got any popcorn?"

"We haven't had dinner yet. I'm not—"

"Then let's grill some burgers." Royce pushed up the sleeves of his cotton, Western shirt. "I could use a burger. How about you, Alec?"

"Sure. Burgers sound good." So did watching videos of Stephanie, especially since she seemed hesitant. Did she have something to hide?

"Well, I'm not sticking around for this," Stephanie warned.

"Aren't you hungry?" asked Royce.

She stuck her freckled nose in the air. "I'll get something at the cookhouse."

"Suit yourself," said Royce, and Alec caught the faintest glimpse of satisfaction on the man's face.

What was going on here?

Stephanie stuffed her feet into a pair of worn leather boots, shrugged into a chunky gray sweater and stomped out the door.

"I thought she'd never leave," said Royce.

Alec peered at the man. "What's going on?"

Royce turned down the short passage to the kitchen. "We're grilling burgers and watching family videos."

Twenty minutes later, Alec bit into a juicy, flavorful burger. He had to admit, Royce really knew his way around an outdoor grill. Alec was starving, and the burger was fabulous, slathered in fried onions, topped with a thick slice of garden fresh tomato, and encased in what had to be a homemade bun.

Beside him in the opposite armchair, Royce clicked the remote control on the television. "If anyone asks," he said, settling down to his own dinner. "We were simply eating burgers and watching home videos."

Chewing and swallowing, Alec glanced from their plates to the television and back again. "No problem. I've got your back."

Royce nodded.

They made their way through their meals as a young, red-haired Stephanie bounced over foot high jumps on a white pony. Her small hands were tight on the reins, her helmet was slightly askew, and her face was screwed up in determination as she cleared the rails.

Alec couldn't help but smile, and he wondered why Stephanie objected to him watching. She was adorable.

In his short time he'd spent down at the main house on the Ryder Ranch with Royce and his fiancée, Amber, Alec definitely got the sense that both Royce and Stephanie's oldest brother Jared were in the habit of indulging her. Looking at this video, and knowing the age difference between Stephanie and her two brothers, it was easy to see how that had happened.

Turning toward a crisscrossed jump, the pony gathered itself. Stephanie stood in the stirrups, leaning across its neck. The animal's front legs lifted off the ground, back feet kicking out. The pair sailed over the white painted rails, jolting to the dirt on the other side.

The horse came to a halt, but Stephanie kept going, flying over its head, arms flailing as she catapulted forward, thudding into the dirt. Luckily the horse veered to one side, stepping neatly around her little body.

Jared and Royce both ran into the frame. The two teenagers gingerly turned their sister over, talking to her—though Alec couldn't make out the words—brushing the dirt from her little face.

She sat up. Then she nodded, bracing herself on Jared's shoulder and coming to her feet.

Her brothers kept talking, but she shook her head, walking determinedly toward the pony, taking the reins, and circling around to mount. She was too short to put her foot in the stirrup, so Royce gave her a leg up.

Jared kept arguing, looking none too happy. But Stephanie got her way. She turned the horse, heading to the end of the arena. The camera followed her as she restarted the course.

Alec shook his head, his feelings a cross between admiration and amusement.

Suddenly Royce set his plate aside and lifted the remote control, muting the sound.

Alec turned his attention.

"There's something you need to know." Though Royce's tone was even, his expression was narrowed and guarded.

Alec arched a brow.

"This needs to be kept in the strictest confidence," Royce warned.

"Everything you tell me is kept in the strictest confidence." It was a hallmark of Alec's business.

Royce nodded sharply.

Alec waited, his curiosity growing.

"Right," said Royce, fingers drumming against the

leather arm of the chair. He drew a breath. "Here it is then. We're being blackmailed." He paused. "It's Stephanie."

"What did she do?" Dope a horse? Fix a competition?

Royce scowled. "She didn't *do* anything. She's the one in the dark, and we're keeping it that way."

Right. Stupid conclusion. Alec tried another tactic. "Who's blackmailing you?"

"I'd rather not say."

"Okay…" Alec wasn't sure where to go with that.

"It's the biggest drain on the cattle ranch's account."

At least that explained why Amber thought Alec ought to know.

"How much are we talking about?" he asked.

"A hundred thousand a month."

"A *month?*"

Royce's expression was grim as he nodded.

Alec straightened in his armchair. "How long has this been going on?"

"At least a decade."

"*Excuse* me?"

"I know."

"You've spent *twelve million dollars* keeping a secret from Stephanie?"

Royce rocked to his feet, shoulders square, hands balled.

"Must be one hell of a secret."

Royce twisted round to glower at Alec.

"Sorry. None of my business," said Alec.

Still, he couldn't help sifting through the possibilities in his mind. Was there a shady business deal in their past? Did the family fortune originate from an unsavory source? Gambling? Bootlegging?

"You won't figure it out," said Royce.

"I might."

"Not this. And I don't want you snooping around."

"I won't snoop," Alec agreed. He'd respect his client's wishes. "But I might think."

Royce gazed at the silent screen where an elevenish Stephanie was taking yet another spill. "Suppose you can't stop a man from thinking."

"No, you can't."

"Aw, hell." Royce heaved a sigh and sat back down.

Alec gave him a moment. "How bad can it be?"

Royce scoffed out a harsh laugh. "My father was a murderer and my mother was adulterous." He paused. "We're being blackmailed by her lover's brother. The lover was also the murder victim." Another pause, and Royce's voice went lower. "*That's* how bad it can be."

Alec's brain filled in the blank. "And Stephanie is your half sister."

Royce drew back sharply, his expression confirming the truth.

Alec shrugged. "That's the only possibility worth twelve million dollars."

"She's *never* going to know."

"You can't keep paying him forever."

"Oh, yes, we can." Royce grasped the back of his neck. "My grandfather paid until he died. Then McQuestin paid. I took over a couple months ago."

Though it went beyond the bounds of his contract, Alec felt an obligation to be honest. "What are you going to do when he ups his price?"

It was obvious from Royce's expression that he hadn't considered that possibility.

"You'll eventually have to tell her, Royce."

Royce shook his head. "Not if we stop him."

"And how are you planning to accomplish that?"

"I don't know." Royce paused. "Got any ideas?"

TWO

Last night's cookhouse burger hadn't measured up to Royce's talents, but it had filled Stephanie's hunger gap. And at least she'd avoided one more screening of *Stephanie Hits the Dirt Across America*.

It was one thing to show that bloopers reel to friends and family, but to strangers? Business associates? She was busy trying to get Alec to take her seriously, and Royce was making her look like a klutz.

Nice guy her brother.

She opened the wooden gate to Rosie-Jo's stall in the center section of the main horse barn and led the mare inside. The vet had given the horse a clean bill of health, and they'd had a great practice session this morning. Rosie had eagerly sailed over every jump.

Stephanie peeled off her leather gloves, removed Rosie's bridle and unclipped the lead rope, reaching through the gate to coil it on the hook outside the stall. She selected a mud brush from the tack box and stroked it over Rosie's withers and barrel, removing the lingering dirt and sweat from the mare's dapple gray coat.

"How'd it go?" Wesley's voice carried through the cavernous barn. His boot heels echoed as he crossed from Rockfire's stall to Rosie-Jo's. He tipped back his Stetson and rested his arms on the top rail of the gate.

"Good," Stephanie answered, continuing the brush strokes.

Though she didn't look up, a shimmer of anticipation tightened her stomach. The barn was mostly empty, the grooms outside with other horses and students. She hadn't talked to Wesley since their aborted kiss two days ago. If he wanted to try again, this would be the opportunity.

"Hesitation's gone," she added. "You tacking up?"

Wesley nodded. "Rockfire's ready to go. Tina has them changing up the jump pattern for us."

Stephanie gave Rosie-Jo's coat a final stroke. Normally she'd do a more thorough job, but she could always come back later. For now, she wanted to give Wesley another chance. Meet him halfway, as it were.

She replaced the brush, dusted her hands off on the back of her blue jeans and started across the stall to where he was leaning over the rail. Suddenly shy, she found she couldn't meet his eyes. Was she being too blatant, too obvious? Should she make it a little harder for him to make his move?

It wasn't like she was experienced at this. Ryder Ranch was a long way off the beaten track. She'd never had a serious romantic relationship, and it had been months— she didn't want to count how many—since she'd even had a date.

She came to a stop, the slated gate a barrier between them. When she dared look at his face, his lips were parted. There was an anticipatory gleam in his blue eyes. And his head began to tilt to one side.

Should she lean in or let him take the lead?

"Am I interrupting anything?" It was Alec's voice all over again, and his footfalls rapped along the corridor floor.

Wesley's hands squeezed down on the gate rail, frustration replacing the anticipation in his eyes.

"Is this some kind of a joke?" he rasped for Stephanie's ears only.

She didn't know what to say. Alec seemed to have a knack for bad timing.

"I'm sorry," she whispered to Wesley.

"Not as sorry as I am."

She turned to face Alec. "Can I *help* you?"

"I hope so." He stopped. After a silent beat, he glanced meaningfully at Wesley.

Wesley glared at him for a moment then smacked his hand down on the rail. "Time for practice," he declared and turned on his heel to lead Rockfire from his stall.

As she watched the pair leave, disappointment clunked like a horseshoe to the bottom of Stephanie's stomach.

"What is it now?" she hissed at Alec, popping the latch and exiting the stall. After securing it behind her, she set off after Wesley.

"Places to go?" asked Alec, falling into step.

"Things to do," she responded, with a toss of her hair. She was going to watch Wesley's practice session. It was part of her job as his coach. Plus, she'd be there when he finished. And by then, Alec should be long gone.

"I'm trying to help you, you know."

"I can tell."

"Is your sex life more important than your company?"

Stephanie increased her pace, stomping forward, ignoring Alec's question.

Sex life.

Ha! She couldn't even get a kiss.

She passed through the open barn doorway, squinting into the bright sunshine, focusing on Wesley who was across the ranch road, mounting Rockfire.

Too late, she heard the roar of the pickup engine, then the sickening grind of tires sliding on gravel.

She had a fleeting glimpse of Amber's horrified face at the wheel before a strong arm clamped around Stephanie's waist and snatched her out of harm's way.

Alec whirled them both, sheltering Stephanie against the barn wall, his body pressed protectively against hers as the truck slid sideways, fishtailing out of control, roaring past to miss them by inches.

"You okay?" his voice rasped through the billowing dust.

She told herself to nod, but her brain was slow in interpreting the signal.

"You okay?" he tried again, louder.

This time, Stephanie managed a nod.

"Stay here," he commanded.

And suddenly, he was gone. Without Alec's physical support, her knees nearly gave way. She grabbed at the wall, mustering her balance, blinking the blur from her eyes while the world moved in slow motion.

As she turned, she took in two ranch hands across the road. Their eyes were wide, mouths gaping. Wesley struggled to control Rockfire, turning the big horse in dust-cloud circles.

Stephanie followed the direction of the hands' attention. A roar filled her ears as Amber's blue truck keeled up on the left wheels.

Alec was rushing toward it

Stephanie tried to scream. She tried to run. But her voice clogged down in her chest, and her legs felt like lead weights.

Then the truck overbalanced, crashing down on the driver's door, spinning in a horrible, grinding circle until it smacked up against an oak tree.

The world zapped back to normal speed. Amongst the cacophony of shouts and motion, Alec skidded to a stop. He peered through the windshield for a split second, then he clambered his way up to the passenger door, high in the air.

He wrenched it open, and Stephanie's body came back to life. She half ran, half staggered down the road, Amber's name pulsing over and over through her brain.

Alec swiftly lowered himself into the truck.

Stephanie grew closer, praying Amber was all right.

Suddenly Alec's sole cracked against the inside of the windshield, popping it out.

"Bring a truck," he shouted, and two of the ranch hands took off running.

Stephanie made it to the scene to see blood dripping down Amber's forehead. The realization that this was all her fault, made her stagger.

Alec met her eyes. "She's okay," he told her, his voice steady and reassuring. "Call Royce. But tell him she's okay."

Stephanie saw that Amber's eyes were open.

She looked dazed, but when Alec spoke to her, Amber answered back.

His hands moved methodically over her body, arms, legs, neck and head.

But then Stephanie saw it.

"Smoke," she tried to shout, but her dry throat wouldn't cooperate.

Alec saw it, too.

People ran for fire extinguishers, while Alec fumbled with Amber's seat belt.

While he worked, he spoke calmly and firmly.

Stephanie couldn't hear the words, but Amber nodded and swallowed. She wrapped her arms around Alec's neck, as the first flames snaked out from under the hood.

He spoke to Amber again, and she closed her eyes, burying her face against Alec's neck. His arms tightened around her, and he slowly, gently eased her through the opening left by the windshield.

Stephanie held her breath, her glance going from the growing flames, to Amber and back again.

Wesley appeared by her side. "You okay?"

The question annoyed her. "I'm fine." It was Amber who was in trouble. And Alec, who might get hurt or worse trying to save her.

The flame leaped higher.

Alec's foot touched the ground outside the truck.

He gripped Amber close to his chest, rising to rush away.

"Get back!" he shouted to the growing crowd, just as the hood blew open, missing the tree trunk and cracking against the roof of the cab.

He staggered forward, but stayed upright and didn't lose his grip on Amber.

Three hands arrived with fire extinguishers, aiming them at the engulfed truck.

Stephanie backed away from the heat. Remembering the cell phone in her hand, she quickly dialed Royce's number.

Another pickup pulled up, and Alec lay Amber carefully across the bench seat.

"Don't try to move," he warned her.

"Hello?" Royce's voice came into Stephanie's phone.

"Royce?" Her voice shook.

"Stephanie?"

She didn't know what to say.

Alec scooped the phone. "Alec here." He took a breath. "There's been an accident. Amber's fine." A pause. "No. No one else was in the truck." He glanced at Stephanie, then down at Amber. "She's conscious."

He moved the phone away from his mouth. "Can you talk to Royce?"

Amber nodded, so Alec handed her the phone. Then he motioned to everyone else to back off. They obeyed, with the exception of Wesley who still hovered next to Stephanie.

When Amber put the phone to her ear and listened, tears welled up in her eyes. Stephanie instinctively moved in to comfort her, but Alec stopped her with his arm.

"Don't touch her," he whispered, keeping his arm braced around Stephanie's waist.

He reached into his pocket, retrieving his own cell phone.

Stephanie looked at him with a question.

"Medical chopper," he said in a low voice, turning away from Amber to speak to emergency services.

Stephanie's attention immediately returned to Amber. Blood was still oozing from the cut on her forehead, and there was a wicked bruise forming on her right shoulder. Her blouse was torn, her knuckles scraped.

Was she really okay? Had Alec lied to Royce? And what did Alec know anyway? He wasn't a doctor.

Okay, so he knew enough to pull Amber from a burning truck.

That was something.

That was huge.

While Stephanie, Stephanie had been stupid enough to march out in front of Amber and cause all this.

Her chest tightened with pain, and a sob escaped from her throat.

Alec turned back. His arm moved from her waist to her shoulders, and he gave her a squeeze. "It's not your fault," he rumbled in her ear.

But his words didn't help.

"Listen to me, Stephanie." He kept his voice low. "Amber is fine. The chopper will be here in fifteen minutes. But it's just a precaution."

"You're not a doctor," she snarled.

"No, I'm not."

"I'm sorry." Stephanie shook her head. "You pulled her out. She could have—"

"Stop."

Amber let the cell phone drop to her chest. "Royce is on his way." Her voice was weak, but just hearing it made Stephanie feel a little better.

"The medical chopper's going to beat him here," Alec told Amber, lifting the phone and gently smoothing her hair away from the wound.

"Want to bet?" Amber smiled, and Stephanie could have wept with joy.

Somebody had located a first aid kit, and Alec gently

cleaned the blood from around Amber's head wound and placed a square of gauze to stop the bleeding.

"Are you okay?" Stephanie dared to ask her.

"Did I hit you?" Amber asked back with a worried frown. "Are you hurt?"

Stephanie quickly shook her head. "No. No. Not at all. I'm perfectly fine. Just worried about you."

"I'm a little stiff," said Amber. She wiggled her fingers and moved her feet. "But everything's still working."

Stephanie mustered a watery smile.

Amber's eyes cut away to focus over Stephanie's shoulder. "I guess that's it for the truck, though."

"It was pretty spectacular," Wesley put in.

Alec frowned at him. "A small fire can do a lot of damage."

Amber looked back at Alec. "Thank you," she told him in a shaky voice.

"I'm just glad you're all right." His smile was so gentle that something warm bloomed to life inside Stephanie.

Amber was going to be okay, and it was because of Alec.

Royce's truck appeared over the rise, tires barely touching down between high spots on the dirt road. A cloud of dust rolled out behind him.

And then he was sliding to a stop at the scene. He burst out of the driver's door, hitting the ground running as the *thump, thump, thump* of the chopper blades sounded in the sky.

Alec watched the towing company employees winch the wrecked pickup onto the flatbed truck. He'd talked to Jared in Chicago, and they agreed to have it removed as quickly as possible. Royce had called to report that Amber would be released from the hospital in a couple of hours. Alec was relieved to learn that Amber's recovery would be short.

She had a few stitches in her forehead, but there were no worries of a concussion. Other than that, she'd only suffered scrapes and bruises. Royce was getting them a hotel room in Missoula, and they were coming home in the morning.

Steel clanked and cables groaned as the half-burned hulk inched its way up the ramps. Several of the ranch employees stood to watch. But it was nearing eight o'clock, and most had returned to their jobs or their homes once they heard the good news about Amber.

Stephanie appeared beside Alec, tucking her cell phone into her pocket and pushing her messy hair back from her forehead. "Amber's making jokes."

Alec was also relieved to see Stephanie getting back to normal. She hadn't been injured, but she'd seemed almost in shock there for a few minutes.

"And how are you doing?" he asked.

"Just a little worn-out." She stilled to gaze at the flatbed that was silhouetted by the final vestiges of a sunset.

"You sure?" he probed.

"I'm sure," she confirmed, voice sounding stronger.

"Good for you."

One of the towing operators was tying down the pickup, while the other started up the engine of the flatbed. Work here was done.

He turned, then waited for Amber to start back to the house with him. Lights had come on in the staff cottages. The scent of freshly cut hay hung in the cooling air. And the diesel truck rumbled away down the ranch road, toward the long hill that wound past the main ranch house to the highway.

"I was looking for a media file," said Alec as the engine faded and the crickets took over.

"A what?"

"That's why I came to find you earlier. Do you have documentation of your jumping career publicity?"

She looked confused.

"I'll need the background information to calculate the dollar value of the exposure," he elaborated.

"I don't understand."

"What's not to understand?"

"You can switch gears that fast?"

It was his turn to draw back in confusion.

"You just risked death to save Amber."

"Risked death?" he chuckled, but then he realized she was serious.

"How did you know how to do that?" she asked.

"It's not exactly rocket science."

She peered at him through the dim glow of the yard lights. "Were you with the fire department or search and rescue?"

"No."

"You pull a woman from a burning truck and carry her to safety only seconds before it explodes. How does that not rattle you?"

"That's the Hollywood version." He steered their course around the corner of the big barn, linking up with the path to her front porch. "I kicked out a windshield. I didn't defuse a nuclear weapon."

"You risked life and limb."

"You know you tend to overdramatize, right?" He did

what needed to be done, and only because he was the closest guy to the wreck.

And, quite frankly, it wasn't fear of the fire and for Amber's safety that had stuck with him. The worst moment had been that split second before he'd pulled Stephanie out of the way of the truck.

"You saved a woman's life, and just like that." She snapped her fingers. "You're working on some mundane report."

"Correction. I'm *trying* to work on a mundane report. Do you maybe have a list or something?"

They'd arrived at the house and mounted the steps, heading in through the door.

Stephanie kicked off her muddy boots, socks and all. "I have a few scrapbooks down at the main house."

"Can we pick them up tomorrow?"

"Sure." She pulled the elastic from her ponytail and ran her fingers through her messy hair. The action highlighted its auburn shimmer, while the pose showed off the compact curves of her body.

It was a struggle not to stare. So, he moved further into the house to where his work was spread out on the dining room table. He dropped into a padded chair, reminding himself of where he'd left off.

"Alec?" she called, coming around the corner.

"Yes?"

When she didn't answer, he couldn't help but turn to look.

She'd stripped off her cotton work shirt and now wore a thin, washed-out T-shirt and a pair of soft blue jeans that hugged her curves. The jeans rode low, revealing a strip of soft, pale skin above the waistband. Her bare feet struck him as incredibly sexy as she padded across the hardwood floor.

"What is it about your past life that led you to rush into a burning vehicle while everybody else stood there and stared in horror?"

"Let it go."

She might look soft and sweet, but the woman had the tenacity of a pit bull.

"I'm curious," she told him.

"And I have work to do."

"It's not a normal thing, you know."

"It's a perfectly normal thing. A dozen guys out there would have done the same."

Stephanie shook her head.

Alec rolled his eyes and turned back to his spreadsheet.

"Let me guess," she carried on. "You were in the marines."

"No."

"The army?"

"Go away."

That surprised a laugh out of her. "It's my house."

"It's my job."

She pondered for a minute. "There's an easy way to get rid of me."

He slid a quizzical gaze her way.

"Answer the question."

He wasn't exactly sure what to say, but if it would get her out of the room and off his wayward mind, he was game to give it a try. "I was in the Boy Scouts."

She frowned. "That's not it."

"Visited dangerous cities?"

A shake of her head.

"Had the occasional bar fight? Never started one," he felt compelled to point out.

She braced her hands on the back of a chair and pinned him with a pointed stare.

"You're not leaving," he noted.

"That's all you've got?" she demanded.

"What more do you want?"

"I don't know. Something out of the ordinary. Something that taught you how to deal with danger."

"I grew up on the south side of Chicago."

"Seriously?"

"No, I'm making that part up."

"Was it in a dangerous part of town?" she asked, leaning forward, looking intrigued.

Alec liked the way her pose tightened her T-shirt against her body.

"Relatively," he told her. Crime had been high. Fights had been frequent. He'd learned how to read people and avoid situations, and how to handle himself when things went bad.

Her voice went low and intimate, as if somebody might overhear them. "Were you like a gang member? In rumbles and things?"

He reflexively leaned closer, lowering his own voice. "No gang. I was raised by a single father, a Chicago cop with very high standards of behavior." Not that Alec had ever been tempted to join a gang. But his father most certainly would have stopped him cold.

"Your father's a police officer?"

Alec sat back. "Not anymore. He's owner and CEO of Creighton Waverley Security."

"So, you work for him?"

Alec shook his head. Work for his old man? Not in

this lifetime. "I do occasional contract work for his company."

"Like this?"

"This is a private arrangement between me and Ryder International."

"There's an edge to your voice."

"That's because you're still asking questions."

"Are you mad at me or your father?"

"Do you ever stop?"

"Do you?"

"I'm paid to ask questions."

"Yeah?" The smile she gave him sent a rush of desire to every pulse point in his body. "I do it recreationally."

They stared at each other in thickening silence, and he could hear the alarm bells warming up deep in the base of his brain. Both Royce and Jared were protective of their sister, and they would not take kindly to Alec making a pass at her.

Not that Alec would ever make a pass at a client.

He never had.

Of course, he'd never wanted to before, either.

So, maybe it wasn't his high ethical standards that kept him on the straight and narrow. Maybe he'd simply never been presented with a client who had creamy skin, deep, cherry lips, perfectly rounded breasts and the wink of a navel that made him want to wrap his arms around her waist, drag her forward and press wet kisses against her stomach until she moaned in surrender.

A sudden rap on the door jolted him back to reality.

It couldn't be Royce. He was still at the hospital. And Jared was in Chicago.

Stephanie hesitated but then turned from Alec and

moved into the alcove off the living room to open the front door.

"I just wanted to make sure you were okay." Wesley's eager voice carried clearly across the room.

Of course.

The soon-to-be boyfriend.

Wasn't that a nice dose of reality.

Three

Brushing her teeth in the en suite bathroom, Stephanie couldn't help but replay Alec's rescue over and over in her mind.

In the moments after the crash, she'd been preoccupied with Amber's safety. And then the helicopter arrived, and the tow truck, and the staff were all anxious and needing to talk. And later she'd been preoccupied with Alec.

But now she knew that Amber was safe. She was alone with her thoughts, and she found herself focusing on those seconds in Alec's arms.

He was surprisingly strong, amazingly fast and obviously agile. His strength had given her a sense of security. Then later, while they'd argued, she'd felt a flare of something that was a whole lot more than security.

She couldn't exactly put a name to it. But it was strong

enough, that when Wesley had showed up, he'd seemed bland by comparison.

She spat the toothpaste into the sink and rinsed her mouth. As she replaced the toothbrush in the charger, she paused, gazing at herself in the mirror.

Attraction, she admitted, glancing at the door that led from the opposite side of the bathroom into the guest room where Alec was sleeping.

She was attracted to him.

She wanted it to be Wesley, but it was Alec.

She gritted her clean teeth, dragged a comb through her curls, braided them tight and snagged an elastic before heading back into her bedroom.

The window was wide, a cool breeze sliding down from the craggy peaks, while the horses blew and snorted in the fields below. Thoughts still on Alec, roving further into forbidden territory, she dropped her robe onto a chair and climbed between the crisp sheets. Her laundry was still behind, and she was prickly warm, so she'd gone with panties and an old tank top, soft as butter against her skin.

She closed her eyes, but nothing happened.

Well, nothing except an image of Alec appearing behind her eyelids.

When he first showed up, he was just a good-looking city guy. There were plenty of those in magazines and on television. And she'd never been particularly attracted to men based on looks alone.

But now she knew his business clothes masked solid muscles. Worse, she'd learned he had a quick mind and a whole lot of courage. And he'd likely saved her life—which was probably a classic aphrodisiac.

Whatever the cause, she could tell she wasn't getting to sleep anytime soon.

She tossed off her comforter, letting the breeze cool her skin, staring out at the three-quarter moon, trying not to think about Alec in the next room. So close.

No. Not so close. So far.

It was fine for her to lay here and fantasize, she told herself. It was perfectly normal and perfectly natural. In real life, it needed to be Wesley, but here in the dark of night…

She flipped onto her stomach. Then she fluffed her pillow and searched for a comfortable position.

She couldn't find one. She flipped back again, reaching for the water glass on her bedside table. It was empty.

Sighing in frustration, she clambered from the bed and crossed the carpet to the bathroom. Opening the door, she flicked on the light.

That exact moment, the door from Alec's room swung open. They both froze under the revealing glare, staring at each other in shock. Her hormones burst to instant attention, and she nearly dropped the glass.

Alec's chest was bare, the top button of his slacks undone. His hair was mussed, and his chin showed the shadow of a beard. As she'd guessed from his embrace, his shoulders were wide, his biceps bulged, and the pecs on his deep chest all but rippled under the light.

His gaze flicked down her body, stopping at her panties, and tension flicked in the corners of his mouth. "Is that from today?"

Her heart pushed hard against her ribs, knowing the skimpy outfit was very revealing.

"Did I *hurt you?*" he demanded.

And then she realized he wasn't salivating over her

bare legs, her skimpy top or the high-cut panties. His gaze had zeroed in on the bruise from where she'd fallen off Rosie-Jo.

She couldn't decide whether to feel relieved or disappointed. "It wasn't you," she assured him. "I fell off my horse."

He took a step forward. "Have you seen a doctor?"

"It's just a bruise."

"It looks deep. Do you need some ice?"

I'm standing here nearly naked. "No."

He moved closer still, and a hitch tightened in a band around her chest, while her hormones raced strategically around her body.

"It'll take the swelling down," he went on. "I can run to the kitchen and—"

"Alec!"

"What?"

"I'm standing here in my underwear."

He blinked. "Right." Then his eyes darkened to charcoal. "Right," he said, his gaze skimming her from head to toe.

She wished she could tell what he was thinking, but his expression gave away nothing. After a long minute, he drew a breath. "Sorry." He took a step back.

"Alec—"

He shook his head, holding up his palms. "Let's just forget this ever happened."

He was right, of course. But she couldn't seem to stop the thick layer of disappointment that slid its way through her stomach. Did he not find her even remotely attractive?

She guessed not, since he hadn't even noticed how she was dressed until she'd pointed it out.

He might have saved her life. He might care about

her physical safety. But apparently it was in a purely platonic way.

"I wasn't—" He took another backward step. "I didn't—" He shook his head. "I'm sorry," he repeated. Then he shot through the doorway to firmly click the door shut behind him.

Stephanie was sorry, too. But she suspected it was for an entirely different reason.

Alec spent the next few days working as fast as humanly possible and avoiding Stephanie as much as he could— which didn't turn out to be difficult, since she was an early riser, and she worked long hours.

Keeping himself from thinking about her proved a considerably tougher challenge. The picture of her in her tank top and panties was permanently seared into his brain stem.

Her face had been scrubbed and shiny, not that she ever seemed to wear makeup. Her shoulders were smooth and lightly tanned, her breasts were perfectly shaped, barely disguised under the thin, white fabric of the well-worn top. Her legs were long and toned, accented by the triangular, flat lace insets of her panties. And her waist was nipped in, stomach flat and smooth.

It had taken all of his willpower not to surge across the tiny bathroom and drag her into his arms.

He drew a shuddering breath, pulled the borrowed ranch truck transmission into fourth gear, and sped up on the final stretch of the road between Stephanie's equestrian stable and the main cattle ranch.

Business Consulting 101, he ruthlessly reminded himself. *Keep your hands off the clients' sister.* His business had been built on integrity. His clients trusted him with sensitive problems that were often high stakes and high risk. If he tossed his principles and made a pass at a client, no one would ever be able to trust him again.

In a self-preservation move, rather than talk to Stephanie face-to-face about her publicity history, he'd mentioned the scrapbooks to Amber. Amber had helpfully offered to hunt them down.

He'd already developed a comprehensive picture of the Ryder Equestrian Center from a business perspective. Not that he was under any illusion that the Ryder brothers wanted to learn the truth about their sister's profitability.

In any event, once he finished with the scrapbooks, he'd head back to the safety of his Chicago office, away from the temptation of Stephanie. The report would stand on its merits. Jared and Royce could use it or ignore it. It was completely up to them.

The main ranch house came into view, and he geared down to control the dust, bringing the truck to a smooth stop on the circular driveway between the house, the barns and the corrals.

Like Stephanie's place, the original ranch house was set on the Windy River. Groves of trees and lush fields stretched out in all directions. There was a row of staff cabins accessed by a small bridge across the river. Working horses were corralled near the house, while clusters of brown and white cattle dotted the nearby hillsides.

Jared Ryder appeared on the porch, coffee cup in hand, and Alec drew a bracing breath as he exited the truck.

He waved a greeting, slammed the door and paced across the driveway. "Didn't know you were in Montana," he said to Jared as he mounted the front steps.

"Just overnight," Jared returned. "Melissa and I wanted to check on Amber."

"How's she doing?"

"She's good. Thanks again, by the way."

"Not a problem."

Despite Stephanie making such a big deal about it, Alec suspected her brothers were both the kind of men who'd rescue anyone in need without a lot of fanfare.

Jared's matter-of-fact nod told Alec he was right.

"I should be done at the Equestrian Center tomorrow," Alec offered. With some hard work, he could wrap things up tonight.

"Glad to hear it. The sooner you get started in Chicago, the better." Then his expression turned serious, voice going lower as he glanced around them. "I hear Royce told you about our little issue."

Alec lowered his own voice in response. "About the blackmail?"

"Yeah."

"He did," Alec confirmed. "And I advised him to come clean with Stephanie."

Jared scoffed out a laugh. "Yeah, that's not going to happen."

"That's exactly what Royce told me."

"He thought you might help?"

"If I can."

Jared gave another considered nod. "Personally, I suggested we hunt him down and—"

"That's not the kind of work I do," Alec quickly put in, on the off chance Jared was serious.

"I wasn't going to suggest we harm him. Though I can't deny the idea has merit. I was thinking more along the lines of explaining to him in excruciating detail what each of us has to gain by ending this, and what each of us has to lose if he keeps it up.

"But it's a moot point anyway. We can't do anything until we find him. And, so far, we haven't been able to find him." Jared gave Alec a significant look.

A moment of silence passed.

"You want me to check into his whereabouts?" asked Alec.

"Amber's friend Katie says you have contacts."

Katie Merrick was a lawyer working for Alec's father's firm, Creighton Waverley Security. Where Creighton Waverley was conservative and by the book outfit, Alec had contacts who could be a little more creative.

"His name is Norman Stanton," Jared offered. "Frank Stanton, Stephanie's biological father, was his brother. The blackmail payments are all tied up in some off-shore company called Sagittarius Eclipse. That's pretty much all we know."

"That's a start." Alec nodded decisively. He'd be more than happy to help track down the man who had targeted Stephanie.

Stephanie needed to purge her wayward fantasies once and for all. And Wesley was the key. Across the arena, he was calling her name, making his way toward her through the soft, deep dirt.

"I've been looking for you," he gasped, as he grew close enough to speak. He ducked through the rails, rising up beside her.

Stephanie was observing Brittany, one of her youngest students, in the starting area of the jumping course.

She smiled briefly at Wesley then nodded to Brittany's trainer, Monica, where she held the bridle of Brittany's horse. Monica stepped back and gave the start signal, and Brittany cantered her horse toward the first two-foot plank.

"How was California?" Stephanie asked Wesley, glancing his way again.

He truly was a fine looking man. His blond hair curled around his ears. He had bright blue eyes and an aristocratic nose. And his quick sense of humor and easy laugh had made him friends throughout the stable.

"It was a long three days," he responded with a warm smile. "My sister has boyfriend trouble. My mother cooked five meals a day. And I missed you."

"I missed you, too." Stephanie told herself it wasn't really a lie, since she wanted so much for it to be true. She rested her elbow on the second rail, tipping her head to look at him.

Truth was she hadn't thought much about him while he was away. Her only excuse was that she'd been busy training. The Brighton competition was coming up in a few short weeks, and it was the unofficial start of qualifying for the Olympic team.

Training was important. It was hard to find time to think about anything else.

Well, except for Alec.

She clamped her jaw down hard, ordering herself to forget about Alec. He'd been skulking around the stable all week, asking questions, printing financial reports, and generally making a nuisance of himself.

Wesley did his part. He took a step closer to her, his shoulder brushing against her elbow.

Brittany turned her horse and headed for jump number four.

Wesley brushed his fingers along Stephanie's bare forearm, easing closer still. He touched the back of her hand, turning it to feather his fingertips across her palm, before cupping her hand and giving her a squeeze.

It was a gentle touch. A pleasant touch. She forced herself to concentrate on enjoying it.

"We need to talk, Stephanie." His blue-eyed gaze went liquid.

"About?"

His smile widened. "About us, of course. I'm dying to kiss you." He moved her hand from the rail and turned her, tugging her toward him, voice going breathy. "I've been thinking about you for three long days."

Stephanie opened her mouth, but the words she wanted to utter wouldn't come out. She hadn't been thinking about Wesley for three long days. And she wasn't dying to kiss him.

Okay, she wasn't exactly opposed to kissing him. But the rush of excitement she'd felt the last two times they'd come close was decidedly absent.

"Tell me how you feel," he breathed.

Brittany cantered past. The clomp of her horse's hooves tossed sprays of dirt, while the *whoosh* of its breathing filled the air. Stephanie used the instant to pull back.

"I really like you, Wesley," she told him.

"That's good." He smiled confidently and moved in again.

"I'm…" Curious? Hopeful? Desperate to have you erase Alec from my thoughts?

"You're what?" he prompted.

"Worried." The word jumped out before she could censor it.

He frowned. "About what?"

"You're my student."

It was a lame excuse, and they both knew it.

Jessica Henderson had been her now husband Carl's student for three years before they announced their engagement. Nobody had been remotely scandalized by the relationship. In fact, half the state horse jumping community had attending their wedding.

"You make me sound like a kid," said Wesley.

"You're younger than me," Stephanie pointed out, feeling suddenly desperate to get out of the kiss she'd been planning for so long.

"Barely," he told her, the hurt obvious in his tone.

"Still—"

"Stephanie, what's going on?"

"Nothing," she lied again.

"I *missed* you."

She tried to come up with something to say.

He stepped into the silence. "You're beautiful, funny, smart—"

"I have a business to run and a competition to train for."

"What are you talking about? What happened while I was gone?"

"Nothing." It was the truth.

His lips puffed out in a pout. "I don't believe you."

Stephanie took a breath and regrouped. "It's just… I need to focus right now, Wesley. And so do you. Brighton is only a few weeks away."

She sped up her words, not giving him a chance to jump back in. "And we both need to nail it. It's your first major, senior event, and I need the ranking."

"I still don't see why we can't—"

"We can't, Wesley."

He reached for her hand once more, squeezing down. "But we're so good together." With the sun slanting across his tousled hair, and the pleading tone in his voice, he suddenly struck her as very young.

"We can be friends," she offered.

His brow furrowed. "I don't want to be friends."

"Yes, you do. We're already friends. We're going to train together and nail Brighton."

"And then what?"

"What do you mean?"

"After Brighton? If we still feel the same way?"

She didn't know what to say. She didn't feel the way she wanted to feel, and she didn't see that changing.

He grinned, obviously taking her silence for agreement. The eager, puppy-dog look was back in his eyes. "I know we have something special."

"We have friendship and mutual respect," she offered carefully.

"There's more than that."

Stephanie took a step back. "Seriously, Wesley, I can't let you—"

"Not right now. I get it." He gave a vigorous nod. "But we both know—"

"No, we don't know—"

Brittany shrieked, and Monica shouted, and Stephanie whirled to see the horse shy to one side. It refused the jump and sent Brittany bouncing into the soft ground.

The girl's breath whooshed out as she landed with a thump on her rear end.

By the time Stephanie was through the fence, Brittany had grabbed two handfuls of dirt and tossed them down in disgust.

She was obviously more angry than injured, but Stephanie rushed to assist just in case.

* * *

Stephanie was angry with herself.

But she was also angry with Alec.

What was he *doing* to her? Why did he have to usurp Wesley? Why couldn't she get the bare-chested image of him out of her head. And *why* hadn't he been interested in her when she was standing half naked in front of him?

All he'd noticed was her stupid bruise.

It was the end of a long, frustrating day, and she marched through the front door. She stripped off her gloves and boots then came around the corner to find the object of her frustration stationed at the dining table, stacks of papers fanned out in front of him. There were magazines, newspaper clippings, financial reports and reference books.

He glanced up, expression unreadable.

She tried to think of a clever greeting, but nothing came to mind. She stood there in silence, her heart beating faster, her hormones revving too high, and her brain tripping up over itself.

"I finished the publicity and promotion calculations," he finally offered. He slid a piece of paper in her direction. "Amber gave me your scrapbooks."

Stephanie ordered her feet to move forward, keeping her attention fixed squarely on the printout as she crossed the hardwood floor. She lifted the paper, scanning to the bottom where each of the past ten years were listed with a corresponding total.

"That can't be right," she found her voice. The numbers were ridiculously low.

"You did get quite a lot of coverage," Alec admitted, setting down his pen and crossing his arms over his chest. "But it's in random placements."

She glanced at him. "Some of those magazines charge tens of thousands of dollars for a single ad. I had the cover. I had the center pages. That's priceless. Ryder International was mentioned over and over again."

"As a targeted placement. Sure, you're going to pay a premium price. But the Ryder International demographic is no more likely to be reading *Equine Earth* as they are to be reading *People* Magazine."

"That's not true."

Alec scraped his chair backward and came to his feet.

"Horse people have money," she repeated her earlier assertion. "They own businesses. They rent real estate."

"Maybe," he agreed. "But maybe not. Now, if Ryder International was in the equestrian equipment business, *Equine Earth*—"

"We're in the equine *breeding* business."

"Revenues from your breeding sales are a tiny fraction of the revenues from the real estate division."

"You're out to get me, aren't you?"

"I'm not—"

She thrust the paper back on the table. "From the minute you walked onto this ranch, you've been out to prove that I'm not a valuable partner in this corporation."

"These numbers aren't my personal opinion—"

"The hell, they're not."

"They're generally recognized calculations for determining—"

"Shut up."

He stiffened. "Excuse me?"

She moved in. "I said shut up. I am so tired—"

"Of what?" he asked incredulously.

"Of you! Of you and your—" She ran out of words. What was she trying to say? That she was tired of being attracted to him? Of knowing that he wasn't attracted to her? Of having his presence at the stable mess with her mind?

He waited, staring hard.

She mustered an explanation. "Of you trying to prove I have no value."

His look turned to confusion. "Is that what you think?"

She gestured to his work with a sweep of her arm. "That's what all this says."

"It says you're a financial drain on the corporation. And you are."

"I'm an asset."

"Not a financial one."

Her throat closed up with emotion, and she hated it.

Why did she care what he thought? Her brothers weren't going to accept this. What could it possibly matter that some opinionated, hired gun of a troubleshooter thought she wasn't pulling her weight?

It shouldn't.

And it didn't.

But then something shifted in his expression, and he cursed under his breath. "I'm trying to be honest, Stephanie."

She didn't trust herself to speak, and she needed him to think it didn't matter, so she waved her hand to tell him to forget about it. She wished he'd back off now and leave her to wallow.

But he took a step closer, then another, and another. His eyes went dark, from pewter to slate to midnight.

She stilled, unable to breathe. Her chest went tight. Her heart worked overtime to pump her thickening blood. And she found herself gazing up at him, feeling the pinpricks of longing flow over her heating skin.

Suddenly he clamped his jaw and his hands curled into fists. "We *can't*."

No, they couldn't.

Wait a minute. Couldn't what? Did he mean what she thought he meant?

"Stephanie. You're my *client*."

Yes, she was.

And that mattered.

At least it should matter.

Shouldn't it?

But a kiss wouldn't hurt. A kiss was nothing. She'd kissed a dozen men, well, boys really. A kiss didn't have to lead anywhere. It didn't have to mean anything.

And then at least she'd know. She'd know his touch, his scent, his taste.

She subconsciously swayed toward him.

"Stephanie." His voice was strangled.

The world seemed to pause for breath.

And then he was reaching, pulling, engulfing her, plastering her body against his, flattening her breasts, surrounding her with his strong arms. His mouth came down on hers, open, hot, all encompassing.

Passion shot through her body, igniting every nerve ending, every fiber from her hair to her toes.

He tipped his head, deepening the kiss. She opened her mouth, shocked that these intense sensations could come from a simple kiss. Her arms stretched around his neck, and her body instinctively arched against him.

His hands slid down her spine, lower, and lower still. She gasped at the sensation, moaning when the heat of his palms cupped her bottom.

She curled her fingertips into his hairline, struggling for an anchor, her knees going weak, as the subsonic vibrations of arousal sapped the strength of her legs. She kissed him harder, her thigh relaxing, allowing his own to press between, sending shock waves through her torso.

"Stephanie," he rasped, and she loved the breathless sound of his voice.

He groaned then, breaking away, reaching backward to unclasp her hands.

But she fought back, shaking free from his grasp, cupping his face and peppering his mouth with quick kisses. She did *not* want this feeling to end.

He gave a guttural groan, enveloping her again, taking over the rhythm, bending her backward and thrusting his tongue deep into her mouth while one hand slid up her rib cage, surrounding her breast.

She kissed him fervently, fists tightening, toes curling, as she struggled to get closer and closer.

Then suddenly, she was lifted from the floor, scooped into his arms. The kisses continued and sensations built as he carried her up the stairs to her bedroom. There, he set her down, and his fingers swiftly scrambled with the buttons on her blouse.

Yes. Skin to skin. They absolutely needed to be skin to skin. She fumbled with the knot in his tie, making little progress. She switched to the buttons on his white shirt.

He chuckled deep in his chest as he swooped off her blouse, removing her bra in one deft motion. "I win," he breathed in triumph.

Then he helped her out, and tore open his shirt, discarding it on the floor.

She sighed in sublime satisfaction as his hot body came

up against hers. Her breasts and belly tingled, and her skin flushed with pleasure.

He lifted her once more, sinking onto the bed full-length. His hand found her bare breast, strumming the nipple to exquisite arousal. His kisses roamed from her mouth to her neck to her shoulder, and finally to the hard beads of her sensitized nipples. She was restless, itchy, and her hands felt empty, but she didn't know what to do with them.

She buried them in his short hair, convulsively tightening her fingertips against her scalp. Her thighs twitched apart, and he settled between them. A burst of desire rocketed through her belly. She reached for the waistband of his slacks, certain they needed less clothing between them and more heated skin.

He helped her out again, rising to strip off the rest of their clothes. He paused then, his gaze sweeping hotly over every single inch of her nakedness.

She loved the way he was looking at her, as if he liked what he saw. She loved that she was naked, loved that she could stare right back at his glorious, hot, sculpted body.

He slowly lowered himself against her, one palm running from her knee to her breasts, then back again. He gently eased her legs apart, watching her expression. Then he kissed her eyelids, took her mouth once more in a deep, lingering, passionate kiss.

His touch became firm, his movements more hurried, and when he tore open a condom, she experienced a moment of fear. But then he was back, and his kisses were magic, and her body took over, spreading and arching and welcoming him.

She expected a pain, but it was minor and fleeting, and the building sparks of desire quickly filled her mind. He adjusted her body, and the sensations intensified. She dragged in labored breaths, hands convulsing against his back, toes curled and hips arching to meet him with every stroke.

They rode a wave that stretched on and on, until his body tensed. His rhythm increased. He cried out her name, while lights and sound exploded in her mind, making her weightless, suspended in time, before she pulsed back to earth and felt the weight of Alec on top of her.

His breathing slowed, and he kissed her temple, her ear, her neck.

Then he dragged in a labored gasp. "Stephanie Ryder, you blow my mind."

She struggled to catch her own breath. "If I could talk," she panted. "I'd tell you exactly the same thing."

He chuckled deep, rolling over to put her on top.

Her limbs felt like jelly. But now that it was over, a soreness crept in between her legs. She shifted to ease it.

"Careful," he warned, reaching his hand between them. He eased out of her body.

But then he frowned, lifting his fingers to peer at them in the bright moonlight. "What the hell?"

He whirled his head, pasting her with an accusing look. "You're a virgin?"

"Not anymore."

He recoiled in what looked like horror. "Why didn't you *say something?*"

"Why would I?" It was her problem, not his. Besides, it wasn't like she was saving herself for some mythical future marriage.

"Because..." he sputtered. "Because..."

"Would you have done something different?" Personally she wouldn't have changed a thing. Virginity wasn't a big deal in this day and age.

"I wouldn't have done *anything at all*."

"Liar," she accused. Half an hour ago, neither of them had been thinking past sex. "Did you tell the first woman you slept with that she was the first?"

He frowned in the starlight. "That's completely diff—"

"Ha! Double standard."

He raked a hand through his mussed hair. "I can't believe we're having this argument."

"Neither can I."

"You'll argue about anything, won't you?"

"Takes two to tango, Alec."

He curled an arm around her shoulders and pulled her tight. "You are impossible."

"And you're inflexible."

"You really should have said something." But his voice was starting to fade as a pleasant lethargy took over her body.

"I didn't," she muttered. "Get over it."

His voice dropped to a whisper next to her ear. "I doubt I'll be doing that for a very, very long time."

Her eyes fluttered closed, and her body relaxed into sleep.

Then, after what seemed like only seconds, there was a loud knock on her bedroom door. She blinked, and the bright sunlight stung her eyes.

"Stephanie?" Royce's voice demanded.

Alec was on his feet, clothes in hand, and through the connecting door to the bathroom in a split second.

"Hang on," she shakily called to her brother.

"Something wrong?"

"Why?" She blinked again, struggling to adjust her eyes.

"It's after nine."

She sat straight up and glanced around, grabbing her discarded clothes and stuffing them under the covers just in case Royce barged in. "I overslept."

"Have you seen Alec?"

"Uh, not since last night." Technically, it was true, since she'd had her eyes closed for the past few hours.

"He's not in his room."

The water came on in the bathroom.

"I hear the shower," she called to her brother. "Meet you downstairs?"

There was a pause. "Sure."

Stephanie flopped back down on her pillow, blowing out a sigh of relief. Not that her sex life was any of her brother's business. But, wow. She'd hate to have to listen to the shouting.

Four

As Alec approached the kitchen, he heard both Royce's and Jared's voices. He adjusted his collar, straightened his cuffs and shoved his guilt as far to the back of his mind as humanly possible.

Then he cringed as he passed the messy dining room table. They all would have seen it on their way to the kitchen, and it was completely unprofessional to leave his work scattered like that.

"We're all heading out there in an hour," Jared was saying.

"Good morning," Alec put into the pause, glancing at the faces around the breakfast bar, first at Jared and Royce, then Melissa and Amber, checking for anger or suspicion.

Nothing he could detect, so he allowed himself a quick glance at Stephanie.

Damn it. She looked like she'd made love all night long. And her gaze on him was intense.

When Amber turned toward her, Alec quickly cleared his throat, moving toward the coffeepot, hoping to keep everyone's attention from Stephanie. The woman had no poker face whatsoever.

"Heading where?" he asked Jared as he poured.

"The airport. We can give you a lift."

Alec didn't dare look, but he could feel Stephanie's shock. It wasn't perfect timing, but he couldn't very well refuse the offer after telling Jared he was leaving today. There was work to do in Chicago, and there was also Norman Stanton to deal with.

Besides, what was he going to do if he stayed? Make love to Stephanie again? If they were alone in the same house, odds were good it would happen. His professional ethics were already teetering on the edge of oblivion.

"Thanks," he forced himself to tell Jared. Then he turned, casually taking a sip from the stoneware mug. "Stephanie? I've got a couple more questions before I pack things up." He nodded toward the dining room, hoping she'd get the hint. It might be their one chance to say goodbye alone.

Standing at the opposite side of the breakfast bar, she was blinking at him like a deer in the headlights.

This time Amber did catch Stephanie's expression, and she frowned.

"Stephanie?" he repeated. If she didn't snap out of it, they were going to have one hell of a lot of explaining to do.

"What?" She gave her head a little shake.

"In the dining room? I had a couple of questions."

"Oh. Right." Now she was looking annoyed with him. That was much better.

She followed him out, but Amber came on her heels, followed by Royce and the rest of the family. Alec was stuck with asking Stephanie some inane business questions, to which he already had answers, as he packed the papers away in his briefcase.

In no time, they were heading out the door to Jared's SUV. Alec hung back, but he only managed the briefest of goodbyes and apologies to Stephanie before he had to leave.

Stephanie spent the next few weeks training hard with Rosie-Jo for the Brighton competition. At first, she'd been angry with Alec for his abrupt departure. Then she'd been grateful. After all, there was no sense in prolonging it.

They'd had a one-night stand, no big deal. She couldn't have asked for a better lover. And, though it was short, it had been wonderful, physically, at least.

But then the gratitude wore off, and she felt inexplicably sad and lonely. She found herself remembering details about him—the sound of his laugh, how his gray eyes twinkled when he teased her, his confident stride, his gentle touch, the heat of his lips and the taste of his skin.

She knew she was pining away for something that couldn't be, for something that had never existed in the first place, except in her own imagination.

She didn't think she felt guilty about making love to him. But maybe she did. Maybe that was why she was pretending their relationship was something more than a fling.

Cold fact was, she'd given her virginity to a man she didn't love, a man who was little more than a stranger.

It was the end of another long training day. She stabled Rosie-Jo and double-checked the feeding schedule. Leading up to Brighton, everything about Rosie's regime had to be perfect, as did Stephanie's.

She pressed her hands against the small of her back, arching as she sighed. Her period was a few days late, and she was getting frustrated with the wait. It was only a small difference, but competing at the most favorable hormonal point in her cycle could be the edge she needed to win. If she didn't get it by the weekend, she could be jumping with PMS.

She pulled her ponytail loose, finger-combed her hair and refastened the rubber band as she made her way to the barn door. She was exhausted, almost dizzy with fatigue today. And she was famished.

She took that as a good sign. It wasn't uncommon for her to polish off a pint of ice cream and a bag of potato chips the day before her period started. Not that she'd indulge in either this close to a competition. She'd have some grilled chicken and a big salad instead.

The thought of the food had her picking up her pace across the yard. But by the time she got to the front porch, she'd changed her mind. Chicken didn't really appeal to her. Maybe she'd do a steak instead.

Then she opened the door and caught the aroma of one of her housekeeper Rosalind's stews. She gripped the door frame for a split second. Okay, definitely not stew. She'd sit out on the back veranda and grill that steak.

The next morning, Stephanie blinked open her eyes, surprised to find it was nine-fifteen. The training schedule was obviously wearing her out. Fair enough. Her body was telling her something. She'd make sure she incorporated an extra hour sleep in her routine for the next two weeks.

She sat up quickly, and a wave of nausea had her dropping right back down on the pillow.

Damn it. She could not get sick.

Not now.

She absolutely refused to let a flu bug ruin the competition.

She gritted her teeth, sitting up more slowly. There. That was better. Wasn't it?

She gripped the brass post of her bed, willing her stomach to calm down.

It wasn't fair. First her period screwup, and now this. She needed to do well at Brighton. She'd trained her entire life for this year of all years. But it was as if the stars were lining up against her.

She started for the en suite, telling herself it was mind over matter. She was young and healthy. And she had a strong immune system. She was confident she'd quickly fight off whatever it was she'd picked up.

She stopped in front of the sink, pushing her messy hair back from her face, groping for her toothbrush and unscrewing the toothpaste cap.

She caught a glimpse of herself in the mirror. Her face was pale. Her eyes looked too big today, and the smell of the toothpaste had her rushing to retch into the toilet.

There was little in her stomach, but she immediately felt better. What the heck was wrong—

She froze.

"No." The hoarse exclamation was torn from her.

Her hand tightened on the counter edge and she shook her head in denial. She could *not* be pregnant.

They'd only done it once. And they'd used a condom.

Okay. She breathed. She had to calm down. She was only scaring herself. How many crazy thoughts had popped into her head since Alec left? This was simply one more in the series.

She drew another deep breath. The nausea had subsided.

It had to be psychosomatic. Her period would start today, maybe tomorrow. Her hormones would get back on track. She'd stick to her training regime, and she'd kick butt in Brighton.

Anything else was unthinkable.

On morning four of the nausea and exhaustion, Stephanie dragged her feet to the bathroom, staring with dread at the home pregnancy test she'd picked up the afternoon before. Even before she followed the directions, she knew what the answer would show.

Sure enough, the two blue stripes were vivid in the center of the viewing window. She was pregnant.

She plunked the plastic stick in the trash bin and moved woodenly to the shower.

As the warm water cascaded over her body, she let a tear escape from her eye. Then another, and another.

What oh *what* had she done? This was her year, first the nationals, then the European championships and finally tryouts for the Olympic team.

The moment she'd trained for, longed for, prayed for her entire life was upon her, and she was going to have a baby instead, without a father. Her brothers would be furious on both counts. They'd be so disappointed in her.

Her mind searched hopelessly for a way to keep it secret.

Maybe she could fake an injury and take herself out of competition. Then she would find an excuse to stay in Europe for six months. And, then... And, then...

She whacked the end of her fist against the shower wall in frustration.

What would she do? Come back to Montana with a baby in tow? Tell them she adopted some poor orphan in Romania?

It was a stupid plan.

Defeated, she slowly slid her way down the wall, water drizzling over her as she came to rest on the bottom of the tub. She wrapped her arms around her knees, staring blankly into space as the water turned from hot to tepid.

"Stephanie?" Amber's voice surprised her. It was followed by a rap on the bathroom door.

"Just a sec," Stephanie called out, rising to her feet, swiftly spinning off the now-cold water.

"You okay?" Amber asked.

"Fine." Stephanie flipped back the curtain and grabbed a towel, scrubbing it over her puffy cheeks and burning eyes.

What was Amber doing in Montana?

"You've been in there forever," Amber called.

"What are you doing here?"

"Royce got restless in Chicago. It was either this or fly to Dubai for the weekend. You want to come down to the main house for a while?"

Stephanie pressed her fingertips into her temples. The last thing in the world she needed was one of her brothers hanging around. She needed to be alone right now.

"I have to train," she called through the door.

"You decent?" asked Amber.

"I'm—"

The door opened, and Stephanie quickly wrapped the big bath towel around her body.

"Morning." Amber grinned.

"You never heard of privacy?"

"We're practically sisters." Then Amber's grin faded. She cocked her head, staring into Stephanie's eyes. "What on earth?"

Stephanie quickly turned away, coming face-to-face with her own reflection in the mirror. Her eyes were bloodshot. Her cheeks had high, bright pink spots, but the rest of her face was unnaturally pale.

"I had a rough night," she tried, but her voice caught on her raw throat.

Amber's arm was instantly around her shoulders. "What's wrong? Did you get bad news? One of the horses?"

"No." Stephanie shook her head.

Then Amber's gaze caught on something. Her eyes went wide, and her jaw dropped open.

Stephanie looked down to see the home pregnancy test box on the counter.

"You can't tell Royce," she croaked.

"You're *pregnant*."

Stephanie couldn't answer. She closed her eyes to block out the terrible truth.

"Is it Wesley?"

Stephanie quickly shook her head.

"Who—"

"It doesn't matter."

There was a silent pause, then Amber touched her shoulder. "Alec."

Stephanie's eyes flew open. "You can't tell Royce."

"Oh, sweetheart." Amber pulled Stephanie into her arms. "It's going to be okay. I promise you, it's going to be okay."

It wasn't often that Alec spent time in his Chicago office. For one thing, his jobs rarely kept him in the city.

He preferred to be on the ground, gathering information from real people in different places around the world.

Consequently his office was stark, almost sterile. In a central location between the river and the pier, it was a single room on the thirty-second floor. The view was spectacular. The desk was smoke glass and metal, with sleek curves and clean lines. Matching chairs were thinly padded with charcoal leather. He used his laptop everywhere he went, and his file cabinets were stainless steel, recessed into the wall.

There was no need for a receptionist, since his phone number wasn't published. He wasn't listed on the building's lobby directory, and he rarely had more than one job on the go at a time.

So, it was a surprise when the office door swung open.

Alec glanced up to see Jared fill the doorway. He walked determinedly inside, followed closely by Royce, their faces grim.

They shut the door and positioned themselves on either side, folding their arms across their chests, as Alec came to his feet. There wasn't a doubt in his mind that they knew he'd taken Stephanie's virginity.

"Stephanie told you," he stated the obvious. He wouldn't lie, and he wouldn't deny it. If they fired him, they fired him.

Jared spoke. "Stephanie doesn't know we're here."

Alec nodded and came out from behind the desk, ready to face them.

Royce stepped in. "Stephanie's pregnant."

The words stopped Alec cold.

Seconds dripped like icicles inside the room.

"I had no idea," he finally said.

"You're not denying you're the father," Jared stated.

"I'm not denying anything. Whatever Stephanie told you, you can take as true."

"Stephanie didn't tell us anything," said Royce.

Then Alec wasn't about to add to their body of knowledge. What happened between him and Stephanie was private.

She was pregnant, and he'd absolutely do the right thing. And her brothers had every right to call him on it. But they didn't have a right to anything more than she was willing to voluntarily share.

Jared took a step forward, and Alec wondered if he was going to take a swing.

"Here's what we're going to do," Jared said.

"I *will* marry her," Alec offered up-front.

"Not good enough," said Royce, squaring his shoulders to form an impenetrable wall next to his brother.

Alec didn't understand. There were limited options at this point.

"We don't want to see Stephanie get hurt," said Jared.

Alec's mental reflex was to make a joke about that being the understatement of the century. But he held his tongue.

"No woman wants a marriage of convenience," said Royce.

Alec still wasn't following.

"She wants a love match."

Alec peered at Royce. "Are you saying you want her to marry someone else?" His thoughts went to Wesley, and he found his anger flaring. Wesley wasn't the father of her child. *Alec* was the father of her child.

His mind wanted to delve into that unfathomable concept, but he forced himself to focus on Jared and Royce.

"We mean a love match with you."

Alec gave his head a little shake.

He'd step up. He'd provide financial and any other support needed, but he and Stephanie barely knew each other. They weren't going to settle down and live happily ever after just because her brothers decreed it.

He would never put any woman in that position. He knew from the catastrophe of his own parents' marriage, exactly what happened when you tried to fake it.

"I hope that was a joke," he intoned.

Jared took yet another step forward. "There is nothing remotely funny about any of this."

Alec looked into the man's eyes. "No, there's not. But you can't control people's emotions. She's no more in love with me than I am with her."

"You can change that," said Royce. "Tell her you love her, and make her fall in love with you."

Alec slid his glance sideways. "No."

Not a chance in hell. There was not a freaking chance in hell he would set Stephanie up for that kind of heartache.

Royce squared his shoulders. "It wasn't a question."

Alec could well imagine that few people said no to the Ryder brothers. They were intellectually and physically powerful men. Add to that their economic wherewithal, and they were pretty much going to get their own way in life.

But Alec didn't intimidate easily, and he had a set of personal principles that stopped well short of duping a woman into falling in love with him.

"I'll marry Stephanie," he told them both. "I'll respect her. I will provide for our child. And I'll lie to the world about it if she wants me to. But I won't lie to her."

He gave a harsh laugh. "You two might think you're protecting her by—"

"We *are* protecting her," said Royce, and Jared's expression backed him up.

"Nevertheless," Alec articulated carefully. "*I'm* going to be honest with her."

Since Alec spent most of his life on the road, a marriage of convenience would be fairly easy to pull off. And after the baby was born, she could decide what she wanted. If it was a quiet divorce, no problem.

Jared and Royce glanced uncertainly at each other. It was obvious the meeting wasn't going the way they'd planned.

"May I assume I'm fired?" Alec put in.

The two men exchanged another glance.

Royce cleared his throat.

"I think we'll leave that up to Stephanie," said Jared.

This time Alec did laugh. "Then you might as well take your files with you when you go. She's pretty ticked off about my valuation of her publicity."

The two men hesitated again.

"It is right?" asked Jared.

"It's right," Alec confirmed.

"Let's maybe leave the business arrangement as is for now," said Royce.

Alec glanced from one man to the other. "You sure?"

They both nodded.

"No point in disrupting everything at once," said Jared. Then he clapped a hand down on Alec's shoulder. "You can come back to the ranch with us."

"You afraid I'm going to try to run off?"

"We don't want Stephanie to be upset any longer than necessary."

"She'll still be upset after I get there." Alec tried to picture their conversation. Then he wondered how Stephanie felt about the baby. Then, finally, he let his mind explore how he felt about the baby.

He'd never planned to have children. The genetics in his family did not lend themselves to quality parenting. His father was incapable of love, and his mother had been unable to put her child's welfare ahead of her own misery.

At least Alec's child would have Stephanie.

For some reason, the thought warmed him. Stephanie might be indulged and impulsive, but she was also sweet and loving. He'd seen her work with both animals and children, and he knew instinctively she'd be a great mother.

And he was going to be a father.

As he exited the office with Jared and Royce, he tried hard to keep the prospect from terrifying him.

At the front of the stall, Stephanie rested her forehead against Rosie-Jo's soft nose. She placed her hand on the horse's neck, feeling it twitch and pulse with strength beneath her fingertips.

"I went to see the doctor today," she told Rosie-Jo, wrapping her hands around the mare's bridle.

Rosie-Jo nickered softly in response, bobbing her head up and down.

Stephanie slowly drew back, gazing into the horse's liquid, brown eyes. Her throat closed over. "I'm definitely pregnant, girl."

Rosie-Jo blinked her lashes.

"And that affects you," Stephanie forced herself to continue. "Because he's afraid I might fall off. He's afraid

I'll hurt the baby." Stephanie closed her eyes and drew a bracing breath. "I'm so sorry, Rosie. I know how you love the crowds. And you've worked so hard. And I've worked so hard. For so long."

Rosie snuffled Stephanie's shoulder.

Stephanie opened her eyes to the blur of gray horse hair, her voice catching. "So, he doesn't want me to jump anymore."

"That sounds like good advice to me," someone rumbled behind her.

Rosie snorted, while Stephanie startled. She turned and came face-to-face with the man who'd haunted her dreams.

"Alec?" She struggled to make sense of his presence in the barn. "What are you doing here?"

"Your brothers picked me up in Chicago." His gaze scanned her thin cotton shirt, blue jeans and worn boots.

The implication of his arrival, and the meaning of his opening words penetrated Stephanie's brain.

He knew she was pregnant.

And her brothers must know, too.

She felt the walls close in. She hadn't prepared for this moment, hadn't had any time to even think about it. She'd assumed it would be weeks, even months before her pregnancy was general knowledge.

"I believe Amber gave you up," Alec offered.

Stephanie didn't respond, her mind still grappling with the fact that he knew, that he was here, that the secret was out.

"When were you planning to tell me?" he asked, face impassive, tone guarding his mood.

The word *never* sprang to mind. Though she knew she wouldn't have kept it from him.

"I don't know," she managed, answering him honestly. "I hadn't thought about it." It was enough of a challenge coming to terms with the situation herself.

He shook his head and gave a scoff of disbelief. "You hadn't *thought about it?* You're unexpectedly pregnant, and it's not on your mind twenty-four seven?"

"I just found out."

"You told Amber a week ago."

"And I saw the doctor this morning. I hadn't even decided—"

"Decided *what?*" His voice went deadly low, and his gray eyes turned to black.

"What to do." She had her riding career, her students, her business. Not to mention a baby, then a child. She'd never even known her own mother, how would she handle it all?

He wrapped his hand firmly around her upper arm. "Stephanie, if you even think about—"

She blinked up at him.

"—harming our baby."

Harming? What was he talking…

Then her eyes went wide, and she jerked her arm from his grip. "What is the *matter* with you?"

"Me? You're the one who hasn't made up her mind—"

"How to *raise* the baby." She smacked him on the front of his shoulder. "Not whether to keep the baby."

He didn't even react to the blow. "You can't be happy about this."

"Of course I'm not happy about this. I'm not ready to be a mother. I have a business to run. My jumping career is ruined. And my brothers know I slept with you."

"Your brothers will get over it."

Her brothers. She groaned inwardly.

Royce and Jared knew Alec had made her pregnant.

Wait a minute. She looked him up and down. "You're still standing."

"I am."

She cocked her head. "How come you're still standing?"

"You thought your brothers would kill me for sleeping with you?"

"I never thought my brothers would find out."

"Yeah." He glanced away. "I was kind of counting on the same thing."

Then the fog lifted, and a picture came clear in her mind. Of *course* her brothers hadn't harmed him. They needed him alive.

She didn't know whether to be furious or mortified. "You're here for a shotgun wedding."

"Something like that," he admitted.

She felt guilty on a whole new front now. Alec was a decent guy. He didn't deserve this.

She shook her head. "Don't worry about it."

"Do I look worried?"

"You definitely look worried."

"It doesn't have to be a big deal."

"It doesn't have to be anything at all." Making up her mind, she turned decisively and started down the corridor.

Alec settled in beside her.

She finger-combed her hair and refastened her ponytail at the base of her neck. "Thanks for stopping by, Alec. You're an honorable man. But your baby is safe in my hands. I'll drop you a line once it's born."

He coughed out a laugh. "Yeah, right."

"Your life is in Chicago. Leave this to me." In this day and age, a reluctant husband was a complication not a benefit. What had her brothers been thinking?

"Not quite the way things are going to happen," he said.

"They can't make you marry me."

"Now that part's debatable."

"Okay. Maybe they can make you. But they can't make me." She spotted a length of binder twine on the floor and reflexively stooped to pick it up.

"They want what's best for you, Stephanie."

She wrapped the orange twine neatly around her hand. "No, Alec. They want you to pay for your sins."

"They want to protect you."

She gave a dry chuckle. "From what? A scarlet letter?"

He didn't respond.

"I'm a big girl, Alec. I made a mistake, and I'm going to pay. But it doesn't mean you have to get dragged along for the ride." She peeled the loop of twine from her hand and reached for the door latch.

His hand shot out, blocking the door shut. He stared down at her with an intense singularity of purpose. "Get this straight in your mind, Stephanie. You *are* marrying me."

She squinted at him in the dim light. "That was a joke, right?"

"Am I laughing?"

"I don't know what they threatened you with."

"Nobody threatened me with anything."

"Then why are you talking crazy?"

"I'm talking logic. It doesn't have to be forever."

"And what girl doesn't want to hear *that* in a marriage proposal?"

"Stephanie."

His words shouldn't have the power to hurt her. She barely knew the man. And she needed to keep it that way.

She stuffed the twine in her pocket and crossed her arms over her chest. "Marriage would make a bad situation worse."

He imitated her posture, crossing his own arms. "Marriage would make things right."

Suddenly the entire conversation seemed absurd, and a cold laugh burst out of her. "How do you figure?"

His jaw clenched. "I'm the baby's father."

"Yes?"

"I have a responsibility."

"To do what?"

"I don't know," he practically shouted. "Provide for it."

"You can write a check without having a marriage license."

"Is that what you want?"

"Yes."

"And I have no say?"

"Not really."

He glared at her for a long moment. Then he smacked the door open and marched out of the barn.

As she watched his retreating back, Stephanie realized she had won.

She tried to feel glad about that, but somehow the emotion wouldn't come.

Five

"Well, what was I *supposed* to say?" Stephanie challenged. Sitting on a submerged ledge, water to her waist in the ranch swimming hole, she stared at Amber over the rippled surface of the water.

"Yes?" Amber suggested as she pulled the last couple of strokes across the small, cliff bordered pool and settled on the ledge next to Stephanie. Her forehead was completely healed, and the cut from the accident would barely leave a scar.

The swimming hole was a favorite place for Stephanie. Water from a small tributary to the Windy River trickled down a waterfall and gathered in a deep pool, hollowed out over millennia. The semicircle cliffs were open to the east, so the morning sun soaked into the granite, heating the water, keeping it comfortable all summer long.

It was near noon, and the sun streamed down on Amber's wet, blond hair, reflecting in her jewel-blue eyes.

"And actually *marry* him?" Stephanie swiped her own wet hair back from her forehead, tucking it behind her ears.

"You are having his baby."

"And, we're practically strangers."

"Not completely." Amber's eyes took on a meaningful gleam.

Stephanie glared in return. "Nobody gets married because of a baby anymore."

Amber didn't answer, but an opposing opinion all but oozed from her pores.

"What?" Stephanie prompted.

"You're pregnant, Steph."

"I know that." Stephanie had tried hard to push it from her mind. But the reality wasn't going anywhere.

"A husband might not be such a bad thing."

"I thought you'd be on my side."

"I *am* on your side."

Stephanie snorted her disbelief.

"We're only suggesting you give it a try."

"And if I fail?" Which was a foregone conclusion in Stephanie's mind. And therefore the entire exercise was a waste of time.

"Then you fail. Nothing ventured—"

"We're talking *marriage,* Amber." Stephanie couldn't believe her future sister-in-law could be so cavalier about something so serious. Maybe Stephanie was a hopeless romantic, but she didn't want to stand up in front of God and her family and take vows she didn't mean.

"It doesn't have to be a traditional marriage."

"Maybe that's what I want."

Amber cocked her head, silent for a few moments. "Are you saying you have feelings for Alec?"

"No!" Stephanie's denial was quick. Her emotions caught up a split second later. She didn't have feelings for Alec. She wouldn't allow herself to have feelings for Alec. "I just want…"

"What?"

"Normal. I want something about this entire mess to be normal."

"Define normal." Now Amber was being deliberately obtuse.

"A date? A candlelight dinner? Maybe a movie? Something, anything even a little bit romantic."

Amber snorted out a laugh. "What's romantic? Melissa went undercover and spied on Jared, and Royce picked me up in a bar." She snapped off a twig and tossed it into the pond. "I was a one-night stand that never went home."

Despite herself, Stephanie's interest was piqued. "You and Royce had a one-night stand?"

"Not the first night."

"Which night?"

"None of your business."

"Did you know you loved him?"

"Not at the time."

"Were you a virgin?"

"No."

"But you loved him later. So, somewhere, deep down inside, you must have known."

"Don't do this, Stephanie."

Stephanie clamped her jaw. Amber was right. Comparing herself to Melissa and Amber was futile. They were with men that they loved, men who would stick around, share their lives forever.

Leaves crackled on the trail behind them, and Stephanie turned to see Alec emerge from the trees.

His attention was fixed on Stephanie. "Royce told me I'd find you here."

Amber made to stand up, but Stephanie grabbed at her arm. "Don't go."

"You two have a lot to talk about."

"We've already talked." Stephanie had no desire for a repeat argument. She didn't have the energy.

Amber glanced up, obviously assessing Alec's expression. "I don't think you're done yet." She came to her feet, stepping her way out of the pool where she snagged a towel from a rock. Then she stuffed her feet into a pair of bright blue thongs.

Stephanie braced herself as Alec crouched down beside her. He was wearing a pair of lightweight khakis and plain, white dress shirt. His shoes were too formal, but at least he'd forgone the tie.

"Swimming?" he asked conversationally.

"No. Riding a bike."

"You think sarcasm's going to help?"

"I don't think anything's going to help."

"Right." He shifted. "So, your long-term plan is to wallow in self-pity?"

Stephanie refused to answer. Instead she swung her legs back and forth in the water.

She heard a rustle, then he stepped onto the ledge to sit. He'd stripped down to a pair of black boxers, and she quickly shifted her gaze to the other direction.

"You've seen me naked," he rumbled, amusement clear in his tone.

She might have seen him that way once, but she didn't

intend to see him that way again. She scrambled to put her feet under her.

His hand came down on her shoulder. "Oh, no you're not."

"You're going to hold me prisoner?"

"If I have to." The hand remained firmly in place.

Stephanie gave an angry sigh.

"I was thinking a garden wedding would be nice."

"What part of no didn't you—"

"We could do it here, if you like. Or in Chicago."

"Alec, we can't—"

"There's a ring in my pocket. Simple, but a couple of carats. It should impress your friends." He glanced across the shiny surface of the pool. "Probably not a good idea to give it to you here."

Despite herself, she turned to look at him. "You bought me a diamond?"

"Of course I bought you a diamond. We're getting married."

"You can't bribe me with jewelry, Alec."

"I'm bribing you with a name for our baby."

"I'm hardly a fallen woman."

"This isn't about you, Stephanie."

"Of course it's about—" She almost said me, but she clamped down her jaw instead. Her jumping career was ruined, and that was that. The baby was her priority now.

He smiled. "Ah. A glimmer of responsibility."

"Of course I'll do what's best for the baby." Beneath the water, her hand moved subconsciously to her abdomen.

"Marrying me is best for the baby."

She didn't answer.

"I'm under no illusions that we can 'make it work,'" Alec continued.

"Ah. A glimmer of reality," she mocked.

He frowned at her. "We barely know each other."

"You got that right."

"This isn't my first choice, either."

She stifled a cold laugh, but he ignored her silent sarcasm.

"I'll be honest with you, Stephanie. When it comes to women, I'm not a long-term kind of guy. And I don't see that changing."

Wow. This proposal just kept getting better and better.

Did he mean he'd continue dating? She supposed there was nothing to stop him from doing just that. He had an apartment in Chicago, and he traveled on business most of the time.

She shouldn't care. She had no right to care. Though it would be embarrassing if he was seen in public by someone she knew.

"Will you be discreet?" she asked him.

"Excuse me?"

"With the other women. Will you be discreet?"

His brows knit together. "What other women?"

"You just said your lifestyle wouldn't change."

"I didn't—"

"I assume that means I'm free to see other men," she added defiantly. "Although it would be more complicated for me to—"

"Whoa," he roared. "You are *not* going to be seeing other men."

"Isn't that a double standard?"

"Double *standard?*"

"I'm trying to understand how this will work."

Perhaps refusing Alec had been the wrong strategy. Maybe agreeing to marry him and pressing on the details would be more effective. She'd bet it wouldn't take him long to back out.

"Well, one way it will work, is that my pregnant wife won't be sleeping with other men."

"So, I'll be celibate then?"

"Damn straight."

"For how long?"

"For as long as it takes. It worked just fine for the first twenty-two years of your life."

"That was before."

"Before what?"

Frustration goaded her. "Before I knew how much fun it was to have sex."

Alec's eyes frosted to pewter. His mouth opened then closed again in a grim line.

She didn't care. Let him think she was embarking on a spree of debauchery. So long as it changed his mind about the wedding.

"You're lying," he finally said.

"That sex is fun?" she deliberately misunderstood, crossing her arms beneath her breasts. "You were there, Alec. Do you think I'm lying?"

"You are impossible." But his gaze dipped to her cleavage and the clingy one-piece bathing suit.

The heated look brought a rush of memories, and she realized that talking about their sex life might not be the brightest move. It had been far better than mere fun. And the experience was still fresh in her mind. And, given different circumstances, she'd definitely be in favor of repeating it.

"I'm merely pointing out some of the impracticalities of your master plan," she told him.

"Stephanie, in five or six years, you are going to have a

child in your life asking about their family. Do you want to tell them Daddy was a one-night stand, or do you want to tell them Mommy and Daddy had a fight and don't live together anymore."

Stephanie's brain stumbled on the picture of a five-year-old. There *would* be a five-year-old. And she'd be solely responsible for raising him or her.

Panic rose inside her. How would she manage? Her only role models were a grandfather and two teenage boys.

"I can't—" She came to her feet, water rushing down her legs and dripping from her suit.

Alec rose. "Don't you dare—" But then her expression seemed to register. "Stephanie?"

She was going to have a baby. She was honest to God, going to have a baby.

She felt the blood drain from her face.

She'd never fed a baby, burped a baby, changed a diaper. What if she did something wrong? What if she forgot something important? What if she inadvertently harmed the poor, little thing?

"Stephanie," he sighed in obvious exasperation. He reached for her, pulling her to his body. His bare chest was warm from the sun, and his arms were strong around her. She had a sudden urge to bury her face and hide there forever. His deep voice vibrated reassuringly in her ear.

"Marry me, Stephanie. It won't be perfect. It won't be romantic. But we'll at least be honest with each other."

His sincerity touched her and, miraculously, she didn't feel so completely alone. She let herself sink into Alec's strength. Then she gave in and nodded against his chest.

Stephanie had preferred to hold the wedding at the ranch, and that was fine with Alec. He'd done his duty and informed his father, omitting the fact that Stephanie was pregnant. History might be repeating itself on one level, but the unplanned pregnancy was the only thing his marriage would have in common with his parents'.

Jared and Melissa had flown to the ranch. Then Melissa and Amber had joined forces to convince Stephanie to put on at least a cursory show for the ceremony. It would only be the six of them and a preacher, but they couldn't completely hide the event from the ranch workers, nor should they. It was better if it looked natural.

In the end, they'd chosen a quiet spot by the river. It was a couple of miles up a rutted, grassy road from Stephanie's house, out of sight from the working areas. A field of oats rippled behind them, while horses grazed on the hillside, and the river burbled against a backdrop of cottonwood trees.

Alec and the preacher arrived first, but within minutes, Jared's SUV pulled up with the rest of the party. The men all wore suits, while Amber and Melissa chose knee-length dresses, Amber in bronze, and Melissa in burgundy.

Stephanie was the last to emerge from the backseat. But when she did, Alec couldn't stop staring.

Her white dress was simple, strapless with a high waist and a sparkling belt below her breasts. The skirt fell softly to her knees, showing the curves of her slim, tanned calves. Her shoes were pretty, white satin ballet slippers against the long green grass.

Her hair was upswept, brilliant auburn under the deep, blue sky. She wore diamond earrings and a delicate, matching necklace, and subtle makeup had toned her freckles to nothing. His gaze was drawn to her graceful neck and smooth, bare shoulders.

Alec was far from a romantic man, but he was forced

to fight the urge to sweep her up in his arms and carry her off on a honeymoon.

She took a tentative step forward, and then another.

It was no traditional march down the aisle, and she seemed uncertain of what to do.

Alec moved forward, meeting her halfway, taking her hand so that they approached the preacher together. Her fingertips trembled ever so slightly against his skin, and he fought a thickness in his chest and the desire to pull her tight against him and reassure her. His reaction was ridiculous. The ceremony was as simple as they could make it. They were here to get the job done, nothing more.

The preacher began speaking, and everyone went still.

Stephanie stared determinedly at Alec's chin while she spoke her vows.

Alec by contrast watched her straight on, continuing to marvel at how stunning she looked. He realized that he'd never seen her in a dress, never seen her in jewelry, or with her hair in such a feminine style.

He'd known she was beautiful. He'd been physically attracted to her from minute one. But this incredible creature standing in front of him surpassed any dream or expectation he'd ever had. Once again, he found his imagination moving to a wedding night and honeymoon.

He ruthlessly shut that thought down. He had to keep a distance between them. Royce and Jared's plan to make her fall in love was both foolish and dangerous. Alec's mother had loved his father, and his father's indifference had destroyed her.

Then the preacher was finishing, inviting Alec to kiss the bride.

It seemed silly to do it, but churlish to skip.

So Alec bent his head. He struggled for emotional

distance as he rested a hand on her perfect shoulder, slid the other arm around her slim waist and touched his lips to hers.

It was a tender kiss, nothing like the ones they'd shared when they made love. But sensations ricocheted through him, nearly sending him to his knees.

He held it too long.

He kissed her too hard.

He just barely forced himself to pull back.

When he did, she finally looked at him. Her cheeks were flushed, her mouth bright red, and her silver-blue eyes were wide and vulnerable. Something smacked him square in the solar plexus, and he knew he was in very big trouble.

Even in the midst of her stressful wedding day, Stephanie's heart lifted when she saw McQuestin sitting on the front porch of the main ranch house. The old man was like a second grandfather to her, and she'd missed him while he'd been in Texas recovering from his broken leg.

She rushed out of Jared's SUV, leaving Alec in the backseat.

"You're home," she called, picking her way carefully along the pathway in her thin, impractical shoes.

The old man's smile was a slash across his weather-beaten face. His moustache and thick eyebrows were gray, and his hair, barely a fringe, was cut close to his head. His battered Stetson sat on his blue jean covered knee, while a pair of crutches were leaned against the wall next to his deck chair.

"Married?" he asked gruffly.

"I am," she admitted, giving him a hug and a kiss on his leathery cheek. She hoped her brothers hadn't told McQuestin about her pregnancy.

"How's the leg?" she asked, brushing past the subject of the wedding.

"Be right as rain in no time. This your gentleman?" He nodded past Stephanie.

Her hand still resting on McQuestin's shoulder, she turned to see Alec mount the stairs a few feet in front of Jared and Melissa. Royce's truck came to a halt behind the SUV.

"That's him," said Stephanie.

McQuestin looked Alec up and down. "She's too young to get married." An accusation and a challenge were both clear in his tone.

Alec stepped forward and wrapped an arm around Stephanie's bare shoulders. His hand was warm, strong and slightly callused, and her skin all but jumped under the touch.

"Sometimes a man has to move fast," he responded easily. "Couldn't take a chance on somebody else snapping her up."

McQuestin's faded blue eyes narrowed. "You're not stupid. I'll give you that."

"I told you you'd like him," Jared put in.

"Never said I liked him. Said he wasn't stupid. Now this one, I like." He nodded to Amber as she joined the group. "Got a good head on her shoulders."

"That she does," Royce agreed, and Stephanie realized McQuestin would only have met Amber today. Melissa on the other hand had been engaged to Jared before McQuestin's accident.

McQuestin glanced around at the circle of six. "You go away for a couple of months, and look what happens?"

The comparison of the three relationships made Stephanie uncomfortable. She shrugged out of Alec's embrace and backed toward the door. "I'll go see how Sasha's doing."

"She's got that table all decked out in delicates," said McQuestin. "I'm afraid to touch it."

"We're celebrating," said Melissa, giving him a hug on the way past. "It's good to have you back."

McQuestin winked at her. "A poker game with you later, young lady."

"You bet." Melissa fell into step behind Stephanie, passing through the doorway. "I think he lets me win," she confessed in a whisper.

"If you're winning, he's letting you," Stephanie confirmed.

"Who is he?" asked Amber as the door closed behind the three women. "We only had time for 'hi, how are you,' before we left for the ceremony."

"He's been the ranch manager forever," said Stephanie, slowing her steps as she approached the dining room table.

It was set with her mother's china, the best crystal wine-glasses, an ornate, silver candelabra and low bouquets of wildflowers. Sheer curtains muted the lighting, and Sasha had baked a stunning, three tiered wedding cake. It was pure white, decorated with a cascade of mixed berries and was sitting on the sideboard with an ornate silver knife and a stack of china plates.

Stephanie gripped the back of a chair. "I feel like such a fraud."

"You're not a fraud," said Melissa, coming up on one side.

Amber came up on the other, flanking Stephanie with support. "And it looks delicious."

The unexpected observation made Stephanie smile. "Are we looking at the bright side?"

"No point in doing anything else."

"I suppose that's true," Stephanie allowed as she wandered over to the cake.

It did look delicious. She reached around the back, and swiped her fingertip through the icing then licked the sweetness off with her tongue.

"I can't believe you did that," Melissa laughed.

But Amber followed suit, tasting the icing herself. "Yum. Butter cream."

"It's good," Stephanie agreed.

"I love cake," Amber snickered.

Stephanie lifted the knife. "Let's cut it now."

"Oh, no, you don't." Melissa trapped her wrist.

Stephanie struggled to escape. "What? You worried it's bad luck."

"I don't believe in wedding luck," said Amber, swiping another finger full of icing. "My fiancé saw the wedding dress before the ceremony *and* slept with the bridesmaid. And that turned out to be good luck."

Stephanie and Melissa both blinked, round-eyed at Amber.

"Royce slept with a bridesmaid?" Stephanie asked in astonishment.

"Not Royce. My old fiancé, Hargrove. He slept with my best friend Katie. So I say to hell with luck. Let's eat the cake."

"Hello?" came Alec's censorious voice from the doorway.

Stephanie and Melissa both dropped the knife, and Amber guiltily jerked her finger away from the bottom layer.

"Amber has a thing for cake." Royce's tone was dry next to Alec, but there was a twinkle in his eyes exclusively for Amber.

"That's true," Amber admitted, grinning right back at him, making a show of licking the tip of her finger.

Something about their easy intimacy tightened Stephanie's chest. She didn't dare look at Alec, knowing his expression would be guarded. There was no intimacy between them. They were barely acquaintances.

A few words, no matter how official, couldn't make this a real marriage.

She knew she'd repeated the vows, and so had Alec, because the preacher had pronounced them husband and wife. But there'd been a ringing in her ears, and she'd had trouble focusing her eyes. She couldn't honestly say she recalled any of it.

Except the kiss. She remembered the kiss all too well. And she remembered her body's reaction to it—the arousal, the yearning, the fleeting fantasy that he'd scoop her into his arms and carry her off on a honeymoon.

"Stephanie?" Alec interrupted her thoughts.

Before she could stop herself, she glanced his way and caught his neutral expression, no twinkle, no teasing, no private message.

"The cake," he prompted. "It's up to the bride."

Amber playfully elbowed her in the ribs. "Let's do it."

Stephanie forced a carefree laugh, turning away from Alec. "I don't care if we cut it before dinner."

"Not without a picture," said Melissa.

Stephanie kept the smile determinedly pasted on her face. "Sure."

Alec dutifully moved up next to her and the ornate cake, draping an arm around Stephanie's shoulders.

Despite her vow to remain detached, she flinched under his touch.

"It'll all be over soon," he promised in a whisper.

"Maybe for you," she snapped. "You go right back to your regular life."

He stiffened. "You want me to stay?"

"Of course not." But she realized it was a lie.

She desperately wanted him to stay.

Six

It had been two weeks since Alec had seen or heard from Stephanie. Back in his compact, Chicago office, he'd filled every spare second with reviews of the various Ryder International divisions and queries to the possible whereabouts of Norman Stanton. He'd called in every outstanding favor and, quite literally, had feelers out all over the globe.

But no matter how hard he concentrated, he couldn't get Stephanie off his mind. He knew he had to stay well away from her for both their sakes, but he couldn't help wondering what she was doing. Was she still battling morning sickness? Was she picking out baby clothes? A crib? Thinking about a nursery? Had she been to the doctor again?

He was tempted to call, but he had to be strong. He'd seen the loneliness in her eyes and caught her fleeting glances his way after the wedding ceremony. She was vulnerable right now, and Alec couldn't risk having her look to him for emotional support.

His instinct to care for his wife and unborn child might be strong, but if he gave in, it would be Stephanie who got hurt in the end.

A news update droned in the corner on his small television set, while the cordless phone on his desktop sharply chimed.

It was an unfamiliar area code, and he snapped up the receiver. "Creighton here."

"Alec. It's Damien."

Anticipation tightened Alec's gut. "What've you got?"

"We found him."

Alec rocked forward in his chair, senses instantly alert. "Where?"

"Morocco."

Alec closed his eyes for a brief second of thankfulness. "Good. Great. What now?"

Damien Burke was a decorated, former military man. He'd done tours in both special forces and army intelligence, and there was nobody Alec trusted more.

"The U.S. doesn't have an extradition treaty with Morocco. Not that I'm suggesting we involve the Moroccan authorities. But Stanton will know that. You can bet that's why he's here. And that limits our bargaining power."

"It's not like we didn't expect this," said Alec. The man was smart enough to illegally drain millions of dollars from the Ryders then hide out in a foreign country. It stood to reason he'd done his research on extradition laws.

"I may be able to get him to Spain," Damien offered.

Alec was cautious. "How?" Kidnapping was not something he was prepared to authorize.

Damien chuckled, obviously guessing the direction of Alec's thoughts. "Margarita Castillo, Alec. Trust me, I'm not about to break the law and get myself thrown in a Moroccan jail."

"Who is she?"

"An associate who, I promise you, will have Norman Stanton on an airplane within twenty-four hours."

"And then?"

"And then a friend from Interpol will lay out the man's options."

Alec battled a moment's hesitation. "You won't do anything… You know…"

Damien scoffed. "'You know' won't be even remotely necessary. I've watched the man all day. He's soft as a tourist. We're shootin' fish in a barrel here."

"Good." A tentative satisfaction bloomed to life inside Alec. He might not be able to be with Stephanie in Montana, but he could do this for her.

Not that she'd ever find out.

"Touch base again tomorrow?" asked Damien.

"Thanks," said Alec, signing off and sliding the phone back into the charger.

"—arrived at Brighton earlier this morning," said the female, television news announcer, "and seen here heading for the barn area with her mare Rosie-Jo."

At the sound of the familiar name, Alec's gaze flicked to the television set.

"Anyone who follows the national circuit will remember this pair from Caldona where Stephanie Ryder and Rosie-Jo took first place."

Alec reflexively came to his feet, drinking in the sight of Stephanie's smiling face. She was dressed in faded jeans and a white cotton blouse. Her auburn hair was braided tight, and her amazing clear blue eyes sparkled in the Kentucky sunshine.

"She's had an extraordinary year," the male co-anchor put in.

"And an extraordinary career," said the female. "If they take the blue ribbon this weekend, you have to expect the pair to be a shoe-in for the Olympic team."

If they *what?*

"People are calling Rosie-Jo a cross between Big Ben and Miss Budweiser," the announcer continued.

Alec gave his head a startled shake.

This was Brighton.

It was live.

Stephanie wasn't allowed to jump. It was too dangerous for the baby.

"High praise, indeed," the other answered.

Alec knew she was unhappy about the pregnancy, and he knew how desperately she wanted to compete. But she wouldn't… She couldn't…

She stepped past a cluster of reporters, Wesley beside her, leading Rosie-Jo.

"What would it mean to you to win at Brighton?" one reporter asked her.

"I'm sorry?" she cocked her head to better hear above the noise.

"What makes Rosie-Jo so special?" asked another, drawing Stephanie's attention.

"Ambition." She smiled. "She's a powerful jumper, and she loves her job, so she's always totally enthusiastic. But she's still very careful."

Stephanie took a step back, giving a friendly wave but ignoring the rest of the questions.

Alec flipped open his cell phone, dialing hers as he

powered down his computer. He got her voice mail, left a terse message to call him then tried Royce.

By the time Royce's voice mail kicked in, Alec was out the door on his way to the airport. He didn't know what the hell she was thinking. Forget about who was vulnerable and who might get hurt, his job was to protect his unborn child.

The reporter's question had startled Stephanie, so she'd pretended not to hear it. Word that she'd scratched from the competition had obviously not yet leaked out. But it would be common knowledge by Friday at the latest, and there would be questions, although she had no idea how she was going to answer them.

Wesley turned Rosie-Jo into her appointed stall at the Brighton grounds. His shoulders were tense, and he'd barely said a word since they boarded the plane in Montana.

She'd been waiting since the wedding for his sullen mood to lift. She kept thinking another day, another week, and he'd stop acting like she'd kicked his dog.

He unclipped Rosie's lead rope, and the horse startled.

"Wesley," Stephanie sighed, knowing time was up. He needed to focus completely on jumping, and that meant she had to confront the situation head-on.

"Yeah?" He concentrated on coiling the lead rope in his callused hands.

"You can't ride like this."

He didn't look up. "Ride like what?"

"You know what I'm talking about."

He crossed to the stall gate and slipped the catch. "I'm fine."

"You're not fine."

He set his lips in a thin line, opening the gate.

She followed him out. "We need to talk—"

"It's none of your business."

"I'm your *coach*."

He glared at her, obviously struggling to mask the hurt with anger. "And I guess that's all you ever were."

Guilt tightened her chest. "Wesley, I never—"

"Never what? Never said we had a future? Never said you liked me? Never rushed off to marry that—"

"Wesley," she warned.

"Why did you lie?" The pain was naked in his eyes now. "All that stuff about us talking about it later. Why didn't you just tell me up-front it was him?"

Wesley was in worse shape than she'd realized, and she knew she had to talk him down. Riding Rosie-Jo at Brighton was a once in a lifetime chance for him to make a splash in front of a huge, national class audience.

"I didn't lie," she told him sincerely. "I do like you."

His lips thinned, and he turned to walk away.

She rushed after him, pushing her hesitation to a far corner of her mind. It was time to be completely honest. "I married Alec because I'm pregnant."

Wesley's head jerked back.

"We got married because of the baby."

He stopped and blinked at her in stunned silence.

"I don't know where it's going, or what will happen in the long-term. But I didn't lie to you, Wesley."

He glanced reflexively at her stomach. "That's why you're not riding."

"Yes."

"You mean…" His brain was obviously ticking through the math, going back to Alec's first visit to the ranch.

"Don't even go there," Stephanie warned, already

regretting her impulse. Her behavior was none of Wesley's business.

"Right." He squared his shoulders. "So it's a marriage of convenience. You're not in love with him."

She didn't answer.

After a beat of silence, the pain and anger cleared from Wesley's eyes. Then he smiled. "So, afterward…"

In an instant, Stephanie realized her error. His hopes were up all over again.

It took Alec the rest of the afternoon to get from Chicago to Lexington and take the short hop to Cedarvale and the Brighton facility.

He tried Stephanie's cell phone again, then tracked down her hotel and had the front desk try her room. In the end, he was forced to talk his way into the restricted area of the grounds and walk methodically through the horse barns looking for her.

He finally spotted her in the distance, outside, next to a white rail fence line decorated with sponsor bulletin boards.

Even at this distance, she took his breath away. The late day sunshine glinted off her hair. She was silhouetted against a dark background, her jeans and white blouse accentuating the body that he adored. He swore he could hear her voice, her laughter, her gasps when he drew her against him and kissed her.

It was all in his mind, of course. He was deluding himself if he thought she'd ever laugh with him again after this.

He wished he didn't have to be mad at her. He didn't want to fight. He wanted to hold her in his arms, caress her and kiss her, tell her everything was going to be okay. Then he wanted to figure out a way to make it okay.

For a moment he wondered if he'd played it wrong at their wedding. She'd asked him to leave, but if he'd stuck around, maybe she wouldn't be here. Their baby would be safe. And he wouldn't be headed for a confrontation that was sure to hurt them both.

As he drew closer still, he saw she was talking to a couple of reporters. Despite his simmering anger, he had to give her kudos for that.

But then he saw who was standing beside her. Wesley again. And the kid was way too close. They were practically touching. While Alec marched forward, Wesley reached up and cupped his hand over her shoulder, giving it a squeeze.

Alec quickened his pace.

The sun was setting, but the barn area was still alive with activity. Grooms walked horses, stable hands moved feed and manure, while technicians worked in the broadcast tents, setting up sound and video equipment for the weekend.

Alec halted beside Stephanie, and in one swift motion wrapped his arm around her shoulder, dislodging Wesley's hand.

Stephanie turned to stare at him. While Wesley's head whipped around. Both reporters immediately stopped talking. And the television camera swung to Alec.

"Alec Creighton," he introduced himself with a nod. "Stephanie's husband."

Stephanie froze beneath his embrace, while the two female reporters' jaws dropped open.

"Sorry to interrupt, darling," he put in easily.

One reporter recovered more quickly and stuffed her microphone in Alec's face. "You're married to Stephanie Ryder."

"Stephanie Creighton," Alec corrected, though they'd never actually discussed her changing her name.

"When did you get married?"

"Tell us about the wedding."

"We were married in Montana. At the Ryder Ranch." Alec made a show of smiling down at Stephanie. "It was a simple ceremony, just the family."

The reporters switched their attention to Stephanie.

"This is big news. Were you planning a formal announcement?"

Alec didn't give Stephanie a chance to speak. Not that she seemed particularly capable of joining the conversation.

"You can take this as a formal announcement," he told them. "You can also take this as notification that Stephanie won't be competing this weekend."

Both microphones went to Stephanie. "You're not competing?"

"Thank you," said Alec. "That's all we have to say for the moment." He swiftly turned her away and started back across the yard.

"You *did not* just do that," Stephanie rasped as they angled across the lawn to the nearest building.

Wesley seemed to have found his feet and was struggling to catch up with them.

"What are you doing here?" Alec demanded of Stephanie.

"What do you mean?"

Wesley caught them at a trot, and Alec pasted him with a warning glare.

Was the kid suicidal?

Stephanie was Alec's wife. Wesley had absolutely no right to be touching her.

"This is a private conversation," Alec announced.

Wesley looked to Stephanie for confirmation, and it was all Alec could do not to send the man sprawling.

"It's okay, Wesley," said Stephanie. "I don't know what he's doing here, but—"

"Goodbye, Wesley," Alec interrupted.

Wesley hesitated a second longer in a transparent and hopeless attempt to pretend he had a choice. Then he shot Alec a hostile look and peeled off to one side, tracking for one of the technical tents.

Stephanie stopped dead. "What is the *matter* with you?"

"Not here," Alec growled, scanning the grounds, looking for a place that offered privacy. It didn't seem promising.

"We'll go back to the hotel." He switched their direction.

"Those were reporters," she hissed under her breath.

"No kidding."

"An hour from now, everybody's going to know we're married."

"Were you planning to keep it a secret?"

"No. I don't know. I hadn't really thought about it."

"What about the baby? Were you planning to keep that a secret, too?"

"Yes. For now anyway."

He grunted, struggling to hold his temper.

She didn't seem to feel guilty. She didn't seem contrite. Had she somehow convinced herself it was okay to fly eight feet in the air and come crashing down on the back of a eighteen-hundred-pound animal? He'd seen her last bruise. The sport was bloody dangerous.

They took a stone pathway to the main hotel tower, crossed the lobby and entered an elevator.

As the elevator filled up, Alec nabbed her hand and

tugged her close beside him. She pressed the button for the twenty-sixth floor.

It was a short walk down the hallway to her room. She inserted the key. He opened the door. Then he shut it behind them.

She immediately turned on him, back to the picture window that looked over the arena. "Are you out of your mind?"

He ignored the question. "Do your brothers know you're here?"

"Of course they know I'm here. Why are you acting like I've done something wrong?"

He advanced on her. "Because you're *pregnant*."

"I know I'm pregnant. That doesn't mean my life stops."

"*This* part of your life stops."

She paused. Her eyes darkened. Then she waggled her finger at him, stepping three paces backward as she shook her head. "Oh, no, no, no. I am not going to sit home in Montana twiddling my thumbs for the next seven months."

He stepped forward once again. "Well you're sure as *hell* not sitting on the back of a horse jumping six-foot oxers."

She blinked. "What?"

"I know you can be reckless. I've heard you're irresponsible. But honest-to-God, Stephanie—"

"*What?*" she shouted.

"You are *not* going to compete in show jumping while you're pregnant with my baby."

She stared at him like he'd grown two heads. "What makes you think I'm competing?"

He gestured out the picture window. "You're here."

"I'm coaching Wesley."

Nice try. "With Rosie-Jo?"

"Wesley's riding her."

"No, he's not." The woman was caught. She might as well own up to it.

"Yes, he is."

"Rosie-Jo is your horse."

"She's also a once-in-a-lifetime jumper. She's not taking a year off just because I'm forced to."

Alec stopped. A chill of unease spread through him. "You're not jumping?"

"Of course I'm not jumping, you idiot. It's dangerous."

"I *know.* That's why I'm here."

Her shoulders relaxed. "To stop me from jumping?"

"Yes."

"I don't understand, Alec." She gave her head a little shake. "Where did you get the idea…?"

He raked a hand through his hair. "I saw you on television this afternoon. You were here. You had Rosie-Jo. The reporters—"

"And you jumped to a conclusion."

"Apparently."

Her eyes narrowed. "Where were you?"

"Chicago."

"And you flew all the way to Cedarvale?"

"What was I supposed to do?"

"Phone me?"

"I tried."

"Trust me?"

Alec didn't have an answer for that. How could he trust her? He barely knew her.

"It's my baby, too, Alec."

"I know."

"I'm not going to hurt our baby."

Alec drew a breath. He supposed he knew that now. But he had no way of knowing that back in Chicago when the evidence had stacked up against her.

The hotel room telephone jangled.

Stephanie kept him in her sights with a censorious expression as she crossed to answer it.

"Hello?"

She paused. "Yes."

She nodded. "Okay… I know… Thank you."

She hung up the phone then turned to Alec.

"What is it?"

"Word's getting around. You've just been included on a VIP reception invitation for tomorrow night."

She waited, and Alec wasn't sure what to say.

"What are you going to do?" she finally asked.

He knew what he should say, knew he should get his butt back on that plane and leave her the heck alone. But now that he was here, he couldn't bring himself to leave. He found his emotions making deals with his conscience.

He promised himself it would only be for a day or two. He'd get them a suite, so they both had privacy. He wouldn't let her get close, wouldn't let her depend on him. He wouldn't do anything to mislead her.

But when he spoke, his voice came out soft and deliberate. "I guess I'll stick around and be your husband."

"This way," Stephanie said to Alec, pointing to an aisle that stretched between two racks of clothes in the exhibition hall in the basement of the hotel. For the first time in weeks, she felt lighter, almost happy. She'd always enjoyed the social events around major jumping competitions, and she woke up this morning vowing to enjoy them this weekend.

It would be odd hanging out with Alec, odder still that people would know they were married. But at least she'd have a dancing partner.

She supposed there was always a silver lining.

"You have got to be kidding me." Alec stopped dead in his tracks in the middle of the exhibition hall entrance, staring in obvious disbelief at the racks of costumes, hats, shoes and accessories.

"Our party's a 1920s theme," she offered, halting beside him.

He gazed deliberately around the barnlike costume rental setup. "They bring all this in for horse jumping?"

"Tonight isn't the only theme event. And with this many wealthy people in one place, it's a prime opportunity for fund-raising."

People were starting to pile up behind them, so she snagged his arm and tugged him forward.

"You mean I have to dress up in a costume *and* give away my money?" he asked.

"You really don't get out much, do you?" she couldn't help teasing him.

"Not like this," he told her, gazing around the jumble of merchandise taking up about a quarter of the cavernous room. "I'm more a dinner at Palazzo Antinori or a cruise on the Seine kind of guy."

"A closet romantic," she reflexively observed, then cringed at the unfortunate choice of words.

His expression turned serious. "No, Stephanie. I'm not a romantic of any kind."

She sensed some kind of a warning in his words.

"Over there." She cheerfully pointed, changing the subject as they made their way past a suit of medieval armor and a shelf of colored wigs and sparkling Mardi Gras masks.

Alec leaned in close, his tone still dire. "I don't want you to…" He obviously struggled for words.

She refused to prompt him. She really didn't want to pursue this line of conversation.

"To get caught up—"

"In the 1920s?" she wedged in.

"In our marriage," he corrected.

She let sarcasm color her tone. "You afraid I'll mistake a dance for a declaration of undying passion and devotion?"

He backed off a little. "You seem…"

"What?" she demanded.

He shrugged. "Happy. Animated."

"And you attribute that to *you?* Wow. That's some ego you've got going there Alec."

"It's not my ego."

"Right."

He clenched his jaw. "Forget I said anything."

"I will."

"Good."

"You're faking, Alec. I get that. I'm faking it, too." She might have let her emotional guard down for a moment, but she wouldn't make the mistake of enjoying herself again.

He searched her expression. "Fine."

"Fine." She nodded in return. Just flipping fine. Bad enough she had to fake a marriage. Now she wasn't allowed to smile while she did it.

She put her attention on the costume racks again, now simply wanting to get this over with. "You might as well pick something?"

He glanced around. "I'm not a fan of costumes."

"Yeah? Too bad."

He shot her a look of annoyance.

What? She was supposed to get happy again? "Be a man about it," she challenged. "Put on some pinstripes and spats. Be grateful it's not superhero night."

His look of horror almost made her smile.

"You'd look good in red tights."

"Not in this lifetime."

"Check those out." She gestured to a rack of suit jackets.

For herself, she moved further down the aisle, finding a selection of flapper dresses.

She started through them one by one. After a few minutes, she came across a sexy, silky black sheath, dripping with shimmering silver ribbons that flowed from the low-cut neckline, past the short hem of the underdress to knee-length.

With a spurt of mischievousness, she held it against her body. "What do you think?"

His gaze traveled the length of the garment, eyes glittering with what looked suspiciously like humor. "You show up in that, doll-face, and I'd better be packin' heat."

This time, she did crack a smile.

She pulled the dress away from her body, turning it and making a show of taking a critical look. "Too much?"

"Not nearly enough."

She could have sworn there was a sensual edge to his tone. But his cell phone chimed, cutting it off.

She hung the dress back on the rack, battling a wave of prickly heat that slowly throbbed its way through her system. Faking, she reminded herself ruthlessly. Faking, faking, faking.

"Alec Creighton," he said into the phone.

His glance darted to her for a split second, then he turned away, lowering his voice.

She told herself to focus on the costumes and give him his privacy. He had his own life, and she had hers. As he'd so clearly just pointed out, this intersection between them was completely temporary.

Still, she couldn't help catching snatches of the conversation. She heard him say tomorrow, then airport, then Cedarvale.

It sounded like he was leaving, and a wave of disappointment surprised and worried her. It was good that he was leaving.

But then she heard him say her brothers' names. She blinked at his back, listening unabashedly to the final snatches of the conversation.

As he signed off, she quickly grabbed another dress, pretending to be absorbed by it.

"This one?" she asked.

It was a soft, champagne silk, with a low V-neck, spaghetti straps and covered in sparkling, criss-cross beading. The silk came to midthigh, while a wide, sheer, metallic lace hemline, slashed to points, rustled around her knees.

"They don't have anything with sleeves?" he frowned.

"It's the roaring twenties," she told him, trying not to wonder about his phone call. "I'm supposed to look like your moll. What do you think? A wide choker and a long string of pearls?"

"I think you'll be the death of me."

"What about the red one?" she lifted another from the rack. "It comes with satin gloves and a feather boa.

Alec's nostrils flared. "Better stick with the gold."

"It's champagne."

"Not the red, and definitely not the black."

"Fine." She put the red one back, wishing she was brave enough to ask about the phone call. Was he leaving? And why had he mentioned her brothers? "What about a long cigarette holder?" she asked instead.

"Absolutely not. You're pregnant."

"Shhhh." She glanced quickly around, worried someone would overhear.

He moved closer, leaning down to whisper. "You're pregnant."

"I wouldn't really smoke anything."

"Don't even joke about it."

"Who was on the phone?" she blurted out.

"A friend."

"Does he know my brothers?"

Alec's brow furrowed. "No. Why?"

"No reason," she lied, glancing away. "I thought it might be about the Ryder International review. Are you leaving tomorrow?"

"You trying to get rid of me?"

She looked back up at him again, puzzling over why he'd hold back the truth about the phone call. If the friend didn't know her brothers, Alec wouldn't have mentioned their names. "I need to get Wesley prepared," she told him.

Alec's jaw tightened, eyes squinting further. "I'm staying."

"Okay," she agreed.

He gave a sharp nod of acknowledgment.

Moving away from yet another uncomfortable moment, she gestured to the rack of suits. "Did you find something to wear?"

"I'm not wearing pinstripes."

"How about a hat?" She selected one with a center dent and a wide, satin band and tried to place it on his head.

He jerked sideways, out of the way. "How about a suit jacket and a pair of slacks, and I write a check big enough that nobody cares?"

Seven

Chandeliers dangled from the ballroom ceiling, while massive ice sculptures and floral arrangements decorated white linen tables. The waiters wore period tuxedoes, and a big band played a jazz tune on a low stage in one corner of the room.

On Alec's arm, Stephanie glittered. Her rich, auburn hair bounced in a halo of tight curls to her bare shoulders. It was pulled back on one side by an elaborate, rhinestone clip, which matched her ornate necklace and dangling earrings. Her makeup had been done in a bright twenties-style, and the shimmering, champagne dress clung to her lithe body.

Alec couldn't help a surge of pride as people turned to stare. His marriage might be a sham, but he was the envy of every man in the room.

He leaned down to whisper. "You should dress up like a girl more often."

"They're not looking at me," she whispered back, smiling politely at the onlookers.

"Yes, they are." More people turned to stare.

Up to now, it hadn't occurred to Alec to wonder how Stephanie had made it to twenty-two as a virgin. But now it sure did. He also realized men would be lining up to take his place the minute he was out of the picture.

It was not a pleasant thought.

"They've heard," she told him in an undertone.

"Heard what?"

"About us. That we got married."

He disagreed. "It's you." Still, at the mention of his temporary position, he couldn't stop himself from curling his arm around the small of her back.

"Oh, sure," she mocked. "Really give them something to talk about."

"I could give you a kiss."

"You're incorrigible."

"Just playing my part."

"Play it from over there." She quickly sidestepped out of his embrace.

He followed, snagging her around the waist once more. "And how will that be convincing?"

"Give it your best effort."

"Oh, I intend to," he drawled.

"Stephanie," purred a woman in a floor-length, peacock-blue, sequined gown. She swept in front of them with a flourish, looking to be about sixty-five, though very well preserved. Her streaked blond hair was decorated with blue feathers, and she brandished a matching fan like a weapon.

"Mrs. Cleary," Stephanie greeted with a smile, and the woman's gaze immediately jumped to Alec. She raised her sculpted brows.

"This is my husband, Alec Creighton," Stephanie supplied smoothly.

Alec liked the sound of that. He let his hand slip to hers, and he stroked the pad of his thumb across her diamond ring and the matching wedding band.

Stephanie jolted her hand away. "Mrs. Cleary is the president of the Brighton Fund-raising Committee." The tone told him he ought to be impressed.

"A pleasure, Mrs. Cleary." He gave her a warm smile and used his newly freed hand to shake with her.

She checked him over carefully. "Please, call me Bridget."

"Bridget," he obliged.

"I hear congratulations are in order." The words were more an accusation than a tribute.

"Indeed, they are." Alec drew Stephanie firmly to his side, feeling her soft curves beneath the sexy dress. There was no law telling him he couldn't enjoy his acting role. "We're looking forward to starting a family."

He felt her stiffen, but how could she complain? He was simply smoothing the pathway for the inevitable announcement of her pregnancy.

"Stephanie?" came a second voice, a younger woman this time. "Are you going to introduce me?" She offered Alec a gleaming white, perfectly straight orthodontic smile.

She looked to be in her late twenties and wore a bright purple, beaded dress, and a matching headband. She held a long cigarette holder, and her blond hair was upswept in a riot of curls. Her lashes were dark with heavy makeup, and she wore fishnet stockings with high-heeled, black shoes accented by an oversize silver buckle on the sexy ankle strap.

In another time and another place, he would have smiled right back at the undeniably beautiful woman. She was the stuff of erotic dreams. But Alec found he preferred Stephanie's more understated look. And it wasn't just the fake husband in him speaking. Interesting.

"Rene," Stephanie greeted, her voice slightly tight, features carefully neutral. "This is my husband, Alec."

There was a proprietary inflection on the word husband. Nice.

"Pleasure to meet you, Alec the husband," Rene giggled as she extended the back of her hand, wiggling her fingers in an obvious invitation.

He ignored the hint, and shook her hand instead of kissing the back.

She gave a mock pout with her jewel-red lips.

A tall, thin man appeared. He wore an outrageous purple velvet coat with leopard-print trim and matching slacks.

"Rene," he admonished, from beneath a broad brimmed hat. Then he glared a warning at Alec.

Alec had to bite down hard to keep from laughing. It was tough to take a man seriously when he was dressed like a sitcom pimp.

"Alec Creighton," he said instead and extended his hand. "I believe our wives know each other."

The man's eyes went round.

"Wife?" Rene cackled. "That'll be the day."

"My apologies," said Alec. Then he smiled warmly down at Stephanie. "But I highly recommend it." He glanced back at the man. "You should think about asking her."

The man looked like a deer in the headlights.

Alec could feel Stephanie's body vibrate with repressed laughter.

"What do you think, sweetheart?" Alec asked her.

"Dance," she sputtered, grabbing Alec's arm and turning him away from Rene.

Alec quickly took the lead as they wove their way through the crowd.

"You are *bad*," Stephanie accused.

"They deserved it. So, who is she?"

"She's the princess of the circuit. Her father owns a stable of jumping horses."

"Big deal. So do you."

Stephanie snorted out a laugh. "Not like he does."

Alec drew her into his arms and swung her into the latest song in a Duke Ellington tribute. "You're not intimidated are you?"

"By Rene?" Stephanie easily followed his lead.

"Yes." He waited. He'd learned to recognize it when she was stalling.

She paused. "Maybe once. She's been glamorous since she was twelve."

"You're glamorous now."

Stephanie coughed out a laugh. "Not like her."

Alec let his hand trail along the smooth silk of Stephanie's dress, letting the tactile memory remind him of exactly how gorgeous she'd looked walking out of her hotel bedroom earlier. She'd positively taken his breath away.

Now, his voice went husky. "Better than her."

She didn't answer, but she seemed to mold slightly closer against him. He gathered her tight, ignoring the warning that was sounding in his brain.

"Besides," he forced himself to joke. "She's obviously jealous of your husband."

"Ego, Alec?"

"A man can tell these things."

"Because she was flirting with you?"

"Exactly."

Stephanie chuckled. "She flirts with everyone."

"I'm quite a catch," he protested, telling himself to put a little distance between their bodies.

He ignored himself.

"You have quite the ego."

"Part of my charm."

"You have charm?"

He didn't answer. Instead he savored the feel of her in his arms, inhaling the scent of her hair, letting the haunting strains of a saxophone solo carry them away.

"I suppose you do," she said softly.

"What?"

"Have charm."

He drew back. "You're conceding a point?"

"You also have looks," she continued. "But you already know that. Every woman in the room is envious of me right now."

"You mean every man is envious of me." He drew a breath. "How is it," he struggled to frame the question that had been nagging at him for weeks. "That you stayed a virgin all those years?"

"I don't get out much."

"I'm serious."

"So am I."

"Stephanie?"

She shrugged against him. "I honestly never had any offers."

Now that was ridiculous. He chuckled low. "Maybe there weren't any verbal offers. But, trust me, there were offers. You've had at least two dozen since you walked into this room."

She pulled back. "Where?"

"Never mind."

"You're crazy."

"I'm just smarter than you."

She rolled her eyes.

"More observant," he amended.

"You have a vivid imagination."

"And you have a sexy rear end."

"You keep your mind off my— *Hey,* there's Royce. What's he doing here?"

Alec didn't know whether to resent the interruption or be grateful Royce had arrived so promptly.

Before he could make up his mind, Stephanie was out of his arms and heading off the dance floor.

Alec followed closely behind.

She glanced from her brother to Amber. "Where did you guys come from?"

Amber grinned, but her quick glance at Alec told him she knew they were here about Stanton.

"We were in Chicago," she told Stephanie. "But you know your brother. I mentioned you might need moral support, and the next thing I knew we were taxiing down the tarmac."

Stephanie's brows knit together. "But I'm not even riding."

"Exactly," said Amber, drawing Stephanie a small distance away from Alec and Royce.

Royce gave him a nod. "I got your voice mail."

"Damien has news," Alec returned. "Amber knows?"

Royce stepped closer and kept his voice low. "Amber's the brains of the outfit. She was the one that noticed the resemblance between Frank's sister and Stephanie."

Alec nodded. "You have an intelligent fiancée."

"I have an amazing fiancée."

Alec's gaze strayed to Amber's black and red costume. The women were drawing more than their share of appreciative male glances. "You might want to hurry up and marry her."

Royce looked around, clearly making the same observation as Alec. "She's having trouble deciding on the wedding location." His shoulders squared. "But we might have to make a detour through Nevada on the way home."

Alec gave a chopped chuckle, while Royce took a half step toward Stephanie and Amber to stare a man down.

The man moved on, and Royce drew back. "What time's the meeting?"

"Wesley has a warm-up scheduled at three. Stephanie has to be there. I told Damien I'd call when the coast was clear."

"He's here?"

"On his way." It would be good news. Alec might not have heard the details yet, but if Damien was finished in Spain, Norman Stanton was no longer going to be a threat to the Ryders.

"How do we know Stanton won't go back on his word?" Royce asked Damien.

Alec had waited until Stephanie was occupied in the arena with Wesley and Rosie-Jo, then he'd given the all clear signal to Damien, Jared, Royce, Melissa and Amber. The group had assembled in the hotel suite's living room.

Jared nodded to back up his brother's question. "The man's a blackmailer and a thief."

Damien cast a fleeting glance to Alec. He wasn't used to having his situational assessment questioned. But he was also a consummate professional, so he wouldn't make an issue.

"Norman knows we can reach out and touch him in Morocco," he answered simply.

Alec straightened from where he'd propped his shoulder against the arched entryway to the dining area. "There aren't a lot of places left for him to hide."

"He must be pretty ticked off," Melissa put in. "What's to stop him from calling a tabloid and exposing it to the world?"

"Arrest and incarceration," said Alec.

Jared elaborated. "Stanton must have thought he was safe in Morocco. Yet Damien tracked him down and lured him to Spain. He knows we're tenacious, and he has to be feeling like there aren't a lot of places left to hide."

"Could the police really extradite him from Spain?" asked Royce.

Damien gave a little half smile. "Technically, yes. Practically... It's hard to say. But if you're Norman Stanton, do you take that chance?"

"We've got him trapped in a standoff," Alec clarified. "He talks to Stephanie, we press charges."

"A smart man takes the money and runs." Jared nodded.

"Any chance we can get the money back?" asked Amber. Then she glanced around at the blank faces. "We're talking about twelve million dollars here."

"I can look into it," said Damien. "But he'll have spent a lot of it already."

Royce shook his head. "I'm done. Stephanie's the important thing. I say if he walks away, we walk away."

Melissa's eyes went wide. "Excuse me? Twelve million dollars?" She glanced to Jared, and it was obvious the sum was news to her.

"Paid out over at least ten years," Jared told his wife.

"It was Grandpa Benteen and McQuestin," Amber elaborated. "They didn't know how else to—" She stopped, suddenly casting a guilty glance to Jared, obviously realizing Melissa might not know about Stephanie's illegitimacy.

"We have another problem," Alec told the gathering.

Everyone went silent.

He snagged one of the dining room chairs, straddling it backward in the archway and propping his elbows on the back.

Damien backed off a few steps, positioning himself near the glass patio door.

"Your mother was six months older than your father," Alec explained to Jared and Royce, trying to keep it as straightforward as possible. "Since they died together, she was deemed to have predeceased him."

Both men watched him, expressions growing wary.

"In his will, should his wife predecease him, your father asked that his estate 'be divided among my children, then alive.'"

There was a split second before the words sank in.

"Stephanie's not his child," said Jared.

"Frank Stanton." Melissa shook her head.

"But we can fix it?" Royce asked.

"I talked to Katie Merrick. It'll take a few lawyers, and a stack of contracts, but it's doable. Trick is, you'll have to get Stephanie to sign them without reading them."

"Too late for that." Stephanie's terse voice intruded.

Alec jerked his head toward her.

Stephanie stood in the foyer doorway. Her face was pale, but her eyes glittered with anger.

"Oh, no," Amber rasped.

Alec came to his feet.

Stephanie stared at her bothers. "I'm…" That was as far as she made it.

Both of them stood, but she held up a hand to stop them. "And nobody was going to *tell* me?" She turned her accusing stare on Alec.

"What did you hear?" he asked, his mind scrambling for a damage control plan.

"Is this a conspiracy?" She glanced around the room. Her gaze stopped on Damien. "Who's this?"

Damien glanced to Alec.

"He's yours," Stephanie scoffed at Alec. "Of course he's yours. Is this why they hired you?"

Alec took a step forward. "Stephanie."

"Wow." She gave a shaky laugh. "Is that what you're doing for us? Is Ryder International even *in* financial trouble?"

"Stephanie," Jared began.

"You should sit down," Royce put in.

Stephanie rounded on him. "*You* should start talking."

The two stared at each other for a moment.

"We were being blackmailed," said Royce.

"By Alec?"

"*No*," Alec jumped in, unable to remain silent any longer. "By Norman Stanton. I *was* looking into your finances." He wasn't about to hit Royce and Jared with an *I told you so*, but it was darn tempting.

"So you claim." Stephanie glared at him. "But we both know you can fake pretty much anything."

"Alec's not the bad guy," said Amber.

"Then who's the bad guy?"

"Frank Stanton," said Royce.

"And he's my father?"

"Can we talk about this later?" asked Royce, his gaze going pointedly to Damien.

"Sure." Stephanie shrugged. "Don't mind me." She crossed to a desk and picked up some papers. "I just dropped by for the insurance forms. Let me know how this all turns out. I'll sign anything you want."

"Don't start sulking," warned Jared.

Alec felt a flash of anger. He moved to position himself between the two. "I think she's got a right to be a little upset," he told Jared.

Jared's eyes narrowed down. "Stay out of it."

"I don't believe I will." Alec folded his arms across his chest. They were the ones that hired him. They insisted he marry Stephanie. Convenience or not, she was his wife.

Royce stepped up beside his brother. "It's a family matter."

"I'm family."

"Not really."

"I have a piece of paper that says so."

Stephanie stepped back in. "And they have a piece of paper that says *I'm* not. Procured by *you,* if I overheard correctly."

"You're still our sister," Jared hastily put in.

"Half sister. Out of the will."

"There you go again," Royce all but shouted. "The most dramatic possible—"

"I think you'd better leave," Alec said to the brothers.

"Us leave?" Jared's voice was incredulous. "*You* leave."

"It's my hotel room. And she's my wife—"

"Give me a break!" Stephanie threw up her hands. "*I'll* leave."

"No." Alec's hand shot out to stop her. "We need to talk." Past today, they were still having a baby, and they still had to make that work.

"Let go of Stephanie," Royce growled.

Amber came to her feet, voice commanding. "Stop this. All of you. I mean it."

She placed herself between Alec and Royce. "Alec wants to talk to Stephanie."

Royce clamped his jaw in silent protest, but everyone filed out. Alec was left alone with Stephanie. "For the record," he told her, "I advised them to tell you the truth."

She didn't turn around. "Why didn't you tell me the truth?"

"I promised I wouldn't."

She was silent for a moment. "So a business contract is more important to you than your wedding vows?"

Alec drew a breath.

"Never mind," she continued. "Don't answer that."

He moved a few steps toward her. "It was complicated. I had no right—"

She turned. "No right to be honest with your wife?"

"Don't twist things to score points."

The woman had enough on her side of this argument without doing that.

She dropped into one of the French provincial chairs. "So, I guess I'm a bastard."

He pulled out another chair and angled it toward hers, sitting down. "So am I. It's not so bad."

"I meant literally, not metaphorically."

"So did I."

Her expression softened ever so slightly. "Really?"

"My father eventually married my mother." Though that had turned out to be more a curse than a blessing.

Stephanie slumped back in the chair. "My mother had an affair."

"So it would seem."

"I've had her up on a pretty high pedestal all these years."

Alec leaned forward, covering Stephanie's hands where they rested in her lap. "She was human."

"You accept infidelity?"

"I understand weakness and imperfection."

"Are you imperfect, Alec?"

"I took your virginity and made you pregnant while I was working for your brothers. Then I lied to you. Well, held back the truth anyway."

"And you'll eventually be unfaithful."

He drew back. "What? No. Why would I—"

"Can you really stay celibate for months on end?"

"I don't know," he admitted. He'd never tried.

It had only been a couple of weeks since the wedding, but so far he hadn't had any overwhelming desire to sleep with other women. Ironically the only person he wanted to make love to was Stephanie.

"You'll eventually give into temptation," she determined.

"Where is this coming from?"

"My mother did. Your parents did. We did."

"You've really wandered off on a tangent here." He wanted to talk about her family, to make sure she was coping okay with the truth.

"I'm merely pointing out that we both have the infidelity gene."

He coughed out a surprised laugh. "It comes down to principles and personal choice."

"*We* slept together."

The reminder made him aware of their joined hands, her sweet scent and those cherry-red lips that were slightly parted with her breath.

"Yes, we did," he agreed.

"When we shouldn't have."

"That's debatable. We didn't betray anyone."

"Except maybe ourselves."

Alec shifted his chair closer and raised their joined hands. "Do you feel guilty, Stephanie?"

She gazed into his eyes. "Do you?"

He shook his head. "I don't have a single regret about making love to you. And I don't hate Frank Stanton. And I'm glad your mother gave into temptation. If not for that, you wouldn't be here."

"So, I should be grateful?"

"You should be sensible. Don't rail against things you can't change. Just make the best of what you have."

She seemed to think about that for a minute. Then her lips softened, and her voice went low. "I miss you, Alec."

Desire instantly overran his brain. "I'm right here."

"That's not what I meant."

"I know." He steeled himself against the urge to drag her into his arms. "But you're upset and vulnerable, and I still have a few principles left."

Silver sparkled to life deep in her eyes. "How can I get rid of them?"

Simply by breathing. His hands convulsed around hers. "You can't."

A sharp rap sounded on the suite door, and Stephanie frowned.

Alec felt like he'd been saved from himself. They were only going to stay away so long.

Eight

"You know Stephanie's going to see him," Amber warned Royce in an undertone.

Alec slowed his steps, not wanting to intrude on what was obviously a private conversation, but wanting to know about anything that involved Stephanie.

She and her brothers had talked late into the night. Then Alec had seen her briefly at breakfast. But Wesley was in final preparation for competing tomorrow, so Stephanie's entire day was being spent at the arena. It annoyed Alec that Wesley was still flirting with her.

Royce gave Alec a nod of welcome. "I'm half tempted to buy it for her," Royce said to Amber.

"You know you can't do that," Amber returned. "The price tag's up over a million dollars."

"Hey, Alec," Royce greeted, and Amber turned around to face him.

Alec wished he could ask what they were debating. He hoped there weren't any more family secrets being kept from Stephanie.

He settled for, "What's up?"

"Blanchard's Run is here," said Amber.

Alec nodded, hoping to bluff his way through the conversation.

"Stephanie's still upset," said Royce.

"You can't buy her a million dollar horse to make her feel better," warned Amber, jabbing Royce with her elbow. "Tell him, Alec."

"She's right," Alec agreed. Stephanie didn't need monetary bribes from her brothers. She needed them to respect her enough to be honest with her.

"She's had her eye on him for months," said Royce.

"Here she is now," Alec warned them, as Stephanie approached from the opposite end of the barn. Her smooth, sexy stride carried swiftly along in her tooled cowboy boots.

Amber and Royce both turned.

"Uh-oh," Amber breathed.

Stephanie's attention had been caught by one of the stalls. She stopped and drew back in obvious surprise. Then she turned to walk to the gate.

She stood there for a few moments staring at the horse inside. Then she squared her shoulders and resumed walking toward them.

Nobody said a word as she approached.

"You knew, didn't you?" she asked her brother.

"We just found out," Amber quickly put in.

Stephanie cocked her head as she gazed steadily at Royce.

"We just saw him," he backed Amber up.

"But you weren't going to tell me."

They didn't deny it.

"Was that for my own good, too?"

When nobody immediately answered, she shook her head in disgust then paced off down the center aisle of the barn toward the hotel and the main offices.

Alec went quickly after her. "What was that about?"

She didn't break her stride. "Blanchard's Run."

"He's a horse, right?"

"He is."

"And you want to buy him?"

"I do."

"But he's expensive." Alec had the full picture now.

"He's a bargain."

"A million dollars?"

"You're just like the rest of them."

"Hold up there for a second." He snagged her arm, tugged her to a stop before she could exit the barn and join the crowds outside.

She stopped, but turned on him, eyes blazing.

"Is this important?" he asked.

"Not at all," she denied.

"Stephanie?"

She drew in an impatient sigh and crossed her arms beneath her breasts. "Why do you want to know?"

"Because I do. Because you're not mad at me, you're mad at them." He jabbed his thumb back in Royce's direction. "And because I hate it when you act like a spoiled kid."

Her eyes narrowed.

"You're not, you know. You're an intelligent woman who knows what she wants and how to work for it. You want this horse, and I'm curious to know why."

"Fine." She drew a breath. "I've been interested in

Blanchard's Run for nearly a year. I've studied his blood-lines and the conformation of his offspring, along with their competition records. And I think the combination of Blanchard's Run and my retired mare, Pinnacle, would produce fast, smart, high jumpers. If science and genetics has anything to say about it, the EBVs of their offspring would be off the charts."

"EBVs?"

"Estimated Breeding Value."

"Oh."

"In technical terms, they would be worth a whole lot of money."

"Really?"

"Yes, really. I can also breed him to three other mares I've bought this year, partly in anticipation of a future acquisition of Blanchard's Run. Then, three, maybe five years from now, if his existing offspring prove out the way I expect them to, and if the Ryder foals show promise, we'll be able to get top dollar for the animals."

Alec was impressed. "So, why don't your brothers want you to buy the horse?"

"Because they've never listened long enough to know my plan is based on concrete science. They assume I'm operating on emotion instead of intelligence."

"They're wrong," said Alec.

"Yeah? Well, since I'm out of the will, I don't have much of a leg to stand on anymore."

"There is that." Even as Alec was agreeing with her, he was coming to a decision.

It had nothing to do with guilt. And it had nothing to do with his feelings for Stephanie. And it wasn't to help her feel better after yesterday's revelations. It was a good business decision, plain and simple.

* * *

Stephanie blinked in disbelief at Blanchard's Run's ownership papers. They'd been delivered to the hotel suite five minutes ago, with her name on the envelope.

She squeezed her eyes shut and shook her head against what had to be an illusion. But, no, she wasn't crazy. That was her name, and Ryder Equestrian Center, and Blanchard's Run's pedigree.

The suite door opened.

Alec strode in and glanced at the papers. A grin spread across his face.

"You?" she asked in amazement.

"I thought you made a convincing case."

She stared up at him, her brain grappling with the situation. "You bought Blanchard's Run?"

He tossed his key card on the table near the foyer. "Was it all true? The EBV thing?"

"Of course it was."

"Good. 'Cause if it's not, I just made a very big mistake."

"It's all true," she assured him with a nod, emotion stinging the backs of her eyes. Nobody had ever trusted her like this before.

"I'll expect him to make money," Alec warned.

She nodded. "He will."

"Are you hungry?"

Suddenly she was. "Starved."

"You want to go out or stay in?"

"Could we eat out on the balcony?" she asked, warm feelings for Alec blossoming inside her. It was a gorgeous night, and she loved the view across the grounds to the arena. She felt like celebrating. And she felt like being alone with Alec.

"I'll call room service," he offered.

"I'm going to shower." She hugged the ownership papers to her chest, smiling all the way to her bedroom.

Alec had made a business investment in her. He trusted her to make good decisions, to make money.

She set the papers carefully on the bedroom desk, smoothing them out. Then she stripped off her work-worn clothes and headed for the shower.

She scrubbed her hair and rinsed it with conditioner. Then she shaved her legs and used some of the rose scented shower gel and body lotion provided by the hotel. After blow-drying, she wrapped herself in a fluffy robe and wandered back into her bedroom.

The windows were open, letting in the fresh night air.

She felt light and happy, optimistic about the future for the first time in weeks. Blanchard's Run would kick Ryder Equestrian Center to a whole new level.

She pulled open the dresser drawers. Her choices were limited, but she was in a mood to dress up.

She found a matching set of underwear, white lace panties and a low-cut bra. She pushed a pair of pearl earrings into her ears, fastened the matching necklace and bracelet, then crossed to the closet for the single dress she'd brought along on the trip.

A soft, clingy knit, it had narrow straps, a low square-cut neck and crisscrossed ties decorating a tapered V back. The skirt flared over her hips, cascading softly toward her knees. She quickly realized the bra wouldn't work and tossed it back in the drawer.

In the bathroom, she put on a little makeup. She tied her hair up, then brushed it back down, then twisted it in a messy knot at the back of her head, letting wisps curl across her forehead and along her temples.

She heard a knock on the suite's outer door. Alec's footfalls told her he was answering, and she gave the waiter a few minutes to finish setting up. Then she slipped her feet into little black sandals and left the bedroom.

Alec wasn't in sight, but the glow of candlelight flickered through the glass, balcony door.

She wandered outside to find hurricane lamps decorating the patterned, white, wrought-iron tables. Linen and silverware was set out, and plump, peach colored cushions softened the chairs. Salad had been served, while a low wreath of flowers surrounded the glass chimney candle at the center of the table.

"Madame?" came a low voice as a tuxedoed waiter appeared.

He pulled out her chair as Alec arrived in the doorway.

He'd also showered and shaved. He wore charcoal slacks and an open collared, white, dress shirt.

His gaze took in her outfit. "You look very nice." The words were reserved, but there was a burn in his eyes that warmed her from head to toe.

She sat down, and Alec took the chair opposite.

The waiter poured them each a glass of ice water to go with their salads, then melted away, closing the glass door behind him as a chorus of crickets ebbed and flowed from the shrubs and grass far below.

"Do my brothers know you bought Blanchard's Run?" She tried a bite of the fresh greens, avocado and raspberry vinaigrette salad.

Alec shook his head, tasting the salad himself. "You can surprise them."

"They'll be very surprised."

Alec shrugged. "It's your horse, your stable."

She took a few more bites, then dared a personal question. "How did you afford him?" She loved the horse, but she didn't want Alec going out on a limb financially.

He stared levelly at her.

"I'm sorry," she quickly apologized. "Was that too personal?"

"No. It just hadn't occurred to me that you didn't know."

"Know what?"

"Anything about my financial status."

"Or your family. Well, except for that little bit about your parents."

"Where I know pretty much everything about you."

She set down her fork. "More than me, as it turns out."

He gave a rueful smile.

The waiter reappeared, removing their salad plates and replacing them with chicken and pasta before disappearing once again.

"Financially I'm perfectly comfortable," said Alec.

Stephanie wasn't sure what that meant.

"I didn't have to borrow money to buy Blanchard's Run," he elaborated.

"So, you didn't marry me for my money?"

He smiled at her. "I didn't marry you for your money."

She cut into the tender chicken. "You know, we never signed a prenup."

"Are you worried?"

"Not anymore," she deadpanned.

"You could come out ahead on this," he speculated.

"Good to know. Since I have very expensive taste in horses."

Alec coughed out a laugh, and she smiled along with

him. His slate eyes reflected the glint of the candlelight, and the flicker of the flame bounced off the planes and angles of his face. He was a spectacularly handsome man.

Her gaze was drawn to his open collar, pushing her thoughts to his muscled chest and impressive shoulders. She couldn't help but remember him naked, in the pale light of her bedroom, his touch, his scent, his taste.

She moved on to his hands, stilled now on the silverware that rested against his plate. The things those hands had done to her.

"Is Madame finished?" The waiter's voice startled her.

"Yes, please." She drew a ragged breath, shifting in her chair as she became aware of the prickled heat chafing her skin.

"We'll skip dessert," Alec told the man. "Thank you for your time."

"Very good, sir." Once more, he disappeared, this time leaving the suite. They were alone.

A full minute of silence ticked by while the breeze freshened, and candlelight flicked across the planes and angles of Alec's face.

"You bought me a horse," she sighed, still not quite believing it could be true.

He shrugged. "I know most guys go with flowers."

"But you're not most guys."

"I guess not."

"*Definitely* not."

He bunched his napkin and tossed it on the table. "So, what did you get me?"

"I was supposed to buy a gift?" She feigned alarm.

He nodded. "It *is* our anniversary."

"What anniversary is that?"

"Fifteen days."

"Ahh," she nodded. "The little known fifteen-day horse-themed anniversary."

"Celebrated from Iceland to Estonia."

"We're in Kentucky."

"So, no present for me?"

She tucked her hair behind her ears. "I saw a ten-gallon hat in the gift shop downstairs."

He grinned. "Not my style."

"A silver, long-horn steer belt buckle?"

He rose from his chair. "Try again."

"I've got a nice riding crop in the trailer."

"Did you mean that to be sexy?"

"Noooo," she chuckled as she shook her head.

"Thank goodness." He made his way around the table. "I mean, *ouch*."

"You'd prefer sexy underwear to leather?"

He held out his hand. "Sexy underwear would definitely be my first choice for a gift."

She placed her hand in his, taking a deep breath and screwing up her courage. "Had to go without a bra tonight," she confessed.

His gaze dipped down. "Guess that saves me some unwrapping."

She rose to her feet, heart pounding, perspiration beginning to glow on her skin. "Yes, it does."

"I've missed you," he said.

"I'm right here," she parroted.

He smiled at the joke. "That's not what I meant." And his gaze did a tour of her body. His eyes darkened to pewter, going molten with desire.

"It's not what I meant, either," she whispered, zeroing in

on his lips, coming up on her toes, while his hand wrapped around to the small of her back and drew her close.

She stroked her palms up the length of his chest, reveling in the play of muscles beneath the thin cotton. She curved over his shoulders, to the back of his neck, into the rough texture of his hairline, while his mouth slowly descended to hers.

She parted her lips, her entire body softening in reaction to her nearness, his touch.

He stopped, lips a fraction of an inch from hers. "Tell me this isn't gratitude."

"Would it matter?" she couldn't resist asking.

"I know I should say yes." He sucked in a breath. "But, honestly. Maybe."

"It's quid pro quo," she teased.

"Sex with you is worth a million dollars?"

She drew back. "Sex? I thought we were talking about a kiss."

"We can stop at a kiss," he assured her, settling his arms more comfortably around her waist.

"I think we should do that," she responded.

"You're lying."

"Absolutely." She inched back, pasting a sultry smile on her face and sliding one of her straps off her shoulder. Then she pushed down the other. The slinky fabric caught on her hardened nipples, clinging there in the candlelight.

Alec glanced around, obviously confirming they had privacy. Then he drew her into the shadow of the over-hang.

"For a million dollars," he whispered, as his lips finally came down on hers in an explosion of taste and texture. He kissed her deeply and thoroughly, and her body nearly melted when his fingers found her zipper and pushed it down.

Her dress fell away, the breeze of the night caressing her skin. He surrounded her near naked body with his strong arms, hands roaming everywhere as he pressed her against the smooth, warm concrete wall.

She squirmed against him.

And his breathing rasped. "For a million dollars, I think we're going to have to do it twice."

Twice turned out to be essential for Alec. Because the first time was over far too fast. And he was convinced he could make love to Stephanie all night long.

In his bedroom now, he kissed the damp skin at the back of her neck, drawing her heated body more solidly into the cradle of his own. She fit perfectly. Everything about her fit perfectly, and he was beginning to wonder if he'd ever grow tired of holding her in his arms.

"Tell me about your family," she said softly, toying with the sheet he'd drawn over them both. The comforter had long since hit the floor, and most of the pillows were scattered around the room.

"Not a good time," he breathed. He wanted to focus on here and now, not on the past, and not on the future.

She eased onto her back. "Why not?"

He gazed down at her incredibly gorgeous face. There were two freckles nearly merged together on the cheekbone below her right eye. He kissed them, loving that he was close enough to observe that and so many other intimate and delightful things about her.

"Alec?" she prompted as his hand slid over her hipbone, wandering down her thigh.

"What?"

"Why not?"

He drew back a few inches. "Let me see... Maybe because I've got a beautiful, naked woman in my arms?"

"We already made love."

"We're doing it twice, remember? You insisted."

"I need a rest."

"Liar."

She grinned but didn't give in. "You have to tell me something about your family."

"I was an only child, and my father was a hard-ass."

"How so?"

"He was harsh and demanding, with expectations that nobody could ever hope to meet." Alec kissed her ear, letting his fingertips flutter over her flat stomach.

It blew him away to think of his baby in there. It also blew him away to have her in his bed again. He'd slept with plenty of women, but he'd never felt this close to any of them. And he'd never felt so protective and so completely privileged.

"Did he hurt you?" she asked in a small voice.

Alec drew back again. "You mean physically?"

She nodded.

"Of course he did. But I was a teenager by then, and I could take it."

Her eyes widened in sympathy, and she wrapped her arms around his neck, squeezing tight.

"I love the effect," he told her, hugging her back. "But I'm not crazy about the motivation."

"Oh, Alec."

"Don't do this, Stephanie. It was a long time ago. It wasn't that bad, certainly nothing to turn into a movie of the week."

"Nobody ever hit me," she told him.

His hug tightened reflexively. "They'd better not have."

"It's not fair."

"Nothing's fair. But I got the girl in the end, so I win."

It was her turn to draw back. "You mean me?"

"Who *else* would I mean? How bad do you think I am at this?"

That coaxed a smile out of her. "You mean pillow talk?"

"Like I'm going to lay in bed with you and talk about some other woman."

She shrugged. "How should I know?"

Her question brought a warm glow to his chest. "I love it that I was the first."

"You didn't seem that thrilled at the time."

"I was feeling freaking guilty at the time."

The sympathy was gone from her eyes, and the teasing light was back. "For taking advantage of my innocence?"

"For not having properly appreciated the privilege of being your first lover."

"What about your mother?" she asked.

"You're not going to let this go, are you?"

"No."

He hesitated for a long moment. But Stephanie deserved to know the truth. "She died when I was ten."

Her eyes clouded. "Oh, no. What happened?"

This time, Alec's hesitation was even longer. "She swallowed a bottle of sleeping pills."

Stephanie's eyes went wide. "She killed herself?"

He nodded. "Very few people know that."

Stephanie shook her head to assure him she'd keep the secret. "Do you know why?"

"My father was a hard-ass," Alec repeated.

She closed her eyes and drew him close. "Oh, Alec."

"It was a long time ago." It truly was. "I don't even know why I told you."

"Quid pro quo," she whispered against his shoulder, kissing him softly. "You know all my secrets."

"I do." He skimmed his hand over her belly, along her thighs and around to cup her bottom, feeling so incredibly lucky to be so close to her. "Have I ever told you how grateful I am that you'll be my baby's mother?"

She drew back, giving him an astonished gaze. "Seriously?"

"Seriously." He hesitated.

"Why?" she finally whispered.

He gave in to complete honesty. "Because you're everything I'm not."

Her eyes went round, and he bent to kiss her smooth stomach.

"You hear that, kid?" His voice unexpectedly thickened. "You're going to have the best mother in the world."

She stroked her fingers through his hair, and he kissed her again, softly and leisurely. Then he pecked and suckled his way over her stomach to her breasts. She gasped as he took one pebbled nipple into his mouth, and his body instantly reacted to her taste and texture. Stephanie arched her back, and a small groan came from her lips.

He slipped an arm beneath the small of her back, moving to the other breast, while his hand went on an exploration of its own. After long minutes, he kissed his way to her mouth. She tasted sweet, hauntingly familiar, and he battled a dread of letting her go.

He thrust his tongue into her mouth, feeling a desperation

to brand her as his own, wanting the memory of tonight to be seared indelibly into both of their brains.

She kissed him back, deeply and thoroughly, her palms sliding down his back, over his buttocks, along his thighs. He didn't want to rush her, but the urge to push inside grew stronger and stronger.

Then he felt her thighs twitch. They eased apart, welcoming him. It was all he could do to fight the freight train of desire as instinct took over, and his hips automatically flexed forward.

She bent her knees and rose to meet him, the heat of their bodies searing against each other. He drew his head back, watching her wide eyes as he slowly eased inside. Her cheeks were flushed, her dark lips parted in small gasps, and her pupils dilated as she stared deep into his soul.

He stilled, his voice a rasp. "I could do this forever."

"Please do."

"Oh, yeah."

He watched her intently, while his need built, and the tension in his muscles coiled to painful. Still, he refused to move. A single movement would be the beginning of the end. And he didn't want this to end. He quite literally wanted to stay right here for the rest of his life.

"Oh, Alec," she moaned, and a lightning flash of lust shot through him.

"I know." He held fast.

But her eyes fluttered shut, and her hips flexed forward, and her legs wrapped around him, catapulting his subconscious into action. There was nothing he could do to stop the long strokes of pleasure propelling them forward.

Her nails dug into his back. Her gasps were music to his ears. He inhaled her scent, reveled in her hot, moist core, guiding them both as long and as high as he could manage. Then her cries rocked his world, and her body convulsed against him, and his name on her lips sent him over the edge into rhythmic paradise.

Nine

The scattered showers of the new day made the jump course heavy and less than ideal. But Rosie-Joe had excelled in worse conditions than this.

"Make sure you give her time to get her footing before the triple combination," Stephanie told Wesley.

He was dressed, pressed, trimmed and ready to go, his round coming up in only minutes.

"The rain won't spook her," Stephanie continued. "Keep her balanced, and she should run clean. Just keep your head in the game."

Wesley nodded, his gaze suddenly focusing on something in the distance. A smile grew on his face that seemed just a little too confident.

"Are you listening to me?" she asked, as horses, grooms and competitors shifted around them. The announcer's voice was clear on the PA. The crowd applauded as Bill Roauge and Zepher made it cleanly over the water jump.

"You worry too much."

"Wesley—"

He leaned in close, brushing her arm. "Just wish me luck," he whispered. Then he brushed something from her cheek and tucked her hair behind one ear.

Suddenly a blur of movement crossed her vision. Alec's big hand wrapped around Wesley's arm. Wesley staggered backward, as Alec propelled him ten feet to stop abruptly against the wall.

Stephanie was too stunned to move.

Had Alec lost his mind?

She couldn't see his face, and she couldn't hear his words. But she could see the set of his shoulders, and the width of his stance, and his hand was clamped tight around Wesley's arm. Wesley's cockiness turned to shock, while most of the blood seemed to drain from his face.

The groom holding Rosie-Jo stared in stupefaction, while Stephanie finally spurred herself to action, marching across the floor.

"Do you understand?" Alec ground out in a harsh voice she'd never heard before.

Wesley gave a rapid nod, and before Stephanie could say anything, he broke away from Alec and brushed past her.

She turned, torn between going after him and demanding answers from Alec. But Wesley was already mounting Rosie-Jo, and she couldn't think of a single thing to say to him that might help. So, she rounded on Alec.

"What is the matter with you?" she hissed, moving close to face him.

"Not a single thing."

She gestured to Wesley. "He's about to ride."

"So what?"

"You've completely blown his concentration."

Alec pasted her with a hard stare. "He should have thought of that before coming on to another man's wife."

"What?" she sputtered. What on earth was Alec's problem? After last night, how could he possibly think she had any interest in Wesley?

"You going to watch him?" Alec grimly nodded to where Wesley was entering the ring.

She had to watch.

Of course she had to watch.

"We are not through here," she warned Alec.

"We never are," he sighed as she turned for the fence.

Alec fell into step beside her.

"What are you doing?" she asked.

"I'm coming with you."

"It's probably better if you—"

"This isn't negotiable, Stephanie."

"Then at least stop scowling."

They stopped at the fence as Rosie-Jo cleared the first jump.

"He wasn't coming onto me," she muttered in an undertone.

"I agree," said Alec.

And she turned to him with frank astonishment.

"He was testing *me*," said Alec.

The crowd cheered as Rosie-Joe cleared the next jump.

"Testing you for *what*? You were there last night, Alec. You already won." She reflexively scrutinized Wesley's lineup for the vertical.

"To see what I'd do if he made a move on you. He saw

me coming, Stephanie. He looked me straight in the eyes, launched that smug grin and moved in on you."

Stephanie clearly remembered Wesley's touch and his whisper. "I had dirt on my cheek," she defended.

"No, you didn't. You had a husband within eyeshot and a young pup looking to test the waters."

The crowd cheered again.

"You're paranoid." But she had to admit, something had seemed off about Wesley's gesture. And there was no denying he'd been pushing the boundaries with her since she'd told him about being pregnant.

"I'm not paranoid. I'm realistic."

"He knows it's a marriage of convenience," she felt compelled to defend Wesley. It was probably her own fault for not being clear with him three days ago.

"It doesn't matter."

"It does to him."

Butterflies formed in Stephanie's stomach as Rosie-Jo lined up for the triple. She held her breath.

Oxer, vertical, vertical.

He'd done it. Stephanie let out a breath and applauded along with the rest of the crowd.

But on the next jump, Rosie-Jo rubbed a rail.

Stephanie swore under her breath as the announcer acknowledged the fault.

They made the last three jumps clean, their time putting then in eighth place. A respectable showing.

As the pair approached the exit gate, Stephanie and Alec stepped to one side. Alec tossed an arm over her shoulder.

She knew what he was doing, but she also knew it was what she'd signed up for. And, while she wasn't sure Wesley had deliberately taunted Alec, it was probably better if he understood the boundaries up front, particularly while they were working together.

Wesley scrutinized Stephanie. Then his gaze shifted to Alec. It immediately dropped to the ground. She smiled and congratulated him as he passed, but he didn't look up again.

"What did you say to him?" she couldn't help asking Alec.

"That another man would have taken his head off. And he would have."

"I can't believe this has got blown so far out of proportion." She needed to talk to Wesley. The sooner, the better.

"He's a punk kid," said Alec, drawing her further back from the gate, out of the way of the horse and groom traffic, turning to face her. "It's past time for him to learn right from wrong."

"It's partly my fault," she acknowledged. "For telling him we were getting married because of the baby."

Alec's steel gaze burned into hers. "That doesn't change our vows."

"It gave him expectations."

"Are they valid, Stephanie?" The noise of the crowd and loudspeaker disappeared under Alec's intensity.

The question annoyed her. "What do you think?"

"Then tell him."

"I did. I tried. He refuses to understand."

Alec's jaw went hard. "He understands now."

She couldn't help but worry about Wesley. "Did you scare him?"

"Absolutely. And I wasn't bluffing. If he comes near you again—"

"I'm still his coach."

"You know what I mean. And he knows what I mean."

The crowd applauded, and Stephanie glanced behind herself to the board, seeing a new leader. Wesley was bumped to ninth.

She turned back to Alec and heaved a sigh. "This is going to be very complicated."

"No, it's going to be very simple. You'll be professional. He'll be professional. And nobody will get hurt."

"Sometimes you sound like my brothers."

Alec unexpectedly twitched a grin. "That's definitely not what I was going for."

And suddenly last night was between them, as vividly as if they'd had videotape. She remembered his body, the feel, the taste, the sound of his voice and the intimate things they'd said.

It was a crazy situation, a confusing situation. They had one last night before they separated and went back to their individual lives. She hadn't the vaguest idea what would happen to them then. The only thing she knew for sure was that she'd spend this last night with Alec.

In the morning, Alec watched Stephanie preparing to load the Ryder stables trailers on the Brighton grounds. It was overcast, with rain threatening again. He'd pretty much blown his flight out of the Cedarvale Airport, but he didn't care. He was staying right here until she was on the road.

Stephanie had flown in last week, but she was traveling home with the horses, a couple of grooms and Wesley. Alec wasn't crazy about the arrangement, but he was the one who'd bought Blanchard's Run. And now she insisted on accompanying the stallion back to Montana.

She was dressed in blue jeans, scuffed boots and a navy

T-shirt, and he couldn't help but contrast it to the way she'd looked last night. She'd worn a sexy, white nightie—for a short time, anyway. Then they'd made love and retired to the deep whirlpool tub. Afterward, they'd wrapped themselves in the plush robes provided by the hotel.

They'd sat up late on the balcony, talking about family, music, even politics. Anything to avoid the real topic, which was what happened next in their relationship. Afterward, she'd slept in his arms, while he let his imagination explore risky and unlikely scenarios, involving him and Stephanie, and their baby.

He was playing with fire here, and he knew full well somebody could get hurt. He only hoped it was him and not Stephanie.

Rosie-Jo's hooves clanked on the ramp up to the cavernous trailer, while Royce appeared at Alec's side.

"Any updates on the money?" asked Royce.

Alec nodded. "Damien called last night. Since Stephanie knows the truth, our negotiating position has changed, He thinks he can get back a million or two."

"That's it?"

"He thinks Norman Stanton liked women, ponies and high living. There's a house in Miami, a sports car and an astonishingly small bank account."

Royce crossed his arms over his chest. "Not enough to impact the corporation's bottom line."

"Nowhere near," Alec agreed. "But I'll have some final numbers on that for you in my formal report next week."

Royce nodded, glancing at his watch. "You flying out of Cedarvale?"

"I am."

"The Lexington flight leaves from there in forty minutes."

"I'll catch the next one."

"The next one's tomorrow."

Alec shrugged. "I'll get there."

"I've got the jet. You need me to drop you off somewhere?"

There was something odd in Royce's tone, and Alec searched the man's expression.

Was there something he wanted to talk about in private?

Did he have more secrets?

If he did, Alec wished he'd do them both a favor and keep them the hell to himself. The last thing he wanted was to get embroiled in Ryder family politics again.

"I hear you put Wesley into a wall yesterday," said Royce.

"That's an exaggeration."

"Not from what I heard."

"Who'd you hear it from?"

"It wasn't Stephanie."

Alec hadn't thought it was, particularly since he hadn't left her side for nearly twenty-four hours. He did wonder if it was Wesley himself.

"He was out of line," he told Royce.

Royce gave a thoughtful nod. "I know how that goes."

Alec wasn't sure what Royce was getting at. Was he annoyed because Alec had gone after one of their stable clients?

"What did he do?" asked Royce.

He touched her cheek? He touched her hair? Both of those things sounded lame when they were out of context. "None of your business," said Alec.

"Then, tell me something." Royce turned away to watch the Ryder crew, prepping the trailer, widening his stance, stuffing his hands into the front pockets of his blue jeans.

Alec followed his line of vision to where Stephanie was coiling a lead rope. Wesley was packing up the ramps in preparation to leave.

"About my sister." Royce continued, tone thoughtful. "Would you shoot any guy who touched her?"

"In a heartbeat," said Alec.

Royce clicked his cheek. "That's how it starts."

It wasn't exactly a trick question. "Name one guy who wouldn't?"

Royce turned back to Alec. "So, I take it you're going with Plan A."

"Plan A?"

"The one where you make her fall in love with you."

"I'm not going with Plan A." Plan A was fraught with peril.

Then again, he wasn't going with Plan B, either—the one where he disappeared from her life for months at a time.

He hadn't come up with any plan that seemed workable under the circumstance.

"I'm going to say goodbye," he told Royce. Then he left him behind, crossing the small chunk of parking lot that brought him to Stephanie.

"We're about ready to take off," she informed him as he approached, smiling openly, her face scrubbed fresh, her auburn hair flowing in the wind.

"Are you sure you wouldn't rather fly?"

She cocked her head. "Didn't we already have this debate?"

"I wasn't happy with the outcome."

"I'm staying with Blanchard's Run. I'm going to protect your investment."

But his investment wasn't the most valuable thing involved in this package. "You hired his personal groom to take care of him."

"I'm driving to Montana, Alec." Her expression sobered, and her clear blue eyes reflected the gathering clouds. "What about you?"

"Back to Chicago."

She nodded, and her smile came back. It looked a little forced to him, but he couldn't be sure.

"For a week," he elaborated, watching her closely. "Then I'm coming to Montana."

She sobered then swallowed.

"My report will be ready."

"Oh. Right." She gave a little laugh. "Of course."

He wanted to say more. He wanted to tell her he was coming for *her,* not for the damn report. He wanted to tell her they would work this out, that he was falling fast and hard for her, and he was having trouble picturing his life without her.

But it was too soon. And he couldn't risk hurting her. He had no idea how she felt. And half a dozen people were watching them.

He should have asked her last night. But, the truth was, he was afraid of her answer. She'd told Wesley it was a marriage of convenience. And it was. And it might never be anything else.

"See you in Montana?" he asked.

She nodded. See you in Montana.

Ten

Stephanie wished she'd had at least five minutes alone with Alec before the meeting convened around the dining room table at the main ranch house. She's been on the road for days, arriving home last night with Blanchard's Run. Her cell phone conversations with Alec had been sporadic and brief during the long stretches of isolated highway. And there'd been little privacy for evening conversations, since she was sharing motel rooms with the female groom.

She missed him. And she was beginning to doubt her memories. She'd tried to cling to the intimacy they'd shared in Kentucky, but as the days rolled by, she began to fear she'd imagined it.

She'd wanted to talk to him alone before the meeting, but his plane had been late. It was raining hard. And her truck got stuck in the mud on the way down the hill from her place in a pocket where there was no cell signal.

She was the last to arrive. She was wet through to her underwear. Her hair was stringy, and mud caked her boots. Her shower had been a waste of time, and the makeup she'd applied after lunch was long gone. So much for hoping Alec might find her attractive.

"There you are," said Royce as she kicked off her boots in the front hallway.

"Got stuck on Moss Hill," she explained, swiping her hands over her riotous hair, hoping against hope she didn't have mascara running down her cheeks.

"Just got here myself," McQuestin put in, in an obvious attempt to make her feel better.

Stephanie's gaze skipped around the long, rectangular table, Jared, Melissa, Royce, Amber, McQuestin, ah, finally, Alec at one end. The last time she'd seen him here was their wedding. And she couldn't quite contain her smile. He looked so good, immaculate suit, fresh shave, trimmed hair.

He smiled back and gave her a nod, but something about him seemed reserved.

She quickly schooled her features, taking an empty chair halfway down one side.

"Are we ready?" asked Jared where he was positioned at the other end of the table.

There were several nods.

"Then let me start by thanking Alec for his hard work. We know this won't be easy. And we understand we're not going to like everything you have to recommend. But I'd like to say on behalf of my family, that we'll take a serious look at all of your suggestions."

Alec nodded his head in acknowledgment. "I appreciate that, Jared." He shuffled a stack of papers in front of him. "Perhaps I'll start with the ranch." He looked to McQuestin.

"The cattle operation has lost money for several years in a row."

McQuestin screwed up his weathered face, narrowing his eyes.

"However," Alec continued. "Beef prices are on the rise. While land values are at a low. So selling doesn't make sense—"

"'Course it doesn't," said McQuestin.

"With some streamlining to management," Alec continued, "the ranch ought to be able to break even."

"Streamlining?" McQuestin challenged.

"You've stopped paying the blackmail, for starters," said Alec. "And best practices have come a long way in the past thirty years. I'd suggest hiring an agricultural studies grad and—"

"An academic?" McQuestin spat.

"McQuestin," Jared warned. "We said we'd listen."

But Alec was smiling. "Unless you'd like to enroll in college yourself."

McQuestin's bushy brows went up, while everyone else tittered with laughter.

"The details are in my report." Alec flipped a page. "On to the real estate division. As I'm sure you're all aware, it's had the highest profitability for the past few years. But that's about to be challenged. Rental rates are on a downward trend in Chicago, and vacancies are expected to rise."

Stephanie glanced at Jared, but his expression gave away nothing.

"You have a couple of choices there," said Alec. "Ride it out, or sell off either or both of the Maple Street and industrial properties. I'd absolutely recommend keeping everything you've got in the downtown core. When the market recovers, that will go up first."

Jared nodded, but didn't venture an opinion.

"*Windy City Bizz* magazine," said Alec. "Sell that puppy just as fast as you can."

Royce sat up straight. "No. That's Amber's—"

"No, Royce." Amber put her hand on his shoulder. "You should sell it."

"There's no saving print publications," said Alec. "Particularly periodicals."

Stephanie drew a sigh, gauging Amber's expression. She looked sad, but not hugely upset. Stephanie, on the other hand, was getting more uncomfortable by the minute.

Ryder International had been a strong and growing company for as long as she could remember. Jared was an amazing entrepreneur, and Royce seemed to excel at acquisitions. She couldn't quite believe they were in this much trouble.

"What about the jet?" asked Royce, tension evident around his mouth.

"You're going to need it," said Alec. "I know it feels like an indulgence, but you've got interests in half a dozen states. You need to be mobile."

Amber gave Royce's arm a squeeze.

"On the legal issues with your father's will." Alec's gaze flicked to Stephanie for a split second. "I'd recommend vesting Stephanie with nonvoting shares."

Stephanie was sure she couldn't have heard right.

"She doesn't have time to pay attention to the corporate issues—"

"Wait a minute," Stephanie blurted out. She glanced from Jared to Royce, and then to Alec. "You don't want me to vote?"

"I don't want you to *have* to vote. There are a myriad of things that you—"

"How is that different?" What was the matter with him? How could he have blindsided her like that?

He directed his next words to Jared. "You and Royce should have an equal partnership. Frame up a dispute resolution process if necessary, but don't make Stephanie the swing vote."

"Wait a minute," Stephanie shouted.

Jared shot her a look. "We'll give it some thought."

"How can you—"

"Stephanie," Jared warned. "We can discuss it later."

She compressed her lips then turned her cold glare from Jared to Alec. "It's a stupid idea."

"Steph," Royce put in kindly. "You can convince us of that later."

"Fine," she huffed. Her brothers would never go for it anyway. She might only be a half sister, but they loved her. They wouldn't strip away her power for no reason.

What was *wrong* with Alec? What could have changed between the time he bought her Blanchard's Run and now?

"High tech is the future," said Alec. "I wouldn't recommend selling, but you might want to look at some international licensing deals. You can maximize your sales without growing the division to an unwieldy size."

Nobody answered to that.

"On sports and culture." Alec flipped a page in front of him. "I'd suggest standing pat."

Stephanie blew out a sigh. It wasn't relief. It was, well, okay, it was relief.

"Except for the jumping stable."

She stilled, feeling all gazes land on her.

"It's a cash drain, and there's no end in sight." He looked up, taking Stephanie in along with everyone else, pausing no longer, no shorter on her stunned expression than on any of the others. "You need to sell off the entire operation. The sooner the better."

Stephanie found her voice. "Wait just a—"

"May I please finish?" he cut in.

"No, you may not finish. You've just recommended selling something that I spent half my life—"

"Stephanie—"

"—building!" She came to her feet.

"I don't expect you to—"

"How could you *do* this?"

"Will you have a little faith?"

"No. I will not." She rapped her knuckles down on the polished tabletop. "Is there any part of my life you're *not* planning to destroy?"

Alec's lips compressed, eyes darkening to pinpoints.

Stephanie turned on Jared. "Since I have no voting privileges, I guess you two can do whatever you want. But I'm not going to sit around and listen to this guy pick over our family like a vulture."

"Stephanie," Royce tried.

"No!" She turned on her second brother, backing up, scraping her chair legs against the wood floor as she pushed it out of the way. Then she pivoted on her stocking feet and stalked for the door, grabbing her muddy boots on the way out.

"Excuse me," Alec's voice intoned to the group behind her as she slammed the door.

She quickly stuffed her foot into the first boot. Then hopped in place on the porch as she struggled with the other.

The door opened and Alec stepped out. "What the hell is the matter with you?"

"With me? With *me?*" She rammed her foot down to the sole, straightening and flipping her hair over her shoulder. "You're the one out to destroy my life."

He folded his arms over his chest. "You are rushing to preposterous conclusions."

She leaned in. "Tell me one thing, Alec. Why did you buy me Blanchard's Run?"

"Why do you think I bought you Blanchard's Run?"

She gave the only plausible answer she'd come up with. "Because you felt guilty."

"It was not guilt."

"Why then?" she rattled on. "So I'd sleep with you?"

He sputtered out a cold laugh. "Yeah, right."

She forced a note of contempt into her voice. "Well, congratulations, Alec. It worked. I slept with you because you bought me a horse."

"No, you didn't."

"Oh, yes, I did." She glared straight at him, and his eyes flickered with uncertainty.

"What?" she asked sarcastically. "Did you think I'd fallen for your good looks, wit and charm? Think again, Alec. I wanted the horse. You got me the horse. I figured I owed you. And since we'd done it once already—"

"Stop it."

"Truth hurts?"

"Lies hurt, Stephanie."

"Yeah. They do. And we've been a lie from minute one. I'm sorry I forgot about that."

She nodded toward the door behind Alec. "Better get back to your job. My brothers can let me know what they decide." Then she turned, searching for every scrap of dignity she could muster as she paced down the stairs.

As Alec reentered the house, the faces staring at him from the dining room table alternated between condemnation and frank curiosity.

"We stopped them from going after her," Amber informed him.

"I'm sure you did." Alec could well have imagined Jared and Royce's first reaction was to rush outside and save their sister from him. "Thank you," he finished, including both Amber and Melissa in his gratitude.

"We're not selling the jumping stable," Royce informed him, clearly ticked off.

Alec shook his head in disgust. When he'd planned his little speech, he'd planned it all the way to the end, where he revealed his master plan and became Stephanie's hero. He hadn't counted on her being so dogged in her interruptions. And he sure hadn't counted on hearing such a painful truth about her feelings for him.

He'd been looking forward to getting back to Montana from the minute he left Stephanie at Brighton. Now all he wanted to was get the hell out of the state.

He dropped back into his chair. "I want you to sell the jumping stable to *me*."

They all blinked at him in silence.

He threw up his hands, spelling it out in detail. "I'm married to Stephanie. It'll be half hers. This way, Ryder International won't be stuck with the financial liability, but she'll still—".

"Did you tell that to Stephanie?" Amber asked.

He glared at her but didn't answer the question. "I can afford the cash drain. I'll be a silent partner."

Jared snorted. "That's why you don't want her to have voting shares in Ryder International."

"She's going to be a little busy with other interests," said Alec. That, and he'd selfishly assumed she might want a little time left over for him.

"You need to tell her," said Melissa.

"So she'll be grateful?" His voice was sharper than he intended, and Jared frowned at him.

"Sorry," Alec apologized. "You all know my marriage to Stephanie is a sham—"

"Say what?" McQuestin seemed to come back to life.

"She's pregnant," said Alec, not willing to keep any more secrets.

"And you did the right thing?" asked McQuestin, lined face screwing up as he narrowed his eyes, sizing up Alec as if he was debating getting his shotgun. A little late for that.

"I did the right thing," Alec confirmed. "I'll live up to my responsibility, including providing for her and my child by buying and financing the Ryder Equestrian Center. But there's nothing more than that between us."

"Are you sure?" asked Amber.

"Positive," said Alec.

Royce looked to Jared. "Yeah. Except that he'll shoot any man who touches her."

Jared's eyebrows shot up, and he turned his attention to Alec. "You poor bastard."

"What?" asked Melissa.

"It's a joke," said Royce. "A bad joke."

"Explain," demanded Amber.

Alec gathered his paperwork. Jared and Royce's pity was the final straw. If a man had to have his heart broken, he could at least do it in private. "I'll leave a copy of my recommendations for your review. You are, of course, welcome to use or discard anything."

"Explain," Melissa echoed.

Jared gave in. "You know, when Dad murdered Frank Stanton—"

McQuestin rocked forward. *"What?"*

Royce jumped in. "It's a barometer of how much you love your wife."

"Alec's in love with Stephanie?" asked Melissa.

"Alec is saying goodbye," said Alec, turning for the door.

McQuestin jumped into the fray. "Your father didn't murder Frank Stanton."

Everybody went silent and stared at McQuestin. Even Alec froze then turned back.

"It was self-defense," said the old man. "Your mother had changed her mind. She refused to leave with Stanton. Stanton got mad and shot at your dad. He hit your mother by accident in the shoulder, and your father shot back. Your father was rushing her to the hospital when the truck went into the river."

"Then why did Gramps hide the gun?" asked Jared.

"Make it look like a robbery." McQuestin gave him a stern look. "Trials are unpredictable."

And the affair would have been public knowledge. Alec didn't agree with the action, but he thought he understood the motivation. Still, it didn't change anything for him. His hope of a future with Stephanie was over. The sooner he got back to Chicago, the better.

The room went silent as everyone digested the revelation.

"I've got a plane to catch," Alec put in. He didn't exactly

have a ticket, since he'd been hoping to stay here with Stephanie. But nobody needed to know that.

"If you leave," Amber ventured, cocking her head sideways. "How are you going to shoot any man who touches her?"

"Nobody's shooting anyone," he returned. And Stephanie didn't want or need his protection.

Royce came to his feet. "You're just going to abandon her?"

"What part of marriage of convenience don't you understand?"

"The part where you fell in love with my sister."

Alec opened his mouth to deny it, but he found he couldn't lie. There was no point in even attempting to salvage his pride. "She doesn't love me."

"Are you sure?" asked Amber.

Alec gave a sharp nod.

"Then change her mind," Jared put in mildly. "Melissa didn't start off loving me."

Royce grinned. "And Amber took some convincing."

Amber socked him in the arm. "I loved you, dummy. I just didn't tell you about it."

It was painful for Alec to watch the interplay. "It's better if I just leave."

"You sure?" McQuestin put in gruffly, his pale gaze boring into Alec. "Because if you're wrong, and you break that little girl's heart. *I'm* the one who'll be shooting at *you.*"

Two miles from the main ranch, Stephanie jerked her car to the side of the muddy road and brought it to an abrupt halt.

Her hands were shaking. Her stomach ached. And she

couldn't seem to muster up enough strength in her leg to push the clutch and gear down for the hill.

What was she going to do?

She'd come home with such high hopes. But the days and nights at Brighton now seemed like a cruel dream. She'd fallen fast and hard for her husband, and it had seemed like he was falling for her. She'd even dared to hope it was love.

But he didn't love her. He didn't even like or respect her. Why else would he have stripped away her business?

There had to have been other options.

Why was it *her* who had to sacrifice everything?

She gripped the steering wheel, her anger reviving, blocking out her heartache.

But then she remembered *Windy City Bizz*. Amber loved that magazine. Yet, she'd quickly agreed to sell it. And Royce had offered up the jet. And Jared had spent years building up their Chicago property inventory. He had huge plans for construction in the next decade, yet he was looking at selling.

Stephanie swallowed, a horrible thought creeping into her mind. Had she just let her brothers down? Was this why they kept secrets from her? Did they think she couldn't handle the hard truths?

She sat back, shoulders drooping, considering for the first time in her life that she might have some responsibility to turn a financial profit, not just to provide theoretical PR and goodwill. She had an obligation to her family. And she had an obligation to Alec.

Another ranch truck rocked to a halt beside her. But she didn't even look up.

Moments later, Amber banged on the window.

"Stephanie!"

Stephanie blinked blankly at Amber. Her pride was in tatters and her heart was broken to bits.

She loved Alec.

She realized he wasn't trying to hurt her. He was trying to treat her like an adult, a functioning partner. He'd done her the courtesy of telling her the hard truth about her stable, instead of trying to sugarcoat it so she wouldn't get hurt.

She loved him, and he respected her. And she'd just destroyed any chance they might have had at building a future together.

"Will you open—" Amber grabbed the door handle and yanked the driver's door wide. "You have to come back."

Stephanie shook her head. She couldn't go back. She was mortified by her behavior, and she needed to go home and bury her head.

"He's leaving," Amber rushed on. "He's leaving now. McQuestin threatened to shoot him, but he's still leaving."

"What?" Stephanie managed to say, completely confused by Amber's agitation.

"Stephanie." Amber took a breath. "Listen to me. Alec wanted to sell the stable—"

"He was right," Stephanie nodded, swallowing her pain.

"—to *himself*."

Stephanie struggled to make sense of the words.

"*He* was going to buy it. *You* were going to run it. Hell, you were going to own half of it, since you're his wife."

Stephanie felt the blood drain from her face, while the roar of a hurricane pounded in her ears.

Amber grabbed her hand, tugging on it. "You have to come back. *Now*."

Stephanie fumbled with her seat belt catch. "I don't understand."

"He loves you."

"Who loves me?" Stephanie pushed off the seat, landing on the muddy road.

"Alec. He loves you."

Stephanie didn't believe that for a minute. And even if he had, he didn't anymore. Still a little part of her heart couldn't help holding out hope. "He said that?" she dared ask as Amber bundled her into the passenger seat of the other truck.

"He said he'd shoot any man who touched you." Amber swung into the driver's side and put the truck in gear.

"That's not exactly the same thing," Stephanie pointed out.

"It's some kind of a joke. But Royce says it means he loves you. But he's convinced you don't love him. And he's heading for the airport. From there, with his job, who knows where he'll end up." Amber glanced across the seat, voice lowering. "So, if you love him, Stephanie…"

Stephanie stared back. She slowly nodded.

"You need to tell him. And you need to do it right now."

"I'm sorry," Stephanie mumbled. "I wasn't thinking. You gave up the magazine. Royce offered the jet. Of course I'll give up the stable. I didn't mean to sound so spoiled and selfish back there."

Amber unexpectedly smiled. "Me giving up the magazine is nothing compared to you giving up the stable. Your brothers were never going to let that happen. Of course, as it turns out, that wasn't what Alec meant anyway."

"He wants to *buy* the stable?" Stephanie turned the revelation over in her mind.

"And he made it clear you'd be half owner. And he'd be a silent partner. And he was doing it to provide for his wife and his child."

"Oh, no." Acute regret slid through Stephanie's stomach.

"But it's good news."

Stephanie blew out a sigh. "I said some things. To Alec. When I thought he was out to get me."

"What things?"

Stephanie groaned. "He must hate me."

"What things?"

"That I only slept with him the second time—"

"You slept with him a second time?"

"And a third and a fourth and a fifth. Maybe more. I kind of lost count."

Amber laughed. "Well, that sounds promising."

"No." Stephanie shook her head. "I just finished telling him I'd only done it because he bought Blanchard's Run. It was gratitude sex, and I didn't find him either handsome, funny or charming. I may have said I didn't like him. I definitely implied he should get lost."

"Do you think he believed you?"

"I was pretty convincing."

"But you're in love with him?"

Stephanie moaned, bending forward around her stomachache. "Yes."

"Maybe try telling him that." The truck rocked to a halt. Stephanie looked up to see Jared, Melissa, Royce and McQuestin standing in the front driveway.

She glanced frantically around for Alec, opening the door, stepping out.

"He's gone," said Jared.

"How long?" asked Amber.

"Twenty minutes, at least." Royce shook his head.

"I'm going after him," Stephanie decided. Amber was right. While Stephanie had been dead wrong. She owed him an apology, and she was going to suck up her pride and tell him she loved him.

She was sure it would be nothing but a lesson in abject humiliation, because no man was going to love a woman who'd behaved the way she did. And despite his joke to Royce, she was sure Alec would be happy to put as much distance as possible between himself and her.

She looked to Amber. "Give me the keys."

"You'll never catch him," said Melissa. "And it's dangerous to try."

"Take the Cessna," McQuestin put in.

Royce looked at the old man, then grinned. "We'll take the Cessna." He grabbed the keys from Amber and headed to the truck at a trot. "Come on," he called to Stephanie.

She sprinted after him.

It was a five-minute drive to the ranch airstrip. Royce sped through his pre-flight checklist. Stephanie slapped on the earphones and strapped into the seat and braced herself for takeoff.

In no time, they were skimming a thousand feet above the ranch road. The road met the main road, and they banked east. There'd be little traffic before the Interstate, so Alec's black car should be easy to spot.

After they found him? Well, things were definitely going to get tough. She tried to come up with a speech in her mind, something, *anything* that might help him forgive her. But she was drawing a blank.

"Painful, isn't it?" asked Royce through the radio.

"I was so stupid."

He laughed. "We all are. I told Amber she should marry her former fiancé. I could have lost her right then and there."

"But you didn't."

"No, I didn't."

Stephanie peered out the small windshield, scanning the length of road in front of them. Range land whizzed by, with the occasional barn or stream. "We don't know how this one's going to turn out."

"He loves you, Steph."

"I may have killed that."

"You can't kill it. Believe me, you can't kill it."

Stephanie drew a breath, desperately trying to convince herself that Royce knew what he was talking about. But the fact was, he didn't. His and Amber's relationship was unique and special. It wasn't representative of every other relationship in the world.

"There he is," said Royce, pointing to the road. And Stephanie's heart went into overdrive.

Royce overflew the car, checked for traffic, then turned the Cessna in a tight circle, bringing it down on the pavement of the road. They coasted to a stop, and he shut off the engine.

Stephanie removed her headphones, unclipped the harness then clambered out of the small seat, stepping on the wing strut before dropping down to the pavement.

"Go get 'em, tiger," Royce called with an encouraging grin.

Stephanie couldn't muster up a smile in return. Her palms were sweating and her knees were weak. She took a few trembling steps along the centerline, watching for Alec's car to come into view. She didn't have long to wait.

The black car coasted to a stop, but Alec didn't get out.

Squinting, at the tinted windshield, Stephanie forced herself to walk toward it.

Finally the door opened, and Alec stepped out, frowning. "What the hell?"

"I'm sorry, Alec."

He looked at the plane, then back to her. "What the *hell?*"

"It's Royce. We were afraid you'd beat us to the airport and get on a plane, and I wouldn't be able to find you."

"So you landed on the *highway?* Have you lost your mind?"

"I came to apologize."

He was still frowning. His eyes were squinted down in anger. "It never occurred to me in a million years that I'd have to make this rule. But don't you ever, *ever* take my baby up in an airplane and land on a public roadway."

"It's perfectly safe. We checked for traffic."

"Stephanie."

"Okay. Okay. I won't." She paused. "But don't you want to know why I'm here?"

"To say you're sorry?"

She screwed up her courage. "To say I love you."

His expression never flinched. "They told you about me buying the stable?"

She nodded.

"And you're grateful for that?"

"It's not about gratitude."

His look turned skeptical. "Really?"

"It was never about gratitude for Blanchard's Run."

"That's not what you said an hour ago."

"I lied an hour ago."

"But you're not lying now?"

"No."

He took a step forward, jaw clenched, expression grim. "Explain to me, Stephanie. How exactly am I supposed to tell the difference?"

It was a fair question. She moved closer to him. "I guess you can't."

His expression softened ever so slightly. "So, when you tell me that you love me? Which, by the way, I desperately want to believe—"

"But you need proof?" she ventured.

"And it can't be sex."

"Too bad." Her voice dropped low. "I've been thinking about sex all week."

Something twitched in his expression.

"I missed you so much," she told him. "I thought about you all morning. I imagined you pulling me back into your arms, holding me tight, and telling me everything was going to work out for us."

"And instead I threatened to sell your home out from under you."

"I should have listened longer. And it shouldn't have mattered. I should have been able to handle the hard truth."

"I should have started with the punch line."

"I love you, Alec. I don't know how to prove that to you, but I'm willing to do anything you say."

A grin twitched the corners of his mouth. "Marry me?"

"I already did."

He reached out and took her hands in his. "Have my baby? No. Wait. You're already doing that."

She couldn't help but smile.

"And since we're already having amazing sex…" He drew her in closer. "I can't come up with a single thing that would definitively prove you love me."

"I could shoot somebody," Stephanie ventured.

His hand slipped to the back of her neck, fingers burrowing into her hairline. "What are you talking about?"

"Amber said it was some kind of a joke. It meant you loved me."

"I do love you," he admitted, and a heavy weight lifted from Stephanie's chest. "But there'll be no shooting involved."

"Okay by me. Hey, I have an idea."

"Shoot."

She rolled her eyes. "What if we live happily ever after? We pull that off, you can be sure that I love you."

Alec smiled as he leaned in. "Deal." Then his lips came down on hers, and he drew her tightly into the circle of his strong arms.

She pressed her body against him, clinging to him, loving him with ever fiber of her being.

Epilogue

After considering nearly every wedding location on the planet, Amber had finally decided on a casual wedding at the ranch. She and Royce were married in the meadow overlooking Evergreen Falls.

She'd confided in Stephanie that it was as far removed as she could get from a cathedral and a ballroom in Chicago—the plan she'd had in place with her former fiancé, the one who was now married to Katie, her best friend and maid of honor.

It was full on summer, a year since Stephanie had met Alec. Their baby girl was now three months old, and little Heidi had slept the ceremony away in her father's arms. Now she was resting her head on his shoulder, staring wide-eyed at the lively country band that had taken over the deck of the ranch house.

The patio had turned into a dance floor, with the overflow spilling onto the lawn.

"You going to start riding again?" Royce asked Stephanie as he twirled her in his arms to the sweeping strains of a breakup song.

"I just got the okay from the doctor."

"But did you get the okay from Alec?"

Stephanie laughed. "Did you get the okay from Amber to keep flying?"

Her brother frowned.

"Same thing," she pointed out.

"Not exactly."

"Yes, exactly."

"How many times have you fallen off a horse?"

"Dozens," she responded. "Hundreds."

"I rest my case. I've never once fallen out of my airplane."

Stephanie caught the warm gaze of her husband, and he playfully waved Heidi's hand in her direction.

"Alec wants me to ride," she informed her brother.

"Alec wants you to smile. Trust me, he doesn't want you to ride."

"He can't stop me."

"He can get you pregnant again."

"He would nev—" Stephanie frowned. Wait a minute. Was that why he was being so cavalier about birth control?

Royce started to laugh.

Stephanie stopped dancing and drew back from his arms. She turned, eyes narrowing in Alec's direction.

Alec shot back a look of confusion.

"Melissa," Royce sang, drawing his six months pregnant sister-in-law into his arms.

"What did you say to her?" Melissa's laughing voice followed Stephanie to the edge of the patio.

Alec's brows narrowed in confusion, while Heidi gurgled and waved her arms toward Stephanie.

"How many kids do you want?" she asked Alec, retrieving her daughter and settling Heidi against her shoulder.

"As many as I can get," he answered with a grin.

"I'm not giving up riding."

"Huh?"

"You can't keep me pregnant all the time."

"Who says I'm trying to keep you pregnant?"

"Royce."

Alec's gaze shot past her. "Well, what the hell does Royce know?"

She leaned in. "You didn't want to use a condom last night."

Alec lowered his voice. "You're still breast-feeding."

"It's not foolproof."

"Nothing's foolproof."

"I'm jumping Rosie-Jo tomorrow," she warned.

"Go for it. I'll baby-sit."

"Really?"

"Yes, really. And stop listening to your brother. He's trying to stir up trouble."

Stephanie glanced to where her brother had switched dance partners once more. He now held his bride, Amber, in his arms, her gauzy white dress flowing around the satin slippers on her feet. He whispered something in her ear, and she smacked him in the shoulder. He just grinned and winked.

That was her brother Royce, all right, stirring up trouble.

"I think our princess is tuckered out," said Alec,

smoothing his hand over Heidi's silky hair as her mouth stretched in a wide yawn.

Stephanie smiled. "Home?"

"Home." He nodded.

She turned and caught Amber's gaze, giving her a little wave.

Amber mouthed, "thank you," keeping her head tucked against Royce's shoulder. They'd see each other for a proper goodbye in the morning before the couple left on their honeymoon.

"Want me to take her?" asked Alec as they made their way toward the stairs to the deck. Through the house was the fastest way to the driveway and their truck.

"I'm fine," Stephanie answered, starting up the short staircase while Alec kept close behind.

Heidi's warm little body relaxed into sleep, even as they passed the drummer.

"Keys in the truck?" asked Alec as they crossed the living room.

"Should be." Stephanie snagged a final cheese puff from the buffet on the dining room table.

"You're *still* hungry?" Alec teased.

"You try feeding a baby." She took two steps back and washed the cheese puff down with a strawberry.

Alec pulled open the front door and stood aside to let her pass.

"Thank you, sir," she mocked as she sashayed through.

"I just like the view from—" Alec nearly barreled into the back of her where she'd frozen still on the top step.

"Hello, Alec." Damien gave him a nod.

But Stephanie's gaze was fixed on the man standing next

to Damien. He was older, clean shaven, his jawline softer, face wrinkled and shoulders stooped.

The front door banged open to Royce's jovial voice. "You trying to sneak—" Royce stopped, too. Then a lighter set of footsteps came to a halt on the porch.

"Stanton," Royce growled.

Alec stepped around Stephanie and Heidi, putting his body between her and Norman Stanton.

"We'd hoped the party would be over," Damien apologized.

"What the hell are you doing?" Alec demanded of his friend.

Royce took a step forward, coming parallel with Alec, while Jared appeared out of nowhere.

Norman Stanton cleared his throat. "I'm sorry—"

"You're *sorry?*" Royce roared.

Norman swallowed convulsively, and Stephanie found herself pitying the man.

"I didn't mean to intrude."

"This is my *wedding.*"

"I knew you were leaving tomorrow," said Damien, stepping forward to hand Royce an envelope.

Alec stepped up to Damien, voice low. "Start talking."

Norman spoke up. "I never meant to hurt any of you."

Jared stepped forward. "If you're not hightailing it off Ryder land in about thirty seconds, you're the one who's getting hurt."

"It was Clifton," said Norman.

"Don't you *dare* speak my father's name."

"Damien?" Alec warned in another undertone.

"I thought he murdered Frank!" Norman all but wailed.

Everyone stilled, and Stephanie found herself mesmerized by the pain in the older man's eyes.

"He was my brother. And he was murdered. And I went after revenge."

Stephanie glanced at her brothers to see them exchange a look.

"I told him the truth," said Damien.

"I know now that it was self-defense," Norman clarified. He peered between Alec and Royce, seeking out Stephanie's gaze. "He loved your mother."

Alec stepped sideways, blocking Norman's view.

"And he loved you."

"Don't you speak to my wife," said Alec.

Stephanie touched Alec's arm. "It's okay."

Alec didn't move. "No, it's not."

Royce's incredulous voice rang out. "This is *ten million dollars*."

Stephanie turned to see the envelope flutter to the ground.

"I wanted to pay you back," said Norman.

"I helped him liquidate," Damien put in.

"I'm sorry," Norman repeated. "I wanted to make him pay. But I never meant to hurt any of you."

His gaze once again sought out Stephanie. "Frank was my brother, and you were my niece. He talked about you all the time. I couldn't wait to meet you. He said he was bringing you home." The man's voice caught. "Instead I claimed his body."

Tears gleamed in Norman's eyes, and something tugged at Stephanie's heart.

The man looked old and broken, nothing like his picture, nothing like the villain she'd expected.

"I'll get you the rest of the money," Norman told Royce and Jared.

"How?" Royce demanded.

"I gave him a job," said Damien.

"You *what?*" asked Alec.

"I was wrong." Damien shrugged. "He didn't blow the money on women and ponies."

Stephanie moved her attention to her husband.

"No?" Alec asked, watching Damien closely.

Damien gave him a meaningful smile and shook his head. "Let's just say my organization can use his talents."

"Did you steal it from someone else?" Jared demanded.

"It's your money," said Stanton. "I've been holding it for you."

"We'll be looking for interest," Royce put in.

Alec transmitted a silent question to Damien, and Damien's smiled broadened.

Norman's hungry gaze was glued to Stephanie.

She could feel his loneliness and sorrow pierce straight to her soul.

He was her uncle, the brother of a father she didn't remember. She found herself wondering what Royce would do if he thought someone had killed Jared, or the other way around, or what both of them would do if they thought someone had harmed her.

She shifted around Alec, gazing into Norman's lined face in the pool of lamplight.

His eyes went wide, darting to Heidi as she drew closer.

Royce shot forward, but Alec's arm reached out to block him.

Stephanie smiled gently at Norman. "Would you like to meet your grandniece?"

Twin tears slipped out of his blue eyes, trailing swiftly down his pale, sagging cheeks.

Stephanie eased Heidi away from her body, exposing her little pink face. "This is Heidi Rae Creighton. Heidi, this is your uncle Norman."

She felt Alec's gentle hands close around her shoulders.

Norman stood frozen for a full minute.

Then he lifted a shaking finger, gently stroking the back of Heidi's tiny hand. "Heidi Rae." His voice was strangled with emotion.

Stephanie's chest tightened, and tears stung the backs of her eyes.

Royce appeared in Stephanie's peripheral vision. She braced herself, but Royce's body language was no longer hostile.

"This check good?" he asked gruffly.

Norman didn't take his eyes off Heidi. "It's good," he affirmed.

Royce gave a sharp nod as Jared joined them.

Alec's hands squeezed Stephanie's shoulders, and he leaned down to whisper. "You are an amazing woman. And I love you *so* much."

* * * * *

Warning bells rang out in his head. His mind screamed, Off-limits.

He wasn't ready for any relationship, much less one with his employee. How many times had he reminded himself of that?

Joe stepped out of his car and leaned against it.

"Thank you for following me home, Joe. It wasn't necessary, but I do appreciate it."

"Just wanted to make sure you got home safely, Ali."

She faced him and leaned over to give him a little kiss on his cheek. "That's sweet."

Sweet? Joe's hackles went up. He spread his legs and braced Ali's waist with his hands, pulling her closer. Her exotic scent went straight to his brain. "Can you forget that I'm your boss for one night?"

His gaze dropped down to the ripe fullness of her mouth.

Ali blinked. Then a beautiful smile emerged. "I think so. Why?"

Joe answered her by cupping a hand around her neck and bringing her mouth to his. "To show you I'm not that sweet," he whispered before he crushed his mouth to hers.

SEDUCTION ON THE CEO'S TERMS

BY
CHARLENE SANDS

DID YOU PURCHASE THIS BOOK WITHOUT A COVER?

If you did, you should be aware it is **stolen property** as it was reported
unsold and destroyed by a retailer. Neither the author nor the publisher
has received any payment for this book.

All the characters in this book have no existence outside the imagination of
the author, and have no relation whatsoever to anyone bearing the same name
or names. They are not even distantly inspired by any individual known or
unknown to the author, and all the incidents are pure invention.

All Rights Reserved including the right of reproduction in whole or in
part in any form. This edition is published by arrangement with Harlequin
Enterprises II B.V./S.à.r.l. The text of this publication or any part thereof may
not be reproduced or transmitted in any form or by any means, electronic or
mechanical, including photocopying, recording, storage in an information
retrieval system, or otherwise, without the written permission of the publisher.

This book is sold subject to the condition that it shall not, by way of trade or
otherwise, be lent, resold, hired out or otherwise circulated without the prior
consent of the publisher in any form of binding or cover other than that in
which it is published and without a similar condition including this condition
being imposed on the subsequent purchaser.

® and ™ are trademarks owned and used by the trademark owner and/or its
licensee. Trademarks marked with ® are registered with the United Kingdom
Patent Office and/or the Office for Harmonisation in the Internal Market and
in other countries.

Published in Great Britain 2011
by Mills & Boon, an imprint of Harlequin (UK) Limited,
Eton House, 18-24 Paradise Road, Richmond, Surrey TW9 1SR

© Charlene Swink 2010

ISBN: 978 0 263 88237 7

51-0711

Harlequin (UK) policy is to use papers that are natural, renewable and
recyclable products and made from wood grown in sustainable forests. The
logging and manufacturing processes conform to the legal environmental
regulations of the country of origin.

Printed and bound in Spain
by Blackprint CPI, Barcelona

To Bill, Carol, Angi and Eric—the Petti.
Thanks for being my biggest fans and source of
love and support. I'm happy to call you family!
With special gratitude to my sister Carol
and brother-in-law Bill for making me an auntie!

Award-winning author **Charlene Sands** writes bold, passionate, heart-stopping heroes and always…really good men! She's a lover of all things romantic, having married her school sweetheart, Don. She is the proud recipient of the Readers' Choice Award and double recipient of the Booksellers Best Award, having written twenty-eight romances to date, both contemporary and historical Western. Charlene is a member of Romance Writers of America and belongs to the Orange County and Los Angeles Chapters of RWA where she volunteers as the Published Authors Liaison.

When not writing, she loves movie dates with her hubby, playing cards with her children, reading romance, great coffee, Pacific beaches, country music and anything chocolate. She also loves to hear from her readers. You can reach Charlene at www.charlenesands.com or PO Box 4883, West Hills, CA 91308, USA.

Dear Reader,

I have always loved fairy tales. *Cinderella* and *Beauty and the Beast* count among my favorites, so when I wrote Joe Carlino and Ali Pendrake's story it was with those two tales in mind.

Ali, the beautiful Cinderella, must transform into Plain Jane to catch the eye of the man she loves. Her "makeover in reverse" is fun to watch. You'll find yourself cheering Ali's last-ditch attempt to get her boss, hunky computer-genius Joe, to notice her.

Like the Beast in Disney's fairy tale, Joe doesn't know he wants love in his life. His vow to never engage in an office romance spurs Ali's clever plan to change his mind.

I hope you enjoy *Seduction on the CEO's Terms*. Sit back, kick your shoes off and sip from a glass of great California wine.

Fall into the fantasy!

Happy reading,

Charlene

One

Ali Pendrake sat at her desk at the Carlino Wines office, hitting the computer keys in rapid succession. She'd been at the top of her keyboarding class in college seven years ago, being not only a speedy typist but an accurate one. Today her usual tenacious focus waned and mistakes abounded.

"Darn it, Ali. You dummy," she muttered under her breath. She hit the backspace key and fixed her error, her concentration lost today.

Stealing a glance at her boss, Joe Carlino, Ali sighed. Joe's attention was glued to the computer screen in his executive office as he mumbled and crunched numbers. Deliberately, she'd positioned her desk in the outer office to afford herself this view of him.

No matter how hard she'd tried, she couldn't get Joe off her mind. Working alongside him in New York last year for a software giant, Ali had come to know him fairly well. Tall, dark-haired and extremely handsome behind the glasses he wore, Ali admired his intelligence, dedication and honest work ethic more than his good looks. He'd always treated her with respect, and Ali appreciated that.

Usually men took one look at her and discounted her intellect and ability. All they saw was a rather buxom auburn-haired woman with a pretty face and nice legs, so of course, she couldn't possibly have any brains. Most male employers had never given her a chance. Oh, they'd pretended to hire her for her capabilities, but all too soon harsh reality would set in when they made nonprofessional overtures.

The last thing Ali wanted was to be like her mother. Umpteen boyfriends and five husbands later, Justine Holcomb, a one-time beauty queen, gloried in the attentions of men. The former Miss Oklahoma never missed a chance to scope out wealthy, powerful men and manipulate them into marriage.

Ali only wanted *one* real good man. And that man wouldn't look at her twice.

"Ali, could you come in here?" When Joe popped his head out of his office, his thin black-rimmed glasses slipped down his nose Clark-Kent style.

Excitement buzzed within her at the sound of his voice. She'd never wanted her feelings for Joe to show. She'd enjoyed working with him in a professional manner in New York. It had been a rarity and an experience she'd valued. But then his father died, and he'd been called home to help run the family wine empire.

She'd driven him to LaGuardia Airport as her last official act as his personal assistant. He'd taken her in his arms and kissed her goodbye. Now memories of the exquisite press of his mouth on hers, his musky scent, the scratch of his day-old beard on her skin and the way he held her tight in his arms flashed through her mind. In that instant, everything inside her had gone hot; her body had oozed with desire. She'd looked up and met the gleam of desire in his eyes.

They'd stared at each other for a long time, saying nothing. She didn't know what to say. He'd obviously felt the same awkwardness in the situation after that kiss and had left her standing there pondering what had happened.

Since then, there wasn't a day that went by when she didn't think of him, and to her great surprise those thoughts weren't G-rated. In fact, her traitorous mind conjured up sexy images of Joe that stole her breath.

So when he'd called, offering her the opportunity to uproot her life and work to join him in northern California, the decision hadn't been difficult. She'd been ecstatic and jumped at the offer. She figured she'd have another chance with Joe. She happily left the Big Apple's rat race behind.

But after three weeks on the job, Ali was sure the potted plant in the corner of the room got more attention from Joe than she did. He was all business, pretending that the kiss they'd shared at the airport hadn't blown them both away. In truth, no man she'd met recently had been *less* interested in her.

"Sure, Joe. I'll be right in." She picked up her notepad, her BlackBerry and her wits and followed him into his office.

He waited for her to sit down before taking a seat behind his desk. His warm smile devastated her. "I realized that I haven't asked you how you're settling in here in Napa." He leaned back in his leather seat, waiting for her to reply.

"Just dandy, boss." She returned his smile. "It's different and all, but you know what they say, a girl's gotta do what a girl's gotta do."

Joe peered over his glasses at her. "How's that?"

She shrugged, and her white peasant blouse slipped off her shoulder. Joe didn't appear to notice when she adjusted it back into place, his focus staying on her face. "I like working with you," she said truthfully. "I'm glad to be here. I think we make a good team."

Joe nodded slowly. "I appreciate that. So you have no problems? No questions?"

Yes, you don't seem to know I'm alive.

"Not really. Not about work. I would love to learn more about the Napa area, though. I thought I'd start venturing out on the weekends."

"Sounds like a good plan."

She straightened her calf-length skirt. She'd gone for the gypsy look today. Hoop earrings and her bright auburn hair down in curls added some flavor to her outfit. She had smarts and was proud of her achievements, but she also loved fashion. Her flamboyant style often garnered compliments from the other Carlino Wines employees. If nothing else, it was an icebreaker and a way to meet people who had worked for the family for a long time.

Joe stared at her for a moment. She sat, waiting for him to voice the reason he'd called her into his office. Usually, it was to go over accounts, check monthly reports or give her an assignment. His silence made her wonder. "Is there anything I'm doing wrong?"

"Hell, no," Joe said. "You're the best employee we have on-site."

"Well, thank you."

"That's the reason I've asked you in here today. I, uh, well, I have a favor to ask. And I won't hold it against you if you can't help me out with this."

Ali waited for a moment before the suspense got to her. She gestured impatiently with both hands. "Spit it out, Joe."

He chuckled and shook his head.

She grinned.

"Okay, okay. I've offered to give Rena and Tony a wedding reception. You've met my brother and sister-in-law, right?"

"Great people," Ali said.

"It's a long story, but they got married secretly a short time ago, and well, now they want to renew their vows and have a reception."

"You offered to throw it for them?"

"More like my brother Nick roped me into it. What do I know about planning a party like that, right?"

She nodded.

"That's where you come in. I need your help. I'll understand if you're too busy to help me out with this—"

"Are you kidding?" Ali stood, excited at the prospect. "I love a good party. You won't have to ask me twice. What's the timetable on this?"

"Well, the sooner the better. Tony mentioned he wanted to do it ASAP. Say, in three weeks?"

"That's doable."

"Really?" Joe stood, too, an expression of relief washing over his features. "It may mean working together some weekends—that's if you're not too busy."

"I'm not too busy." *Was he joking?* She'd sat around her apartment at night bored to tears. Not that she couldn't have company, but the men who'd asked her out didn't compare to the computer brain—she refused to call Joe a geek—who seemed to occupy her mind lately.

"You might not have time to check out the sights around here."

Ali's mind clicked into high gear. "I'll make you a deal. If I help plan this successfully, then you can show me the sights in wine country. Fair is fair, Joe."

Joe adjusted the glasses on his nose, and Ali recognized that sign. Whenever Joe needed extra time to contemplate a question, he played with those glasses. "I can show you the inner workings of a computer better than I can be your Napa Valley tour guide."

"Joe," Ali said, refusing to let him off the hook, "you grew up here. You *know* this area." This was her opportunity to see Joe in less sterile surroundings. She really wanted to get to know him better. Her recent work relationship with Dwayne Hicks made her extremely wary of all men. Dwayne had exacted more from her than secretarial skills, and things had gotten ugly. Joe was the only man she'd trusted to take a chance with. And she really did love a good party. "Are we on?"

"I really appreciate this, Ali. Yes, we're on."

After returning to his office, Joe picked up his phone and dialed Nick's number. He reached him on the second ring.

"Hey, Joe. What's up?"

"Tony's wedding reception is in the works as we speak."

"That's good news. I knew you'd come through."

"Hey, not me. I'm not the wedding planner. I've got a one-woman task force, and I know she'll do a great job."

When his father died, his brother Tony had called both he and Nick home to honor the terms of Santo Carlino's will. All three sons were to take the helm at Carlino Wines for a period of six months and figure out which son would be better suited to run the family empire. It was his father's dying wish. Joe had left his life behind on the East Coast to help Tony and Nick, but he'd never have guessed part of his job description would be as a wedding planner.

Secretly, Tony had married his first love and high school

sweetheart, Rena Fairfield, shortly after her husband's death in order to save her winery and provide for her unborn child. After they fell back in love with each other, Rena had finally come around to letting their secret out. And Tony didn't trust anyone outside the family to see that his renewal of vows and reception were done right. He'd entrusted his brothers with the honor.

Joe sighed with relief. With Ali's help now, he knew it all would work out. She was always up for a challenge, and he had faith that she'd do a superb job.

"And you're going to come in on deadline with this?"

"Yeah, we'll be in the right time frame," Joe replied.

"You talked your gorgeous assistant into helping you, didn't you?"

"Nick." Joe sighed. "Her name is Ali Pendrake. And yes, she's taking on the project. We'll need a female's input, and she's very capable."

Nick chuckled. "So you've told me about a hundred times. Beauty and brains is a dynamite combo in a woman, Joe."

"I guess so," Joe said, fidgeting with his computer keyboard. He didn't like the direction this conversation was taking.

"So, you're *really* not interested in her?" Nick asked.

"No, of course not. She's my employee. I thought I made myself clear on that."

Joe dismissed the one time he'd held Ali in his arms and kissed her. His gesture of farewell at the New York airport that day had gotten a little out of control. But his emotions had been running high at the time. His father had just passed away, and he'd been called home. His life had changed drastically, and Ali was there for him, lending support and comfort. Kissing her had been impulsive—and so damn good that his head had spun.

He'd thought of her often after that. But after his assistant and ex-fiancée Sheila's betrayal, an office romance of any kind was out of the question. She had cut his heart out when she'd dumped him for another man. Joe had a will of iron, and though Ali was beautiful and had traits he admired, he knew he'd never pursue anything with her but a working relationship. He'd offered her the job in Napa only because he knew he could work beside her and not get emotionally involved. It was hard for both of his brothers to understand that he just simply didn't see Ali that way.

"So, you wouldn't mind if I asked her out?" Nick questioned.

Joe furrowed his brows. He hadn't seen this coming. Nick had his fair share of women. He wasn't one to spend his nights alone. But Ali and *Nick?* Joe couldn't picture them together. His jaw clenched, and he contemplated for a moment.

"Joe? Did you hear me?"

"I heard you, little brother."

"We've never stepped on each other's toes when it came to women, but if you're clearly not interested in Ali—"

"I'm not."

"So, I can ask her out without causing you sleepless nights?"

"No, you can't ask her out."

"I can't?" Nick didn't sound too upset. "Why?"

"No offense, but I wouldn't subject any of my employees to dating you, especially Ali. You'd likely break her heart. And then she'd leave town, and I'd be out one damn good personal assistant."

"You don't give me much credit."

"History doesn't lie."

"Maybe I'm a changed man."

"Maybe...but I don't want you to use one of my employees as your test subject."

Nick laughed. "Man, you really don't have a good opinion of me, do you?"

"In any other arena, you're a great guy. Just *not* when it comes to women." Joe was ready to leave this subject behind. "So when are you leaving for Europe?"

"In a few days. But have no fear, I'll be back in time for the big hoopla. I wouldn't miss Tony's wedding reception."

"Yeah, your timing is impeccable. Leaving me to deal with all the details, while you're off—"

"Selling wine, schmoozing with customers and making sure Carlino Wines stays on top."

"Among other things," Joe muttered.

In truth, it bothered him how glad he was that Nick would be out of the picture for a couple of weeks. If he wasn't around, he couldn't be romancing Ali. In his analytical mind, that shouldn't be a factor. But he was damn glad of it just the same.

"I'll see you at home tonight," Nick said.

"I'll be working late with Ali."

"Hey, I can't blame you, bro." Joe visualized his brother's smirk. "Regardless of all your denials."

Joe hung up the phone and shook his head.

Ali came in then, holding a calendar in her hands. "Joe, I think we'd better set a date for the wedding reception."

Ali's darn blouse had slipped down again, and it was all he could do to keep from staring at her soft shoulder. She had such beautiful creamy skin. He'd have to be blind not to notice.

Every day with Ali was a fashion extravaganza. Today she looked like a gypsy princess—a very sexy, approachable one. He'd never noticed her style much in New York, but now, Nick and Tony's prodding was making it hard for him to *keep* from noticing her.

But the more he noticed, the more he was determined to keep her off-limits. She wasn't his type of woman anyway. She reminded him too much of Sheila with her quick wit, flamboyant nature and sense of adventure. He'd been playing with fire in his office relationship with Sheila, and he wasn't about to jump back into the flames anytime soon. A broken engagement and being left for a flashy billionaire wasn't his idea of a good time. Joe had been smacked down by that betrayal, and he had no intention of bounding up on the ten count to take another knockout punch.

"I think that's a good idea. Sit down, and we'll go over some dates. Then I'll check with Tony to make sure it'll work for them."

"I'm already on it. I just spoke with Rena. She's coming into town today, and we're having lunch. I'll cross-check the dates with her once you and I come up with something feasible."

Joe smiled and leaned back in his seat. He wasn't sorry he'd asked Ali to come work for him. Time and again, she'd proven to him that hiring her was the smartest thing he'd ever done. "I'm glad you took me up on my offer to come to Napa, Ali."

Ali's jade-green eyes lit up. "You are?"

"Yeah, you're in line for employee of the year."

Ali's gaze dropped to the calendar in her hands. "How nice."

Joe drew his brows together. Ali wasn't thrilled with his pronouncement. Somehow he'd disappointed her, but he couldn't figure out how. If anyone understood an honest work ethic, it was Ali Pendrake.

He thought she'd be happy that he'd recognized her many capabilities.

Rena Carlino was beautifully pregnant. The minute she walked into the office, Ali noticed the bright beam of happiness on her face and the lightness in her step despite sporting a rounded belly.

From all she'd gathered from Joe, Rena hadn't had an easy life and Tony had caused most of her trouble. The former race car champion had left Rena in the dust years ago to pursue his dream of racing stock cars. Jilted and heartbroken, Rena had married David Montgomery, Tony's best friend. She'd come to blame Tony for David's untimely death, faulting him for her heartache and the terrible things done to ruin her family's winery.

But when Tony returned to Napa twelve years later and honored the vow he made to Rena's dying husband to marry his pregnant wife, their rocky road had smoothed out. To his credit, Tony had come through in the end. Now, Tony loved both mother-to-be and baby and the evidence of that love beamed in Rena's eyes.

"Hi, Ali."

Ali stood and smiled. "Hi." She walked around the desk to embrace Rena. "You look fabulous."

Rena rubbed her belly and grinned. "Thank you. Most days, I'd disagree with you. But I made an extra effort today, since I was meeting you for lunch."

"I don't believe that for a minute."

"Oh, believe it. I feel *fine,* it's just that I'm moving so much slower these days. I'm used to doing a lot of work. I was always up early, working hard at the winery, but now things have slowed down. It's to be expected. And Tony is so protective that he won't let me lift anything heavier than my purse."

Ali chuckled, and a slight wave of envy coursed through her system. Tony adored Rena, and Ali wondered when her time would come to feel that same sort of love from a man. "I hear the baby's healthy as a horse."

"Yes, and I plan to keep it that way. Did you hear we're having a boy?"

"Oh Lord, love him. Another male Carlino in the world? I feel sorry for the next generation of baby girls."

Rena grinned. "I know what you mean. The Carlino men are a handful. I guess I'll have my work cut out for me."

Ali really admired Rena. She'd been given a lot to deal with lately, and she'd taken it all in stride. She'd finally come to accept the role as Tony's wife without giving up her own dream of saving her family's legacy, Purple Fields Winery. But even more amazing was that she'd forgiven Tony for all the hurt he'd caused and accepted him as the father of her child.

Ali grabbed her knockoff Gucci handbag and her briefcase. "Excuse me a second. I'll just let Joe know we're leaving for lunch." Ali turned and bumped smack into Joe, stepping on his toes and bumping heads. "Oh!"

Joe grabbed her arms to steady her, his touch sending lightning bolts straight through her. She was so close to him that their breaths mingled. The subtle scent of Hugo cologne was heaven to her senses.

"Are you okay?" he asked with concern.

Ali stared at him and nodded. "I didn't see you. That's what you get for sneaking up on me."

"I wasn't sneak—" But he stopped when he noticed her smile.

"I'm fine, Joe," she said. "You?"

Joe straightened. For a computer whiz, Joe didn't have an ounce of jelly on his body. He was granite hard, but rather than speculate, Ali would like firsthand knowledge. *If only...*

Joe dropped his hands from her arms, blinked and then took a step back. "I'll let you know if I develop a headache later."

"I'm really sorr—" Then Ali stopped when she realized Joe was joking, something he rarely did.

He walked around her to give Rena a hug. "Hi, sister-in-law. How's my brother treating you?"

Rena sighed. "Like a queen. I've got no complaints, Joe. And I can't thank both of you enough for taking on the wedding details. I'm afraid with all the construction we're doing to the house now it's a bit much for Tony and me."

"No problem," Joe said. "With Ali's help, it should run like clockwork." Joe glanced her way, and her heart did a little flip.

"You're welcome to join us for lunch, Joe," Rena said, "but I'll warn you, we'll be talking wedding and baby, and there's no getting around it."

Fear entered his eyes for a moment. "I'll leave you two to hash out the details. Once you have a plan, then I'll chime in. Thanks, anyway."

"Sure, Joe." Rena glanced at Ali and they both giggled.

"What's so funny?"

"Having three root canals without anesthesia sounds better to you than having lunch with us today. Admit it, boss."

Joe shrugged his shoulders in feigned innocence, which made him look sexier than all get-out. "Have a nice lunch, ladies."

They bid him farewell, and twenty minutes later after a nice walk along the main street of town, they were seated at an outside café that served sandwiches, salads and specialty coffees.

Ali ordered a double vanilla latte, while Rena opted for a glass of cranberry juice. They sipped their drinks while waiting for the salads they'd ordered.

"So how do you like Napa?" Rena asked.

"From what I can tell, I like it. It's a far cry from New York."

"Did you grow up there?"

She shook her head. "Heavens, no. I'm a southern gal from Oklahoma originally. My mama and daddy divorced when I was just a kid. Seems Mama wanted a better life for us, and Daddy just wasn't up for the task. She was Miss Oklahoma after all and figured she deserved better than a man who worked for the county as a deputy sheriff. As soon as she could, she moved us to the East Coast. I grew up in a string of big cities from Boston to New York. We never really settled anywhere for long."

"Sounds like you had it tough as a kid."

She shrugged. "It is what it is. I still keep in touch with my dad. He's remarried now and perfectly happy and still working in law enforcement."

"And your mom? Do you see her?"

"We see each other whenever we can." Ali wouldn't tell Rena her mother was on husband number five now. Ali had been bounced around from one household to another, from city to city, her mother never finding satisfaction in the men she married. She'd always wanted to elevate herself and thought money and power would be the ticket. Now, she was married to a millionaire attorney with political ties. "My mama leads a very busy social life." Ali shook her head and shuddered. "That life's not for me. So yeah, Napa's a nice change of pace."

"I wondered why you'd agree to uproot your life to work here…for Joe." Rena's brows raised, and her blue eyes beamed with clarity. "Can I ask you a personal question?"

Ali nodded.

"Are you and Joe…"

She shook her head. "Nothing."

"Really?" Rena sounded truly puzzled. "Because I swear, I thought I saw sparks between you two at the office."

"That's just me being me. Joe isn't interested."

Rena opened her mouth to reply but then clammed up.

"Were you going to say something?"

Rena stared at her for a moment. "No, it's not my place."

Darn it. "I understand," Ali said.

Ali opened her briefcase and took out her calendar. "Shall we set a date for the big occasion?"

"Sure," Rena said, and leaned over to glance at the calendar.

They settled on a Saturday three weeks away. The celebration would be held on the Carlino estate, the renewal of vows under an arbor of flowers in the backyard and the reception on the grounds.

"I'm doing this for Tony," Rena said. "For years, I wouldn't step foot on Carlino land. This is one way for me to show Tony that I've truly let the past go."

"You're very lucky to have this second chance, Rena." Ali cast her a small smile, suddenly feeling that life was passing her by.

Rena reached over and took her hand. "If I've learned one thing about life it's that you've got to make the best out of every moment and go after what you want." She lowered her voice. "If you have a goal in mind, don't let anything stop you."

Ali blinked. It was a lightbulb moment for her. She'd never been a quitter. Joe Carlino had enticed her to come to Napa, and she'd jumped at the chance because she cared about him. Ali wasn't one to wait around for things to happen.

If Joe needed a little push, then Ali wouldn't mind giving her sexy employer a shove in the right direction.

Two

As soon as Ali opened her front door, Joe realized his mistake in coming to her apartment tonight.

"Hi, Joe." She beamed him a smile. "I can't thank you enough for coming by. I'm in computer hell at the moment. Your timing is perfect, I just finished my Pilates workout."

He'd *noticed*. She wore spandex, a tight midriff top that pushed her cleavage to its limits and black pants that hugged her tiny waist. A glittering sheen of moisture coated her exposed skin.

Damn Nick and his constant jabbing. Joe didn't want to notice Ali as anything but his assistant. Feeling beholden to help when she'd complained about her computer problems today, he'd offered to stop by to look at it. "Happy to help out, Ali."

She stepped aside to let him in as she sipped from an Arrowhead water bottle. "I don't know what happened to it. Like I explained at the office, it just froze up on me. But I'm glad you came by anyway. You've never seen my apartment."

"River Ridge has a great reputation," Joe said. He'd gone out of his way to find her a good location that suited her when she'd accepted the job.

"It's a great place. I've always wanted a fireplace. I love the view from my living room window, too. Come take a look," she offered, and walked over to a wide picture window overlooking a garden setting. "There's a little pond out there. Can you see it?"

Joe stepped beside her and gazed out the window, indulging her. He'd made sure she'd gotten an apartment with the best view. He'd checked out this apartment before Ali had moved in. Adjusting the glasses on his nose, he narrowed his eyes. "I see two ducks splashing around."

"Let me see," Ali said, brushing up against him. "Oh, how sweet."

Her joy at such a little pleasure touched him. Joe stepped away from the window. "Different from living in New York, isn't it?"

"That's an understatement," she said with a groan. Then she sipped her water again. "Well, I'd better get showered and changed. I'll show you my computer, and maybe you can work your magic while I'm cleaning up. Can I get you anything?"

Joe kept his focus on her face and shook his head. "No, I'm good." He wouldn't allow his mind to conjure up images of her showering.

"Okay, then follow me." She walked down a short hallway. "This is my bedroom," she said, pointing and continuing to move.

Joe caught a glimpse of soft yellow hues, a large inviting bed and mismatched furniture that somehow looked perfect together. A fresh scent of lavender emanated from the room.

He followed her into a smaller bedroom down the hall. "I haven't fixed it up yet. It's sort of my office, slash, junk room, slash, guest room."

Joe scanned the room. "It's not very messy."

"You haven't seen what's stashed in the closet." She grinned.

"Shoved everything in there, did you?"

"*And* under the bed."

"All this to impress me?"

"Well, I didn't want you to see how unorganized this room is. I have a rep to protect, you know."

Joe shook his head in amusement.

"Okay, boss. I'll get out of your hair now. Just twitch your nose and fix the darn thing."

"I'll try."

Ali turned to exit the room and offered as a parting shot, "If you can't fix it, nobody can."

Joe grinned. He appreciated the compliment. Joe was good with computers and had been fascinated with them since he was a young boy. While all the other kids were involved in sports or getting into mischief, Joe stayed at home, learning the intricacies of the newest form of technology. He'd never felt he'd missed out on his childhood, though his father would often look in on him in his bedroom and frown.

Fifteen minutes later with the computer problem solved, Joe strode out of the office/junk room/guest room and walked down the hallway, passing Ali's bedroom. The door was closed, the shower had stopped and a vision of Ali towel-drying her naked body entered his mind.

His will of iron allowed him only two seconds to enjoy that image before he proceeded to the living room. He sat down on the sofa, picked up a *People* magazine then flipped through the pages. When the doorbell rang, Joe stood, glancing at Ali's room down the hallway.

"Ali," a male voice carried through the doorway. "It's Royce. And I have something for you I think you're going to like."

Joe stared at the door for a moment. When Ali didn't come out of her room to answer it, Joe walked over and yanked the door open.

A man wearing oven mitts holding a casserole dish raised his eyebrows. "Sorry, I didn't know Ali had company. I'm Royce."

"Joe."

The shaggy blond-haired Brad Pitt lookalike didn't seem happy to find Joe in Ali's apartment. And Joe didn't make it easy on him.

"I'm Ali's neighbor."

Joe nodded.

"I brought her my newest creation. Ali tests out some of my meals for me."

Joe narrowed his eyes. "Hold on. I'll get Ali."

"I'm here," Ali said, coming into the room dressed in jeans and a white knit top, still towel-drying her gorgeous auburn hair. As she whizzed by him, he caught the scent of fresh citrus. "Oh, hi, Royce. What did you bring me this time?"

Royce seemed relieved to see her. "Champagne chicken with a touch of cognac."

"Yum. Smells great. Come in and set it down on the stove. Joe, this is Royce, my neighbor. He's a chef at Cordial Contessa. Royce, this is my…uh, Joe."

"We've just met," Joe said, watching how Royce's gaze fixed on Ali. "Ali works for me at Carlino Wines," Joe said.

Ali furrowed her brows and stared at the two of them. "Well, thanks, Royce. I'll give you my review of your latest creation tomorrow. Unless you want to join us?"

"Join you? What are you two doing?"

Ali looked his way. "Joe's a computer genius. He's fixing my senior-citizen computer. Poor thing is on its last legs."

"*Fixed* your computer," Joe corrected.

"You fixed it already?" Ali's eyes lit up, and Joe took immense satisfaction in her reaction. "There, you see," she turned to Royce. "He *is* a genius."

Ali returned her attention to Joe, her green eyes round and bright. "Thank you so much."

"No problem. Your computer has a lot of life left in it. You just need to upgrade a few things." Joe took the list he'd jotted down out of his pocket and handed it to her.

Ali's smile faded when she glanced at the items he'd listed. "Okay."

Joe gently grabbed the list from her hand. "You know what, I'll take care of it for you."

"Really? But you've already—"

"It's not a problem, Ali. Consider it payback for helping me with the wedding."

"The wedding?" Royce interrupted, casting Ali a curious look.

"Joe's brother is getting married, and he needs a little help with the planning."

"Is that part of your job description?" Royce asked with a disingenuous smile, directing his attention solely to Ali.

"She's doing this off-the-clock, as a favor to me. Not that it's any of your business," Joe said.

Ali intervened, appearing a little nervous. "I'm happy

to do it. I love planning fun events. I know parties the way
Joe knows computers."

Joe met Royce with a hard stare. Who the hell was this
guy anyway? Why was he so damn protective of Ali? He
tested Joe's even-keeled temper in the span of just a few
minutes.

Ali placed her hand on Royce's arm and guided him
toward the door. "Thanks for the champagne chicken,
Royce."

"Anytime, Ali," he said. "Let me know what you
think."

"I will," she said, closing the door behind him.

Joe walked up to her. "Is he your boyfriend?"

Ali shook her head. "No."

"Gay?"

She laughed. "Hardly."

From her laughter and the surprised expression on her
face, Joe surmised Royce had ulterior motives for bringing
Ali his latest culinary creation.

"I think he's just a little protective of me."

"You think?" Joe asked between tight lips.

She shrugged. "I've confided in him about some things
in my past, and well now, I think I shouldn't have."

What sort of things? Joe had been work-close to Ali, but
they'd never confided in personal matters before. He felt
a twinge of jealousy that shouldn't be. But still, it gnawed
at him all the same.

"He's interested in you, Ali," Joe said with blunt honesty.

"I've made it clear that we're just friends."

Hell, men never took that "just friends" garbage seriously. If they were interested in a woman, eventually it
would come out.

Ali walked over to him and stared straight into his eyes.

Her fresh scent surrounded him. Her hair had dried in curls around her pretty face. She glanced at his mouth, and Joe had a difficult time keeping his focus. If she made another move toward him, he didn't think he'd stop her. And that could spell disaster.

He reminded himself that office romances never worked out. An image of Sheila flashed in his mind. He and his bright, feisty, flamboyant onetime fiancée were complete opposites. It had taken months to realize that marrying her would have been a big mistake.

"Can we forget about Royce?" Ali asked. "We have work to do on the wedding."

"Right, the wedding." Joe pushed his glasses farther up his nose and nodded. "Royce who?"

Ali went to bed that night thinking of Joe. For once, she noticed a chink in his armor. He'd actually seemed perturbed with Royce showing up. She could only find a bit of hope in that.

Royce had offered friendship when she'd first moved into River Ridge. He'd helped her settle in and was always around if she'd needed anything. After a couple of weeks, he began asking her out, but Ali had always made it clear that she wasn't looking for a relationship.

Royce had backed off and offered his understanding. He'd been so compassionate, and one night over a bottle of zin and his delicious shrimp scampi à la Contessa, Ali had confided in him about her past history. She'd explained about her tumultuous childhood with her mother and her latest office fiasco with her employer, Dwayne Hicks, a man who'd hired her under false pretenses, pursuing her sexually and giving her grief at the office because she'd denied him.

She'd filed harassment charges against him, and the

whole ordeal had left her somewhat scarred. No matter
the right or wrong of it, lawsuits against employers didn't
build great resumes.

That's why working for Joe Carlino had appealed to her.
He'd been flawless as a boss and seemed to have no other
agenda. Working alongside him, her feelings had grown
out of respect and admiration.

Ali snuggled deeper into her bed. Joe was becoming
more and more important in her life. Instead of fearing
those feelings, she welcomed them with her whole heart.
He was the only man on her radar, and she wished they'd
met outside of the office environment. They'd had a strictly
professional working relationship. Until he'd kissed her at
the airport, Ali held no hope for a relationship with him.
But after that kiss—and if she'd read his jealousy right
tonight—all was not lost.

The sun shone warm and bright into her apartment when
Ali rose from bed the next morning. The Napa news report
called for record-high temperatures today. With that in
mind, Ali slipped on a sleeveless white eyelet sundress,
tied it at the waist with a red leather belt, added beaded
red jewelry around her neck and wrists and tucked her feet
into matching three-inch sandals.

After a quick slurp of orange juice, Ali set out for the
Carlino estate for her morning meeting with Joe. If she
was going to plan a renewal of vows and a reception at the
estate, she needed to see the house and grounds. When
she'd come up with the idea last night, Joe hadn't balked.
Always logical, Joe saw the value in her visit.

After being buzzed inside the gates, Ali drove up
the stone driveway and parked the car. The estate and
well-groomed grounds were massive, and the colorful

rolling vineyards beyond lent a beautiful backdrop for the house.

A housekeeper named Carlotta met her outside the arched Mediterranean-style breezeway and showed her inside the house. She found herself face-to-face with Nick Carlino, who'd just descended the stairs. "Hey, Ali."

"Hi, Nick."

"You're here early. Joe said you'd be coming over for a meeting." He cast her an assessing look. "You look beautiful today."

"Thank you."

"What's the meeting about?" he asked.

"We're going over plans for the wedding before our real workday begins."

"Joe would be lost without you." He eased into a smile. "He really relies on you, doesn't he?"

"I guess so."

"He's always singing your praises to anyone who's willing to listen."

"And is that all he says about me?" The question slipped out much to her surprise "Sorry, I shouldn't have asked you that."

"No need to apologize. As far as I'm concerned, Joe's got rocks in his head." Nick winked. "Come on, I'll take you to him."

Nick led her outside to a covered stone deck overlooking a swimming pool that blended into the landscape so well it appeared born of the earth rather than man-made.

"Joe does laps in the pool every day. Clears his mind for all the numbers he crunches," Nick explained.

Ali spotted Joe gliding through the pool. Sleek and well-muscled, Joe dipped in and out of the smooth blue waters, and Ali's heart swelled.

"Hey, Joe. You have company," Nick called out. He

turned to Ali. "Unfortunately, I've got a plane to catch. Thanks for helping Joe out. He needs it." Again, Nick winked, and before he turned to walk away, he offered one last parting comment. "Just so you know, my brother isn't as noble as he seems."

"Meaning?"

"Don't give up on him."

Ali opened her mouth in denial, but Nick's astute look spoke of the futility in that. He wouldn't buy it, and Ali wasn't all too sure she could sell it to him.

Oh God, was she that obvious?

"I'll be right there," Joe called to her from the far end of the pool.

Joe bounded out of the pool, and she caught her first real glimpse of another side of Joe—the stunning, well-built, tanned and gorgeous man who looked as if he could conquer an enemy in one fell swoop.

Ali's throat constricted.

Her Clark Kent had just transformed into Superman.

Three

Morning sunshine cast a golden sheen over Joe's entire body as he stood by the pool's edge. Water dripped from his hair to his shoulders and then slowly drizzled down his rock-hard torso. She could compare him to a Greek god, but nothing topped Superman in her estimation.

She watched him towel off, then throw his arms into a shirt and head her way. Ali got a grip real fast. She couldn't be caught drooling.

"Sorry," he said as he approached. "I didn't realize the time."

"How many laps do you do?"

"One hundred."

Her mouth gaped open. "One hundred? Every day?"

"Just about."

"No wonder."

"No wonder what?" He looked puzzled.

Ali had to learn to stop thinking out loud. "Oh, um. I

was thinking about your stamina...you must have great stamina."

Joe smiled. "I've built it up over the years." He walked over to a large inlaid stone and iron patio table and picked up his glasses. Taking a second to clean them with the end of his shirt, he narrowed his eyes. "So what do you think?"

"About your stamina? Very impressive."

"No," he said, running a hand through his hair. He put his glasses on, and this was the Joe Ali had come to know. "I mean, about using this place for the wedding."

"Are you kidding? It's a girl's dream come true, Joe. Your home is amazing, and I've only seen a small part of it."

"I'll rectify that in a few minutes. First let me shower and change. In the meantime, have a cup of coffee. I cooked you up some breakfast to have during our meeting."

"You cook, too?" Ali couldn't believe Joe had culinary skills, as well as his other talents.

"I get by. After my father died, our longtime cook retired, and we just never replaced her. Tony's living at Purple Fields now, and Nick and I are rarely home."

Joe walked over to a coffeepot on the patio counter. "What'll you have?"

"I'll get it, Joe. Don't worry about me."

"Okay, I'll be back in five, then I'll give you the grand tour."

Ali watched him leave, her heart in her throat. She couldn't fight her feelings any longer. All shreds of rationality escaped her. She'd never before met a man like Joe Carlino. Before, she'd welcomed the challenge to get him interested in her. But now, it went deeper than that. She admired Joe, found him unique and intelligent and sexy as sin. Emotions washed over as a question entered her mind.

Could she be falling in love with her boss?

"I think your home will work out nicely," Ali said after a cup of coffee and not-half-bad eggs Benedict. Joe cooked like he did everything else, with honed precision and accuracy.

She sat at the patio table after he'd given her the grand tour of his home. Stunning was an understatement. Joe's mother must have had a hand in decorating the house. He'd always spoken so fondly of her sweet, calming ways, and her talent for making a house a home was evident everywhere.

The entire home, though updated with modern conveniences, oozed warmth and love, giving off a Mediterranean flair from the polished carved wood furniture and colorful sofas to the pale golden walls and inlaid stone flooring.

Where the first floor was set to bring in the harmony of the family, the upstairs was laid out to accommodate privacy, each wing being a home within a home. The parents and three sons could enjoy their private suites and never bump into one another.

Silly, but Ali pictured herself here with Joe, living in the east wing of the house. It wasn't the grandeur that appealed to her but the sense of stability. Seeing Joe's brothers interact with each other—witnessing their family ties—had touched a sentimental chord within her.

She'd never had a real place to call home.

She fought her resentment tooth and nail, yet Ali couldn't forgive her mother for her lifestyle. She'd dragged her young child from town to town, marrying men who'd

look upon Ali as a burden. At least, she'd always felt like a
necessary evil that Justine's husbands had to endure.

Ali had inherited her mother's feisty, bubbly nature. She
wasn't shy by any means. But unlike her mother, Ali had a
career that she enjoyed. She'd worked hard for everything
she'd achieved in life including her bachelor's degree in
business. She had brains, thank goodness, and liked to use
them.

But now, she was at a complete loss with her strong
feelings for Joe. She'd never been in love before and wondered if the impeding sense of dread and earth-shattering
excitement she felt was normal. The conflicting mix of
emotions put her on unsteady ground.

And other than that one kiss, he really hadn't laid a hand
on her. She'd never want to resort to her mother's means
for snaring a man, and therein was her problem.

"Where should we hold the renewal of vows?" Joe asked,
his focus and those dark piercing eyes intent on her. He'd
changed from his swim trunks to black casual trousers and
a white button-down shirt. Joe the Hunk had changed back
into Joe the Boss.

She came out of her stupor to reply to his question.
"Poolside. I think that'll be perfect," she said, the notion
in her mind gaining momentum. "The sound of the rock
waterfall and the glistening water below will be a great
backdrop. We'll have a flower archway made for them to
say their vows underneath but nothing too elaborate. The
grounds are enough."

Joe looked out at the pool, giving a nod of agreement.
"I think you're right."

"I'm always right," she teased.

"I know." Joe didn't blink as he shot back his response.

Ali stared into his eyes. Did he really have that much

faith in her abilities? "I think Rena will be pleased with what I have in mind. Do you think Tony will like my ideas?"

"Without a doubt. He has the woman he loves. That's all he cares about."

"I wish," Ali began, then bit down on her bottom lip.

"What do you wish?" Joe asked, touching a finger to his glasses. Ali knew his gestures and that one meant true curiosity. She couldn't relay her innermost wish, but she could turn the tables on him.

"Have you ever been in love, Joe?"

He blinked and shot his head back in surprise. "Me?"

She held her breath and nodded.

Joe pursed his lips and answered in a clipped tone. "Once. It didn't work out."

Ali was floored by his admission. He was a gorgeous, thirtysomething man who had a lot going for him, but somehow she couldn't picture Joe being in love.

Unless of course, it's with you, Ali.

"I'm sorry."

"Don't be," he said. "It was for the best." He dismissed the subject by flipping through a batch of menus she'd brought with her. "Now, what about the reception? Any ideas?"

"I have a few thoughts on the subject."

He nodded. "Good."

Ali stood and walked around the grounds, conjuring up images of how to best use the backyard and surrounding vineyards for the reception. But more so, she had to move away from her sexy boss to come to grips with the fact that Joe had been in love once. And maybe, he was holding on to that love. Maybe that's why he'd kept his distance. A knot twisted in the pit of her stomach.

Joe came up behind her. His nearness made her heart pound against her ribs. "What's your plan, Ali?"

In the world-according-to-Joe, you always had to have a plan.

Ali turned to find him close enough to touch. She searched his eyes, dying to know the truth. Ali made a decision right then and there to go for broke. "I'm working on it. But you can be sure when I come up with a good plan that you'll be the first to know."

Ali stood in the wine-tasting room at Purple Fields, browsing through the items on the shelves. The quaint shop spoke of decades of winemaking, a family legacy that Tony Carlino had a hand in saving.

Ali looked out of the shop's window to view the construction crew outside. It appeared every effort was being made to update the house without losing its original rustic style.

"Hello, Ali. This is a pleasant surprise."

Ali turned to face Rena, who had walked in from the backroom. "Hi," Ali said. "I hope you don't mind me stopping by."

"Not at all." Rena walked over to her. "It's good to see you again. Sorry about the mess outside. Tony needed more space. And with the baby coming, we thought it best to do the construction before he's born. Tony wanted to add a playroom for the baby, an office for himself and a full remodel of the kitchen for me."

"Wow! All that will be done before your little bambino enters the world?"

Rena nodded. "Carlinos have a way of making things happen."

Ali glanced out the window again and sighed. "If they want something badly enough I suppose."

Rena stared at her, furrowing her brows. "Ali, is something wrong?"

She shook her head. "No." She plastered on a big smile. "I came to give you an update on the wedding plans."

"Wonderful. I'm getting excited about it. Come, have a seat and let's talk."

Rena guided her to one of the three small round tables set in the corner portion of the room. "I'll get us something to drink first. Grape juice for me and our best merlot for you."

Rena returned shortly, handing her a wineglass. Ali sipped from it. "This is fabulous." She set the glass down on the cheery cornflower blue-and-white tablecloth and waited for Rena to take her seat. "Thank you."

"I should be thanking you for all you're doing. I hope Joe isn't working you too hard on this."

"Not at all. I, uh, listen, Rena, I have a confession to make," Ali said. She was never good at fibbing. "I could have called you with the update. We're just beginning with the plans, and there's not much to tell."

"Okay," Rena said, looking a little confused. "But you don't need a reason to stop by to say hello. You're new to Napa, and I'm happy to be your—"

"I do have a specific reason for coming here. Dang it, I'm so confused, and now I'm confusing you!"

Rena chuckled. "Ali, just tell me."

Ali chewed on her lower lip and took a deep breath. She was never one to hesitate about anything. "Okay, I think I'm in love with Joe," she finally blurted out.

Rena's eyes snapped wide-open. "Oh, wow."

"Yeah, wow. It's wonderful and terrifying."

Rena smiled and nodded in full agréement. "I know. That's exactly how I felt about Tony. I didn't want to love him, but those feelings just creep up on you and there's no denying them."

"Joe doesn't suspect anything. He barely knows I'm alive."

"Joe's involved in his work, but he knows you're alive, Ali. I can guarantee it."

"Yeah, I'm nominated for employee of the year."

Rena's smile faded and she cast her a solemn look. "You're serious about this? About him?"

"Very. I've never been in love before. I think Joe's perfect for me. Unfortunately, the only sheets he's interested in me slipping between are the Carlino Wine's tally sheets."

A chuckle burst from Rena's lips. "Sorry. You do have a way with words, Ali."

"It's a curse. I spit out exactly what I'm thinking."

"But not in a demeaning way. You're honest, and that's refreshing."

"Do you think I scare Joe?"

Rena thought about it a few seconds, and Ali was sorry she asked. Perhaps, she didn't want to know the answer to her question.

"No, it's not that," Rena said finally. "I know you don't frighten Joe. He may be a computer geek, but women don't intimidate him. In case you haven't noticed, beyond those brains, Joe's quite a hunk."

"Oh, I've noticed. But that's not the reason I think I love him."

Ali went on to explain to Rena that her reasons for loving Joe went way beyond his sexy good looks. What she'd noticed about him first and foremost was that he'd always taken her seriously, respecting her intelligence, treating her as an equal and *not* coming on to her five minutes after she'd been hired. Ali explained about her former employer. For all intents and purposes, she'd never thought she'd ever get involved with someone in the workplace, much less her boss. But she and Joe had a unique work relationship.

"I flat-out asked him if he's ever been in love, and he told me that he had, once. He didn't want to talk about it. Do you think he's still in love with her?"

"No," Rena said adamantly, bringing hope to her heart. "He's been over Sheila Maxwell for quite some time."

"So what is it?"

"Well, I can tell you this. Joe was burned really badly. Apparently, he became engaged to Sheila while she worked for him at Global Software. She was very beautiful and clever, from what I've been told. Joe thought the sun rose and set on her shoulders. His millions hadn't been enough for her. As you know, of all the Carlino men, Joe is the least flashy. He drives a hybrid car, wears conservative clothes and doesn't have a pretentious bone in his body.

"It wasn't enough for Sheila, though. As soon as an oilman from Texas with billions became interested in her, she dumped Joe like a hot potato."

"How awful for him."

"He didn't take it well. He felt duped and foolish for falling for her. I think Joe is just a little gun-shy right now. And for the record, Ali, he's vowed to never get involved with someone who works for him ever again."

Ali put her head down. "I get it now."

"Well, that's the bad news. The good news is that I think Joe is way off on this. If the right woman comes along—no matter where, when or how—he should act on it. I think he's interested in you, but he's holding on to the promise he made to himself."

"Nick told me Joe's not as noble as he seems. Maybe that's what he meant?"

"Maybe. You're a beautiful woman, Ali. You have flair and style, and if you don't mind me saying, you're sassy. I think Joe looks at you and warning bells go off in his head that scream, 'Stop!'"

"Wonderful," Ali said, feeling hopeless.

"All is not lost. Nick told me he wanted to ask you out, and Joe wouldn't hear of it. Joe was pretty adamant about it."

Ali's antenna went back up. "Did he say why?"

"Something about not wanting Nick to break your heart, but I think it's more than that. I think Joe was jealous."

"That's something," Ali acknowledged. She sipped her merlot, contemplating. "But what can I do about it other than jump his bones?"

Rena shook her head. "I think the opposite approach would work much better. We've got to remove that stop sign in his head. You've got to tone down your appearance and become less of a threat in his mind."

"You mean, a makeover in reverse?"

Rena smiled. "That's one way to put it. But yes, he may notice you more, if you're not on his mental do-not-touch list. Sort of like Cinderella turning back into a plain Jane."

Blood surged through her veins as Ali mulled the idea over. "I think it might work. I'm ready to try anything at this point."

"Trust me, Ali. If I didn't see sparks between you, I wouldn't encourage this. But Joe's a great guy and deserves love in his life again," Rena said, daring Ali with the gleam in her eyes.

"Nothing I've been doing so far has worked."

"If you decide to do this, I'll help in any way I can."

"Hah, so *Ali,* has an *ally.* Okay, I'll do it. If I succeed, I'll name our firstborn after you."

"And I'll hold you to that."

"When should this all happen?" Ali asked.

"Well, I think you should make a few subtle changes during the next few weeks."

"Like toning down my hair and makeup and my sass mouth?"

Rena shook her head with laughter. "Yes, but slowly. The change should happen over time and then—"

"Then?"

"The real transformation will happen when it will be noticed the most." Rena leaned in and curved her lips into a wickedly satisfied smile. "Cinderella will turn into a plain Jane, at the ball…my wedding!"

Four

Dressed in a Brooks Brothers suit and ready to stand up for Tony as best man, Joe glanced around the grounds of the Carlino estate. The backyard had been transformed into an elegant wedding venue, the changes subtle and well-designed thanks to Ali Pendrake.

Joe had spent the past weeks working on the wedding details with her, but she hadn't really needed his input. Ali's organizational skills and her instincts were right on. She'd ordered the cake, taken care of table seating arrangements, hired a five-piece band and a florist and arranged for her neighbor, Royce, to head up the catering.

Joe hadn't said much about her choice of chef, but he hadn't loved the idea.

She'd gotten here early this morning, dressed in jeans and an old sweatshirt, making sure everything would go according to plan. Joe couldn't commend her highly enough, but he also felt a personal sense of pride in her accomplishments. He hated to admit it, but Ali would make an expert wedding planner. Thank goodness, she seemed content working at Carlino Wines with him. He'd never be able to replace her.

"The place looks great," Tony said with a smile, coming to stand beside him on the patio. Guests milled around the grounds, conversing.

"You should tell Ali that. She did it all."

"I will. She's in with Rena now, getting dressed. They've become friends."

"Ali has no trouble making friends." Satisfaction hummed through him. Inexplicably, that his sister-in-law liked Ali made Joe feel good.

"Rena and I owe you both a big thank-you."

Joe nodded. "It wasn't as hard as I thought it'd be."

"Hell, I wouldn't think so. I hear you spent your weekends with Ali."

Joe shot his brother a warning glance. "It's not like that."

Tony shook his head. "I know, and I can't figure that out."

"Sometimes, neither can I." Joe muttered aloud what he'd kept his mind from thinking.

The band started playing, and guests began to take their seats. Tony straightened his tie and took a deep breath. "It's time to do this. I'd better get Rena."

Joe embraced his brother. "I'll see you up there," he said. "I'm happy for you, Tony."

Ali's plan was for both Tony and Rena to walk down the white aisle runner together. They'd had a hard road getting to this place, and their trip down the aisle together would be more meaningful and show unity.

Joe had the urge to grab Ali from the dressing room and have her stand beside him. He wanted her next to him.

They'd been together in this from the beginning, but he held back. Logically, his place was beside his brothers and not with his personal assistant. And damn it, if Ali had a way of making him think illogically.

Joe took his place next to Nick to the left of the flowery archway. The setting sun reflected off the pool waters, and he squinted as he waited for the wedding couple. The band stopped playing, and the entire group of guests hushed their voices. Then a harpist began playing a melodic tune.

Joe searched the dozens of guests for Ali. When he spotted her standing by the last row of chairs, their eyes locked.

His heart pounded.

His breath caught in his throat.

Dressed in a soft jade-colored satin dress, covered with a jacket of the same material, her hair spun up in a demure twist and her face nearly free of makeup, Joe almost hadn't recognized her. Her appearance stunned him. Flashy Ali, usually with all the bangles, beads, boots and exotic hair, looked soft and elegant tonight.

"That's a new look," Nick whispered. "Ali sure can keep a man on his toes."

Irritated by the truth of that comment, he ignored his brother and focused on Ali. She'd been on his mind too much lately. True, they'd spent a good deal of time together these past three weeks planning the wedding. Joe hadn't faltered, keeping his relationship perfectly professional the entire time. Whenever his mind would wander, he reminded himself that she was his employee and a woman who was off-limits. He denied feeling anything but pride for Ali and her accomplishments here today.

Joe turned his attention to his brother, who had reached the arbor of flowers along with Rena. Without the benefit of clergy, they renewed their wedding vows to each other with deep emotion and honesty. At times, they laughed; at times, tears stung their eyes. When it was all said and done, Tony took his pregnant wife by the hand and turned to their guests, receiving a round of applause.

Rena's face beamed with joy, and Tony looked happier than Joe had ever seen him. A bit of envy crept into his heart. At one time, Joe thought he could be that happy. But he'd learned a hard lesson. No woman would ever make a fool of him ever again.

After shaking his brother's hand and hugging Rena, Joe turned to face Ali, who had walked up and also congratulated the couple.

"You did it, Ali," he said.

"*We* did it, Joe," she said softly.

"You did most of the work. The place looks great. I can't give you high enough praise."

Ali put her head down, then glanced out toward the vineyards. "Thank you."

Joe was at a loss for words. Usually Ali did most of the talking. Today she appeared unusually melancholy. "Can I get you a drink?"

"That would be nice."

"I'll be right back."

Joe flagged down a waiter holding a tray of bubbly champagne and returned to Ali with two flutes. "Here you go." He handed her one and then made a toast. "To you, Ali, for all your hard work. The wedding was perfect."

Ali touched his glass and then sipped champagne.

Joe stared into her eyes, wondering what was up.

Ali smiled softly at him, and for some odd reason, dread entered his heart.

Ali's neighbor, Royce, came out of the kitchen and approached them. "Ali, can I speak with you for a minute? I need your opinion about something."

"Sure," she said to Royce. "Excuse me, Joe."

The chef put his hand to Ali's back and escorted her into the kitchen. With a clenched jaw, Joe watched Ali walk away from him. He polished off his champagne in one huge gulp and searched for something stronger.

He headed for the bar inside the house and poured himself two fingers of Scotch. It went down smooth and easy, and Joe sighed, relaxing his tense body.

Laughter from the kitchen had him walking that way. He stopped just outside the door, recognizing Royce's amusement and Ali's quiet chuckling. He heard Ali reassuring Royce about the main dish he planned to serve, complimenting his choice, and then they seemed to share another private joke.

Jealousy burned in his gut.

He clenched his teeth again and headed outside, his blood boiling.

Ali sat next to Joe at the Carlino table during dinner. She met Rena's good friends, Solena and Raymond, who worked at Purple Fields, and several of the Carlino cousins as they dined on Royce's amazing dinner. She'd had her doubts about hiring him since she sensed Joe didn't like him, but Royce's entrées were a big hit, and she felt justified in her choice.

She was sure she was only asked to join the head table because of the work she'd done on the wedding, yet everyone she'd met had been cordial to her. She'd bitten her tongue a dozen times dying to dive in and get to know her dining partners better, but she'd taken Rena's advice to stay under the radar instead of flashing her friendliness like a neon sign.

She'd spent the past three weekends with Joe, creating a wedding and reception that Tony and Rena would cherish in their memories. All that time, Joe had been eager to help, but he hadn't shown one iota of interest in her personally, even though she'd become more reserved, put her hair into sedate styles she'd never have dreamed up before and dressed herself like a churchgoing schoolteacher.

Her ego had taken a deep plunge.

This was her last-ditch effort to get Joe to notice her as more than his employee. If the makeover in reverse was her ticket to gain Joe's attention, then she'd give it her best shot. Unfortunately, patience was a virtue she hadn't been born with. She'd wanted this to happen the second she'd slipped her feet into her first pair of lackluster pumps.

"In case I haven't said it yet, you look very beautiful tonight," Nick said from across the round table. Rena had done the seating cards and had deliberately put Joe next to her and Nick as far away as possible. "Joe, don't you think so?"

Joe shot Nick a hard look and then turned to Ali. Needlessly, he pushed his glasses up his nose. They were already as far as they could go. "Yes, Ali, you look very pretty tonight."

Nick grinned, and Ali didn't know which Carlino brother she should clobber first.

"Thank you both."

Ali looked at Rena, who gave her a nod of approval. Rena had been a saint, helping her pick out a new conservative wardrobe and giving her tips on how to subdue her outgoing personality. Rena warned it might take some time for this plan to work, but Ali wondered how long she could endure loving Joe and not having that love returned.

After dinner, the band started up again, and people began to approach the large redwood decking overlooking the vineyards, which served as the dance floor.

Ali rose from the dinner table to listen to the music,

and immediately, a friend of the family approached her. "Would you care to dance?"

Ali didn't have time to respond. Joe appeared beside her and clasped her hand in his. "I think she promised me the first dance, Allen."

Ali's heart pumped overtime. Joe squeezed her hand tight, and she nearly stumbled when he brought her onto the dance floor. "I don't do fast," he warned.

How well she knew. But she was sure he meant fast *dances.*

"But I think I can manage not to break your toes with this song." He pulled her up against him, and she thought she'd died and gone to heaven. Hugo cologne and dancing practically cheek to cheek with Joe was a sexy mix. Consumed with being in his arms, she couldn't name the artist or the song they danced to, barely hearing the music at all as Joe swirled her slowly around the dance floor.

"You're a good dancer, Joe."

"Am I?" he asked, his voice a low rasp in her ear.

Tingles broke out all over her body, and she relished each amazing second of the dance.

Joe tightened his hold on her. "How can I thank you for tonight?" he whispered.

She had a few suggestions that didn't involve touring Napa. Lusty images filled her head. She could barely put together a coherent thought with him holding her so close. But she couldn't push her luck. She had to stick to the plan. "You didn't forget our bargain, did you?"

"No. I'm a man of my word."

"I know that about you."

Joe pulled away to gaze into her eyes. He blinked a few times and then shot her a killer smile. That smile, his sexy scent, the way he held her—Ali wanted to pull him into his bedroom and make love to him until the sun came up.

"I'm glad, Ali, but I just don't know how much you'll get out of me being your tour guide."

Nick and Royce both offered to show her the sights, but Ali was holding out for numero uno. She wanted to spend time with Joe and only Joe. Ali had pressed him to this bargain, and she couldn't let him off the hook now. Normally, she'd goad him into it—a promise is a promise— but the new Ali had to take a different turn. "It's all right if you'd rather not. I understand."

Joe's brows arched. "I wasn't weaseling out of it, Ali. I'll do my best to show you around."

Ali smiled, warmth overflowing. "That's all I ask."

Joe seemed satisfied with that and took her back into his arms until the dance ended. When they parted, Ali hated the separation. She could have stayed on the dance floor with Joe all night.

"Thanks for the dance," he said, escorting her back to their table.

"It was nice, Joe. Thank you."

Joe nodded, and when he pulled out her chair to sit down, Ali changed her mind about staying at the table. "I think I'll take a little walk."

"Would you like some company?"

She would love it! She hesitated one second then with a slight tilt of her head, she answered. "Okay."

They walked past the reception area lit with twinkle lights and lanterns, down an inlaid stone pathway that led to steep steps. Only moonlight guided their way now, the party music fading.

"They're tricky without much light." Joe took her hand and helped her down steps that seemed to go on forever. He'd touched her more today than in the past year since she'd met him. Ali held out some hope that progress was being made, small as it may be.

Once they reached the floor of the vineyard, which was still pretty high up on the hillside, he released her hand. Ali gazed out at the endless rows of vines that columned Carlino land. She sighed in awe. "Most people have swing sets in their backyards."

"We had those, too. We were privileged as kids, but believe it or not, we had a pretty normal childhood. My father was a taskmaster. We had chores to do and had to bring home good grades, just like anybody else. We got grounded. Well, I didn't so much, but Nick and Tony? They were always causing the old man conniptions."

Ali wished her childhood involved having a mother and father who loved her unconditionally. Someone who loved her enough to ground her or make sure she was doing her homework. She'd never had stability in her life. There was never much normalcy, either. Joe—living up here on a hill, with all his wealth and privileges—probably did have a more normal childhood than she had.

"He cared about the men you were to become."

Joe scrubbed his jaw. "I guess so. He was a hard man. My mother softened him, though. He loved her so much. He'd have died for her."

"They were lucky to have each other."

Ali turned from Joe to absorb what he'd just said. She pretended to look out at the vineyards, but she looked beyond them to her own life. That kind of love—that close family bond—was completely foreign to her. People looked at her and assumed she had everything she wanted. But that was far from the truth. Her childhood hadn't been a fairy tale. She wanted the kind of love that Joe's mother had—that unconditional commitment and devotion. Ali had been on her own in one way or another most of her life.

She could easily live a superficial life, the kind her mother lived, bouncing in and out of relationships, grasping for the brass ring that would make her happy momentarily, but never fully content. Ali had vowed to never be like her mother. She wanted something real. Money didn't matter to her. Oddly, she'd fallen for Joe, a man worth millions, but he could just as well have been broke and she still would've loved him. That was the difference between her and her mother.

"Ali, are you okay?" Joe came up behind her, his voice soft and tender. She felt his solid presence at her back. Maybe that's why she loved him. Joe was a rock of stability. "You're different tonight."

Tears entered her eyes, and she fought them. She couldn't break down in front of him. She didn't want his pity. She didn't want to tell him about her mother, her past and the love she'd never received as a child.

Taking a deep breath, she turned to him and gave a little shrug. "Weddings do that to me. I'm fine."

"You're quiet. I thought you loved a good party." Joe searched her eyes. He looked puzzled and sweetly concerned.

Oh, how she hated all this deception. She just wanted to blurt out that she loved him. She loved him, and her heart was breaking. But it was the last thing Joe would want to hear. She'd destroy their relationship. She had to follow through with "the plan."

"I'm enjoying myself."

Joe cast her a dubious look. "Have I done anything to upset you?"

She shook her head. "No."

To her surprise, Joe reached for both of her hands, clasping them tight. An unexpected jolt shot clear through her. She held her breath, her heart hammering.

Joe slanted his head, staring deep into her eyes and

leaned toward her. "Maybe I'm about to," he whispered into her mouth.

Then he pressed his lips to hers.

The kiss was gentle and giving, but that didn't stop fireworks from exploding in her head. She could hardly believe this. Joy entered her heart, and she wanted to wrap her arms around his neck and press her body against him.

Please let this moment never end.

Joe must have heard her silent plea. He slid his hands up her arms and gently squeezed, tugging her closer, his hips crinkling her satin gown as he deepened the kiss.

The rich taste of liquor made her head swim, and images of bedrooms and silken sheets flashed in her mind. Joe parted her lips and their tongues mated, then a deep groan of pleasure rumbled from his throat and Ali's joy doubled.

It was finally happening.

"Hey, Joe? You down there?" Nick called from above. "It's time to toast the bride and groom."

Ali gasped when she heard Nick's voice and backed away.

"I'll be right there," Joe called toward the stairs. She couldn't see Nick, which meant he couldn't have seen what Joe and Ali had been doing.

Joe turned to her. "Sorry. We'd better get back. You okay?" he asked, blinking behind his glasses.

She couldn't utter a word, so she bobbed her head up and down.

"I, uh, should explain," Joe began, his voice a rasp in the breeze. "You looked like you needed…comforting." Joe's brows furrowed as if he was as confused by his confession as she was.

"Comforting?" Ali questioned on a low breath.

"Yeah." Then Joe turned his attention toward the stairs. "C'mon." He took her hand, and they climbed up the steps, Ali following behind him. Before they reached the top of the stairs, he turned to her, his gaze fastened to her mouth. "When I said I was sorry, I didn't mean about kissing you. I meant sorry we were interrupted."

"I think I knew that," Ali replied, just catching her breath.

Joe's lips curled up slightly. "You're astute, Ali, but if I was out of line, you'd tell me, right?"

Heavens, he was so *in* line, it wasn't even funny. "Yes, I'd be sure to tell you."

Joe looked at her mouth one last time with regret in his eyes, and Ali wanted to skip right over the moon.

After the toasts were made by Joe and Nick, everyone sipped champagne and wished the newlyweds the best. Rena sidled up next to Ali by the dance floor. "How's it going, my friend?"

Ali beamed her a smile. "I'm no longer in the potted plant category."

Rena's brows rose, and she looked on with interest. "Really?"

"Joe kissed me down in the vineyards," she gushed out. She'd wanted to scream it from the rooftops that Joe Carlino finally showed some interest in her. "It was *the best*."

"What did he say?"

"Not much. He was worried about me. I think this change really threw him off. He's looking a little bit puzzled."

"He noticed you. That's all that matters."

Ali drew in a deep breath and sighed. "Oh, I know, but I'm not patient enough to wait. I want more."

Rena's chuckle turned a few heads in her direction.

"Calm down, Ali. You're doing fine. And you look stunning in that dress."

"Who knew that I could wear something so…not me and pull it off?"

"I did."

"Well, I'm not counting my chickens yet."

"It takes time, Ali. If it's meant to be, it'll happen." she said. "And look who's coming straight toward us, with you in his sights."

Ali glanced across the decking and spotted Joe, heading her way. Every time she looked at him dressed in that striking black suit, his dark hair groomed just so, his handsome face marred by just a hint of a beard and wearing those glasses that made him look sexier than a man had a right to look, her heart rate sped up like crazy.

Rena leaned over to whisper. "Remember, weddings have a way of bringing out the best in people."

Ali swallowed hard.

Joe focused his attention on her as he approached. "Is it time to cut the cake?"

Joe was always spot on when it came to schedules. "Yes, I think it's time." She turned to Rena. "Ready?"

"I'm ready. I'll find Tony and meet you over by the cake table."

Both watched as Rena walked away. "I think everyone had a great time tonight," Joe said.

"I know I did."

Joe gazed into her eyes. "I'm feeling a little bit guilty," he began, and Ali prayed he didn't regret their kiss from a few minutes ago. She waited for him to explain. "A few people asked me if you were a party planner. You could have a very lucrative business here, if you wanted it."

"So why are you guilty?"

"Because I told them you're not interested in outside work. You did this as a favor to the family."

"That's not a lie."

"Well no, not technically. But I shouldn't have answered for you. The fact is, I don't want to lose you," then Joe hesitated before adding, "as my personal assistant."

Ali smiled inwardly. Joe was slowly coming around. "You won't."

Joe stared at her, unblinking then glanced at her lips. She returned his stare, wishing he'd kiss her again. But she knew that he wouldn't in full view of the guests at the reception. Too many people knew Ali worked for Joe, and his reputation was at stake, along with hers.

The irony struck her anew. Ali never wanted an office romance. She'd shied away from them all of her adult life, wanting to be treated as an equal in business and respected for her intellect. And as soon as she found a man who'd done that, she'd fallen hard for him.

"I'm in the mood for something sweet," Joe said, still glancing at her mouth.

"Hmm?" She cast him a curious look. It wasn't like Joe to make innuendo. Could he have been teasing?

He gestured with a slight nod toward the fondant cake decorated with white roses and greenery. "Cake. Let's go and see how good your pastry chef is."

He's not *her* pastry chef. She'd simply hired him, but Ali stifled her comment. "I'd like that. Royce recommended him highly."

Joe's lips twisted but he didn't reply.

And ten minutes later, Ali sat at their table in sugar heaven. The mango-filled white cake was too delicious for words. "Mmm."

"It's pretty damn good." Joe had his piece of cake polished off in seconds.

Ali scooped up the last bit of frosting with her fork, relishing every bite, aware that Joe watched her every move. When the owner of a neighboring winery stopped by the table asking to speak to Joe for a second, he agreed and rose from his seat, bending to whisper in her ear. "Excuse me, I'll be right back."

Goose bumps erupted on her arms, and Ali's body sizzled. She cast him a quick acknowledgment and watched him leave. This was new for her. She'd never received so much attention from Joe, and she wanted it to continue. The handsome prince had kissed her and stolen her heart. But she feared her reverse Cinderella night was quickly coming to an end. Now what?

The final dance of the evening was announced. Everyone stopped their conversations and mingled around the dance floor. The band played an old classic tune "I Want to Walk You Home," and Rena, dressed in an ivory-colored satin maternity dress, swirled around on Tony's arm, glowing with joy.

Their happiness was contagious, and as Ali glanced around, she found smiles on all the guests' faces. Out of the blue, Royce appeared next to her.

"Give me a rain check on a dance," he said. "I couldn't get away long enough to show you my dance skills."

He'd changed from his chef's uniform into dark slacks and a black shirt. She couldn't deny her neighbor his good looks. She'd noticed more than one female's head turn in his direction during the night.

"That's okay, Royce. You showed me your culinary skills."

"Well?"

"Absolutely perfect. Every dish was delicious."

Royce closed his eyes, savoring the compliment. "Thank

you, Ali. You recommended me for this event, and I didn't want to let you down."

"You didn't," she said. Then she tilted her head. "In fact, you exceeded my expectations."

"The same can be said about you. You put this party together in record time, and it looked as if you'd worked on it for months instead of weeks."

They shared a moment of mutual admiration.

"Let me finish up in the kitchen, and I'll drive you home," Royce said.

"I'm taking Ali home."

Ali turned to find Joe beside her, his jaw tight as he faced Royce. Where had he come from? Ali hadn't seen him since he'd taken off to speak with that elderly winemaker.

"It's not a problem," Royce said. "We live in the same building."

Joe removed his glasses slowly, squaring off with Royce. Neither one of the men looked like they'd back down. Ali felt like a pawn in some macho game. "Actually, I have my own car. But thank you both for the offer."

There, she'd settled it.

Joe hesitated, eyeing Royce, then slipped his glasses back on. "The food was exceptional tonight."

Royce seemed surprised at the compliment. His rigid stance relaxed some. "Thank you."

That's what she loved about Joe. He was fair-minded. "Ali recommended you, and I trust her judgment."

"I'm happy to have the honor." Royce glanced at Ali. "I've got to see to the cleanup in the kitchen. Catch you later, Ali."

"See you, Royce."

Ali turned to face Joe, his expression noncommittal. "I'll be leaving shortly, unless there's anything else you need me to do?"

"No, you've outdone yourself with this party. Tony and Rena are thrilled with how it all turned out. I am, too."

"It was a pleasure," she said. "Well, then I'd better say good-night to them." She turned to leave.

"Wait," Joe said firmly. "It's a difficult drive down the hill at night. You don't know the roads. I'll follow you."

"But you don't have—"

"No arguments, Ali. I'm following you home."

Five

Joe followed behind Ali's car until she parked in her garage. He watched her get out. He debated for a half second whether to get out of the car and walk her to the door, a little war waging in his head.

The kiss they shared earlier was still on his mind. He'd been foolish to do it, yet he hadn't been able to stop himself. Ali had looked vulnerable and a little sad, something he'd not recognized in her before. The change in her made him want to comfort and console her. He'd meant to plant a little peck on her lips, but the minute he'd taken her into his arms, something snapped inside him. He wanted to hold her and go on holding her. To kiss her and go on kissing her.

He wanted to do more.

Warning bells rang out in his head. His mind screamed that she was off-limits. He wasn't ready for any relationship, much less one with his employee. How many times had he reminded himself of that?

Joe stepped out of his car and leaned against it. "Thank you for following me home, Joe. It wasn't necessary, but I do appreciate it."

"Just wanted to make sure you got home safely, Ali."

She faced him and leaned over to give him a little kiss on his cheek. "That's sweet."

Sweet? Joe's hackles went up. He spread his legs and braced Ali's waist with his hands, pulling her closer. Her exotic scent scurried up his nose and went straight to his brain. "Can you forget that I'm your boss for one night?"

His gaze dropped down to the ripe fullness of her mouth.

Ali blinked. Then a beautiful smile emerged. "I think so. Why?"

Joe answered her by wrapping a hand around her neck and bringing her mouth to his. "To show you I'm not that sweet," he whispered before he crushed his mouth to hers.

A tiny whimper of pleasure arose from Ali's throat, her lips inviting and lush. Joe deepened the kiss and brought Ali even closer, meshing their hips together.

Pressure built in his groin, his breathing sped up and the urge to take Ali inside her apartment and finish this overwhelmed him. He mated their tongues, all the while stroking his knuckles along her smooth cheekbones and then capturing her face in his outspread hand.

"Still think I'm sweet?" he asked, nipping at her lower lip.

"Not at the moment," she answered without hesitation.

"Am I out of line?" he whispered.

She sighed into his mouth. "Very."

But she wasn't complaining, and that's all the fuel Joe

needed to continue. His mind went on autopilot, and he kissed her again and again, each time bringing her closer, crushing her beautiful breasts to his chest, his arousal hard to restrain.

He stroked her lower back, gliding his hands up and down, damning the satin material and wishing he could put his palms to her creamy skin.

Ali pulled away slightly, her breathing labored, a soft sheen on her face. She searched his eyes and shook her head. "I don't do one-night stands, Joe."

Joe loosened his hold on her. It was hard to let her go. Already, he missed the sweetness of her mouth on his and her erotic scent filling his head. He pursed his lips and nodded. He'd let his lust get in the way of what he knew to be right. "When I asked if you could forget that I was your boss for one night, that's really not what I had in mind. I, uh, things got a little carried away."

"They seem to, whenever you kiss me," Ali stated quietly.

Joe knew better than to mess with Ali's emotions. Nothing could come of their relationship. He was her boss, and she was his most trusted employee. "Listen, uh, I, don't believe in workplace relationships. I did that once, and let's just say that it was painful and destructive."

Ali listened patiently, her gaze intent on him. She looked so lovely tonight, and any other man would have found it easy to seduce her into bed. Joe still wanted to. He wanted to make love to Ali tonight.

But it wasn't fair to her, and he'd vowed that he'd never put himself in that situation again.

He reached into his pocket and pulled out a jewelry box made of gold velvet. "This is what I'd meant." He handed Ali the box, laying it on her palm. "It's a thank-you for all you've done to help me."

Ali gazed at the box she held. "I don't understand."

"A pay bonus didn't seem quite right in thanking you for what you've done tonight. You helped my family, and that called for something more personal. I can't tell you how much I appreciate, well…you. Open it."

With trembling hands, Ali opened the box. The look on her face made it all worthwhile. "It's beautiful."

"I picked it out, but I wasn't sure you'd like it."

Joe had gone to the best jeweler in the county to find just the right gold and diamond bracelet. He was used to seeing Ali wearing bangles and jewelry that made a big statement. But that wasn't what he'd wanted for her. When he'd spotted this bracelet, he knew it was right for her. It wasn't gaudy—the small, but perfect diamonds were set within the gold framework of the delicate piece.

"I love it," she said softly. Then her eyes filled with moisture. "This is a thank-you?"

He nodded. "For everything, Ali. But mostly for making my brother's wedding so memorable. Do you want to try it on?"

She nodded and Joe lifted the bracelet from the box and took her wrist in his hand. He secured the clasp, his head bumping hers as they looked on. Her subtle exotic scent dazzled him. Their heads came up at the same time, and they stared into each other's eyes.

Joe's heart thumped, a spark of something more than lust making its way in. He kept thinking of the torturous night ahead while he slept alone in his bed, yet knowing he'd made the right decision.

I don't do one-night stands.

And that's all Joe could offer her. He released her hand.

"It fits perfectly." Ali's voice lowered until it was barely audible. "You *are* sweet."

Joe cringed inwardly.

Ali smiled, and he wasn't sure what to make of it. She blinked and took a deep breath that was almost a sigh of disappointment. "Well, I'd better get inside. I'll probably fall asleep the minute my head hits the pillow."

Joe wished he'd be that lucky. He already knew what his night would be like. "Good night, Ali."

"Good night, Joe."

He waited for her to get inside and close her garage door before he got into his car and drove away.

Ali leaned against the garage door of her condo, listening as Joe drove off. She fingered the bracelet on her wrist, with love bursting from her heart. She'd never been given such a beautiful, thoughtful gift and yet, she'd let Joe leave tonight, making it clear that she wasn't a woman who slept with men unless there was a commitment.

It was the vow she'd made to herself after watching her mother's social-climbing ways. If Joe wasn't ready to give her more, then Ali would have to wait.

But the waiting was killing her! She could be in bed with Joe, making love with him at this very moment if she hadn't stopped him, yet she'd had to express her feelings. He hadn't offered her more than a night of passion, and Ali wouldn't settle for that. She wanted Joe—but not just for one night. She wanted his love and respect, too.

She learned a hard lesson allowing a man to call all the shots. Ali knew better now. Judging by the press of Joe's arousal while kissing her, Joe would have definitely made her night memorable. Sadness filled her heart for a moment, but then she remembered what Rena said.

Be patient.

She realized Rena was right. After all, she'd made progress, and turning Joe away tonight might not have been a bad thing. All things considered, the night had been magical, and Joe had certainly noticed her.

Ali took a quick hot shower and dressed for bed. She climbed in, tucking herself in cozily, and laid her head back, relishing the softness of her pillow. When the phone rang, she groaned and let it ring again, pretending she hadn't heard it. On the fifth insistent ring, she grabbed for it grudgingly, glancing at the clock. It was after midnight, and she couldn't imagine who'd be calling this late. "Hello."

"Ali, it's me."

Those three words instilled fear in her heart when she recognized the voice. She bolted up from bed. "Mom, what's wrong?" Her mother lived on the East Coast, and it was three in the morning there. Concern rippled through her. Guiltily she realized she hadn't talked to her mother in over a month. "Are you okay?"

"No, I'm not okay. I'm terrible." Her mother sobbed into the phone, alarming Ali all the more. Visions of her contracting a rare disease or having a car accident flashed through Ali's mind.

"What is it?"

"It's Harold. He's being impossible. I don't think I can live with him anymore."

Ali's rigid shoulders slumped.

Not this again.

She recognized her mother's tone and the sobs that were more complaint than anguish. What was it this time? Was his work interfering with their playtime? Or was Harold smoking too much? Maybe he liked his dog more than her. Ali had heard it all before. Her mother's need for attention and adoration was monumental, and whenever she didn't get it from one husband, she'd move on.

At forty-nine, her mother was still a beauty, and she had no trouble attracting men. Her problem was keeping them.

She expected perfection from her mate, when she was far from it herself. She wanted to be placed on a pedestal and admired by her man. It had become increasingly clear to Ali that the main trouble with her mother's relationships with men was that *life* got in her way.

There were times when her mother couldn't be the main focus in her husband's life. Times when their work took precedence and times when outside influences that couldn't be helped, interfered. Ali had always believed that the men Justine had married truly loved her, but they couldn't keep up with Justine's need for attention.

"Mom, what's wrong with Harold?" Ali had actually *liked* Harold Holcomb. He was a man of honor and integrity and had always treated her mother well in their three years of marriage.

"He's being so...so, stubborn."

"Mom, please stop crying."

"Okay," she said immediately, catching a sob. "I know you hate when I cry."

"I do. You know I've always liked Harold. I think you should calm down and think about what's important in life. *Really* important."

"I know you think I'm flighty, but this time I'm really worried. We're always fighting and... Ali, *I really love Harold.*"

Her mother seemed a little stunned by her own revelation. Maybe she'd finally figured out what love was all about. "He loves you, too, Mom."

"I know."

"Then whatever it is, you two can work it out."

"I know, I know. You've already said you won't come to any more weddings so I'd better make this one stick."

"Mom," Ali said, sighing into the phone, "can we discuss this in the morning? I'm really tired."

"It's only midnight there, sweetie."

"That's late for us working girls."

"But surely you're not working tomorrow—on Sunday?"

"No, I'm not." Yes, she actually was. She'd brought home a stack of work to look over. She'd been so busy with the wedding reception this week that she'd put a few projects on hold, knowing she'd get to them on Sunday.

Not that her mother had asked her how she liked her new job or her new home. When Ali had moved here from the East Coast, her mother had called her once to make sure she was settled and safe. Once she was assured of that, she hadn't called again, leaving it up to Ali to make the calls from then on.

Her mother really did love her, but she showed it in odd ways sometimes. This call tonight was a perfect example of her love. Justine confided in Ali when she wouldn't confide in anyone else. Ali had always shared that bond with her mom. She'd listen to her and give advice and encouragement, and her mother always made it clear that Ali was the only one she trusted to vent her frustrations.

Maybe Ali had been far too understanding with her mom over the years. Justine needed a hefty dose of reality. "I had a big day today, Mom. I helped my boss plan a wedding reception all week, and tonight was the big event. I just got in a few minutes ago, and I'm really pooped."

"Your boss? You mean, Joe Carlino?"

"Yes, I mean, Joe."

"How was the affair?"

"Spectacular, even if I do say so myself."

"If you had anything to do with it, I'm sure it was stylish and fun."

"Thanks, Mom." Justine was loyal and thought Ali could

conquer the world. Another example of how she showed her love.

Ali wondered what her mother would think of the "new-and-improved" Ali Pendrake, the one with the conservative clothes and reserved demeanor. The one who'd sink to fraudulent behavior to ensnare the man of her dreams.

Justine never had to resort to such measures. She'd simply flirt and tease a man to garner his interest, but Ali was sure her mother had never come up against anyone like Joe before. A man like Joe wouldn't interest her enough to make overtures.

Yet, Joe held Ali's heart in the palm of his hand.

"Okay, sweetie," her mother said. "I'll call you in the morning." She sniffled. "It was good to hear your voice. I miss you, Ali."

Ali closed her eyes and savored the sentiment. "I miss you, too, Mom."

She really did.

"Good night. Sleep tight. You're my beautiful princess."

Ali smiled into the phone. "I know. Good night, Mom."

On Monday morning, Joe walked into the Carlino Wines office, amazed at how this century-old building had survived to modern times. The building on Main Street was well known as one of the "ghost wineries" of the past that had been nearly crippled by age and ruin. The exterior built of mortar and stone, refurbished to its original vintage architecture, spoke of winemaking in its earliest form in the Napa region.

While the exterior held the ambience of old times, the interior had been transformed into offices that represented the most modern and up-to-date technology and equipment in the country. For all his old ways, Joe's father, Santo Carlino, had also been a forward thinker.

Joe headed past the reception area and aimed his way toward his office, stopping short as he approached Ali's outer office. He blinked his eyes then drew his brows together.

Ali sat at her desk, her gaze focused on her computer screen. Her auburn hair was drawn severely back and clasped at the nape of her neck with a band, and her face, free of makeup was adorned with plain, wire-rimmed eyeglasses. He approached with caution. "Ali?"

"Hi, Joe," she said, barely casting him a glance. "Just catching up on work."

He swallowed. "I didn't know you wore glasses."

Ali stopped what she was doing to grant him a little smile. "My contacts were bothering me under the fluorescent lights. I think I need to see my eye doctor." She shrugged. "It's just easier to wear glasses at work." She tilted her head to one side. "Do you mind?"

"Mind?" Joe stepped back a half step. "No, of course not." He pushed his own glasses farther up his nose. "I just didn't realize you wore them."

Ali stood up and came around the desk. "I came in early to finish up those reports you'd asked for." She handed them to him, and Joe noticed the diamond bracelet around her wrist.

His heart gladdened at the sight.

She wore no other jewelry but a pair of tiny heart-shaped gold earrings.

Joe took the files from her. The brush of her hand against his created an immediate spark. They stared at each other, their eyes behind their eyeglasses, locking. Then he scanned her body, taking in her soft pink knit sweater and straight-leg, gray slacks. Something was way off, and it had little to do with the clothes she wore. Joe couldn't put a finger on it until his eyes ventured farther down her body to her feet.

She wore flats. Aside from the glasses and clothes being different, Joe realized he towered over her by three *extra* inches. "You're shorter today." He hadn't meant to blurt that out.

Ali stifled a giggle. "That's what happens when I don't wear high heels."

Joe smiled, reminded of the night he'd fixed her computer, after she'd come out of the shower. She'd been barefoot, but he hadn't noticed how he'd towered over her. He'd had other things to focus on then. In the workplace, though, it caught him off guard. "I guess so."

"Anything else?" she asked.

"No, not at all." Joe tapped the file against his other hand. "Thanks for this. There was no rush on it."

Ali sat behind her desk. "It wasn't a problem. I came in early."

Joe continued to stare. He couldn't help from peering at her mouth and remembering how her lips felt pressed up to his. The kisses they shared the other night couldn't be repeated, yet they'd stayed with him all weekend long. If he were honest with himself, he'd have to say the memory had haunted him.

He remembered holding her and pulling her against him, having her body pressed to his, his desire evident and obvious to both of them. He shoved that memory aside and instead recalled the joy he'd witnessed on her face when he'd given her the bracelet.

Putting it on her.

Seeing her green eyes sparkle as bright as those diamonds.

Feeling contentment that he'd made her happy.

"Joe," Ali was saying, holding the phone to her ear. "You have a call, line two."

"Oh," he said, coming out of his reverie. "Thanks, I'll get it in my office."

"Mr. Carlino will be right with you," Ali said into the phone, and Joe strode to his office and closed the door.

The rest of the week had been pretty much the same. Joe found himself immersed in Ali. He stole glances at her whenever the mood struck, watched her talk on the phone or interact with other employees. She'd play with a rebellious lock of her upswept hair as she studied something on her computer screen, and Joe's methodical mind would wander to the land of Ali Pendrake.

"This is crazy," he muttered to himself on Friday afternoon. He'd been avoiding spending more time with her than necessary, but he owed her. And Joe was a man of his word.

He shot up from his chair and walked over to her desk. She peered up at him over her glasses, and Joe thought she looked adorably sexy.

Don't go there, Carlino.

Those thoughts were exactly why he'd procrastinated all week long.

"Do you need something, Joe?"

"Ali, this is really short notice."

"What is?" She looked puzzled and glanced at her watch. "If you need those invoices sooner, I'm on top of it. They're almost done."

"No, it's not about invoices." Joe scratched his head. "Do you have plans tomorrow?"

"Saturday? Well, nothing that can't be changed. I can come in if it's urgent."

Joe shook his head and stared at the diamond bracelet

he'd given her. She'd worn it every day this week. "This isn't about work."

She stopped what she was doing and took off her glasses. Her eyes were the prettiest shade of light jade. Joe leaned over her desk, bracing his hands on the edge. "I thought you might like to see some of the sights in Napa."

Realization dawned, and Ali pursed her lips, drawing his attention there. Her mouth looked glossy and soft pink, kissable. He forced his attention back up to her eyes.

Ali drew in a breath, then sighed. "Joe, I know you don't want to do this."

The disappointment registering on her face made him feel like a heel. He shouldn't have waited until the last minute. From the look in her eyes, he could tell she'd let him off the hook. Yet, suddenly, that's the last thing Joe wanted. "I do, Ali."

"Because you owe me?" she asked softly.

"Because we made a deal, and I want to show you—"

"Show me?"

"Around. I'd like to show you around wine country. I've been checking out some places during the week that I thought you'd like to see." The fib flowed easily through his lips.

"Really?"

Joe nodded. "Just tell me what time you can be ready."

"I just need to make a phone call to cancel a lesson."

"A lesson?"

She shook her head. "With Royce. He was going to teach me how to cook a—" Ali stopped in mid-sentence and made a slight gesture with her hand "—it's not important. He can show me another time."

Royce again? Joe was glad he'd foiled her plans with

Royce. He felt no compunction whatsoever, and a sly smile curved his lips. "How strong are your legs?"

Ali snapped her eyes to him. "My legs? Pretty strong, I guess. Why?"

She worked out. Joe remembered the night she'd opened the door to him in her workout clothes, her body gleaming with moisture. He'd also seen her going into the on-site gym during her lunch hour. "We're going on a bike trip. It'll take the whole day and into the evening. Are you up for it?"

Ali's expression brightened, and for a second, he thought she'd jump out of her chair. Then she took a deep breath and sent him a sweet smile. "Yes. I'm up for it."

"I'll pick you up at nine."

"Do I need to bring anything in particular?"

Joe shook his head. "I've got it covered."

Joe walked back to his office and sat behind his desk and waited until Ali left her desk. Then he called his friend from high school who ran the Napa Wine and Dine Bike Tour Company. "Hey, Benny. I'm calling in a favor. I need to arrange a private bike tour ASAP. Can I count on you?"

After his phone call with Benny, Joe leaned back, arms behind his head, and rocked in his leather seat, thinking about Ali and looking forward to spending the entire day with her.

An unexpected peace washed over him.

Joe bolted upright in his seat, coming to grips with what he was feeling for her.

Lust, Carlino, he told himself.

That's all it was.

He could deal with it.

He refused to admit it was anything more.

Six

Ali spent Friday night floating on air. She'd had a dickens of a time restraining herself when Joe had approached her at the office about the bike tour. She'd wanted to jump for joy, but instead she'd kept a reasonable sense of decorum. She sensed that when Joe gave her the diamond bracelet it was his way of getting out of their deal, yet he'd surprised her with the offer.

Excited, Ali picked up the phone and dialed Rena's number. She had to share the news with someone. When Rena picked up, Ali greeted her in a rushed voice. "It's Ali. Guess what? I'm going out with Joe tomorrow!"

"Oh, Ali. That's wonderful. So is our little plan working?"

Ali's joy ebbed a little, reminded of the deception that she'd engaged in with Joe. If there was any other way to get Joe's attention she would have tried it, but she couldn't look this gift horse in the mouth. "Apparently so. I'm so happy now that I could throw a party."

"You already did, for me. And it was perfect, Ali. So tell me all about this date."

Ali told her about the bike tour and then relayed the events of the past week and remarked that Rena had been right. Joe seemed to notice the more demure, subdued Ali more. At least, they'd been interacting on a personal level now.

Ali would do anything within her power to have her love returned by Joe, yet as she spoke with Rena, a thought wiggled into her subconscious that she wanted Joe to love her for herself—the woman she truly was.

Rena's bright voice broke into her thoughts. "I can't wait to see you in glasses, Ali. Nice touch."

"You'd hardly recognize me, Rena."

"You're beautiful with or without glasses, Ali. With or without flashy clothes. Joe will come to see this. Right now, you're giving him a very loud wake-up call."

Ali immediately felt better. Rena was right again. She'd needed to change things up a little to get Joe to look at her as more than his devoted assistant. Who'd have thunk she'd needed a reverse makeover to achieve her goals.

Yet, Joe wasn't like most men. And that's what she loved about him.

"I guess you're right, Rena. I hadn't really thought about it that way. I'm glad I called you. I was about to burst outta my seams."

Rena chuckled. "Hey, you're giving an old pregnant lady a thrill."

"Glad to help. Now, if only I could get some sleep tonight."

"Look who's talking about not sleeping. What if you had

twenty pounds of extra baby weight around your middle and no way to get comfortable."

"I wish," Ali said with longing.

Rena's tone sobered a minute. "You'll get there, Ali."

"Will I?"

"Remember what I said about being patient."

"I'm trying. But with every beat of my heart I want to jump Joe's bones and tell him how I feel."

Rena laughed. "Your time will come. Have faith."

"I do."

After Ali finished her conversation with Rena, she felt much better. She poured herself a glass of milk and grabbed an organic oatmeal cookie Royce had brought over the other day.

She sat down on her sofa, propped her feet up and clicked on the television remote. She found her favorite cooking show, munched on the cookie and sipped milk, settling in for a relaxing evening.

Not five minutes into *The Rachel Ray Show*, breaking news flashed on the screen. Images of a yacht off the Florida waters appeared, and the newscaster's somber tone alerted Ali immediately—she recognized the yacht. She leaned forward and turned up the volume on the television.

"While Senator Rodney Holcomb and his family vacationed off the coast of Florida on his yacht, Harold Holcomb, the senator's younger brother, had what is alleged to be a heart attack. The senator acted quickly administering CPR, but it is unknown whether his attempts helped to save his brother's life. Harold Holcomb was airlifted to West Palm Beach Memorial Hospital, along with his wife. The senator will be making a statement in the morning...."

Ali bounded up from the sofa and reached for her phone, dialing her mother's number. Thoughts of their last conversation ran through her head.

We're fighting all the time.

He's so strong-willed. He never gives in.

Her mother married a powerful man, a man who was accustomed to making all the decisions. Justine wouldn't let him get away with bulldozing her. She needed to have a say-so in their lives. Originally, according to her mother, it was what Harold liked best about her. She'd always challenged him.

And what had Ali told her mother to do?

Take a vacation. Get away from their routine and daily life. Take a cruise and talk things out.

Apparently, that's what they'd been doing, trying to work out their differences, perhaps.

Her mother's cell phone rang and rang. Ali's nerves went raw. After the sixth ring, finally someone picked up. "Mom, Mom, is that you? Are you okay?"

"This is Judy Holcomb. Is this Ali?"

It was the senator's wife. "Yes, it's me, Judy. Where's my mother?" Ali couldn't keep the panic out of her voice.

"We're in West Palm Beach Memorial Hospital. Your mom's in with Harry. She's pretty shaken up."

"And what about Harold? The news report said he had a heart attack."

"Yes, they've confirmed it now. They are running tests."

"I'm so sorry. Mom must be beside herself."

"Well, yes. I won't lie to you. She's quite upset. It was a shock to all of us. We were having such a nice time after dinner. Harold and your mother were walking on deck, and she came running for help, crying that Harry had collapsed. We assumed it was a heart attack, and Rodney gave him CPR. We don't yet know the damage, if any, to his heart."

"Oh, I pray he'll be all right. Thankfully your husband acted quickly."

"That's what the doctors are saying. He may have saved Harry's life."

"I should be there," Ali said, thinking aloud.

Judy didn't hesitate to reply. "Ali, I've never seen your mother so frightened and nervous. I tried my best to calm her down. Perhaps you should come."

"I'll take the red-eye. Please tell my mom that I'm on my way."

"I will. I know she needs you, Ali," Judy said. "She's trying to be so brave, but having you here would really help."

"I should be there early in the morning."

"I'll tell her you're coming. I think it's going to be a long night."

For both of us, Ali thought. She hung up and made reservations at Sacramento International Airport. Then she packed an overnight bag. If she left right now, she'd have just enough time to make her flight.

Ali waited until she checked in for her flight before calling Joe. She'd almost forgotten about him and their weekend plans. She couldn't imagine having Joe show up at her door in the morning and realize he'd been stood up. It was either that or calling him at midnight.

He answered on the third ring. "Hello," he grumbled, his voice raspy. It was clear that she'd woken him up. "Sorry to call so late, Joe."

"Ali?"

"Yes, it's Ali. I'm at the airport. My stepfather had a heart attack. I'm on my way now to be with him and my mom."

"Oh," he said, his voice sounding more alert now. "Sorry to hear that." He seemed a little confused.

"I'll be in Florida this weekend. Just wanted you to know in advance so you could cancel the bike tour for tomorrow. I'm sorry. I was really looking forward to it."

"Yeah, I was, too," he said. "But that can be rescheduled. You need to be with your family now, Ali."

Ali's heart surged. She didn't have much family, and she hadn't had a great childhood, but she loved her mother, even with her flaws. And she knew that she needed to be by Justine's side now. "I hope to be back by Monday."

"Don't worry about it. I can manage at the office without you for a few days," he said, and then added, "barely. Take the time you need."

Ali smiled for the first time since she'd seen that newscast on television tonight, and her mood lightened a bit. "Thank you, Joe."

"Have a good flight. I'll see you when you get back."

"Okay."

Ali hung up the phone, and her good mood immediately vanished. Oh, how she wished Joe were here, lending comfort and holding her, telling her it was going to be all right. How she longed to hear him say he loved her. The bike tour would have been a means for them to get closer, to spend time together outside of work.

Then a distressing thought struck. Could this be an omen of some kind? Maybe the deception and her plans to entice Joe into noticing her were backfiring. Maybe it just wasn't meant to be. After all, she was forcing every situation with Joe, and that's not how she normally operated.

Ali shoved those plaguing thoughts aside when she boarded the plane. She dozed during the flight, and before she knew it, she had arrived in West Palm Beach.

* * *

At precisely 9:00 a.m. Ali walked into the hospital, eager now to see her mother and praying that Harold had held on during the night.

"Ali!" Her mother dashed across the waiting room when she spotted her, tears flowing down her cheeks. Ali feared the worst.

When her mother reached her, she wrapped her arms around her and hugged her tight. "I'm so glad you're here."

"I am, too, Mom. How's Harold?"

Justine began crying again, and Ali walked her over to a bench seat and guided her down. Ali sat next to her and offered her a tissue. "He's holding on. I'm to blame for this. His heart attack is all my fault, Ali."

Ali's mother broke down, crying so hard, Ali had to hold her as if she were a baby. She cradled her in her arms and held her, rocking her back and forth. "No, Mom, it's not your fault. It's not."

"We were always arguing," she said between sobs. "I wouldn't give in."

"But that means he wouldn't give in either, right?"

"Right, but what if I caused this? What if…he dies? Oh, Ali. I couldn't live with myself."

Now was not the time for blame, and Ali understood that. "Let's hope he survives this, Mom. Then you both will have to change your ways. But let's not think about that. Let's focus our energy on Harold getting better."

"I just wanted him to slow down," her mother said quietly, her voice drifting. "We're not getting any younger, and I wanted him to stop working so much. He needed a vacation. We both did. It was the best advice, Ali. I finally got him to go on that cruise and we were having—" she stopped to take a breath and dab at her eyes with the tissue

"—we were having such a lovely time. We hadn't argued once on the yacht. Then all of a sudden, he collapsed, right there on the deck, and I thought he'd died."

"You got him help quickly. The senator might have saved his life."

Justine looked at her with soulful eyes. "I've been praying so hard for him, Ali. Lord, I love him so much."

Ali had never seen her mother react this way. Justine had always been indulged. Her husbands had spoiled her, and she'd relished their attention and gifts. In some ways, her mother had been selfish and self-indulgent.

But Justine Holcomb was a different woman now. Ali saw the truth in her eyes and heard the sincerity in her tone. Her mother had finally and fully fallen in love.

Ali's heart ached thinking her mom might lose Harold now, after she'd found the right man to share her life with. It had taken her five tries to do it and all those years of searching. Ali was convinced that her mother would fall apart if she lost her husband.

Though Ali would never want to walk in her shoes, she believed her mother was ultimately a good person. She refused to believe any of the hushed rumors that Justine was a gold digger.

She shuddered at the thought. It was such an ugly label.

"Mom, let's go grab a cup of coffee. I'm operating on a few hours' sleep."

Her mom nodded and they rose, Justine taking one quick look at the critical care room where Harold rested.

"C'mon, Mom. He's not alone. And I bet you've been in there all night with him. Let's get you some breakfast."

On Saturday, Joe rose early and swam his usual one hundred laps in the pool. He ate a breakfast of cooked oats, toast, eggs and orange juice on the patio then showered and dressed. Glancing at his watch, seeing the time approach when he would have been picking up Ali for their bike tour, disappointment registered.

He admitted how much he'd been looking forward to spending the day with her. He wondered how she was faring, taking the red-eye and flying across the continent in the middle of the night, not knowing what she'd find when she arrived. He realized he didn't really know much about Ali's family life. He'd never asked. Had she been close to her stepfather? How would she handle it if the worst happened?

Joe hoped, for Ali's sake, that she wouldn't have to deal with any loss. Having lost his mother and father, he knew firsthand about grieving and heartache.

He didn't want Ali to go through that alone.

Joe drove to the office and finished up some work he'd had to do. "Busy work," he muttered, staring at his computer screen after he'd accomplished his goal in thirty minutes.

He felt at loose ends today with thoughts of Ali never far from his mind. But Joe was resolute, if anything. His vow to keep his distance and not get involved with her was imperative to his sense of well-being. Unfortunately, he couldn't stop thinking about her. He'd glanced at the phone a half dozen times since walking into his office, tempted to call her.

But wouldn't she read something more into that than he intended?

When his phone rang, Joe's heart sped up. He grabbed his iPhone and quickly saw Tony's image pop up on the screen. He felt a measure of disappointment and almost laughed aloud at how ridiculous that was. Had he really thought Ali would call him? She'd barely been gone twelve hours.

"Grapes to grow," he answered.

Tony chuckled. "Wine to flow."

And Nick's line was always "Cash to blow." Typical of Nick, Joe thought. He shook his head. "I don't know why I said that."

"It's been years. Reminds me of high school."

"Yeah, the old man didn't appreciate our little jingle," Joe mused.

"He was more bark than bite. I'd catch him with a grin, when he thought I couldn't see him."

Joe surmised that people tended to remember the good about a person after they were gone, choosing to forget the bad.

"I thought I'd be speaking into your voice mail. Rena said you had a hot date with Ali today."

"Nothing hot about it, Tony. Unless you call a bike tour around Napa a big deal. Ali had an emergency last night. She flew to Florida."

"What kind of emergency?"

"Her stepfather had a heart attack."

"That's rough. How's he doing today?"

"I don't know. I haven't heard from her."

"You haven't called her?"

Joe inhaled sharply. "No."

Tony was silent for a few seconds. "Okay. So what are you doing today? Don't tell me you're at the office."

"Okay, I won't."

"Joe, you can't spend all your time there. Give yourself a break."

"Just clearing up some last-minute things." Joe didn't know why he had to defend his efficiency, yet both of his brothers taunted him about it, until they needed his help with something. Then, they praised his abilities and work ethic.

"Rena and I are coming into town for lunch. Why don't you join us?"

"Yes, join us," he heard Rena call into the phone.

"There," Tony said. "You can't very well refuse a pregnant lady."

"Well, in that case, sure. I'll have lunch with you."

"My wife's got a craving for Italian food. Meet us in a half hour at the Cordial Contessa," Tony said.

"I'll be there," he said.

Thirty minutes later, Joe strode into the quiet, dimly lit restaurant and found his brother nuzzling Rena's neck at a table set for three. "Maybe I should bow out gracefully and let you two get a room."

Rena chuckled and lifted her arms up in welcome. "Come here, Joe, and give your sister-in-law a hug."

After giving her a gentle embrace, he kissed her cheek. "It's good to see you, Rena." Then he turned to shake Tony's hand.

"I'm glad we dragged you outta that pit," his brother teased.

"You mean, the pit with state-of-the-art technology that keeps a roof over all of our heads?"

"The very one," Tony replied. "What brought you into the office today?"

"I'm finishing up a weekly accounting, that's all. Crunching numbers."

"What else is new." Tony looked at Rena and winked. "You need to get a life, Joe."

"I have a life. *A good life.* And I'm trying to keep it that way."

"Meaning?"

"I've been following current buying trends and working

up graphs. Even in today's lackluster economy, people are still drinking wine—to drown out their troubles, maybe. But sales are holding strong."

"That *is* good news," Rena said. "I'm happy to say that Purple Fields is holding its own, too." Rena glanced at the menu. "I'm famished. It all looks so good. Today, I'm going to eat for two and not feel guilty about it."

They gave their orders to the waiter, and the meal was delivered shortly after. They sat in silence for the most part, gobbling down their meals. The veal scallopini was the best Joe had ever had.

"Mmm," Rena said after finishing off her meal. She leaned back and patted her stomach. "So good."

"My pasta primavera was perfect," Tony said. "This place is giving Alberto's a run for the money."

"Yeah, why aren't we eating there?" Joe asked. The Carlinos owned half interest in an Italian restaurant that served Tuscany fare.

"My fault," Rena said with a quick smile. "After having this yummy lemon sesame chicken pasta dish at our reception, I've been craving it all week. The chef is a genius."

And just as she spoke of him, Royce walked out of the kitchen, holding a tray of pastries. "For the newlyweds," he said, placing the delicate tray onto the table. "I'm so happy you came to the Contessa for lunch."

"I told you we would," Rena said. "I've been craving this dish all week. Oh, and these pastries. I can't possibly pass them up."

Royce looked pleased. "Enjoy them."

"Thank you," Tony said.

Royce glanced at each of them. "Would any of you like some coffee?"

"I'm fine with water," Rena said.

"I'm fine, too," Tony added.

"No thanks," Joe said, inexplicably miffed that Royce had made such an impression on Rena and Tony.

"Royce," Rena began. "I know I told you this before, but I'm very glad Ali recommended you for our reception. Everyone complimented the food."

"That's very nice of you to say. Ali's been a good friend."

Rena nodded. "She's a special friend to me, too. I hope she's doing okay."

"She's fine. I spoke with her this morning."

Joe's head snapped up, and he narrowed his gaze on Royce. "How's her stepfather?" he asked. But what he really wanted to ask was why the *hell* did she call you?

"Out of danger, but looks like he'll have a long rehab period. Ali said her mom was really upset, but they are both relieved that he'll make a full recovery in time."

"Oh, that's good to hear," Rena said, glancing at Joe. She seemed to read his mind. "Did she say when she'd be coming home?"

"Probably in a few days. I'm picking up her mail and newspapers and watering her plants for her."

Joe sat there, keeping a steady noncommittal look on his face, while inside his gut churned. "I told her to take as much time as she needs."

"She's planning on calling you tomorrow."

Joe didn't want Royce's blow-by-blow accounting as to Ali's plans. The guy really irked him. Or rather, as Joe mulled it over methodically in his mind, Ali's relationship with Royce was the true source of his irritation.

He nodded and looked away.

"Well, I'd better get back in the kitchen. Enjoy the rest of your meal."

Once Royce walked away, Rena and Tony stared at him.

Joe adjusted his glasses on his nose then spoke when he couldn't ignore their stares another second. "What?"

Tony grinned. "You should see the look on your face. The Grinch has nothing on you."

"Tony," Rena said, grabbing his arm. "Let's drop it."

"Your wife is a smart lady," Joe said.

Tony aimed a headshake at him before digging into a raspberry tart. "Royce sure knows what he's doing," he added after he finished.

The hidden message in his brother's comment wasn't lost on him. "I told you I'm not interested in Ali."

"Who said anything about Ali?" Tony feigned innocence.

"Joe," Rena began. "I was hoping you could do us a favor. Tony and I were scheduled to go to San Francisco for the Annual Grapegrowers Convention. But I'm really feeling tired lately."

"You are?" Tony looked at her with surprise.

Rena turned to her husband and gave him a small smile. "I am, honey. I didn't want to worry you. It's just a combination of the pregnancy and not getting good sleep. I think the trip would exhaust me." She turned her attention toward him. "Would you mind going in our place?"

"You haven't missed that event since you took over Purple Fields," Tony said.

"I've never been pregnant before, either," Rena shot back a little too quickly. Joe had a sneaking suspicion this was a setup, but he couldn't refuse Rena the favor.

"I'll go. Don't worry, Rena."

"I know it's a lot to ask on short notice." Rena seemed really contrite.

Joe gestured away her worry. "I'll have help. I'll take along a secretary."

"That's a good idea," Rena said, seemingly satisfied.

"I think Jody Millwood might be available."

Rena's eyes went wide with shock, and Joe gave himself a mental pat on the back. Rena's expression spoke volumes. He knew what she was up to.

"The woman from your sales office?" Rena's voice elevated slightly. "She's…well, she's a bit—I think she spends her weekends with her grandchildren."

Grinning, Tony caught on and shook his head. "Sweetheart."

Joe frowned. "You two don't give up, do you?" He didn't give them time to protest. "You know what, if I take Ali to the convention and come out of it unscathed, then will you both get the message and quit matchmaking?"

Rena clamped her mouth shut and nodded.

Tony smiled.

"Fine, then," he said. "I'll hold you to your word."

Seven

On Sunday night, just as Joe was retiring for bed, his cell phone rang. He answered it and heard Ali's voice on the other end. "Hello, Joe. It's Ali." She sounded somber, so unlike herself.

"Ali? Are you okay?"

"I'm doing fine, I guess. Just a little tired." He heard the sigh in her voice and wanted to kick himself for not calling her. He glanced at the clock. It was after one in the morning in Florida. "I wanted you to know that I won't be coming back until Tuesday night. I'll take some personal time, if that's okay."

"Don't worry about that, Ali." Damn it, she sounded so businesslike, calling her boss to report her absence at work. Joe thought they'd progressed beyond that. "Take all the time you need."

"Thank you."

"How's your stepfather?"

"He's out of the woods, right now. There was some damage to his heart, but thankfully he'll recover with rehab and a lifestyle change."

"And how's your mother doing?"

"She was overwrought when I first got here, but she's doing much better now. She's taken hold of the situation, making plans for when Harold comes home and how things will change for the better. I'm really proud of her."

There was a lull, and Joe sensed Ali was ready to end the conversation. But he wasn't. He missed talking to her. During the past four weeks, they'd spent a lot of time together at the office and working on the wedding reception. He didn't like how he felt at loose ends without her. "What are you doing now? It's late there, isn't it?"

"Yes, it's past one. I'm getting ready for bed."

Joe's mind took a U-turn, envisioning her slipping off her clothes, donning a sheer nightie that would keep her cool in the humid Florida climate, her hair unrestrained and flowing in curls past her shoulders. He stifled a groan.

"What are you doing?" she asked softly.

"The same. Getting into bed." He flashed a vision of Ali joining him under the sheets and couldn't deny how much the thought pleased him.

"Sorry if I disturbed you."

"Not at all." He missed her. And it was on the tip of his tongue to say so. He should have called her. He should have at least expressed his concern for her stepfather and checked in on her. But his vow to steer clear of her had stopped him. "I'm glad you called."

"You are?" She sounded doubtful.

"The fact is," he began, fumbling with the right words to say, "it's good to hear your voice. I was concerned for you."

"Oh, well, I'm fine. I appreciate your concern."

Joe winced. They were speaking as if they were total strangers, their conversation stilted and deliberate. And had he heard a note of disappointment in her voice? Should he have said more? "I'd better let you get to sleep."

"You, too. Sleep tight, Joe."

He didn't know how much sleep he'd get, but one thing was certain—his entire body was as *tight* as a hangman's noose.

"Good night, Ali."

Frustrated, Joe climbed into bed, realizing his hands-off approach with Ali was backfiring. The more he kept to his resolve, the more he wanted her.

And this wasn't a problem he could solve with his unique mathematical skills.

As soon as the plane landed at Sacramento Airport, Ali grabbed her overnight bag and scooted down the narrow aisle, glad to be back in California. She'd had an exhausting four days and felt like the scourge of the earth in her clothes. She'd tossed together only one outfit change in her hurry to get to Florida, and she hadn't had time to do any laundry while she was there. The clothes on her back were beyond wrinkled.

Ali walked down the long corridor leading to the airport terminal, her body aching and her eyes burning from the little bit of sleep she'd gotten these past days. But the minute she glanced up and saw Joe, standing there waiting at the gate, a burst of stunned joy entered her heart.

He tipped his head when he spotted her. She'd never been so glad to see anyone in her life. Joe, with his hair slightly disheveled, wearing jeans and a black T-shirt, looking better than any of God's creations, was the one and only person who could lift Ali's spirits. She wanted to run to him with outstretched arms and kiss him silly.

But the new Ali would never do something like that. Fake Ali, as she called herself, would simply approach him with a smile, which was exactly what she did.

"Hi, Joe," she said, her breath nearly catching.

"It's good to see you, Ali."

She blinked and waited. Joe noted her hesitation. Then he opened his arms, and she walked straight into them. "Are you okay?"

She nodded, digging her head into his chest and holding on. Tears stung her eyes. She kept telling herself he'd never be here if she hadn't begun this ruse. Somehow that justified her actions. "How did you know what flight I was on?"

"I didn't. But this was the only evening flight coming in from Florida. It seemed logical."

God, how she loved him. "Thank you for coming. But I have my car here."

"Don't worry about your car. I'll have someone pick it up for you. I brought a limo. Thought you'd like a quiet drive home."

Ali nodded. "Sounds like heaven. This is very kind of you."

Joe squeezed her tight and then looked into her eyes. "You've had a rough few days, haven't you?"

Ali cringed. She must look awful. "Yes."

Joe hadn't called her during those four days, and as ridiculous as it seemed, her feelings had been hurt. She'd thought they were closer than that. She'd thought that Joe would have given her more support. Those few kisses they'd shared had given her hope, but she'd come to realize that maybe Joe would never come around. Not in the way she wanted.

"I'm sorry." There was a depth to his tone she hadn't heard before.

"Sorry?"

"That you had to go through that alone."

She shrugged. "At least, my mother is handling it better now."

"Thanks to you, Ali. I bet you being there meant the world to her. You have a way of making people feel better."

When Joe said things like that to her, it made her want to shed tears. He could be so sensitive at times. "I hope so."

Joe snatched her bag from her hand and guided her out to the parking lot. True to his word, a black limo was waiting with a chauffeur who had opened the door the minute he'd spotted Joe.

"After you," he said to her, then handed over her bag to the driver. Joe slid in beside her, and the door was closed.

Ali couldn't keep from asking, "I thought you were the green guy in the family."

Joe laughed. "I am," he said as if he'd just been caught cheating on an exam. "But some things are just worth the carbon footprint."

Ali smiled. "Thank you, Joe."

"Lean back and relax. You must be exhausted."

Ali did just that. She slid down in her seat a little and rested her head back. "Do I look that bad?"

"No, actually you look amazing."

She tilted her head to gaze at him. Those dark eyes behind the glasses appeared sincere. It was on the tip of her tongue to tell him how much she'd missed him, but Ali held back.

Joe slid a little closer and opened his arms to her. "Lean against me, and close your eyes."

The invitation was too tempting to refuse. Silently, she

did as she was told. The minute she rested her head on his chest and his arm wrapped around her, a sense of peace and fulfillment washed over her. "Mmm."

"Try to sleep," he whispered.

"You make the best pillow, Joe," she said, cuddling into him. "I think I will."

Ali knew the exact moment the limo rolled to a halt. Her eyes snapped open. Joe held her against him as she slept, and now she wished she hadn't woken up at all. She wished she could stay in his arms forever.

"You're home," Joe said quietly.

She *felt* at home in his arms. At least now, she could say she'd slept with Joe—or rather *on* him. She slid out of his grasp and straightened in her seat. Oh God, had she snored? "How long was I out?"

"Just about the entire way, Ali."

"Was I, um—"

"Peaceful. And quiet as a mouse."

Thank God. She blinked then nodded, trying to wake up fully.

"If you need another day to rest, take it."

"No," she said shaking her head. "I'm eager to get back to work. I, uh, missed it."

Joe smiled and looked deep into her eyes. "Good, because things don't run smoothly without you."

Ali searched his eyes. Should she read more into his compliment? "That's nice to hear."

The chauffeur opened the door on her side. "Well, this is my stop."

"I'll walk with you." Joe got out on his side of the limo, grabbed her overnight bag from his driver and then met up with her. They walked to her condo in silence. When she reached her front door, she turned to him. "Thanks for the ride. It meant a lot."

Joe searched her eyes and nodded. "You're welcome."
He hesitated for a moment, then scratched his head and let
go a deep sigh. "Ali, maybe now's not the best time to ask,
but are you free this weekend?"

This weekend? Ali's sluggish body registered a happy
alert. Was he going to reschedule their bike tour? There
wasn't anything she had planned that she wouldn't cancel
for him. "Yes, I think so."

"I'm afraid it's a working weekend in San Francisco.
I'm elected to go to the Annual Grapegrowers Convention.
Rena and Tony were planning on going, but Rena isn't up
to it."

"So, they asked you to go?"

He nodded. "And I need your help, if you're willing to
work the weekend."

Ali held her smile inside. An entire weekend in San
Francisco with Joe? Every tired nerve in her body jumped
for joy. This was a dream come true. "I can manage it. Sure,
I'll go with you."

Joe seemed relieved. "I appreciate it, Ali. You never let
me down."

Ali reached up and kissed him on the cheek. "Thanks
again," she whispered, her breath caressing his throat.

Joe blinked and leaned closer, his intense gaze focused
on her mouth.

Ali opened her door and slid inside, popping her head
out. "I'll see you tomorrow."

She closed the door and held her breath. "Fake Ali," she
muttered, "this better work because you just left the man
of your dreams hanging outside your door."

Friday night hadn't come fast enough for Ali. She'd
spoken with Rena out of concern for her well-being, only
to have been assured that her pregnant friend was doing

just fine. Rena confessed that begging off from this trip was a perfect way to get Ali together with Joe in a romantic setting. She'd been darn proud of her plan, and Ali had thanked her matchmaking friend.

Each day since Ali had returned to work she'd found Joe staring at her from his desk, his expression intense. The minute they'd make eye contact, Joe would glance away as if he'd been caught with his hand in the cookie jar. She'd been encouraged and at the same time, felt like a complete con artist, gaining his attention by deceptive means. The subdued hair, the glasses and the conservative clothes were everything she was not.

But now as Ali put her clothes on hangers, her room just a few steps away from Joe's in San Francisco's luxurious Four Seasons Hotel, hope filled her thoughts. She couldn't keep from smiling. Joe, the rock-solid man who held her heart, would be picking her up soon for the Welcome Dinner in the Grand Ballroom.

She knew Joe didn't like these stuffed-shirt affairs. Neither did she, really. Though she'd never have refused this invitation, she wished that they were here for a romantic weekend rather than rounds of business dinners and lectures. "A girl can only dream," she said softly.

She had just enough time to freshen up and dress before Joe would be knocking on her door.

Ali swept her massive hair back into a tight ponytail, allowing a few curly tendrils to fall demurely along her cheeks. She applied a light coat of makeup, just a hint of green shadow to bring out the color of her eyes and a soft peach lip gloss to tint her lips.

She slipped into a black chiffon dress that Rena helped her pick out for tonight's formal dinner. With a square neckline that dipped just a little below her throat, no one could accuse her of looking indecent. The bodice accented her narrow waistline then flowed in wispy folds to just above her knees. An antique pearl necklace complimented the dress and of course, Ali wore the diamond bracelet Joe had given her. She put her feet into two-inch black pumps and finished the whole look by putting on her glasses.

She glanced in the mirror. "You fraud," she whispered.

The knock at the door came precisely at seven o'clock.

Excitement coursed through her system. She dashed to the door, then remembered to compose herself, taking a steadying breath before opening it slowly.

When she glanced at Joe standing at her threshold in a black tuxedo, his dark hair smoothed back and curling at the base of his neck, his face tanned from morning swims and those dark eyes, intense once again, she might have swooned had she been faint of heart.

"You look very nice, Joe," she said quietly.

Joe's lips curved up in a killer smile. "Thanks. And you look beautiful tonight, Ali."

She did? She thought otherwise—the mundane dress was boring with a capital *B*. "Thank you."

"Are you ready to schmooze?"

Ali smiled. "As ready as you are."

Joe frowned. "Not the best way to spend your weekend, is it?"

Was he kidding? There was no place she'd rather be. Ali tilted her head. "I'll survive."

Once at the Welcome Dinner, Ali remembered that this was indeed a working weekend. She kept her eyes and ears open and networked with several winemakers along with Joe. They took their seats after the cocktail hour and listened to the keynote speaker's views on winemaking and the economy.

They dined at a table with three CEOs and their wives, Ali entering into light conversation with the women about West Coast versus East Coast fashions. Ali engaged them while Joe spoke with the men at the table, and after a sumptuous meal, all business was concluded.

A seven-piece orchestra began playing what Ali could only describe as nondescript music. The mellow tunes allowed for close proximity on the dance floor, and as men swept their partners to the center of the room, Ali found Joe deep in conversation with the head of Paladino Wines.

When she was tapped on the shoulder from behind, she turned to a man with hopeful eyes. "Would you care to dance?"

Ali hesitated for one second, glancing at Joe, who seemed oblivious to anything but the deep conversation he engaged in. She couldn't see refusing the middle-aged man, whose name tag revealed him to be a master sommelier. "Yes, thank you."

The man pulled out her chair and waited as she rose and headed for the dance floor. "My name is Juan Delgado," he said.

"Ali Pendrake."

He nodded with a smile and guided her to the dance floor, then took her into his arms as the music played on and literally swept her off her feet. Juan Delgado was not only a wine professional but a marvelous dancer.

Juan took dancing seriously, and there was no time for talking. Ali was curious about him, the man with kind eyes and exquisite dance steps. She'd never felt so weightless while dancing before.

"You dance with spirit, Ali," he said as the dance ended. "If I could confess, I'd love to dance with you all evening."

Juan continued to hold her waist, and his interest deepened to another level, one Ali recognized as dangerous. She glanced at her table and found Joe gone. Scanning the room, she locked gazes with him on the edge of the dance floor, his face tight, his body held in a rigid stance.

Ali had never seen that expression on Joe's face. Her pulse raced with dread. Had she done something wrong?

She turned back to Juan. "You're a wonderful dancer, Juan, and I did enjoy the dance, but I'm afraid I'm not here to dance. I must get back to my table. I'm...working."

"Aren't we all?" The casual tone in his voice belied the passion in his eyes.

Ali broke all contact with him. "Really, Juan. I have to go. Thank you for the dance."

Ali turned and walked straight into Joe, smacking into his chest. "Oh!"

He took her hand. "I need to speak with you," he said, leading her off the dance floor, then out of the ballroom entirely. Ali's heels scraped the floor trying to keep up.

Joe kept walking at a brisk pace, and Ali's mind whirled with confusion. Once he found a secluded alcove in the hallway, he pulled her inside and turned her, pressing her back to the wainscoted wall.

Ali had no time to react. Joe braced the wall behind her with both hands, brushed his hips against her, then crushed his mouth to hers, claiming her in an all-consuming kiss.

The kiss went long and deep, and tears of joy filled her closed eyes. Her mind screamed her love for him, her body turning to jelly in an instant.

Whatever this was, Ali had never experienced such intense passion. This kiss was urgent and fiery beyond her wildest dreams.

Joe didn't let her come up for air. He kissed her again and again, his musky scent filling her nostrils, his powerful body taking full control. Ali relished every second of his passion. Then finally, when both of them were ragged and nearly breathless, Joe broke away to look at her, his eyes gleaming with dark intensity.

"I like you, Ali."

"I like you, too, Joe."

"Wanna blow this damn convention?"

She thought he'd never ask. "Blow it?"

"I want you, Ali," he said, his voice a deep rasp.

Ali's brows rose in response.

He cupped the nape of her neck and eased her head back, planting tiny mind-blowing kisses along her throat. "I want to make love to you all weekend."

"Oh, Joe," she whispered. Her heart nearly burst from her chest.

"I don't want to see you in the arms of another man. I want that right for myself." His next kiss curled her toes. "You have to know I didn't plan this, but it's happening and I can't stop it."

"I know," she whispered. "I know. I don't want you to stop."

Joe gazed into her eyes for a brief moment and smiled. "Then let's go."

He grabbed her hand and led her to the elevator. They waited impatiently, and once the elevator dinged and the doors opened, Joe strode inside, punched the button and took her into his arms again. He kissed her like there was no tomorrow, and they were both breathless when they reached the sixteenth floor. Joe kissed her all the way to the room, both stumbling, and Ali thought she'd truly died and gone to heaven.

They fumbled with the keycard to open the door between kisses, and once inside, Joe shoved the door closed behind them. "I'm usually smoother than this."

Heart pumping like crazy, Ali smiled. "You're doing just fine."

Joe laughed. "Then in that case." He lifted her up in one fluid motion and strode into the bedroom. She wrapped her arms around his neck. Once he reached the king-size bed, he lowered her gently, and Ali released her hold on him.

He took his glasses off and then reached down to take hers off, as well. Then he pulled off the band that confined her auburn hair. He fingered through her tresses, watching the hair spread out across the pillow. "Amazing." He stood tall, straightening out, his gaze fixed on her. Loosening his tie, he removed his tux jacket and unbuttoned the first few buttons of his shirt.

Ali's breath caught. How many times had she dreamed of being with Joe like this?

Joe kicked off his shoes and joined her on the bed, crushing her again with kisses that left no room for doubt about where they were heading.

All the while, Ali held back. She wanted to strip Joe of his clothes, wiggle out of hers and unleash her own fiery passion. But Fake Ali couldn't do that. She had a role to play, and she reminded herself of the journey that had gotten her to this point.

Let it go, Ali. You're where you want to be.

Ali shoved her guilt and self-loathing out of her mind. With Joe beside her, it was easy to do.

He parted her lips and drove his tongue into her mouth. Ali let out a little moan of pleasure. The kisses went on and on until Joe's body went completely rigid with need.

He pulled away and yanked off his shirt, tossing it aside, then worked the back zipper of her dress. He eased it up and over her head, leaving her naked but for her black bra and bikini panties.

Joe took a good look and inhaled deeply, "Ah, Ali."

Ali gazed at him, consumed with love.

"You're beautiful."

So was he. His chest bare, she filled her gaze with broad shoulders, powerful arms and a ripped torso. Every ounce of her wanted to jump his bones right now, but Ali only reached for him and laid her hand on her breast.

Joe took it from there—his passion intensified, his eyes narrowed. The look he shot her was so steamy her insides melted.

He released her full breasts from their bonds and palmed her firmly, his hand rough against her soft skin. Next he grazed over her nipple, the tip pebbling hard. Over and over he touched her, his hand flat against her skin as he moved, explored, caressed and admired her body.

Her breaths shot out in short bursts, her pulse raced. "Oh, Joe," she murmured.

"Hang on, Ali." And before she knew it they were both fully unclothed. Joe slid his hands all over her naked body, kissing her senseless. Gliding his hand lower, anticipation built and every nerve ending tingled with intense awareness. This is the moment she'd wanted for so long—the moment when she and Joe would come together.

He cupped her between the legs and touched her gently at first, then with more and more intensity. Fireworks shot off in her head, and she moved under his ministrations. He stroked her like he would a keyboard with quickness and efficiency, his fingers masterful.

Ali returned his kisses, moved in harmony with him and clung to him as he lifted himself over her. Protection—that had almost magically appeared—was fixed in place. He spread her legs apart.

Ali held her breath and welcomed him with an arch of

her back. And then Joe was joined with her, his erection full and thick, driving into her with a slow deliberate thrust.

Joe's body shook. A low guttural groan of pleasure released from his throat. The union brought tears to Ali's eyes. Then she forgot all else as Joe deepened his thrust, filling her full.

He cursed, and she knew it was from the sheer awe of satisfaction he experienced. She felt it, too. Nothing in her life would ever compare to this.

He gazed down at her, and she curved her lips in a smile of encouragement. Then Joe let loose, his thrusts quick and fiery. He braced his hands on her hips and lifted her even higher, his body coated with moisture, his expression beautifully intense.

Ali relished his lovemaking, moving with him and enjoying each bit of stirring pleasure he brought her. She gave him full command of her body. His stamina amazed her, and she thought of all those early-morning workouts in the pool.

Ali's body reached an explosive point, and she threw her head back and arched way up, letting go of her control. Her release came in exquisite short bursts of surrender. She huffed out quiet little moans and looked up at Joe.

Controlling his own need, he held back until she'd been fully sated. Then his pace and rhythm changed to a frenzied assault, his thrusts hard and demanding until he, too, met with a powerful orgasm.

She watched his face change, his passion release and his body contract. It was stunning and magnificent, and Ali was sure she'd never witnessed anything so inspiring.

Joe eased down onto her, taking her head in his hands, and kissed her soundly. "Did I mention how much I like you?"

"You mentioned that," Ali answered with a chuckle.

Joe rolled off her, and her heated body cooled considerably without him. He turned toward her, his head braced on his hand. He seemed to have something on his mind. Ali recognized when he was in deep concentration. Then he blinked and shot her a serious look. "Stay with me tonight."

The only way she'd leave is if he threw her out. "Yes."

Joe took her into his arms, and they lay in silence together. Shortly after they climbed under the sheets, Joe fell asleep first and Ali watched him take deep breaths, wrapped in his arms.

She wished every night could be this perfect.

Eight

Joe's natural alarm clock woke him at six in the morning to the soft sound of Ali breathing. Her back was toward him, and the uniquely feminine curve of her body next to his was a sexy sight to behold. Her hair fell in wispy waves past her shoulders. On impulse, Joe reached out and touched a few strands, curling his fingers into the thick locks.

He closed his eyes and breathed in her scent.

He hadn't wanted this to happen. He'd fought it with all of his might, telling himself she was off-limits. And he'd been immune to her for a long while, looking at her through eyes that had once been deceived by a gorgeous face and killer body. He'd associated Ali with Sheila, perhaps unfairly, and he didn't want to go down that road of employer/employee ever again.

As a defense mechanism, Joe had dismissed Ali in his mind as nothing more than his very loyal business associate.

Then something changed.

Ali had changed, and he began viewing her differently. The changes in her weren't subtle, and he hadn't figured them out entirely. But Ali had become important to him—and not just because of how well they worked together.

Her neighbor Royce had given him a nudge, the irritating man who had more than friendship on his mind. Then last night, as she danced with her partner, who had all the grace of a swan, another man had approached Joe and asked if Ali was unattached.

"Is she fair game?" Those were the man's exact words.

Joe shot the guy a hard look, deciding right then and there that he couldn't let Ali go. He'd booted the man with a cold and foreboding "no" and claimed her the moment the dance ended.

Joe nibbled on her shoulder, impatient for her to wake up, and when she turned around, he wasn't disappointed. Her green eyes sparkled when she gazed at him, the light in those orbs as brilliant as the sun.

He smiled. "Good morning, beautiful."

Ali's grin went wide, then as abruptly as she'd brought it on, she pulled back on her smile. The light in her eyes faded. "Good morning, Joe."

They'd had an incredible night of lovemaking, yet all the while, Joe felt something was wrong. Not that he could call her on it. He wasn't going to look a gift horse in the mouth. He was where he wanted to be, in bed with an intelligent, gorgeous woman.

He caressed her arm, gliding his hands up and down. "How did you sleep?"

"Very well. You?"

"I always sleep well. But this morning, I woke up and there you were. Sorry, but I couldn't keep from touching you." He leaned closer and kissed her. "You okay with this?"

Ali smiled again, and Joe felt better seeing genuine joy on her face. "I'm great with this."

She turned and braced up on her elbow, her hair flowing over her bare shoulder. She painted a lovely picture draped in the sheets. He could go on looking at her, but when the sheet slipped down and exposed her full breasts, his body reacted instantly.

She covered up, almost shyly, and Joe's sanity returned. "Ali, listen. I don't know where this is going and I want to be fair to—"

"Shh," she said, pressing two fingers to his mouth. "Joe, let's not analyze this. If this is only for the weekend then I'm good with that. And if Monday comes and we have to go back to business as usual, I'll be fine."

Joe took all of that in, wondering if he'd misunderstood her the other night when she'd told him she didn't do one-night stands—not that Joe wanted that with her anyway. He realized he was ready for more. Maybe even a relationship with Ali.

It'd be tricky at work, but they'd find a way.

"And what if we don't?"

"Don't?" she asked.

"Don't go back to business as usual?"

The brightness in Ali's eyes returned full force, transforming her expression into one of pure joy. "I could manage that, too."

Purposely now, she let the sheet slide lower down, and Joe's mind went on temporary vacation. He kissed her on the lips then rolled them both until she was under him. "How am I going to see you at work and not think of you like this?"

Ali pressed her hands to his chest. Oh God, it felt so

damn good. He wished she'd done more of that last night. "I could ask you the same question."

Joe wanted to make love to her slowly, leisurely this time, and devour every inch of her body. He wanted to kiss her into oblivion and then bring them both to simultaneous satisfaction.

But all of that would have to wait. "We can't do this anymore," he said, climbing off her.

Ali appeared stunned. "The convention?"

"Hell no," Joe said, unable to hide his smile. "We're blowing it off, remember?"

"Then?"

"I need to make a trip to the hotel gift shop. I told you I didn't plan any of this. I'm out of protection."

Ali nibbled on her lower lip in that adorable way of hers. Then she smiled. "I'll be waiting."

"Sleep, Ali. I'll take my swim, make that pit stop and be back here before you know it. I'll send up breakfast."

Joe rose from the bed and then leaned down to kiss her again. She watched him move around the room bare naked, her eyes softly following him, and that was enough to send his wicked mind into overdrive.

He dressed into swim trunks, threw his arms into a shirt and headed out. His mind conjured images of Ali waiting for him in bed. It was damn hard to leave her.

Doing one hundred laps in the hotel's junior Olympic-size pool would be his only salvation.

He needed a cold splash of reality.

Ali rested her head against her pillow and sighed. Blissfully happy, she thought about the past twenty-four hours. Joe had finally come around, but was the cost of his ardor too high? She didn't have an answer, and right now, maybe she shouldn't care. All of her dreams were coming true.

Too restless to lie there, Ali rose from bed and realized all of her clothes were still in her hotel room. She donned the dress she wore last night, finger-combed her hair, slipped her feet back into her pumps and left the room.

Once she got to her hotel room, just steps down the hall, she flopped onto her bed, in a quandary. "What now?"

She didn't want Joe to come back and find her gone. She would love to dress in her sexiest lingerie and seduce him the minute he returned to his room. The whole scene played out in her mind in erotically vivid details.

But that wasn't in the plan. And she couldn't tempt fate. The woman Joe was attracted to wouldn't take the reins like that. She wouldn't be the aggressor and let loose. It saddened her to think that Joe might never be attracted to the Real Ali.

She'd give him more credit than that but for the fact that they'd worked together for one year and the Real Ali had never interested him. She'd fallen in love with her boss, and he'd never known it. He wouldn't allow himself to see the truth, much less give the idea any credence at all. He'd had his heart broken by a woman who'd worked for him, and he wasn't going there again. She understood that.

Ali glanced at the digital clock. She didn't have much time. She rose and quickly showered then dressed in a pair of slacks and a soft scoopneck knit top. She pulled her hair back and put on her fake eyeglasses.

She entered Joe's room, and shortly after, room service knocked. She let the waiter in and watched as he set up the table by the large bay window. The food smelled wonderful, and Ali's stomach growled.

Joe walked in just as she nibbled on toast and sipped orange juice. "Hi," she said. "How was your swim?"

He swept into the room, looking magnificent, his dark hair wet and curling at the nape of his neck, his shirt rumpled and buttoned up only partway. Glancing at the clothes she'd put on, he tossed a bag onto the nightstand then strode over to her. "Too long." He bent down to take her face into his hands. Searching her eyes first, he brushed his lips to hers. "I missed you. Couldn't you sleep?"

"No, I, uh…I couldn't." She was still recovering from Joe's admission that he'd missed her. "I didn't have any clothes and with room service coming—"

"It's okay, Ali." He kissed her deeply this time, his mouth making love to hers in a slow deliberate way that curled her toes. Her mind went on autopilot, and she returned his kiss. She was becoming accustomed to Joe kissing her, taking liberties that only made her love him more.

"You should have seen the look on the clerk's face when I walked in dripping wet and bought condoms."

Ali laughed. "I wish I'd been there." Then she thought about it. "On second thought, no, I don't."

Joe grinned. "No, I guess you don't." He lifted the covers from the food plates and seemed satisfied with what he found. "Go on and eat if you're hungry. I'll take a quick shower and be right back."

"I'll wait for you," she said softly. "We'll eat together."

Joe inhaled and peered at her as if she'd granted him knighthood. "Thanks. I won't be long."

Ali heard the shower going on, and all sorts of erotic images played out in her mind. She imagined steamy water raining down his body, his skin sleek and slippery as he soaped up.

Ali rose from the table and peered out the window, trying to thwart her wayward, X-rated mind. The view from the sixteenth floor was inspiring. She wrapped her arms around her middle and enjoyed the rise of the sun over the

Pacific Ocean. The San Francisco Bay was a sight she'd only seen on postcards.

"I'll take you wherever you want to go today." From behind, Joe put his hands on her shoulders and planted little kisses on the nape of her neck.

Goose bumps rose up her arms from the thrill. He smelled fresh and clean, the subtle scent of lime on his skin.

Could she tell him she only wanted to see him between the sheets again? "I'll go wherever you want to take me, Joe."

Joe chuckled. "Then we won't get very far."

She turned around in his arms and stared into his eyes. "Oh, no?"

"The bedroom beckons, Ali." Then he gestured to the table. "And so does the food. C'mon," he said, taking her hand. It was only then she realized he had nothing on but a fluffy white towel around his waist. How would she get through the meal? "I know you're hungry. Sit," he ordered. "Eat up."

"Yes, boss."

Joe squeezed his eyes shut. "Ouch. Let's forget I'm your boss this weekend."

She wanted to ask him, but then who are you? My boy-friend? My lover? But Ali was too distracted by his ripped upper body to formulate any questions. And his lower body and the pleasures he'd evoked last night made her head swim. "I can do that."

She sat down and he joined her, sitting across the table. She had the most appealing view of a nearly naked Joe with San Francisco's famous skyline in the background. A girl couldn't ask for more.

Joe waited for her to fill her plate before he took his share. They dined on eggs Benedict, roasted potatoes and crepes with fresh summer fruit compote. The coffee was heavenly.

Once they finished the meal, Joe rose from the table and reached for her hand. She lifted up and stood before him, puzzled by the solemn look on his face. "I'm not the crafty old lecher trying to seduce my hot secretary, Ali, but I'd be lying if I said I didn't want to make love to you again."

Ali gulped air. She knew what Joe was trying to say. "I'm not doing anything I don't want to do, Joe. As far as I'm concerned, the sights in this room are pretty darn appealing. I don't need anything else."

He drew her in slowly, placing both hands on her waist. "I know how to compromise. We'll do a little of both. Well," he amended, "we'll do a *lot* of exploring in here and some exploring out there."

He sealed the deal with a long, lazy kiss. "How does that sound?"

Explore away, Joe, and leave no stone unturned, she wanted to say. "Wonderful."

Joe led the way, removing her clothes between kisses, and once inside the bedroom, he backed her up against the bed. They fell down together amid laughter, and Joe took his sweet time, discovering all of Ali's erotic zones.

He stroked her throat, tonguing his way up to her chin. Then he kissed her again and again in a sensual frenzy of lips and tongues. His hands inched their way down, and he caressed her breasts, flicking the tips until she bit down with silent urgent need.

Next, he traveled farther down, kissing her torso, her hips, her navel, gently easing his way lower. When he parted her legs and positioned himself, raising her hips to meet his mouth, he made love to her soft folds, until she nearly melted on the spot.

Joe didn't let up. He touched her everywhere, his hands roaming over her skin as he whispered soft endearments, his words muddling in her mind. He stroked her legs and arms with the same heat and passion, and once she was certain he'd caressed her everywhere, he stroked her apex again and again, this time pressing his palm against her silken, needy flesh.

"Joe," she huffed out, holding back her innermost desire to unleash her passion.

Joe removed his towel, and she watched as he rose above her like a magnificent animal ready to claim his mate. He was so beautiful that she wanted to cry.

Then he made love to her, entering her body and deepening his place in her heart. He owned her soul, and there was nothing she could do about it.

After, they stayed in bed and munched on the leftovers from breakfast, then on each other again. Morning became afternoon, and after they'd dozed in each other's arms for a few hours, she heard Joe stir beside her.

She opened her eyes to find him stretched out before her, his hands clasped behind his head. He'd put his glasses on, and the sexy picture he made with the silken sheet draped across his lower body and a look of pure contentment on his face, stole Ali's breath.

"It's almost three," he said.

Was that a hint for her to leave? She wasn't sure where she stood with him. They'd had hot sex, but he hadn't made any declarations to her other than soft stirring murmurs during the throes of passion. "Hmm. I guess I should go."

Joe turned to her. Shaking his head, his voice soft but commanding. "You're not going anywhere. I'll have your bags sent to my room. I want you here with me."

It was music to her ears.

"Don't you want that, too?" He draped his arm around her shoulder. She snuggled closer.

"Yes, of course I do."

"Look," he began, "I don't know where this is going, but I do know I don't want to waste a minute of this weekend without you. It's been a long time since—"

She lifted her head up to peer at him. "Since?"

"Since I've let myself get involved with anyone."

"Why?" Ali asked, though she suspected she knew the truth.

"Because I was engaged once, and to say it didn't work out would be an understatement."

"Tell me, Joe. What happened?"

Joe looked deep into her eyes with reluctance and regret. Through pain and anger, he admitted, "She wasn't the woman I thought she was."

Ali's heart plummeted. She was filled with dread and self-loathing at her own deception.

"I really loved her, or I thought I did at the time. A man has to think he's in love to offer marriage. It's only logical, right?"

"Right," Ali agreed, her pulse pounding.

"Ali, she worked for me before you came to Global."

He looked at her with guilt as if he'd done something unimaginable, while she was the true guilty one who was playing a dangerous game. "Go on."

"I should have never let it happen. She was a flashy woman, and I knew she was high maintenance when I got involved with her. I should have known better. She wanted me to change. To be someone I'm not. She thought after we got engaged that she'd be able to make me into someone more like Nick, for lack of a better example.

"The truth is, she wanted someone who liked to play at life, someone who tossed his money and power around to climb some sort of social ladder. Well, you know, I'm the green guy in the family. That's just not my thing. When she figured out that it wasn't going to happen, she found someone else. She left me for a wealthier, more powerful man."

"She broke your heart."

"I'm over it now. Have been for a long time."

"Oh, Joe, I'm deeply sorry." Ali meant it. She hated that Joe's heart had been broken, but at the same time she prayed that she wasn't going to do the same thing to him. Her deception haunted her, and she hated the weakness in her that caused her to lie to the man she adored, over and over again.

"I hope not too sorry?" He grinned and caressed her arms until she could barely think coherently.

"What do you mean?"

"You wouldn't be here with me if—"

"Oh." Then she smiled, too. "Yeah, I'm not *that* sorry."

Joe kissed her into oblivion, and she forgot all about her deception, his ex-fiancé and his heartbreak.

Nine

On Sunday morning, Joe took Ali to Chinatown, and as they strolled along the streets hand in hand, window-shopping, Joe found pleasure in buying Ali trinkets that sparked her interest. He held a shopping bag full of hand fans, embroidered handkerchiefs and little China dolls. He'd noticed Ali admiring a jade necklace, the delicate round disk an image of a Chinese garden, and he'd gone back to the store to purchase it.

"Oh, Joe," she said, with surprise in her voice. "I didn't expect you to—"

"I know, Ali. But I saw how much you liked it. I wanted you to have it."

Tears filled her eyes. "Thank you." She held the necklace to her chest. "I'll cherish it forever."

Joe took her hand, touched by her genuine appreciation, and they continued to stroll along. He spotted a shop selling hand-painted tea sets and tugged her along. "You have to have one," he said.

Ali shook her head. "No, Joe." She stopped on the street. "You've already given me too much."

Joe turned to her and cocked his head to one side. "Not as much as you've given me, honey."

And Joe realized the truth of that statement. He couldn't remember a time when he'd been so content. Ali had restored his faith in the opposite sex. He trusted her. They were compatible on every level. She was a decent, hardworking woman who didn't have an agenda where he was concerned.

"What have I given you?" she asked, puzzled.

Joe grinned. "A real good reason to get up and go to work every morning."

Ali let go a little gasp of surprise. "Joe."

"It's true. Now, c'mon. I want to show you the Golden Gate Bridge before lunch."

When they returned to the hotel room after lunch, Joe closed the door behind him and took Ali in his arms from behind. He pressed his body to hers and relished how right it felt to be near her. He kissed the back of her neck. "It was a good weekend." Then a chuckle escaped. "I dreaded coming here. I hate these things. But it turned out almost perfect."

Ali questioned him with a look. "*Almost* perfect?"

Joe nibbled on her neck some more. "You never invited me into your shower," he murmured.

Ali turned around in his arms and gazed deep into his eyes. "You don't need an invitation."

Joe raised his eyebrows. "I don't? Well then, I think you need a shower, Ali. You really worked up a sweat this morning." He sniffed the air around her playfully. "Yes, definitely. Oh, man, you really need to get clean."

Ali turned away from him and headed straight into the bedroom, kicking off her shoes and shedding clothes as she went.

Joe swallowed hard, watching her strip out of her clothes quietly. When she reached the master bathroom, he heard the shower door open then close and water rain down. He wasted no time yanking off his clothes and following her.

He joined her in the shower seconds later, and the sight of her, her hair wet and straight, hanging past her shoulders, her eyes brilliantly green and her body glistening with moisture, stole all of Joe's breath. "I wish we'd thought of this sooner. You're beautiful," he said. "Need some help?"

Ali handed him the bar of fragranced soap. Joe made a thick lather in his hands and stepped behind Ali. Winding his arms around her, he pressed the lather gently to her arched throat, then down along her shoulders, stroking her softly as his body became rock hard. Next, he slid his hands lower, soaping up under her arms and sliding his hands just under her ribs. Her intake of breath amplified his desire. He cupped her breasts, filling his hands with her weight, lathering her in circular motions, giving each perfect globe his undivided attention.

Ali moaned softly as he caressed her. She arched toward him, her body fitting his frame. His lust became almost tangible, his erection straining against her.

Joe spent a good deal of time massaging Ali, teasing and tormenting her breasts until she squirmed under his ministrations and huffed out deep breaths.

Joe was in no better shape. He was ready for more. He slid his hands lower, soaping her navel and just below. Steam built up in the shower, but nothing clouded Joe's vision of Ali, in his arms, bending to his will, allowing him the freedom to bring them both immense pleasure.

Joe cupped her between her legs, and she parted them, her moans of ecstasy mingling with his whispered demands. "Let go, baby. Let it happen."

He stroked her over and over, her body gyrating with his, his finger finding her core and breaching it. Beating rapidly, she moved with him, but Ali held back. He felt her control tight and sure.

Joe wanted to see her release, to see her relinquish that control and let go.

When she called his name like a plea, Joe's control snapped. There was only so much he could endure before realizing his own satisfaction. And Ali had him at his limit.

Joe moved against the thick shower glass and grabbed Ali's hips, sliding a hand along her back, bending her slightly. He leaned over her and cupped her breasts, then entered her soft folds from behind. She accommodated his body and both made quick adjustments to this new position. Then Joe drove a little deeper, holding Ali tight, their bodies joined in an erotic stance that heightened his pleasure even more.

He thrust slowly, deliberately, and Ali's body moved with him in a sensual rhythm. He slid his hand down to torment her most sensitive spot, his fingers urging her to completion as his thrusts grew more rapid, more demanding.

Joe kissed her shoulders, murmured loving words and moved with quicker strokes now, his body at its brink.

"Joe, now. Now," she rasped.

The soft flesh of her buttocks against his groin driving him crazy, he gripped her hips and pulled her against him. He drove deeper into her and split them both in two. Her release matching his, they moved in sync, Joe enjoying every movement, every gyration, until both were spent and fully sated.

They stayed in that erotic position until they caught their breath, then Joe whipped Ali around in his arms. When she wouldn't look into his eyes, he tipped her chin up and kissed her, wondering about her sudden shyness. She puzzled him in many ways, but all that was forgotten when she finally looked at him. Her gorgeous green eyes appeared soft and vulnerable, and a sudden flash jolted him. He was smart enough to realize that what he had with Ali wasn't just about sex.

He cared for her.

Deeply.

And he knew he was in trouble.

Joe left a sizable tip for housekeeping in his suite and then tipped the bellboy with a twenty after he'd brought their bags down to the lobby of the hotel. With Ali by his side, he'd never felt more content, and the staff was reaping the benefits of his good mood. The truth was that he hated to see the weekend come to a close.

As they waited for the valet to bring his car around to the front of the hotel, a familiar voice called to him.

"Joe! Joe, is that you?"

Joe turned around, and his good mood vanished when Sheila Maxwell, his ex-fiancée, strode up, her blond waves bouncing off her shoulders. She walked like a fashion model, her clothes Beverly Hills classy, white on white, and no one could miss the diamonds dripping from her ears and throat.

"Hello, Sheila."

Sheila walked up to him and kissed him on the cheek. "It's good to see you, Joe." She glanced at Ali with assessing eyes before turning back to him.

"This is Ali Pendrake." Joe felt obligated to introduce the women. "Ali, this is Sheila Maxwell."

"Sheila Desmond now," she corrected. "It's nice to meet you, Ali. What are you both doing here? Are you vacationing like I am?"

Ali hesitated, looking to Joe before answering. "No, we're here on business. There's a convention in town."

"Oh, right, the Annual Grapegrowers Convention. I'd heard it was at this hotel. Sorry, I didn't put two and two together. So, you work with Joe in Napa?"

"Yes, I do."

"Ali works for Carlino Wines, and we're lucky to have her," Joe added.

Sheila pursed her lips briefly, looking intently at Ali before focusing her attention back to him. Genuine sympathy softened her eyes, "I'm sorry about your father, Joe. I sent you a note of condolence. Did you ever get it?"

Bumping into Sheila after all this time confirmed Joe's suspicions that he was one hundred percent over her. He decided to put the past behind him. "Yes, I did. Thank you for that."

"So now, you're settled in Napa?"

"For the time being, I am. My brothers and I are running Carlino Wines now." He didn't give her an in-depth explanation. At one time, he'd shared everything with her.

The valet approached Joe, signaling to him. "Well, looks like my car is ready. It was nice talking to you."

"Uh, Joe. If I could have a minute of your time?" She searched his eyes, and he couldn't fathom what she wanted to say to him.

He pushed his glasses farther up his nose. "We really have to get going."

"It'll just take a minute. Would you excuse us, Ali?"

"No," Joe said immediately, glancing at Ali. "You don't have to—"

Ali put her hand on his arm briefly, a gesture Sheila didn't miss. "It's okay, Joe." She reassured him with a smile. "I'll wait in the car."

Joe furrowed his brows and watched her walk off. Then he turned his attention to his ex-fiancée, his annoyance barely hidden. He exhaled and waited.

"She's pretty."

"You didn't ask for privacy to tell me how pretty my assistant is."

"Is that all she is to you? Your assistant?"

"That's none of your business, is it?"

Sheila picked up on his brisk tone. "Listen, Joe, I'm not trying to cause any trouble for you. But as soon as I recognized her—"

"Who, Ali?" Puzzled, Joe frowned. "You know her?"

"Not personally, no. But I know the name, and I've met her mother, Justine. She's known in social circles as the beauty queen, and Ali is the spitting image of her."

Joe jammed his hands in his pockets. "Is there a point to all this?"

"I'm trying to warn you, Joe. Look, I don't want to dredge up past history or anything, but I know I hurt you. I'm deeply sorry about that."

Again, Sheila seemed contrite, which in itself, baffled him. "It's over and done with, Sheila."

"My point is that I don't want you to get hurt again. Ali's mother has dumped more men than a dog's got fleas. Did you know she's on husband number five?"

Joe didn't know that. In fact, every time he tried to ask Ali about her family and her childhood, she evaded the question. He'd figured she didn't like to talk too much about herself.

He remained passive, yet his curiosity was piqued.

"Not to mention how many boyfriends she's had in between her marriages. Each time she married, it was to a wealthier, more powerful man. She's married to Harold Holcomb now. His brother is a senator," Sheila added.

"I know that."

"Okay, just so you know. Justine Holcomb is a social climber. Some have been bold enough to call her a gold digger. Consider yourself warned. You know what they say—the apple doesn't fall far from the tree."

Joe almost laughed. If he wanted to use a cliché, something Sheila was famous for, he'd say her comment was like the pot calling the kettle black. "I've never met Ali's mother, and I'm not going to judge her behavior. But if you're insinuating that Ali Pendrake is going to hurt me, then I'd say you're wrong."

"Okay, Joe," Sheila said on a sigh. "I get it. I'm sorry for intruding. But just remember what I told you. Be careful."

"I'm always careful now. You taught me that."

Sheila blinked.

"Sorry," he said immediately. He'd never been one to retaliate, and oddly enough, he really believed that Sheila had no ill intentions toward him. She was way off base about Ali, though. He surmised that Sheila felt compelled to warn him, out of guilt.

She shook her head amiably. "No, it's probably the truth. I can't fault you for that. But I truly never intended to hurt you, Joe. And if it's any consolation, I'm happy. I'd like to see you happy, too."

"Don't worry about me. Look, I've got to run, Sheila."

"It was nice seeing you, Joe. Take care."

"Same to you," he said, backing away and turning toward the hotel doors. As much as he hated to admit it, Sheila had given him a good deal to think about on the ride back to Napa.

Ali should have been on cloud nine as they drove home from San Francisco. As far as weekends went, she'd never had a better one. The only flaw in her perfect adventure happened at the end of the day, as they were leaving the hotel. What were the chances that they'd come face-to-face with Joe's ex? Yet, there she'd been, holding his attention, looking beautiful.

Sheila had flair. She wore expensive clothes, had perfect hair and makeup and held herself with self-assurance. The twinge of jealousy that Ali felt when Joe introduced them couldn't be helped. Joe had been in love with her once. He'd wanted to spend the rest of his life with her. But it was more than that.

Sheila reminded her of someone. She seemed so familiar. And when it dawned on her, Ali bit down on her lower lip, squeezing her eyes shut. A sense of dread coursed through her system.

She's you, Ali. The Real Ali. The one Joe Carlino had refused to notice.

He'd wanted no part of someone who reminded him of the woman who'd broken his heart. Though Rena had spoken of it, Ali hadn't been quite sure, until she'd seen the woman for herself. It wasn't only that Joe shied away from office romances but it was because Ali had seemed too much like Sheila for him to give her a chance.

Ali snapped her eyes open and glanced at Joe. He was driving his hybrid car down the highway, deep in thought.

A million thoughts flooded her head as Joe remained

overly quiet for the rest of the trip home. Had seeing his ex jarred him? Was he still in love with her?

Oh, my gosh, Ali thought. *I'm the rebound woman and a fake one at that.*

Joe caught her staring at him. He cast her a thoughtful look, then reached for her hand. Entwining his fingers with hers, she felt somewhat better.

"Everything okay?" he asked.

"Everything's fine."

No. No. No, she wanted to scream. I need to know what Sheila really said to you. I need to know if you still love her. Joe's explanation when he got into the car at the hotel hadn't seemed plausible.

"She just wanted to make sure I wasn't holding a grudge," he'd said.

And Fake Ali hadn't probed him for more. She'd merely sat back in her seat and accepted his explanation. The whole way home Ali held her tongue, refraining from asking the questions she had every right to ask.

When they reached her apartment, Joe got out of the car and opened the door for her. He helped her out and then grabbed her bag from the trunk. He took her hand and led her up the path to her front door.

"Here we are," she said, needlessly. She turned to face him.

Joe looked deep into her eyes, removed his glasses, then removed hers and planted a kiss on her to end all kisses. Ali had barely come up for air when Joe kissed her again.

Wow.

Maybe she'd misread him before.

He held her close and nuzzled her neck. "I'm leaving. If I don't, I'd want to stay."

"And I'd want you to," she whispered.

He inhaled sharply and backed away. "It was a great weekend."

"It was," she agreed.

He stared at her mouth, then backed up some more. "I'm going now. I'll have all night to figure out how I'm going to keep my hands off you tomorrow at work."

Ali smiled. "Joe."

"Gonna be a long night." He scanned her body up and down. "A long night," he repeated.

Stay, she wanted to say. Stay and make love to me until the sheets catch fire. But Ali knew they'd have to get back to reality. They'd have to come to grips with their relationship—whatever it was.

"I'll see you tomorrow, Joe. I had a wonderful time."

She turned and entered her home, part of her wanting to jump for joy and part of her ready to shed worrisome tears.

Joe started work early on Monday morning. He'd had a poor night's sleep and figured why not put his energy into something productive. He had Ali on the brain and wondered about Sheila's accusations about her mother. It would be easy to find out more by looking her up on the Internet. He was certain Google wouldn't fail him, but Joe held off. He'd already decided to put no credence in Sheila's comments.

Ali wasn't like her mother, just like Joe wasn't like his father.

Sometimes the apple *did* fall far from the tree.

Joe dug into his work with added ambition, trying hard to concentrate on the task at hand. But the fresh scent of flowers drifted by his nose, and he knew the exact moment Ali had entered the office.

She popped her head inside his doorway, just like she'd done every other day. "Morning, Joe."

Joe sat back in his chair, glad to see her. "Good morning," he said, unable to hide a big smile, but before he could summon her inside, Ali was gone.

"Good thing," he muttered. He'd missed her soft, supple body next to his last night. It had been fantastic waking up with her in the morning and holding her in his arms while in San Francisco. He fought the urge to spend last night with her, because he wasn't sure where it would all lead. An open office romance could spell disaster if it didn't work out. He and Ali had such a fabulous work relationship, and he wanted to keep it that way.

He'd have to be content seeing her after hours, but that didn't stop his imagination from flashing images of hot office sex with Ali that would put his other sexual fantasies to shame.

This morning, he'd lost count during his swim somewhere after twenty-seven laps from thinking of Ali. For a man who banked on his analytical mind, that wasn't a good thing.

Joe ran figures of monthly sales on his computer, getting lost in numbers, but every once in a while, he'd hear Ali's voice as she spoke with a coworker and he'd look up. He found himself staring at her, his heart doing crazy little flips and his body growing tight.

She looked so studious in her glasses, with her hair pulled back with a tortoise-shell clip, wearing a pin-striped skirt and a conservative white blouse.

Ali was beautiful no matter what she wore. Any man with eyes in his head was bound to notice.

And Joe wanted her.

The lust he felt startled him. He wasn't going to make it through the day without touching her. He glanced around his office, cursing the modern decor and glass walls—so much for privacy. The decor had never bothered him before now. Would it be too obvious to lower all the shades in his office and call Ali in?

Hell, why should he care? He was the boss. But he had Ali's reputation to worry about.

He pressed his intercom button. "Hi," he said.

"Hi, Joe." Ali glanced at him from her desk and gave a little wave with her fingers. She was only fifteen feet away in her office, but the distance seemed insurmountable. Employees came in and out of her office almost constantly. Again, he damned the glass walls that allowed them no privacy.

"What are you doing for lunch?"

"I wasn't going to take lunch. I'm swamped with—"

"You're taking a lunch, Ali," Joe rasped.

"I am?"

"Yes, you have to take a lunch break. It's the law, and you wouldn't want me to get in trouble for overworking my employees, would you?"

Before she could answer the rhetorical question, he continued. "Have lunch with me today."

"Yes," she breathed into the intercom softly. "I'd like that."

"Meet me in a half hour."

"Where?"

"At Alberto's."

And a short while later, Joe sat across from Ali in a circular corner booth in the Tuscany-style restaurant the Carlino family had half ownership in. It was just the place for two people who wanted a quiet, candlelit lunch.

"This is nice," Ali said, glancing at the stone fountain that obscured them from view from a good part of the restaurant.

Joe watched her intently as she took a look around. When she finally gazed into his eyes, Joe reached for her hand. "I'm going crazy not touching you." He stroked her fingers, rubbing his thumb over them. "Come closer."

Ali scooted closer to him, and Joe's groin tightened. He leaned over to give her a little kiss, but the minute their lips brushed, his heart rate accelerated, and one chaste kiss wasn't enough.

He took her into his arms and dragged her up against him, driving his tongue into her mouth, taking her in a long, drawn out kiss. He reached down to caress her leg, his hand inching up the hem of her skirt, feeling the soft flesh that had driven him wild over the weekend. He moved his hand farther up her thigh, grazing her skin and inching closer to indecency.

Ali pulled back. "Joe." She glanced around. The waiter was heading their way.

"Hell, I usually don't act like a hormone-crazed teenager, Ali." Joe straightened in his seat and lowered his voice. "I told you yesterday that it'd be hard to keep my hands off you."

The waiter approached their table with menus and offered up the day's specials. "Or anything else, you'd like, Mr. Carlino."

"Thank you, Henry. Give us a few minutes to decide."

"Of course. Would you care for a drink?" he asked Ali first.

"A soda for me, please."

Joe needed something stronger. "Scotch on the rocks."

The waiter left, and Ali peered at him, her eyes soft. "You don't usually drink this early in the afternoon."

"There's a lot of things I don't usually do in the afternoon, like grope my—"

"Your?" Ali appeared curious.

"I was going to say, grope my assistant. But you're more than that to me, Ali. I think the weekend proved that."

Ali put her head down. She sighed deeply and hesitated before lifting up to look at him. "I feel the same way, Joe, but there's something I should tell you about my past."

Joe waited, wondering if she'd tell him about her childhood and what it was like for her having so many stepfathers to contend with and having a mother who bounced in and out of relationships. He wanted Ali to explain to him her mother's motives. He hoped the seeds of doubt that Sheila had planted would be washed away with her explanation.

"I was involved with a man once, at work. He hired me under false pretenses. I thought he'd been sincere, but it turned out he wanted a sexual relationship with me. When I wouldn't comply, he made my life very difficult."

"You're not comparing me to him?" Joe blurted.

"No, of course not. But I'm trying to give you an understanding of why I'm cautious. When I told you I don't do one-night stands, I meant it."

Surprised, Joe frowned. It wasn't what he'd expected to hear. Maybe that's why he'd seen changes in Ali. Had she been scarred emotionally from that incident? Ali took pride in her efficiency and competence in the workplace. He couldn't imagine how much that episode in her life might have hurt her. He had to reassure her that he really wasn't an unscrupulous boss out for a brief fling.

"That's not what this is, Ali. I care about you."

His admission made her smile. He should have made that clearer over the weekend. Maybe that's why he'd sensed her holding back. As good as the sex was between them, Joe knew Ali had more to give.

"I care about you, too, Joe."

"I'm not going to pretend I don't want you every minute

of the day. I'm having a hard time staying focused on work with you just a few feet away."

Ali's lips curled up in a sensual smile. "I know the feeling, Joe."

"Invite me over tonight, and I'll be knocking at your door right after work. Hell, I'll even spring for dinner."

Ali's eyes softened, and his hunger for her grew even more powerful. "You're invited."

Joe nodded, imagining mismatched furniture, soft yellow hues and the scent of lavender drifting by as he made love to her in her bedroom.

That's if they'd even make it that far.

Ten

Anticipation coursed through Ali's body the rest of the day. She hadn't been able to concentrate because she was too focused on the idea of Joe coming over after work. She'd lost her focus countless times during the day, going even as far as forgetting who she'd called three seconds after dialing the phone number. She'd stumbled with her greeting until her mind cleared and she finally remembered. After that first episode, Ali decided it wise to jot down the name of the client she'd called and keep it in front of her before she'd made a fool of herself again.

She lived in a haze of desire and tried to avoid making eye contact with Joe in his office for fear of melting into a puddle of lust. At certain times of the day, she knew he watched her, but she held firm and didn't return his gaze. The clock ticked off the minutes at a snail's pace, and she thought the day would never end.

Finally at six o'clock, Ali straightened some papers on

her desk, filed away the rest then grabbed her purse and
stood up. She finally braved a glance in Joe's direction.
Thankfully, he had his back toward her as he spoke on the
phone.

Ali got in her car and drove home, her nerves raw with
tension. Once she entered her home, she leaned against
the door and breathed in deeply. Joe would be here soon
and Ali would have to hold back her innermost desires.
She'd have to be Fake Ali again, the submissive girl with
no personality and no sense of style. Her reverse makeover
had backfired. The guilt she felt deceiving Joe, the man
of her dreams, continued to plague her. He was too good
a man to dupe this way. "Oh, Ali, what have you gotten
yourself into?"

Ali walked to the kitchen and opened the refrigerator. She
pulled out a bottle of water and sipped as she contemplated
her situation. The only person who would understand all
of this was Rena. She'd have to talk to her again about Joe
and how much she hated what she was doing to him.

To both of them.

Rena would help. She'd been the voice of reason and
a good friend. Thankfully, Ali could turn to her, and she
vowed if things didn't get better by the end of the week,
she'd have to ask Rena for more advice.

Not three minutes later, Ali heard a knock at her door
and her heart skipped a beat. She walked to the front door,
took a deep breath and opened it.

Joe glanced over her body in a quick scan. "Good," he
said in a rasp, his brows raised, his expression like a wild
animal about to devour his prey. "You didn't change out
of your clothes."

"I, what?"

He stepped inside, sweeping her into his arms. Kicking
the door shut behind him, Clark Kent turned into Superman.

"I've been fantasizing about stripping you out of these clothes all day."

"Oh, Joe." Ali wrapped her arms around him.

Joe nibbled on her throat, then positioned her against the door, grinding his hips to hers.

"You do this to me, Ali."

The strength of his arousal pressed against her.

"I barely made it here without embarrassing myself." He cupped her head and kissed her hastily on the lips, his hands reaching for the buttons of her blouse. "I need to touch you."

Ali helped. As they fumbled with buttons, Joe nearly ripped her blouse in two. He pushed the material off her shoulders. Then he touched her skin, his hands covering her breasts, his lips crushing her mouth. "You're amazing, sweetheart," he groaned.

Ali's joy mounted. Joe wanted her, and she felt his intense need with his every touch. Her body welcomed his frenzied caresses and openmouthed heady kisses.

Ali stood pressed against her door, inviting his assault with little moans and cries of need. She wanted to strip him of his clothes the way he did her. She wanted to push him down to the ground and play out her every fantasy. "I need you, Joe."

"I know, sweet Ali. I know."

His kisses stole her breath, and his fiery need became hers.

He unfastened her bra, and her breasts sprang free of their constraints. A guttural sound escaped his throat, the sound primal and urgent. He cupped her breast with one hand and stroked her with his tongue—his hot breath on her creating spasms of heat inside her body. Ali's pleasure escalated.

She grew tight and wanton within seconds.

Joe sensed her need. He unzipped her pants and lowered them down. She stood before him naked but for a tiny black thong, shimmering with tiny rhinestones that spelled out, All Yours—the one part of Real Ali that was still intact. Her act of rebellion, she thought.

"Sexy," Joe nearly growled.

"I wore them for you."

A gleam sparked in his hungry eyes. "Hell, Ali. I'm going to imagine you in these every time I see you behind your desk."

"You could take them off."

"Oh, don't worry. They're coming off." Then Joe picked her up in his arms. "Later."

She threw her arms around his neck and held on. Joe strode down the hall, kissing her as he moved. She gestured to her bedroom. "I remember," he said. "I've been dying to see the inside of this room."

"Really?"

"Yeah, really."

Joe pulled her quilt back and settled her onto the sheets. She gazed up at him and waited. He looked at her, his eyes intense and gleaming with dark, hot desire. "How'd I get so lucky?"

Joe unbuttoned his shirt, and Ali watched with keen interest. His bronzed chest came into view, and Ali's throat went cotton dry. She'd never tire of seeing him this way.

Next, he kicked off his shoes, removed his socks and finally released himself from the pants that held his straining erection.

He stood naked before her, and Ali's blood pressure skyrocketed. Everything below her navel throbbed with desire. Her nipples peaked to rosy buds.

Joe noticed. He smiled at her in a way that had her moist

between the legs. That's all it took. One hot look from Joe and Ali was toast.

He reached into his pants pocket and tossed a half dozen condoms on her nightstand.

Ali looked at them with a gasp. "Really?"

"We might need to take the day off tomorrow."

Ali shook her head and giggled. She loved Joe more and more each day.

She wanted to gesture to him to come take her. She wanted to tell him six times might not be enough, but Ali only laid there, watching him, his naked form so enticing, so beautiful that she could easily reach out and touch him, bring him as much pleasure as he brought her.

Should she do it? Real Ali would have jumped his bones ten minutes ago. Ali sensed that's what he waited for. Joe wanted more from her. But Ali's passion was so intense that if she ever unleashed it, Joe wouldn't know what hit him.

The question was taken from her when Joe climbed into the bed beside her and took her into his arms. His kisses shut down her mind completely, and she fell into his embrace, allowing him to lead her to oblivion.

Ali woke in the wee hours of the morning with Joe beside her. They'd made love during the night, not quite the half-dozen times they'd set out for but two rather long incredible and satisfying times that would stay etched in Ali's memory forever.

She glanced at her digital alarm clock. It was four in the morning, and they'd be rising soon. She hadn't expected Joe to stay the night, but it warmed her heart that he did. After their last bout of lovemaking, Joe had taken her into his arms, laying her head on his chest and almost instantly fallen asleep.

He stirred restlessly next to her, and she froze, not wanting to wake him. "It's okay, sweetheart. I'm awake."

Ali lifted up from his chest to peer into his eyes. "It's early."

"How early?"

"Four o'clock."

"I should leave before nosy neighbors see me sneaking out of here."

"I don't care what my neighbors think."

Joe chuckled. "No, neither do I. Just thinking about you." He kissed her forehead and brushed loose strands of hair from her face. "I'm always thinking about you."

"That's nice to know."

"Let's take the day off. Play hooky or *do something else*." He caressed her breasts and wiggled his eyebrows, villain style.

Ali giggled then flopped her head back against her pillow and stared at the ceiling. "I wish we could, but you can't do that."

"Why not?"

"I've scheduled two meetings for you today. It would be rude to cancel at the last minute."

"What time?"

"One is at eleven and one is at three in the afternoon."

Joe bent over and kissed her soundly. "That's seven hours from now."

Ali wrapped her arms around his neck. "Yes, that's true."

"We could accomplish a lot in seven hours."

Ali stroked his handsome face. "Especially since you're so thorough."

He did the same. "And you're so efficient."

Joe slid his hands over her, gently, sweetly until he'd caressed every inch of her. "I love touching you."

"I love you touching me." But Ali loved more about Joe than that, and she prayed that Joe would return that love someday to the woman she really was.

At ten that morning, Joe was head deep in work at the office. He'd gotten in around nine, and Ali had gone into work a half hour before him. She'd insisted she had work to do, so he'd gone home after they'd made love once more to take a shower and dress. Sometimes he cursed his practical mind. Both he and Ali realized they had obligations at the office that couldn't be ignored.

So much for playing hooky all day.

Sometimes Joe wished he could be a free spirit, acting on a whim like his brother Nick. His younger sibling had no trouble shirking his responsibilities if a good time was to be had.

Yet, Joe wasn't complaining. He glanced at Ali, her head down, going over some papers at her desk. She looked up, and their eyes met. The soft look on her face gave him pause. Something powerful was happening between them. It was more than lust, and Joe told himself to slow down.

There were things about Ali that he didn't understand. He wanted her to talk about her childhood, have her explain about her mother and also explain how suddenly, her entire demeanor had changed, almost overnight. Ali had gone from flashy and vivacious to conservative and subdued in the span of a few heartbeats it seemed.

For all he knew, it was another of Ali's fashion statements. What Joe didn't know about women could fill volumes, so he didn't dwell on it. But he knew one thing: He and Ali were good together—so good that he got a hard-on just looking at her sometimes.

Joe scratched his neck and chuckled. "Get down to

business," he said to himself. "You've got a meeting in less than an hour."

He finished up a call with a client and then his cell phone rang. He took a quick look at the screen and winced. He really didn't want to have this conversation.

"Hey," he said to Tony.

"Hey, yourself. How've you been?"

"I've got no complaints."

"No? Well, I've had a few. Seems the guy I sent in my place to the Grapegrowers Convention was a no-show. You missed a lot of networking, bro. I've been getting calls for two days asking what happened."

"You know that's not my thing."

"But you went, right?"

"Yeah, I showed up."

"So what happened?"

Joe hesitated, refusing to answer.

"Ah, *Ali* happened."

Joe wasn't a kiss-and-tell kind of guy. He kept his mouth shut.

Tony didn't give him the same courtesy. "At least admit Rena and I were right about the two of you. You couldn't go away with her without playing musical beds."

"Isn't that exactly what you and Rena wanted? And listen, Tony, before you go getting ideas, it was just one weekend."

"Yeah, and the moon is made of marshmallows."

"What?" Joe furrowed his brows.

"You care about Ali. Just admit it."

"Of course I care about her. I'm not…Nick."

Tony laughed. "No, you're a far cry from our baby brother. Don't worry. I won't repeat what you said about him. But Ali's a nice girl, and you, Joe, have been alone way too long."

"Leave the matchmaking to someone who knows what they're doing, bro."

Joe didn't need any more encouragement when it came to Ali. He was having enough trouble sorting out his feelings for her. He'd been gun-shy for so long that he wasn't ready to open up his heart again. And there was always the fact that if it didn't work out between them, that he'd lose the best damn personal assistant on the planet.

All of that aside, Joe liked the status quo at the moment. Sex after work hours had its advantages. Joe glanced at his watch. He had a day full of meetings and work to catch up on. Evening seemed a long time away.

Joe took a look at Ali again, never tiring of seeing her. She was laughing at something Randy Simmons said, and then the sales manager touched her arm. An act of friendship he was sure, but Joe immediately turned away from them. A jolting pang of jealousy ripped through him. He squeezed his eyes shut and counted to three. He had it bad if he couldn't stand to see another man casually touch Ali.

"Joe, you there?"

"I'm here. I'm busy, Tony. I'd better get back to it."

"Okay, fine. And listen, don't worry about blowing off the convention. You're the numbers man. You would know whether we're in good shape or not."

"Trust me, Carlino Wines is doing just fine."

"Great then. Say hello to Ali for me. Oh, and be sure not to work her too hard."

Where did that come from? "I...don't."

"Good, and remember women need at least a few hours of sleep at night."

Joe hit the button on his iPhone to the sound of Tony's deep chuckle.

* * *

At home on Friday night, Ali looked at herself in the mirror, and that same sense of self-loathing plagued her. Wearing no makeup but a little lip gloss and a few swipes of mascara, dressed in a tan pin-striped pantsuit with her wild auburn hair confined in one long braid down her back, Ali frowned. She took her glasses off and laid them down on the dressing table. "Who are you, Ali Pendrake?"

But Ali knew the image in the mirror wasn't her. She hated the clothes she wore, and that hadn't changed. She'd hoped that slowly she'd morph into a woman who enjoyed dressing down, who enjoyed the conservative look of a businesswoman.

"You," she said pointing to the mirror, "are not *me*."

It wasn't only the clothes that bothered her. She'd faked her subdued personality, biting her tongue each time a sassy comment came to mind. She couldn't say what she wanted. She couldn't do what she wanted. So many times she wanted to express her feelings to Joe. She wanted to disagree with him about politics and religion and shout at him that rock music wasn't just a bunch of garbage.

She wanted to be herself.

She loved Joe Carlino with all of her heart, but she wasn't being fair to him or to herself with this charade. She was like a little kid who'd caught a big fish and then didn't know what to do with it.

Joe was her big fish. He was the love of her life. But he hadn't been even remotely attracted to the Real Ali Pendrake. One year's worth of hoping had proven that. So why on earth hadn't she let things be?

Now, it was too late. She was in love too deeply to get out without horrid injury. She didn't know if she was brave enough to tell him the truth.

"Who are you?" she asked again to the reflection in the mirror.

The week had been magical on the Joe front. She'd see him at the office during the day, and the hunger in his eyes reassured her that she couldn't let him go. He'd catch her in a private moment at work and steal a quick kiss, saying it was his sustenance until they'd met at night.

He'd come over with dinner each evening after work, but they never managed to eat their meal until the midnight hour, too consumed with each other to feel any other sort of hunger but the sexual kind.

Ali was in heaven while he was with her.

But she was in her own private hell when they were apart.

Tonight, she actually begged off with Joe. She needed an escape from Fake Ali for one night. She needed to be herself.

Joe had frowned when she told him she had a cooking lesson with Royce that would go late into the evening. She could see it was on the tip of his tongue to offer to come over after her lesson, but he'd held back. Maybe he'd hoped she would be the one to do the inviting, or maybe, he realized they needed a short break from each other. They'd been together every day and night for one entire week.

Ali kicked off her brown pumps, slipped out of her pantsuit and unbraided her hair. She ran her hands through the strands, and as her hair loosened from their bonds, so had Ali. She felt free, alive. Herself.

She turned on the radio, and a U-2 song blasted out. Ali danced her way to the shower, stepped inside and sang along with the radio, washing her hair, soaping her body and rinsing off as she moved with the music.

She toweled off, fingered through her hair, allowing it to dry naturally for the time being. Later, she'd take a round brush to it and use the blow-dryer to add more wispy curls.

Ali walked to her closet and spread the hangers wide, ignoring her Fake Ali clothes. She picked out a pair of black jeans and nodded. "I've missed you," she said, stroking the material as she would a long, lost love.

Next she searched for just the right blouse. She found a black silk that had gold tones of op art emblazoned on the front, the neck high on her throat, but the back dipping low with crisscrossing straps. She grabbed her leather boots from the floor of her closet and sighed. "I've missed you, too."

Ali opened her jewelry box and went right to a pair of thin, gold hoop earrings. Without pause, she set them onto her earlobes and stepped back from her dresser to admire them. "Nice."

She put her face on—a little blush on her cheeks, eyeliner and shadow to enhance the jade color of her eyes—and then lined her lips with cherry-red lipstick. She finished off her hair with the blow-dryer, then dressed in the clothes she'd picked out and stepped into her foyer where she could view herself in the full-length mirror. She liked what she saw.

The knock came at her door at precisely eight o'clock, and Ali was ready for Royce.

"Wow," he said, glancing at her with keen interest. He had a nice way about him, and some women might think him incredibly handsome in that blond, surfer looking kind of way. He held a grocery bag full of items for the lesson.

"Come in," she said, allowing him entrance. "What are we making tonight?"

"Well, I uh," Royce didn't take his eyes off her. "You look dynamite, Ali. Are you expecting someone else, later?"

Ali laughed. "No way. I'm up for our cookout."

"Really, because you look too gorgeous to stay home and make dinner. If I had half a brain, I'd offer to take you dancing. I have a friend who plays guitar in a band, and he's got a gig tonight in Yountville."

Ali opened her eyes wide, tempted to take Royce up on it. "Gosh, I haven't been to a concert since I left New York."

Royce narrowed his eyes. "Are you saying you want to go?"

Ali took the grocery bag out of his arms and marched to the kitchen. "How about we make dinner first, and if there's time, I'd love to go."

Royce followed her into the kitchen. "Sounds good to me." Then Royce cast a thoughtful look her way. "Hey, Ali, why'd you call me out of the blue?"

She turned away from the groceries she'd been removing from the bag and smiled. "We're friends, aren't we?"

"Yeah, but you've been busy lately."

"I know I have. The truth is I missed having a friend to talk to."

"You can't talk to your, uh, boyfriend?"

Ali only smiled. She couldn't give Royce a good explanation without spilling her whole sordid deception.

"Is he out of town?"

"No! I wouldn't do that to you, Royce. The fact is, he wanted to come over tonight, but I realized I've been neglecting my friends. Besides," she said, poking him gently in the shoulder, "you need to teach me how to make—" She frowned. She didn't know what they'd be making tonight.

"Beef tenderloin with wild mushroom sauce."

"My mouth is watering already! So go on, teach away."

Royce laughed and gazed at her mouth in a dangerous way. She'd told him countless times they were friends and hoped he wasn't reading more into this evening than that. He'd never really made a pass at her, and she trusted her instincts.

The one really good thing about being with Royce was that he liked her for herself. And she could simply *be,* when she was with him.

Royce immediately began barking commands, teaching her about different cuts of meat and how to look for marbling in the pieces she'd find at the market. He showed her how to prepare it and then went on to teach her how to make the wild mushroom sauce. He was actually a very good instructor, and Ali could tell how passionate he was about cooking.

By nine o'clock the meal was ready and they sat down to eat. Ali felt a measure of guilt when she thought about Joe. What was he doing now? She missed him terribly, but at the same time, she felt good about herself tonight. Like she'd reconnected to Real Ali. So much so, that after they ate the savory meal, she agreed to go dancing with Royce.

"Just for a little while," she said on their way to Yountville. "I've had a busy week, and I'm a little tired," she said.

Royce agreed. "No problem, Ali. We'll have a drink and dance a little. I've been meaning to hear Charley's new band. He'll be glad I showed up. Consider this a favor for the cooking lesson."

Ali relaxed more, glad that Royce didn't view this as any sort of date.

When Royce pulled into the back parking lot of the small club, music blared out from the open doors. He parked the car, and they walked around to the front of the building.

They entered Rock and a Hard Place, and immediately Ali loved the look of the small venue. It wasn't a trendy New York club but a more rustic place with sawdust on the floor and a long wall-to-wall dark oak bar.

"They're on now," Royce said, pushing through a small crowd to bring her closer to the stage. He pointed to a band member with longish hair and ripped jeans. "That's Charley on the guitar."

Royce shot him a quick wave, and Charley nodded.

"What's the name of their band?" she asked.

"Guts and Glory."

Ali laughed and Royce joined in. "I know. Not exactly Bon Jovi or Queen, but they sound good."

"They do," Ali said, clapping her hands and tapping her feet to the music.

Royce leaned over to speak into her ear. "Want a drink?"

Ali had to raise her voice over the band to answer. "Sure. Whatever you're drinking is fine."

A few minutes later, Royce returned with two mojitos. He handed her one, and she took a sip. "It's good. Thanks!"

Royce stood beside her until they'd both finished their drinks. "Want another?" he asked. "Or are you ready to dance?"

"Dance."

Royce took her hand and led her onto the small, crowded dance floor. The band played all fast tunes, and Ali let loose, dancing in sync with the beat, despite bumping into other couples for lack of space. She laughed with Royce over the loud music, tossed her hair to and fro and shimmied with the best of them. After five back-to-back dances, Royce came close enough to ask if she wanted another drink.

Ali debated and finally nodded. "One more. But I'll

get them for us." She felt better about paying her own way. Royce frowned but relented, and she stood at the bar with sweat dripping from her brow. She took a napkin and quickly wiped it away.

She was enjoying herself and burning calories, what more could a girl ask?

The band took a break, and as she waited at the bar for their drinks, she saw Royce speaking with his friend Charley by the stage.

A man sidled up next to her, and Ali turned, coming face-to-face with Nick Carlino.

"You're a great dancer, Ali."

"Nick, hi." Ali kept the panic from her voice. She could only imagine what Nick was thinking. Judging by his compliment, he must have been watching her dance with Royce. "Thanks. I love it."

Nick smiled. "Do you come here often?"

He made his point with the cliché pickup line, and Ali also knew that he was darn curious about her being here with Royce.

"No, I've never actually been here before." Ali brushed her unruly hair from her face, a gesture Nick didn't miss. "My neighbor Royce invited me to see his friend play. He's in the band." She pointed, but Nick didn't bother looking.

"What are you doing here?" she asked.

"I'm on a date."

"Oh, really?" Ali scanned the room but couldn't find the woman he was with.

"She's in the back, taking care of business, I presume. There was a problem with one of her employees."

Puzzled, Ali asked. "What kind of business?"

Nick grinned. "She owns the place."

Ali shook her head and smiled back at him. "I should have known."

"I like you, Ali. In fact, if Joe wasn't in the picture—"

"But Joe's very much in the picture," she finished for him.

"Doesn't look like it tonight."

"We don't spend all our nights together," Ali said in her own defense. Although since their trip to San Francisco, they had been inseparable. "And Royce is a good friend. That's all."

"Hey, I'm not accusing you of anything. I have my eye on your *friend,* though, just in case. If he'd so much as made an improper gesture toward you, I'd have decked him."

"Would you?" Ali asked, not sure Nick was telling the truth. He was a charmer with a killer smile and a man used to getting his own way, yet she didn't figure him as the brute type.

"For Joe. Yeah, I would." Nick braced his arm against the bar and looked her dead in the eyes. "Are you going to tell him about tonight?"

Ali blinked. "I suppose. It's no big deal."

"Just be sure that you do. And don't mention you saw me here."

"Why not?"

"Because then he'd be pissed at me for not telling him I saw you." Nick winked. "He's a good guy, Ali. Don't trample him. He's been there and done that once already."

"I wouldn't hurt Joe for the world."

"Good. Just keep it that way."

Ali sipped the mojito the bartender put in front of her. "You Carlinos stick together, don't you?"

"Like glue."

Ali wished she had someone who watched her back,

the way Nick just had for his brother. Most times she was on the giving end with friends and family. Both her father and mother had sought her out when they needed help, and Ali was glad to give it. But she'd never asked for the same in return. She'd grown up independent of others out of necessity. Her mother's frivolous lifestyle hadn't allowed for her to develop close ties.

It was at this moment that Ali realized that she harbored resentment toward both her parents—maybe a childish notion, but she'd wished they watched her back and put her first, just once.

Nick picked up two drinks the bartender sent his way. "Gotta go find my date." He began to leave, then stopped and turned around, his gaze flowing over her from top to bottom, assessing her hair, her face, her breasts and all the way down to her black leather boots. "I like the look, Ali. I think Joe would, too."

Heat crawled up her neck, and she was darn glad that Nick had taken off before he saw how much his comment affected her. It was almost as if Nick had figured her out.

What if he had? What if he knew the truth? He'd seen her cut loose, dancing like a maniac, drinking and laughing with another man. Did he know she was a fraud? She feared that he did and that would spell disaster.

Ali knew her deception had to end. She had to call it quits and confess to Joe what she'd done. She had to hope he felt enough for her, to give his forgiveness. If she'd injured him in anyway, she'd never forgive herself.

Ali was on unsure footing here. She could think of a dozen worst-case scenarios, and each of them made her cringe with regret and anguish. But one thought preyed on her sense of optimism and gave her hope.

Maybe Joe would laugh it off and tell her he loved her no matter what.

Somehow, she didn't see that happening.

A tremble coursed through her body, a quick shiver of impending doom. Ali couldn't shake off the feeling that things were about to go from bad to worse.

When Royce returned, she handed him his drink. "Please drink it fast," she said to him, urgently. "I need to go home."

Eleven

Ali tossed and turned that night, unable to sleep. She missed having Joe beside her, listening to the sound of his breathing and waking next to him in the morning. She missed his kisses and the steady way he held her.

She finally managed to get a few hours of sleep, and when sunlight beamed its way into her bedroom, Ali glanced at the clock. It was after six, and Joe would be taking his morning swim soon.

Ali rose slowly, reminded of her restlessness from last night by a headache that throbbed in her skull. She rubbed her temples and padded to the kitchen to set coffee brewing. Her motions were by rote, one step in front of the other, and gradually, after she drank a cup of coffee and ate a piece of buttered toast, the ache in her head subsided.

"Okay, Ali. Be brave. Pick up the phone and call Joe."

Ali waited ten more minutes, reciting in her head what she'd planned to tell him. Once she was sure he was out of the pool and dried off, according to his precise timetable, Ali picked up the phone.

She was greeted with a cheerful voice. "Good morning, sweetheart."

"Joe," she said with a sigh. Just the sound of his deep, sexy voice did things to her. "Hello."

"How was your cooking lesson?"

"It went well. I think I could duplicate the dish for you one night."

"I'd like that."

"I, uh, missed you last night."

"Same here, honey."

"What did you do?" *Ali, quit stalling. Tell him about last night and then ask to speak with him in person.*

"Tony and Rena stopped by. They entertained me for most of the night."

"That's nice."

"It was, actually."

"How is Rena feeling these days?"

"She looked great, healthy. She's a lot of fun. She even makes Tony tolerable."

Ali didn't respond to his little jibe. Instead, she began her explanation. "Joe, last night after Royce's lesson, he asked me to do him a favor."

"What kind of favor?"

"Just to go with him to a club. I think it's called Rock and a Hard Place, if you can believe that. He had a friend playing in the band and so I went with him, and we listened to the band and had a few drinks."

"Did you enjoy it?"

Ali decided the truth was her best option. If she was going to come clean with Joe, now was the best time to start. "The band was pretty good, actually. Great dance music. Yes, it was fun."

"You danced?"

"I did, Joe."

She heard Joe take a long, deep pull of air. Then silence ensued for what seemed like an eon. "What are you doing right now?"

"Now? I just finished breakfast. I'm not even dre—"

"Don't go anywhere. I'll be over in less than an hour."

Joe hung up the phone before Ali could respond. "That went well," she said, her body shaking. She couldn't tell if Joe was furious or not. She had no idea what he was thinking. Joe didn't wear his heart on his sleeve. He was steady and even and practical minded most of the time.

Ali hopped in the shower and dressed, with her eyes on the clock. If Joe said he'd be over in less than an hour, she knew he wouldn't be late. She had her clothes all picked out for today. It was Saturday, and she'd thought she'd put on her tight stone-washed jeans and something wild and colorful. But Ali changed her mind at the last minute. She donned a brown knit blouse and beige slacks and then put her curly hair back into a tight ponytail. "You're a chicken, Ali Pendrake," she said, sliding her eyeglasses on.

She paced the room and finally settled down with a *People* magazine. She sat on the edge of her sofa and flipped through the pages until she came upon an article that held her moderate interest. Attempting to concentrate on a blurb about upcoming summer blockbuster movies, the doorbell rang. Ali jumped off her perch and tossed the magazine aside. Her nerves jangling, she strode to the front door.

With one hand on the doorknob, Ali took a deep breath, closed her eyes and said a little prayer. Then she opened the door slowly, afraid of what she might find on the other side.

Joe stood on her doorstep, wearing a grim expression,

yet holding a big bouquet of the most gorgeous white lilies Ali had ever seen. Her mouth gaped open in surprise. Joe strode over her threshold, and after she closed the door, she turned to him in question. Without a second's notice, he pressed his mouth to hers in a long leisurely I-missed-you kind of kiss that would have knocked her socks off had she been wearing any. He backed away after that awesome kiss and handed her the flowers.

"For you, sweetheart."

Tears welled in her eyes. She didn't understand any of this, but she was grateful she'd been given a slight reprieve. "Thank you. They're beautiful. But what's the occasion?"

"No occasion." Joe took her hand in his. "I'm not the most romantic soul, Ali," he confessed, using his other hand to move his eyeglasses up his nose. "But I really care about you, and I don't want to take advantage of our situation. We haven't dated at all. Hell, I've barely fed you dinner this week, much less taken you out."

"We've had other things to do," Ali said aloud.

"Yeah, we have. But you deserve more."

"Joe, if this is about last night, it was completely innocent. Really, I have no interest in Royce. You have to know that."

"I know it, or I'd be beating down his door right now."

Apparently, Nick wasn't the only macho Carlino. Ali almost smiled at the image of Superman Joe, taking on Royce, the surfer dude.

"But it was a wake-up call for me, Ali. I've only been in this partway. It's my fault, and I want to make it up to you."

"It's not your fault. There is no fault." Ali almost couldn't bear to hear him out. *She* was the one at fault, not Joe. Guilt ate at her, weakening her knees. She hugged the lilies to her chest.

"Ali, I've got a vacation coming up in a month. I wasn't going to take it, but I've changed my mind. I want you to come with me to our villa in the Bahamas. I think you'd love it."

Staggered by his offer, and the implications that he wanted to share his vacation with her, Ali needed to sit down. She plopped on the sofa as myriad emotions caught her by surprise. Joy and love burst forth, but then self-loathing and guilt reared its ugly head, destroying her good mood. "Joe, that's so…um, I don't have the words."

"How about yes? That's the word I want to hear."

She couldn't refuse Joe anything, much less a chance to be with him at a tropical paradise. "Yes."

Joe smiled then reached for her, crushing the flowers she held between them, and kissed her again. "Good. I'll make the arrangements. We'll take a week. I'll show you a good time, Ali."

"Joe, you always do."

He grinned and stroked her cheek. "Do you have plans tomorrow?"

She thought for a second, then shook her head. "No."

"Great. I've rescheduled our bike tour. That was our deal, and I'm following through. You still want to see Napa?"

She'd follow him anywhere. "Yes, I look forward to it."

"Great, well, I've got to get busy. How about dinner tonight?"

Ali smiled at him while a little voice in her head nagged that her inner chicken was hiding in the hen house. "I'd love it."

He gave her a quick nod and looked deep into her eyes.

"This time, I'm taking you to the nicest restaurant in Napa."

"But Joe, you don't—"

Joe put a finger to her lips. "Shh, Ali." He bent his head and brushed a soft kiss to her mouth. "I'll be dusting off my tux, so be ready."

Ali leaned heavily on the door as soon as Joe left. Her heart in her throat, she felt as though she'd run a marathon without benefit of water. Everything went limp, including the smile she'd shown Joe.

Tears threatened to spill down her face, but she managed to hold her emotions in check and march over to her kitchen phone. She should have done this much sooner.

"Hi, Rena," she said softly into the phone. "It's Ali, and I need your help."

"It's a good thing I insisted you come over this morning, hon. I could hear by the sound of your voice earlier that you were upset." Rena set a cup of tea in front of Ali on a charming round table for two in the Purple Fields gift shop. "I hated to bother you," Ali said quietly.

"No bother. As you can see, we're not busy this time of day. We have the whole place to ourselves."

"Thanks. But with the baby coming soon and the construction on your house, I didn't want to give you added drama."

Rena chuckled and gestured wide with her arms. "Give me drama. *Please,* give me drama. My life is so sedate these days that I'm ready to pull my hair out. Tony takes care of the business mostly, and I'm done with picking floor samples and paint colors." She patted her rotund belly. "Tony tells me to relax now because when the baby comes, I'll be superbusy, but relaxing isn't easy. I've never been one to sit and let the world go by."

"Right now that sounds good to me," Ali said.

"So, what's going on? I presume there are problems with Joe?"

"Yes, but it's probably not what you're thinking." Ali paused to sigh deeply before sharing with Rena her innermost feelings. "I love him very much. I do, and he's been wonderful to me. We have a great time together. That's why I'm so afraid to tell him the truth. I almost did this morning. I almost told him that I've been deceiving him and that the woman he asked to go away with him to the Bahamas is a fake. He thinks I'm someone I'm not. But I chickened out when he brought flowers and asked me to take a vacation with him. How could I refuse that? It's a dream come true."

"Oh, Ali. Is it really that bad?"

"Yeah, it is." A self-deprecating laugh followed. "Look at me? Look at what I'm wearing." Ali pulled at her preppy-looking cotton blouse. "This isn't me. But worse than the clothes, I'm not being true to myself, and I've hit a wall. I can't stand it anymore. I've bitten my tongue so many times around Joe that it's a wonder I can speak at all. I want Joe but not at the expense of fooling him the rest of his life."

Rena sipped her tea and listened carefully.

"Do you think you and Joe…is it serious?"

"For me, yes. For Joe, I think so. At least I'm hoping so. I know he cares for me." She smiled when she thought about this past week and how hungry they'd been for each other. The overtures Joe made this week had been so endearing and thrilling that she could only assume that their relationship would move ahead.

Yet, she had one more confession to make. "Even in the bedroom I'm holding back," she said bluntly. "I'm not the passive sex partner I've portrayed myself to be." Ali worried that she'd overstepped her bounds sharing that detail, but Rena hadn't even blinked. "Sorry, but I had to tell someone."

"It's okay, Ali. You can share anything with me. I'll keep whatever you tell me confidential."

"I'm such a fraud." Ali stared out the little window she sat beside, looking into flourishing vines in the distance. "And I've been too cowardly to tell him that I'm not the person he thinks I am. I've tried, but I'm afraid of losing him."

Rena took her hand and squeezed. "Ali, if you want my advice, I'll give it to you."

"Please." Ali desperately needed help in sorting this out. "If you have any suggestions, I'm listening."

"Don't tell him."

Ali blinked rapidly a few times. "But that means that I'd have to go on pretending."

"Show him." Rena cast her a reassuring smile.

"Show him?" Puzzled, Ali nibbled on her lower lip and shook her head. "I don't get how."

"Show him who you are. Be yourself, Ali. Dress the way you want. Say what you want, and for goodness' sake, don't hold anything back in the bedroom. If Joe cares enough about you, he'll accept you for you."

Ali saw the logic in that. "It makes sense when you say it, but it still scares me."

"Ali, if Joe can't love you for yourself then do you really want him?"

Ali mulled that over for second or two then nodded in agreement with Rena. "Good point."

"I'm sorry I got you into this, Ali. If I'd known it would have given you so much anguish, I would have never suggested your little makeover in reverse."

"You have nothing to be sorry about. If anything, at least you've given me a chance with Joe."

"I hope so."

Ali gained newfound strength. "I'm going to do it, Rena. I'm saying goodbye to Fake Ali for good. Next time you see me, you might not recognize me." Her mood lightened, and tension released from her body. The cloud she'd been under had lifted. "God, I feel so free, just saying it!" She rose and hugged Rena. "Thank you."

"Let me know how it goes, hon."

"I will. I'm taking a gamble. But that's what I always do. I just hope I snatch the brass ring this time."

"Got a hot date?" Nick sauntered into the living room, just as Joe was pouring himself a drink at the bar.

"Maybe."

"No maybe about it. You don't dress in a monkey suit unless you want to impress the hell out of a woman."

Joe turned to his brother and grinned. "Yeah, I guess you're right." The whiskey slid down his throat easily. He glanced at his watch, wishing the time would go by quickly. He had thirty minutes to kill before picking Ali up.

"I am? You mean, you're admitting it?"

"Yeah, I won't deny it." Joe leaned against the long, polished bar and folded his arms across his middle.

"And you're smiling from ear to ear. Be careful, Joey. You might find yourself—"

"I know all the warnings, Nick. And for once, I don't care. I think Ali is the right woman for me."

Nick walked over to pour himself a drink. He offered Joe another, but he shook his head. "Really? It only took you over a year to figure it out."

"I'm slow on the uptake, but I finish with flying colors," Joe said.

Nick chuckled and took a swallow of whiskey. "I couldn't have said it better myself."

"I said it for you, so you couldn't gloat."

"Oh, don't worry. I'm gloating and a bit envious. Ali's pretty spectacular."

"I agree. She's not like most women."

Nick smirked and shook his head, and Joe didn't know why that look annoyed him so much.

"What?"

"Don't be naive, Joe. One thing I know is women. They all want the same thing—money, power, status and lucky for us, we're in the position to give them that."

"Cynical, Nick."

"Realistic. But hey, I'm glad you're coming out of the cave Sheila trapped you in. I hope it works out for you."

Nick finished his drink, slapped him on the back in a show of real affection and left.

Twenty minutes later, Joe knocked briskly on Ali's front door, anticipating the night ahead. He tucked his hands in his pockets and when she opened the door, Joe's mouth fell open. "Wow."

Ali stood before him, and the first thing he noticed was her auburn hair flowing down her shoulders in a mass of curls. Her hair looked untamed and amazingly free. Glancing from her hair to a face that positively beamed, he peered into jade-green eyes that looked twice their size and weren't hidden behind eyeglasses. Her smile brought his focus to her lips colored to a dark pink hue. Full, lush and so kissable, Joe held his willpower in check, determined to give Ali the romantic night he'd planned.

But as his gaze dipped lower, Joe's intake of breath was loud enough to bring on another smile from Ali. Her sexy black dress clung to her body like a second skin—and how that crisscrossing material kept her beautiful cleavage from spilling out could possibly be the eighth wonder of the world.

Her dress stopped short of her knees. Three-inch black high-heeled sandals supported tanned, gorgeous legs that went on forever.

"You like?" she asked, whirling around in a slow circle.

Joe caught a glimpse of her soft shoulders and lower back and all the skin exposed by her dress before she turned to face him.

"You look beyond beautiful, Ali."

"And you look sexy, Joe. I like the tux." She tugged on his arm and enticed him inside.

"No," he said, stopping short and grabbing her hand. Immediate heat radiated between them. He'd have her out of that dress in two seconds flat if he gave in to what he was feeling.

"No?" Ali asked, her lips forming a pout.

"C'mon, sweetheart. If I come inside, we'll never make dinner. Go get your things. I'll wait for you out here."

Joe stepped outside and waited, telling himself he'd done the right thing. With the way Ali looked tonight, all glittery and beaming, he wouldn't have had a chance if he'd strayed inside her condo with the bedroom only steps away.

Hell, forget the bedroom. He might not have made it that far.

Joe drew in a steady breath, allowing the crisp Napa air to cool his jets. *You promised her a great evening, so stick to the plan, Joe.*

When Ali joined him, holding a small purse and wearing a little black shawl around her shoulders, Joe put his hand to her back and escorted her to the limo.

"I know," he said before she could ask. "I debated, but I conserved water today, recycled cans and planted a vegetable garden."

"With your bare hands?" she asked, looking at him like he could save the world.

"No. The gardener did it, but it was my idea."

Ali laughed lightly, and the sound of her joy made him grin from ear to ear.

"Okay, so you get credit for the idea," she said.

"Is that cheating?"

"Not in my book. It's called clever maneuvering, Joe. To be honest, I'd expect Nick to dream something like that up."

"Hey, at least we'll make up for the limo ride tomorrow when we take our bike ride."

"True," Ali said, and the chauffeur opened the door for them. Ali slipped inside and Joe followed, aware of every movement she made in her dress.

Heat climbed up his neck, and he grew hard instantly.

"What's the matter, Joe?"

"Nothing that can't be fixed in a few hours from now. Just keep to the far side of the seat and don't look at me that way."

"Okay," Ali said with a sweet smile that somehow appeared wickedly sinful.

Joe groaned and kept his focus out the window the entire way to the restaurant.

Joe's blatantly sexy gaze was on Ali as they ate dinner atop a hill in a gorgeous mansion transformed into a top-notch restaurant, called quite simply The Mansion. Ali's mother and one of her right-then husbands had dragged her to many classy country clubs as a child, but no place she'd ever been to could compare to this.

Darkly textured stone walls and romantically lit tables were surrounded by old-world elegance in a tall room with sweeping sheer drapes that opened to the magnificence of the valley below. Crystal chandeliers, plush carpets and waiters dressed in tuxedos made an impressive picture. Soft music played by a five-piece orchestra added to the ambience.

The menu, a leather-bound book of choices, had given her a heart attack as she imagined what each entrée would cost. Joe was a rich man, but this extravagance was totally out of character for him. Yet, he looked good in the surroundings, blending in with the decor and not intimidated at all by the elegance. Thankfully, he'd ordered for both of them and picked a fine wine to go with the meal.

Joe gave her his full attention during dinner, entertaining her with the history of The Mansion and telling stories of his youth, growing up in Napa.

After the meal, Joe stood and reached for her hand. "Dance with me."

Ali rose, and he led her onto the dance floor.

"Is this your first-date way to impress a woman?" she asked as they stepped onto the wooden flooring.

"I don't know." He took her into his arms, bringing her up close. "Am I impressing you?"

"Oh, yeah, Joe. You're impressing the heck out of me."

He chuckled and drew her even closer.

Ali wound her arms around his neck. "You might even get lucky tonight, boss." She nibbled on his throat.

"Ali," Joe warned in a low tone, his sharp inhalation very telling.

"What, Joe?"

"They make a great chocolate soufflé here. I want us to last at least through dessert."

"Then maybe you shouldn't have asked me to dance," she whispered.

"I had to," he said. "In case you hadn't noticed, you turned a lot of heads when you walked in."

How could she have noticed? She only had eyes for Joe. "Oh, so you're staking your claim?"

Joe grinned. "Something like that. And you looked so beautiful in candlelight that I had to touch you."

Ali rested her head on his chest, and he tightened his hold on her. "You're saying all the right things."

"Am I passing the first-date test?"

"With flying colors."

Joe chuckled, and when she peered up at him in question, he simply shook his head, smiling.

"Did I say something funny?"

"Not at all. You just repeated something I'd said to Nick earlier."

Ali let that comment go and didn't question him further. Being held in his arms as the violinist played a sweetly romantic tune was heaven on earth.

They moved slowly, erotically. Ali's hips brushed Joe's, her body flowing into his with intimate little touches—a sort of public foreplay that had her mind whirling.

Joe kissed her forehead, caressed her back and ran his hands through her hair, his body rock hard.

Show him who you are. Rena's advice came through loud and clear, and Ali wouldn't stop now.

"You think we could get the soufflé to go?" she asked urgently in a breathless tone that was true to her nature. "I want to feed it to you myself privately."

Joe stopped dancing and stared at her. He blinked several times and grinned. With a hot gleam in his eyes, he dragged her off the dance floor. "Let's go."

Twelve

They made out in the back of the limo, unable to keep their hands off each other. Ali climbed onto his lap, and Joe's control nearly snapped. He ran his hand underneath her dress and stroked her thigh, skimming the soft flesh. Ali's moan of pleasure had his erection pulsing.

Ali seemed different tonight, but Joe wasn't questioning it. He was as hungry for her as she was for him. They stumbled up to her apartment, Ali tugging at his tie, loosening it. She opened the door, and they fumbled their way in.

When Joe wanted to take her straight to the bedroom, Ali shook her head and led him to the kitchen. "Dessert, remember?"

Joe protested with a groan and wished they hadn't taken the chocolate soufflé to go.

"I promise you that you won't be sorry." She removed

his jacket and then his tie and offered him a seat at her kitchen table.

When he glanced at her puzzled, she gave a little shove. "Sit."

Joe sat.

She came around from the back, her exotic scent invading his senses, and with nimble hands she unbuttoned his shirt. She stroked his chest, running her hands up and down. He loved when she touched him. She rarely took the initiative, which confirmed that something was up with her tonight.

He pulled her down to kiss her, and when he tried to do more, she backed away. "Hold that thought. I'll be right back."

Joe waited just a minute before Ali shut down the lights in the room. She came back with one vanilla scented pillar candle glowing and the chocolate delicacy on a plate with one fork. She set the candle down on the table along with the plate.

Next, Ali stood before him and slipped out of her dress. The material pooled at her feet. She stepped out of it, and Joe looked at the most gorgeous woman he'd ever seen. The strain in his pants was now an ache.

Ali wore a tiny bra that barely contained her ample breasts, the nipples a faint hint through the lacy material. A little black stretch of fabric covered the vee between her legs and enticed him beyond belief. Ali had never undressed before him. She'd never been so bold. "If you're trying to kill me, you're succeeding."

Ali smiled, a sensual curving of her lips. "That comes later, baby. First I'm going to feed you."

Ali straddled his legs and took up the dessert plate. She forked into the chocolate concoction and lifted it to his lips. "Open your mouth, Joe."

Her breasts were at eye level and so beautiful. "My mouth has better things to—"

Ali set the fork into his mouth. The chocolate oozed inside and melted into his mouth.

"How is it?"

Joe glanced at the picture she made straddling him nearly naked. "Amazing."

"Now my turn," Ali said, forking a piece and opening her mouth wide. She inserted the fork in and Joe's throat constricted. She chewed briefly then swallowed, licking her lips. "Delicious."

Then she leaned over to kiss him, and he didn't miss the opportunity to drive his tongue into her mouth. She tasted sweet and sexy, and he took his time with her.

"I think we can do better," she said. She set the fork down and dipped her fingers into the soufflé. She pressed the cake into his mouth then brushed a soft kiss to his lips. He chewed quickly and lifted her messy fingers to his tongue, licking off the chocolate, one finger at a time. The heady maneuver broke him out in a sweat.

"Ali," he groaned. "I can't take much more of this."

She plopped a piece of chocolate cake into her mouth and swallowed. "You have a little on your mouth," she said. She leaned in and swirled her tongue onto his upper lip until he burned with dire need.

Joe's willpower shut down.

He pulled out the chair and grabbed her around the waist. "Wrap your legs around me," he ordered. And once she did, Joe bounded up from the chair, Ali's legs tight around his waist.

He knew his way to the bedroom and made quick work of lowering her down on her bed.

But Ali didn't stay down. She rose up on her knees. "Let me undress you."

Joe surrendered immediately. Ali lowered the sleeves of his shirt and pulled it off. Her hands found his chest again, and her touch made his straining erection throb harder.

She caressed him for a few seconds there before sliding her hands down lower to unfasten his belt. She pulled it free, then brought her tongue to his navel and laved it, moistening his skin thoroughly. Joe kicked off his shoes and slipped his feet out of his socks, waiting. Anticipating. Her next move didn't disappoint. Ali unzipped his pants, lowered them down along with his briefs and then glanced at his manhood. "Impressive," she said with a sexy grin.

Joe didn't need any more encouragement. He was almost at his limit.

Ali cupped him with her hands, and Joe managed to hold on, enjoying every minute of Ali's foreplay. She stroked him gently, her soft hands on his silken flesh. He braced his hands on her shoulders, needing to touch her as she pleasured him. Her hand slid over him in ways that he'd only dreamt about, and he grabbed handfuls of her hair in both hands gently encouraging her to go on. But this was Ali, he kept saying to himself, and he wondered why tonight was different. *She* was different. She didn't hold back in any way. She drove him absolutely wild. The picture she made on the bed was a visual he'd not soon forget.

Then, she took him into her mouth. "Oh, yes," he muttered through gritted teeth. Ali held his hips and worked magic on him with her perfect mouth. Her tongue caressed his shaft and flames erupted. He held her hair tight as she moved on him. Little moans of pleasure erupted from her throat, and Joe's whole body gave in to her, allowing her to have her way. He enjoyed every ounce of her sensual assault, whispering his praise in full surrender.

It wasn't long before he reached his limit. He stopped

Ali, pulled her away and climbed onto the bed, taking her with him. "Hang on to your hat, sweetheart."

He entered her in one fully satisfying deep thrust. She was ready for him, and he could always count on that. He moved quickly, fiercely, his memory of what she'd just done to him, making short work of filling her with his powerful need. They climaxed together, the quick joining just chapter one of a very long night ahead.

Joe dozed after that, with a big smile on his face. He heard Ali rise and the shower go on. He pictured her in there, soaping up, scenting her body with some delicious fragrance, and he thought about joining her. But before those thoughts came to fruition, Ali walked into the room bare naked, wet hair flowing down her back and her face scrubbed clean looking natural and pure. Droplets of water glistened all over her body, her breasts full and ripe, nipples erect. Water clung to the tips, and Joe itched to lick those drops off her.

He lifted from the bed to do just that, but Ali stopped him with a gentle hand. "Lay back, Joe. Tonight I'm the boss."

Joe's eyes went wide. "Sounds good."

"Oh, it *is* good."

Joe imagined the most erotic things a woman and a man could do in a bedroom, and his heart began pumping like an oil rig striking a full-on gusher. And in the next hours, most of those erotic imaginings became staggering and stunning memories.

Joe leaned back with amazed joy as Ali straddled him one more time, riding him up and down, her hair dry now and flowing in wild curls past her shoulders, her beautiful body arching, her breasts tipped toward the ceiling, her face glowing and ready to fracture with the shattering of her next powerful orgasm.

They'd had several through the night, each one different and amazing.

Joe held her, stroked her breasts, flicking the tips, and watched Ali with half-lidded eyes, take him places he'd never gone before with a woman. Not like this. Not this potent and heady and downright sexy.

Ali unleashed her passion and rode him with frenzy. She pleaded and moaned with ahs of sheer breathless delight. Oh God, he'd never seen anything so humanly beautiful.

Joe knew this was it—their last time tonight. There wasn't anything more they could possibly do to each other. They were spent and sated, and so when Ali climbed high, Joe met her there and they shattered together, in unison crying out each other's names.

Ali stayed atop him a minute, looking at him with eyes that were unreadable. Then she climbed off, breaking their connection and lay beside him. Immediately, he wound her in his arms and held her. "That was the best sex of my life, Ali. I'm the luckiest man alive."

With that, Ali burst into tears.

Ali bounded out of bed, her heart broken. Unstoppable tears streamed down her face. She couldn't do this anymore. She hated lying to Joe, and the guilt ate at her each day.

She shoved her arms into her silk robe and walked over to the window, her body wracked with anguish. She hugged her middle tight.

"Ali, Ali, what is it?" Joe came up behind her. He put his arms onto her shoulders. "What have I done to upset you?"

Ali whipped around to face him, wiping her tears with the back of her hands. "Nothing, Joe. You haven't done a thing. It's me. I'm the guilty one here."

Ali moved away from Joe, breaking off all contact. She

put the middle of the room between them. She hated seeing the look of puzzlement on Joe's face. "It's just that I can't do this to you anymore."

"Do what, honey?" he asked, softly, being gentle with her. She was probably confusing the hell out of him.

"I'm not the person you think I am. I'm certainly not the soft-spoken, passive little woman I've been pretending to be since almost the minute you hired me back here. I don't like wearing pencil skirts and business suits and putting my hair up in buns. I don't even *need* glasses. Those are fakes. I always wear contacts."

Joe slipped into his briefs and put on his glasses at the mention of hers. He shook his head. "What's going on, Ali, really?"

"Really? *Really?* I'm in love with you. I mean, the Real Ali is, but you didn't notice her, with her sassy mouth and trendy clothes and flamboyant nature. The whole time when we worked together in New York, you never looked at me as anything but your employee. If my hair caught on fire, you wouldn't have noticed me. And then you kissed me goodbye at the airport, and I knew there could be something great between us."

"It was a great kiss, Ali. But I wasn't looking—"

"I know all about it. I know about Sheila what's-her-name and how she broke your heart. I know you didn't want an office romance and boy, you sure as hell stuck to your guns." Ali softened her voice, "But then you called and asked me to work for you, and I came. I flew across the continent to work for you, Joe."

"Ali, where is this going?"

She shuddered and her nerves went raw. "I'm trying to tell you. You wouldn't notice the Real Ali, so I made up Fake Ali. I changed my whole personality to get your attention. You see, what we have now isn't real. Nothing about me is real."

Joe pointed to the bed. "That's as real as it gets, Ali."

"Yes, that was real. But all those other times, I held back—afraid to show you who I was."

A storm brewed in Joe's dark eyes. "I knew it. I sensed that something was wrong. The question is why the hell you thought you had to deceive me."

Tears pooled in her eyes. "I guess I was desperate to have you any way I could." Ali took a breath to steady her nerves. There was no going back now. She had to own up to all of it. "Tonight I opened up and showed you the real me. I couldn't go through with it anymore. I feel so bad about this, Joe."

He remained quiet, as if trying to absorb her confession.

"I don't want you to fall for a woman who is a fraud. That's what I am, a fraud."

"Noble of you to admit it, Ali." She didn't miss the sarcasm in his voice.

"I've been acting all this time. And I can't do it anymore. I'm sorry, Joe."

More tears spilled down her cheeks. She reached for a tissue and hastily wiped them away. "I'm bold and opinionated, and I say what's on my mind. Men notice me. They want me. But not you, Joe. You never wanted the real me."

"You're blaming me for your deception?"

"No, I'm taking all the blame. It's all my fault."

Finally what she told him began sinking in. He pushed his glasses back and forth on his nose and then shook his head, casting her a look of disdain. "Then what Sheila told me about you was true."

"Sheila?" Ali's heart stopped in that instant. "What, how…"

"In San Francisco. She warned me about you. She told me about your mother—her five husbands and all the men in between. She warned me that you were playing me. I didn't take her seriously. But my curiosity got the better of me. I looked Justine Holcomb up. It's amazing what a person can find out on the Internet."

"You investigated me?" Ali's temper skyrocketed.

"Not you but your mother."

"And what did you find, Joe?" She put her hands on her hips, defying him to answer, while inside her heart was breaking.

"A lot, Ali. Your mother has quite a reputation for her conquests. She did just about anything she could to get a ring on her finger. Oh, I didn't want to believe it. But you," he said, his voice thick with accusation, "you're just like her. You manipulated me, Ali. Admit it."

"You're confusing me with Sheila. She's the one who burned you. And she had the nerve to warn you about *me?*" Ali's shackles rose. The hairs on her arms stood on end.

Joe approached her, his voice firm and filled with disgust. "Sheila isn't the issue here. You are. You knew all along that you were deceiving me, acting out a role to what? String me along?"

"No!"

"Get your hands on my money?"

"No!"

"Blow my mind with sex, so I wouldn't catch on."

She slapped his face.

Joe grabbed her hand and stared at her. Through tight lips, his voice cold and hard, he looked deep into her eyes. "I never wanted to believe it of you, Ali. But it's all clear now. Your clothes, your personality, you changed it all to fool me. Hell, you even changed your bedroom habits. Your mother taught you well."

He dismissed her, just like that. He grabbed his clothes, slipping into his pants quickly, and walked out of her bedroom without a second glance.

She jumped when she heard the front door slam. And burst into tears for the second time tonight.

Tumultuous emotions roiled in Joe's gut. He walked at a fast pace, trying to burn off some of his anger and despair. He'd sent the limo home, thinking he'd be with Ali until the morning. So now he found himself furious, barefoot and half dressed walking down the highway toward home.

It had been on the tip of his tongue to tell Ali he was in love with her. That would have made her charade complete, he thought with disgust.

She'd already made a colossal fool of him.

Yes, he'd noticed changes in her, but who could figure a woman's mind? Joe thought Ali had been a little more contemplative lately due to the newness of her surroundings. Maybe she'd felt out of her element and needed time to acclimate to California living. She had few friends here, and all that combined could have an effect on a woman.

But Ali hadn't felt any of those things. No, she'd simply had one goal in mind—to trick him into a relationship.

She was just like her mother.

Joe had read accounts of how Justine Holcomb left her first husband for a wealthy oilman. Then a few years later, she'd become a caregiver for an ailing supermarket mogul and had divorced husband number two and moved on to husband number three. She had ties to famous male actors, real estate tycoons and clothing designers. More husbands, more boyfriends, the list went on and on. No wonder Ali never wanted to talk about her family. Speaking of it would have tipped her hand.

After Joe's fury subsided a little, he pressed Nick's number on his iPhone. The phone rang several times. "I hope I'm interrupting," Joe grumbled after his brother finally answered.

"What?" Nick sounded flustered. "Joe, is that you? Do you know what time it is? Like two in the morning."

"Early for you. I need a ride."

"Now? What the hell. Can't you call—"

"No, I'm in no mood to explain myself. Just pick me up. And don't keep me waiting." Joe gave him the location and plopped himself down by the side of the road.

Ten minutes later, Nick showed up in his red Ferrari, and Joe got in. "You look like crap, man. Have a fight with Ali?"

"More than a fight. Just take me home, Nick, and don't ask any questions."

Nick cast him a concerned look and didn't offer up any snarky remarks, for which Joe was grateful.

When he got home, he emptied half a bottle of Scotch, drank himself into oblivion, replaying his argument with Ali in his head until he couldn't think anymore. He fell into bed and slept off the effects of the alcohol.

In the morning, he frowned at the clock by his bedside when he saw the time. He'd slept past noon and rose with a splitting headache. Apparently, he hadn't slept off all the liquor he'd consumed. He felt like hell.

He lumbered downstairs for a cup of coffee and found *both* brothers sitting in the kitchen. Tony was here? And Rena, too? They all gazed at him with sympathetic eyes.

He whipped around abruptly to walk away. The quick movement brought pain to his skull. He rubbed his head.

"Sit down, Joe," Nick called to him.

"I'm bad company today," he muttered.

"I'll get you a cup of coffee," Rena said, her voice hopeful.

He turned, and she sent him a sweet look. He could easily blow off his brothers, but his sister-in-law deserved better treatment. "Thanks."

Rena was already up and pouring his coffee. She brought it to him and gestured for him to take a seat at the table. He hesitated a second, then sank down in the seat. He directed his attention to Tony. "What are you doing here?"

"It was my idea to come over," Rena said. "I was hoping you'd come down while we were here."

"Yeah, why?"

"Because, um," Rena began, looking guilty about something. "I know what happened between you and Ali."

"You *know?*" Joe sipped his steamy coffee while holding his head steady. "News travels fast."

"Ali called me this morning. She's very upset."

Joe gave a slight nod. "She should be."

Rena leaned back in her seat and sighed deeply. "Oh, believe me, she is."

"If you ask me, having a woman that amazing go to such great lengths to get you to notice her ain't the worst thing that could happen, man," Nick said. "You've got rocks in that geek brain of yours if you haven't figured that out yet."

"I didn't ask you." Joe sent his brother a grim look.

Nick glanced at Tony, who in turn glanced at Rena. His sister-in-law put her hand on her growing belly, and Joe was reminded to tread carefully with her.

"Joe, she really cares about you," Rena said.

"Until the next sucker comes along." This time he took a big swallow of his coffee and burnt his tongue. "Damn it."

"I think you should hear her out," Rena said quietly.

"If you know what she did, then how can you ask that of me? She's a phony. Just like her mother."

"Oh, Joe," Rena said, nibbling on her lower lip. She glanced at Tony, who sent her a nod of encouragement. "What if I told you I had a hand in that little scheme?"

"I'd say no one forced Ali to follow through with it. You probably thought you were helping. She knew better."

"The last thing Ali wants is to be like her mother. Perhaps you've judged her too harshly."

"I've been burned before, remember?"

Rena flinched. "I know, Joe. But Ali seemed so perfect…"

Joe rose. "Thanks for stopping by. I'll live."

He left the three of them and walked out of the kitchen and up the stairs. At least he had a day to get Ali out of his system—until he had to face her at work tomorrow.

Ali called in sick on Monday. It was the first time she hadn't come to work since Joe had met her. On Tuesday, he walked into his office and stopped short when he spotted a young blond woman sitting at Ali's desk.

He approached her with furrowed brows. "Who are you?"

She smiled wide, showing sparkling white teeth. "I'm Georgia Scott, from the Short Notice temporary agency." She rose from behind Ali's desk and put out her hand. "You must be Mr. Carlino."

"Joe Carlino," he said, still trying to figure this out. He shook her hand absently. "Where's Ali, Ms. Pendrake?"

"I don't know. Ms. Pendrake called our office yesterday and said you needed a temp. That would be me. She faxed me very detailed instructions." The woman lifted up several sheets of handwritten papers.

Joe nodded, unnerved seeing Ali's desk occupied by someone else. "Did she say how long you'd be here?"

The woman shot him a quizzical look. "At least two weeks."

Joe entered his office and listened to his messages. He had four, and the last one was a breathless Ali.

"Hello, Joe. Under the circumstances, it would be best if I didn't work for you anymore. I know you think the worst of me, and I'm not going to beg you for forgiveness. I made a mistake, and I'm truly sorry. I've arranged for a temp and hope she works out until you can find a suitable replacement for me. You'll have my official resignation on your desk tomorrow. If I'm nothing else, I'm efficient." She laughed sadly into the phone before the message ended.

Joe stared at the answering machine for several minutes, feeling a hollow sense of loss.

And that feeling persisted the rest of the week. He'd made several attempts to call Ali, but his pride had him clicking off before the phone could ring. What could he say to her? He didn't even know who Ali was anymore. It wasn't just that the hair, makeup and demeanor had changed but it was the entire idea behind it that galled him. Was she really that calculating and devious?

Made a man think what else she would have done to gain his attention.

By the middle of the next week, Joe dreaded coming into work each day and not seeing Ali behind her desk. He'd thought he'd get used to seeing Ms. Scott there, typing away, bringing him reports, making his appointments, but that surely didn't happen. Worse yet, he hadn't lapped his swimming pool since the day Ali quit her job. He'd lost his desire and found most mornings he dragged himself out of bed and forced himself to go to work. His well-ordered life had taken a nosedive.

This morning, as he walked into the front doors of
Carlino Wines, noting that Georgia Scott wasn't at her
desk, Joe's mood lifted a little. He'd come to resent the
woman who wasn't Ali. Yet as he approached his own
office, he slowed when he reached the doorway. His heart
rate sped, and hope that he never thought he'd feel again
surged forth. Ali sat in his office. Her back was to him,
and she sat erect, holding her head up high, her beautiful
long auburn hair flowing in curls down her back.

He entered quietly. "Ali?"

The woman turned her head and looked at Joe with
stunning jade-green eyes. She smiled Ali's smile, but she
wasn't Ali. "I'm Justine Holcomb, Ali's mother. You must
be Joe."

Shocked by the resemblance, Joe took a second before
acknowledging her. "Yes, Joe Carlino."

She put out her hand, and Joe took it, giving a gentle
shake. "Please, if I may have a minute of your time. I came
a long distance to speak with you."

Her soft, gentle voice surprised him. She didn't sound
like Ali, but she sure as hell looked like her—a slightly
older version but Justine Holcomb was every bit as beautiful
as Ali.

"Of course." Joe took a seat at his desk and waited.

"I can see why Ali loves you," she began, not mincing
words. "And by the hope in your eyes before you realized
I wasn't Ali, I think you feel the same way."

"If you came all this way, to tell me how I feel—"

"No, Joe. I didn't. I came to tell you how *I* feel."

And Justine Holcomb poured out her heart to him,
explaining how she'd grown up poor and wanted so much
from life. She told him how her becoming a beauty queen
might have been the worst thing that could have happened
to her. That she floundered in relationships, never being

satisfied, always looking for something that she could never quite attain.

"I wasn't a very good role model for my daughter. Lord knows, I've finally come to realize that now, in my older years. I'm extremely proud of Ali, Joe. Unlike me, she knows what she wants in life. She's decisive and smart, and she's never wanted to climb social ladders. Believe me when I tell you it's the very last thing on her mind. I know she fears living the same kind of life I've led. She's done everything in her power *not* to be like me, but I know she wants love in her life, Joe. She wants a home and a family."

Joe didn't know what to say to that.

She watched him with assessing eyes. "I see you're thinking this through. That's good. Don't make snap judgments. I've done that all my life, and look where that got me? Finally, after five husbands, I've found true happiness, and it took a near-fatal heart attack for me to see how much I love my husband. Ali's smarter than me. She only wants one good man in her life."

He let go a deep pent-up breath.

"And if you don't believe that and think she's just like me, let me share this with you. Since leaving your employ, she's been approached by two of your most formidable competitors to come work for them. Both have offered her great opportunities with more money and frills than she received working for you, if I might add. Ali turned them both down. My daughter is beautiful, and if I might say, she could have her choice of a dozen rich wealthy men, if that were her goal. She doesn't want that—or them. She only wants you."

Justine rose from her seat and smiled. "Think about it, Joe. Think about Ali and what she really means to you."

Joe stood up. "I will. Thank you for coming by. I know it wasn't easy for you."

"Oh, but it was. For my daughter, I'd do anything. I have a lot of making up to do where Ali is concerned." She cast him a sad smile. "Don't wait too long, Joe. Ali plans on moving back to the East Coast."

And with that, Justine turned and left, again with her head held high.

Joe shuddered as he watched her go.

"I knew that guy was a jerk," Royce said, helping Ali move some heavy boxes into her living room. The movers were coming tomorrow. It had been two weeks since she'd seen Joe on the best and worst night of her life. Two weeks and he hadn't called. Apparently his mind was made up.

"He's not a jerk," Ali said in Joe's defense. "He's just, well, I don't know what he is, but he's not a jerk."

Royce grumbled a reply, but Ali wasn't listening. She focused on her move back to New York. A teeny, tiny part of her thought she should confront Joe and talk it through with him before she left Napa for good, but Ali wasn't sure she could take another rejection from him. The past two weeks had been nightmarish for her. She'd spent all of her tears and had moved on to self-recriminations. She was angry with Joe, but she was even angrier with herself. She should have never concocted that scheme, yet her real anguish came each minute of every day when she realized that they weren't meant for each other.

He doesn't want the real you.

After Royce left to go to work late in the morning, Ali kept busy packing up boxes with her clothes and kitchen items. At noon, when her doorbell rang, she called out, "Coming," and grabbed her wallet for the pizza she'd ordered.

"How much do I owe you?" she asked, opening the door and fumbling with her cash.

"Not a thing. I owe you."

A sharp gasp escaped when Ali recognized Joe's deep voice.

He stood on her threshold, dressed in blue jeans and a black polo shirt, looking more delicious than hot fudge melting over a mound of rich vanilla ice cream.

He smiled, and his dark eyes gleamed; Ali thought she'd be melting soon. "What are you doing here?"

Joe peered over her shoulder, taking note of the boxes she had stacked up. "I owe you two things, Ali. The first one is an apology. I wasn't happy with you the other day. In fact, I was disappointed and well, pissed. No one likes to be made a fool."

"Joe, I said I was sorry. It was a big mistake," she implored. At the very least she wanted him to know she regretted how she'd tried to trick him.

"I know, Ali. But I shouldn't have reacted that way. I didn't let you explain. Instead, I assumed the worst about you. I shouldn't have said those things about your mother, either. She's actually a very honest woman."

Ali put her hands on her hips and ignored the hope that filled her heart. "And you know this how?"

"We spoke."

"You spoke…on the phone? Did my mother call you?" Ali's heart raced.

Oh, God, Mom, what did you do?

"No, she didn't call me. She came to see me. Yesterday. She gave me a lot to think about."

"She was here? In Napa? I didn't know," she said, shocked and fearful of how that encounter went. "I didn't put her up to it, Joe. You have to believe me. I understand how you feel about me. I know we're incompatible. We're different as night and day and you don't want—"

Joe leaned close and put two fingers to her lips. "Shh, Ali." His touch caused a quake to rumble through her body. "You don't know how I feel."

When Joe removed his fingers, she opened her mouth to reply, then clamped it shut.

"I said I owed you two things. The first one is my apology. And I hope you accept it."

Ali nodded. "I do."

"And the second one is our bike tour. I regret not following through on that. I owed you that much for all your help, and I keep my promises."

Her heart could have been swept aside with a broom. All the hope she didn't dare count on faded to nothingness. "It's okay, Joe. As you can see, I'm moving. I don't need to see Napa anymore."

"But you do. At least let me take you to one place that's very special to me." Joe moved away from her door so she could see the two touring bikes with helmets on the seats, waiting for them.

Ali furrowed her brows. He seemed so adamant, and what did she have to lose? At least, maybe the two of them could wind up as friends. Okay, maybe not friends. But they could end their relationship on a better note. It would just about kill her to be with him today, but Ali had always been a fool when it came to Joe.

"Fine. I'll put my tennis shoes on."

And five minutes later, Ali, dressed in her moving clothes, a tank top, workout pants and a slick red-striped helmet followed Joe down the highway. It was a road she'd seen a zillion times. An occasional car whizzed by them, and Joe looked back to make sure she was okay. They'd gotten only a few miles from her condo, when Joe pulled off the road by a white wooden fence that separated two properties. Green grass, with vineyards in the distance, sloped down to a little clearing. There, Ali saw a blanket laid out, with champagne cooling in a bucket and flowers set in a little vase.

Joe removed his helmet and got off his bike. Ali did the same. He approached and led her to the blanket just a few feet off the road. "Joe? What is this?"

"It's the only stop on our bike tour, Ali. Come, have a seat."

Joe waited for her to sit on the blanket and then he took a place next to her. Ali looked out, but all she saw was the road ahead of them and vineyards in the background. Confused, she shook her head. "I don't get it."

Joe took her hand, and a jolt of electricity coursed between them. Ali knew it wasn't one-sided. She could tell by the gleam in Joe's eyes that he felt it, too. "Neither did I for a long time. After our fight the other night—"

"You mean, the night you walked out on me after we nearly burned up the sheets in bed?"

Joe appeared chagrined. "Yeah, that night. I walked and walked and thought. I was angry and hurt. And all sorts of things entered my mind. But the one thing that kept coming back to me, over and over again, was that I was so angry with you because I'd fallen in love with you. It was here, right here, as I waited for Nick to pick me up, that I figured it all out. I was ready to tell you that night, but then…"

"I blew it," Ali said softly.

Joe squeezed her hand. "I was burned really badly with Sheila, and I didn't want to even consider another relationship, much less one with my very best personal assistant. Maybe, I'd been a little obtuse about it."

"You think?" Ali said with a grin, her whole world looking much brighter now.

"Yeah, but I'd always liked you. Maybe too much. That's why I couldn't bring myself to fall for you. I held back, but if you think I didn't notice you, you're dead wrong. I noticed. How could I not? You're smart and fun and gorgeous, Ali. I noticed it all. But I was protecting myself. It wasn't so much that *you'd* changed that drew me to you. It was that *I'd* changed. I was ready to give us a chance, finally. It took me a long time, I know. So sue me. I'm slow on the uptake."

"You make up for it, though. In bed." Ali smiled sweetly, and Joe's eyes widened. Then he chuckled.

"Ali, I don't think I can live without you. You and I are like night and day, but who said that's a bad thing? Opposites attract, sweetheart. And life would never be boring. I love you, Ali Pendrake. Marry me. Be my wife, the mother of my children and please," he pleaded, "come back to work for me."

Ali threw her head back and laughed, her heart filling with joy. "I want a raise."

"You got it."

"And a house of our own."

"You got that, too."

"And children, right away. I'm not getting any younger."

"Right away?" Joe cast her such a loving smile that her nerves tingled. "I'm for that."

"I love you, Joe. With all my heart."

Joe leaned over and brushed a soft kiss to her lips. "I love you, Ali. Just the way you are."

Ali's heart warmed, believing that her mother had finally come through for her this time, and that compounded her joy.

Joe poured champagne, and they toasted to new beginnings. Cars continued to whiz by, but Ali sat back on the blanket off the side of the road in Napa Valley and thought it was the most romantic proposal a woman could ever hope to receive.

* * * * *

2 in 1
GREAT
VALUE

HONOUR-BOUND GROOM by Yvonne Lindsay

Alexander Del Castillo was betrothed from childhood. So the CEO doesn't expect his beautiful bride to get under his skin…

CINDERELLA & THE CEO by Maureen Child

Tanner found himself saddled with a gorgeous housekeeper he couldn't keep his mind—or hands—off, who also turned out to be his annoying neighbour!

BARGAINING FOR BABY by Robyn Grady

Queensland sheep-station owner Jack Prescott was all bad boy sex appeal, but he'd inherited his baby nephew and feisty Maddy!

THE BILLIONAIRE'S BABY ARRANGEMENT by Charlene Sands

Suddenly Nick Carlino was face-to-face with a woman from his past…and her five-month-old baby.

EXPECTANT PRINCESS, UNEXPECTED AFFAIR
by Michelle Celmer

Samuel Baldwin had seduced Princess Anne to quench his own desire. Chipping away at Anne's icy façade had been pure pleasure…

FROM BOARDROOM TO WEDDING BED? by Jules Bennett

He'd been faced with the toughest decision of his life—a future full of wealth and power, or the love of Tamera Stevens. What would it be, love or money?

On sale from 15th July 2011
Don't miss out!

*Available at WHSmith, Tesco, ASDA, Eason
and all good bookshops*

www.millsandboon.co.uk

0711/

MILLS & BOON

Book of the Month

MODERN

BOOK OF THE MONTH

MAISEY YATES
The Highest Price to Pay

We love this book because...

Maisey Yates has an incredible talent for writing intense, emotional romance with a sexy, sassy edge. In *The Highest Price to Pay*, she creates a world of high fashion and even higher stakes!

On sale 15th July

Visit us Online

Find out more at
www.millsandboon.co.uk/BOTM

0711/BOTM

Special Offers

Every month we put together collections and longer reads written by your favourite authors.

Here are some of next month's highlights— don't miss our fabulous discount online!

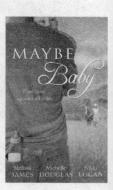

On sale 15th July   On sale 15th July   On sale 5th August

Save 20% on all Special Releases

Find out more at
www.millsandboon.co.uk/specialreleases

Visit us Online

0711/ST/MB346

New Voices is back!

New Voices

returns on
13th September 2011!

For sneak previews and exclusives:

 Like us on facebook.com/romancehq

 Follow us on twitter.com/MillsandBoonUK

Last year your votes helped Leah Ashton win
New Voices 2010 with her fabulous story
Secrets & Speed Dating!

Who will you be voting for this year?

Visit us
Online

Find out more at
www.romanceisnotdead.com

NEW_VOICES

Special Offers
Bestselling Stars Collection

A stunning collection of passion and glamour from your favourite bestselling authors of international romance

On sale 20th May

On sale 17th June

On sale 15th July

On sale 19th August

On sale 16th September

On sale 21st October

Save 20% on Special Releases Collections

Find out more at
www.millsandboon.co.uk/specialreleases

Visit us
Online

0611/10/MB342

BAD BLOOD

A POWERFUL
DYNASTY,
WHERE SECRETS
AND SCANDAL
NEVER SLEEP!

VOLUME 5 – 17th June 2011
HEARTLESS REBEL
by Lynn Raye Harris

VOLUME 6 – 1st July 2011
ILLEGITIMATE TYCOON
by Janette Kenny

VOLUME 7 – 15th July 2011
FORGOTTEN DAUGHTER
by Jennie Lucas

VOLUME 8 – 5th August 2011
LONE WOLFE
by Kate Hewitt

8 VOLUMES IN ALL TO COLLECT!

MILLS &
BOON

www.millsandboon.co.uk

Royal Affairs – luxurious and bound by duty yet still captive to desire!

Royal Affairs: Desert Princes & Defiant Virgins

Available 3rd June 2011

Royal Affairs: Princesses & Protectors

Available 1st July 2011

Royal Affairs: Mistresses & Marriages

Available 5th August 2011

Royal Affairs: Revenge Secrets & Seduction

Available 2nd September 2011

Collect all four!

www.millsandboon.co.uk

0611/26/MB341

LATIN LOVERS COLLECTION

Intense romances with gorgeous
Mediterranean heroes

Greek Tycoons

1st July 2011

**Hot-Blooded
Sicilians**

5th August 2011

Italian Playboys

2nd September
2011

**Passionate
Spaniards**

7th October
2011

**Seductive
Frenchmen**

4th November
2011

**Italian
Husbands**

2nd December
2011

Collect all six!

www.millsandboon.co.uk

11/27/MB343

WEB/M&B/RTL3

Discover Pure Reading Pleasure with

**Visit the Mills & Boon website for all
the latest in romance**

🌹 **Buy** all the latest
releases, backlist
and eBooks

🌹 **Find out** more
about our authors
and their books

🌹 **Join** our community
and chat to authors
and other readers

🌹 **Free** online reads
from your favourite
authors

🌹 **Win** with our
fantastic online
competitions

🌹 **Sign** up for our
free monthly
eNewsletter

🌹 **Tell us** what you
think by signing up to
our reader panel

🌹 **Rate** and review
books with our star
system

www.millsandboon.co.uk

 Follow us at twitter.com/millsandboonuk

 Become a fan at facebook.com/romancehq

FREE BOOK
AND A SURPRISE GIFT

We would like to take this opportunity to thank you for reading this Mills & Boon® book by offering you the chance to take a specially selected book from the Desire™ 2-in-1 series absolutely FREE! We're also making this offer to introduce you to the benefits of the Mills & Boon® Book Club™—

- **FREE home delivery**
- **FREE gifts and competitions**
- **FREE monthly Newsletter**
- **Exclusive Mills & Boon Book Club offers**
- **Books available before they're in the shops**

Accepting this FREE book and gift places you under no obligation to buy, you may cancel at any time, even after receiving your free book. Simply complete your details below and return the entire page to the address below. You don't even need a stamp!

YES Please send me a free Desire 2-in-1 book and a surprise gift. I understand that unless you hear from me, I will receive 2 superb new 2-in-1 books every month for just £5.30 each, postage and packing free. I am under no obligation to purchase any books and may cancel my subscription at any time. The free book and gift will be mine to keep in any case.

Ms/Mrs/Miss/Mr _____ Initials _____

_____

Surname _____
Address _____

_____

_____ Postcode _____
E-mail_____

Send this whole page to: Mills & Boon Book Club, Free Book Offer, FREEPOST NAT 10298, Richmond, TW9 1BR

Offer valid in UK only and is not available to current Mills & Boon Book Club subscribers to this series. Overseas and Eire please write for details. We reserve the right to refuse an application and applicants must be aged 18 years or over. Only one application per household. Terms and prices subject to change without notice. Offer expires 30th September 2011. As a result of this application, you may receive offers from Harlequin (UK) and other carefully selected companies. If you would prefer not to share in this opportunity please write to The Data Manager, PO Box 676, Richmond, TW9 1WU.

Mills & Boon® is a registered trademark owned by Harlequin (UK) Limited.
Desire™ is being used as a trademark. The Mills & Boon® Book Club™ is being used as a trademark.